Following
#1 *New York Times*
Oliver Stone an
return in David Baldacci's most
astonishing thriller yet.

DIVINE JUSTICE

Known by his alias, "Oliver Stone," John Carr is the most
wanted man in America. With two pulls of the trigger, the
men who destroyed Stone's life and kept him in the shadows were finally silenced.

But his freedom comes at a steep price: The assassina-
tions he carried out prompt the highest levels of the U. S.
government to unleash a massive manhunt. Yet behind the
scenes, master spy Macklin Hayes is playing a very personal game of cat and mouse. He, more than anyone else,
wants John Carr dead. With their friend and unofficial
leader in hiding, the members of the Camel Club risk everything to save him. Now as the hunters close in, Stone's
flight from the demons of his past will take him from the
power corridors of Washington, D.C., to the coal-mining
town of Divine, Virginia—and into a world every bit as
bloody and lethal as the one he left behind.

"Cunning chases will keep readers avidly turning the
pages."

—Richmond Times-Dispatch

Please turn this page for more raves
for the books of David Baldacci.

THE CAMEL CLUB

"A terrific read."
—Toronto Sun

"Baldacci knows exactly what his readers want—just enough high-tech suspense to while away a few hours in front of a warm winter fire."
—Fort Worth Star-Telegram

"An original, effervescent thriller . . . page-turning fiction that grips and scares, and offers plenty to think about later."
—Toledo Blade (OH)

"Cleverly constructed . . . If you pick this book up, you'll stick with it all the way."
—St. Louis Post-Dispatch

HOUR GAME

"A thrill a minute . . . King and Maxwell are fictional treats, a fabulously entertaining team, and the action is hot and hard."
—New York Daily News

"Plenty of surprises and suspense . . . rich and deeply textured . . . fast-paced . . . one of Baldacci's strongest thrillers in years."
—Associated Press

"The action is suspenseful and relentless."
—Newark Star-Ledger

SPLIT SECOND

"The action is explosive. Readers will barely have time to catch their breath."

—People

"Excellent . . . a gripping page-turner."

—Associated Press

"Genuinely scary scenes . . . driven by tense action."

—New York Daily News

"A compelling storyteller . . . a supercharged pace."

—Orlando Sentinel

LAST MAN STANDING

"A killer thriller . . . A heart-racer . . . *Last Man* stands tall."

—USA Today

"Engagingly fierce . . . Baldacci's brain-teasing plot leaves you wanting more."

—People

"The action is nearly nonstop and expertly drawn."

—Publishers Weekly (starred review)

WISH YOU WELL

"Compelling . . . stirring . . . an old-fashioned coming-of-age story."

—People

more . . .

"Utterly captivating . . . Baldacci triumphs."
—*Publishers Weekly* **(starred review)**

"Realistic . . . entertaining."
—*Washington Post Book World*

SAVING FAITH

"Plenty of action . . . opens with a bang . . . a joy."
—*USA Today*

"Burns and churns relentlessly forward from the first page."
—*New York Post*

"A lightning-*paced thriller.*"
—*Chicago Tribune*

THE SIMPLE TRUTH

"Compelling . . . finely drawn . . . a page-turner worth losing sleep over."
—*USA Today*

"Baldacci ratchets up the suspense."
—*People*

"Baldacci excels at creating really good guys and putting them at risk."
—*Newsday*

THE WINNER

"Baldacci has come up with another good one."
—*New York Times*

"Aptly named . . . the devilish tale of a heroine who gambles her soul."

—People

"Baldacci pushes the pace pedal to the floor and takes the turns on two wheels."

—New York Daily News

TOTAL CONTROL

"Fast and scary."

—Cosmopolitan

"Moves at the pace of a flying bullet . . . suspense at high speed."

—Orlando Sentinel

"Fast-paced, complex, and totally enthralling."

—Arizona Republic

ABSOLUTE POWER

"Sizzling action."

—USA Today

"A grabber . . . a superior thriller."

—Houston Chronicle

"Fasten your seat belt . . . keeps readers on edge, page after page."

—Associated Press

ALSO BY DAVID BALDACCI

Absolute Power

Total Control

The Winner

The Simple Truth

Saving Faith

Wish You Well

Last Man Standing

The Christmas Train

Split Second

Hour Game

The Camel Club

The Collectors

Simple Genius

Stone Cold

The Whole Truth

DAVID BALDACCI

DIVINE JUSTICE

GRAND CENTRAL
PUBLISHING

NEW YORK   BOSTON

Grand Central Publishing
Hachette Book Group
237 Park Avenue
New York, NY 10017

Visit our Web site at www.HachetteBookGroup.com.

Grand Central Publishing is a division of Hachette Book Group, Inc. The Grand Central Publishing name and logo is a trademark of Hachette Book Group, Inc.

Printed in the United States of America

Originally published in hardcover by Hachette Book Group
First international mass market edition: July 2009

10 9 8 7 6 5 4 3 2 1

ATTENTION CORPORATIONS AND ORGANIZATIONS:
Most HACHETTE BOOK GROUP books are available at quantity discounts with bulk purchase for educational, business, or sales promotional use. For information, please call or write:

Special Markets Department, Hachette Book Group
237 Park Avenue, New York, NY 10017
Telephone: 1-800-222-6747 Fax: 1-800-477-5925

To the memory of my father

DIVINE
JUSTICE

CHAPTER

1

THE CHESAPEAKE BAY is America's largest estuary. Nearly two hundred miles long, its watershed covers an area of sixty-five thousand utopian square miles with more than a hundred and fifty rivers and streams barreling into it. It's also the home of myriad bird and aquatic life, and a haven for legions of recreational boaters. The bay is indeed a creation of remarkable beauty, except when you happen to be swimming in the middle of the damn thing during a thunderstorm in the veiled darkness of early morning.

Oliver Stone cracked the surface of the water and gulped in the thick salty air, a thirsty man in the center of a trillion-ton ocean. The long dive had caused him to go farther down than was particularly healthy. Yet when you throw yourself off a thirty-foot cliff into an angry ocean, you should be thankful just to have a heartbeat. As he treaded water he looked around to gauge his bearings. Nothing he saw was too appealing right now. With each streak of lightning sparking to earth, he eyed the three-story-high cliff he'd been standing on. He'd been in the bay less than a minute yet the chill was already drizzling into his bones despite the full-body wet suit he wore underneath his clothes. He stripped off his waterlogged pants, shirt and shoes and then kicked off swimming east. He didn't have much time to get this done.

Twenty minutes later he cut toward shore, all four limbs cement. He used to be able to swim all day, but he wasn't twenty anymore. Hell, he wasn't even fifty anymore. Now he just wanted land; he was tired of impersonating a fish.

He pointed himself at a cleft in the rock and shot toward it. He slogged free of the breakers and jogged toward a large boulder where he snagged the cloth bag he'd previously hidden. Tugging off his wet suit, he toweled dry and changed into fresh clothes and a pair of tennis shoes. The sodden articles were pushed into the bag, tied to a rock and hurled into the storm-swept bay where they'd join his decades-old sniper rifle and long-range scope. He was officially retired from the killing profession. He hoped he would live to enjoy the experience. Right now it was barely even money on that score.

Stone carefully picked his way up the rocky path to a dirt trail. Ten minutes later he reached a fringe of woods where shallow-rooted pines leaned away from the punishing sea wind. A twenty-minute jog after that carried him to the batch of ramshackle buildings, most closer to falling down than not. The cloud-encrusted light was just beginning to topple the darkness as he slid through the window of the smallest hut. It was no more than a lean-to, really, though it did have such luxuries as a door and a floor. He checked his watch. He had ten minutes at most. Already dog-tired, he once more pulled off his clothes then slipped into the tiny shower with rusted piping that only delivered a thin stream of lukewarm water, like a fountain on its last dying spurt. Still, he scrubbed hard, wiping away the stink and briny clutch of the angry bay— wiping away evidence, actually. He was on auto now, his mind too numb to lead the way. That would change. The head games were about to start. He could already envision the boots coming for him.

Stone was listening for the knock on the door; it came as he was dressing.

"Hey man, you ready?" called the voice. It shot through the thin plywood door like a cat's paw into a mouse hole.

In answer Stone smacked one hand hard against the ragged plank floor as he slipped on his shoes, shrugged into a frayed coat, tugged a John Deere cap low over his head and put on his thick glasses. He ran a hand over the bristly gray beard he'd grown over the past six months, then opened the door and nodded at the short, squat man facing him. The fellow had a beer keg frame and a lazy right eye along with teeth yellowed by too many Winstons and double-pop Maxwell House coffees. This was clearly not café latte land. The top of his head was covered by a Green Bay Packers knit cap. He wore faded farmer's bibs, dirty work boots and a threadbare, grease-stained coat along with an easy smile.

"Cold one this morning," the man said, rubbing his chunky nose and slipping a lit cigarette from between his lips.

Tell me about it, Stone thought.

"But it's supposed to warm up." He drank from an official NASCAR tankard of java, letting some dribble down his chin when he pulled it back.

Stone nodded as his bearded face drooped and his normally attentive eyes grew vacant behind the smudged lenses. As he walked behind the other man Stone's left leg bent outward with a chicken-wing limp that stooped him into being several inches shorter.

They were loading an old banged-up, bald-tired Ford F-150 with firewood when the police car and black sedans slid into the driveway, propelling pebbly gravel in all directions like fired BBs. The trim, muscled men who climbed out of the rides wore blue slickers with "FBI" stenciled on the back in gold lettering and pistols with fourteen-round clips in their belt holsters. Three of them walked up to Stone and his buddy, while a chubby uniformed sheriff with polished black boots and a Stetson hustled to catch up.

"What's the deal, Virgil?" Green Bay asked the uniform. "Some sonofabitch break outta prison again? I'm telling you, you boys oughta start shooting to kill again and screw the pissant liberals."

Virgil shook his head, worry lines rising on his forehead. "No prison. Man's dead, Leroy."

"What man?"

One of the FBI slickers snapped, "Let me see some ID."

Another said, "Where were you and your friend an hour ago?"

Leroy looked from one Fibbie to the next. Then he

stared over at the uniform. "Virgil, what the hell's going on?"

"Like I said, a man's dead. Important man. His name's—"

With a slash of his hand, a slicker cut him off. "ID. Now!"

Leroy quickly slid a thin wallet out of his bib's pocket and handed over his license. While one of the agents punched the number into a handheld computer he'd slipped from his windbreaker, another agent held out his hand to Stone.

Stone didn't move. He just stared back with a vacuous expression, his lips gumming and his bum leg doing an exaggerated deep knee bend. He looked confused, which was all part of the act.

"He ain't got no license," Leroy said. "He ain't got nothing of nothing. Hell, can't even talk, just grunts."

The FBI agents closed around Stone. "He work for you?"

"Yessir. Four months now. Good worker, strong back. Don't ask for much money—room and board is all, really. But he got a bad leg and not too much upstairs. He's mostly what you call unemployable."

The agents looked down at the protruding angle of Stone's leg then back up at his bespectacled face and bushy beard.

One of them asked, "What's your name?"

Stone grunted and made several jerky motions with his hand, like he was showing off a bastardized martial art for the federal men.

"Sign language, least I think it is, or some such," Leroy volunteered wearily. "Don't know sign language myself so's I don't know his real name. Just call him 'Hey man.' Then I show him what needs doing. That seems to work. It ain't like we're doing heart surgery up here, just throwing shit in a truck mostly."

A slicker said, "Tell him to lift up his pants leg on his *bum* wheel."

"What for?"

"Just tell him!"

Leroy motioned to Stone to do so by drawing up his own pants leg.

Stone bent down and, with improvised difficulty, mimicked Leroy's action.

The men all stared down at the ugly scar marching across the kneecap.

"Damn!" said Leroy. "No wonder he can't walk good."

The same FBI slicker motioned with his hand for Stone to roll his pants leg back down. "Okay, fine."

Stone never thought he'd be thankful for the old bayonet wound a North Vietnamese soldier had given him. It looked a lot worse than it actually was because the surgeon had had to fix Stone up on the floor of the jungle in the middle of an artillery barrage. Understandably the doctor's hands had not been at their steadiest.

Sheriff Virgil said, "Leroy and me grew up here together. He was the center and I was the quarterback on the high school football team that won the county championship forty years ago. He's not riding around killing anybody. And that feller there, easy to see he's not the sharpshooting type."

The FBI agent tossed back Leroy's license and looked at his fellow feds. "Clean," he muttered in a disappointed tone.

"Where you headed?" another slicker said as he glanced at the half-loaded truck.

"Same place I'm always headed this time of the morning this time of the year. We take us some wood down to folks who ain't got time to chop their own, and sell it before the cold weather sets in. Then we get down to the marina and work on the boat. Maybe take it out if the seas clear up."

"You got a boat?" one agent said sharply.

Leroy looked over at Virgil with a comical expression. "Yeah, got me a big-ass yacht." He pointed behind him. "We like to take us a ride in that there Chesapeake Bay and maybe catch us a few crabs. I hear tell they like that shit round these parts."

"Cut the crap, Leroy, before you get yourself in trouble," Virgil said quickly. "This is serious."

"I believe it is," Leroy shot back. "But if a man's dead, you best not waste any more time jawing with us. 'Cause we ain't know nuthin' 'bout nuthin'."

"You see anybody pass this way this morning?"

"Not one car till you folks come tearing up. And we both been up before full light."

Stone limped over to the truck and started throwing wood in the cargo bed.

The agents looked at each other. One of them mumbled, "Let's roll."

A few seconds later they were gone.

Leroy walked over to the truck and started tossing wood in. "Wonder what man be dead?" he said, really to himself. "Important man, they say. Lot of important men in this world. But they die just like the rest of us. God's way of making life fair."

Stone let out a long, loud grunt.

Leroy looked over at him and grinned. "Hey man, now that's the smartest thing I heard all damn morning."

When the day's work was over, Stone pantomimed to Leroy that he was heading on. Leroy seemed to take it well. "Surprised you lasted long as you did. Good luck." He peeled off a few faded twenties and handed them over. Stone took the money, patted the man's back and limped off.

After packing his duffel, Stone set out on foot and hitchhiked to D.C. in the back of a truck, the driver unwilling to let the scruffy Stone ride with him in the warmth of the truck's cab. Stone didn't mind. It would give him time to think. And he had a lot to think about. He had just killed two of the most prominent men in the country on the same day, literally hours apart, using the rifle he'd earlier chucked into the ocean before taking the dive off the cliffs.

The truck dropped him off near the Foggy Bottom area of the capital and Stone set out for his old home at Mt. Zion Cemetery.

He had a letter to deliver.

And something to pick up.

And then it would be time to hit the road.

His alter ego John Carr was finally dead.

And the odds were awfully good that Oliver Stone might be right behind him.

CHAPTER

2

THE COTTAGE WAS DARK, the cemetery darker still. The only thing visible was the mist of Stone's exhaled breath as it mingled with cool air. His gaze penetrated to every square inch of the cemetery because he could not afford any screwups now. It was stupid coming here, but loyalty was not a choice he felt, it was a duty. And it was who he was. At least they couldn't take that away from him.

He'd waited nearby for about a half hour to see if anything looked strange. His place had been watched for a couple months after he'd abandoned it. He knew this because he'd been watching the watchers. However, after four months of him not being around, they'd given up their sentinel and moved on. That didn't mean they wouldn't come back. And after the events of this morning, they probably would. All cops would you tell you that every violently ended life was worth the same level of investigation. Yet the reality was, the more important the victim the more diligent the hunt. And based on that maxim they would be bringing an army on this one.

Finally satisfied, he crawled underneath the fence at the back of the cemetery and crept to a large headstone. He yanked it over, revealing underneath the small compartment scooped out of the dirt. He took the box hidden there and put it in his duffel bag, then set the stone back in place. He patted the grave marker affectionately. The name of the deceased who lay here had long since been worn away by time. But Stone had researched the people who'd been buried at Mt. Zion and knew that this was the final resting place of one Samuel Washington, a freed slave who'd given his life to help others like him to freedom. He felt a certain kinship with the fellow because in a way Stone knew just what it was like to not be free.

He eyed the cottage in a dusk rushing headfirst to nightfall. He knew Annabelle Conroy had been staying there. Her rental was parked at the front gate. And he'd been inside the cottage when she'd been absent from it a couple months ago. The place looked far better than when he'd lived there. Yet he knew he could never reside at Mt. Zion again unless it was in a supine position approximately six feet underground. With the two early morning pulls of the trigger he'd become the most wanted man in America.

He wondered where she was tonight. Hopefully, out enjoying life, although since the news of the two murders was everywhere, he knew that his friends would easily deduce what had happened. He hoped they didn't think less of him. That actually was the real reason he was here tonight.

He didn't want to leave his friends hanging out there for him. The feds weren't incompetent. They would be coming this way eventually. Stone wished with all his heart he could do more for the Camel Club, after all they had done for him. He had thought of simply turning himself in. But there was such a core of survivor mentality built into his psyche that his essentially walking to his own execution was not an option. He could not let them win that way. They would have to work a little harder.

The letter he held was carefully worded. It was not a confession because that would put his friends in an even greater dilemma. Granted, Stone was caught in a classic catch-22, but he owed them something. He should have known that with the life he'd led there was only one possible conclusion.

This.

He slipped the letter from his pocket and rolled it around the hilt of a knife he pulled from another pocket, securing it with string. He took aim from the darkness of the side yard and let fly. The knife stuck into the porch column.

"Good-bye."

He had one more place to visit.

A few moments later he was crawling back under the fence. He walked to the Foggy Bottom Metro station and climbed on the train. Later, a thirty-minute walk brought him to yet another cemetery.

Why was it he was more comfortable with the dead than the living? The answer was relatively simple. The dead conveniently never asked questions.

Even in the darkness he quickly found the grave he was looking for. He knelt down, brushed some leaves away and gazed at the tombstone.

Here lay Milton Farb, the other member of the Camel Club, and the only deceased one. Yet even dead, Milton would forever be part of that informal band of conspiracy theorists who'd insisted on only one thing: the truth.

Too bad their leader hadn't honored that principle.

The only reason his beloved friend was dead was because of Stone.

My fault.

Because of him, the brilliant if quirky Milton was resting here for all time now, a large-caliber round having ended his life underneath the United States Capitol. It nearly equaled the grief Stone felt for the death of his poor wife decades ago.

Stone's eyes moistened as he remembered that final, awful night at the Capitol Visitor Center. How Milton had looked at him after the bullet struck; those wide, pleading, innocent eyes. The memory of his friend's last seconds of life would remain with Stone until *his* dying day. And there had been nothing Stone could do, except avenge his friend. And he had. He'd killed many heavily armed, expertly trained men in close confines that night, and he hardly remembered doing any of it, so overshadowed was it all by that one stunningly improbable death. Yet it hadn't come close to making up for the loss. That was what the killings this morning had been about, at least partly. And neither of them had made up for losing Milton either. Or his wife. Or his daughter.

He very carefully cut out a chunk of grass and dirt on top of his friend's grave, laid the box in it, and put the grass back on top, pushing it down firmly with a shove from his foot. He removed all evidence that the ground had been disturbed and then stood very erect and saluted his dead friend.

A few moments later Stone slowly walked back to the Metro and rode it to Union Station, where he bought a train ticket south with most of his remaining cash. There were a few police and plainclothes officers around and Stone duly noted the location of each one. No doubt the heavy artillery was at the three local airports doing their best to nab the killer of a well-known U.S. senator and the nation's intelligence chief. The lowly American train system obviously didn't warrant such a level of scrutiny, as though assassins wouldn't deign to ride the decrepit rails.

Thirty minutes later he climbed on the Amtrak Crescent, destination New Orleans; it was a spur-of-the-moment decision as he had looked up at the marquee. The train was a few hours late leaving, otherwise he would've not been able to take it. Not a naturally superstitious man, he had considered that an omen. He jammed himself into a small bathroom, trimmed off the beard and removed his glasses before going to his seat.

He'd heard construction jobs were still plentiful in New Orleans after Katrina. And people, desperate for workers, didn't ask for tricky things like Social Security numbers and permanent addresses. At this point in his life Stone did not like questions or numbers that would lead anyone to know who he really was. His plan was to lose himself in a mass of humanity trying to rebuild from a nightmare not of its own making. He could relate to that very well, because he was basically trying to do the very same thing. Except for those two final shots. Those he'd intended with every pulsating nerve of anger and sense of justice denied he possessed.

As the train bumped along in the darkness Stone sat in his chair and stared out the window. In the reflection he studied the young woman who sat next to him holding a baby, her feet perched on a battered duffel bag and a pillowcase crammed with what looked to be bottles, diapers and changes of clothes for the infant. They were both asleep; the child's chest nestled against its mother's swollen bosom. Stone turned to look at the child with its triple chins and doughy fists. The baby suddenly opened its eyes and stared at him. Surprisingly it didn't cry; it didn't make one sound, in fact.

Across the aisle a rail-thin man was eating a cheeseburger he'd bought in the station, a bottle of Heineken cradled between bony knees covered by patched denim. Next to him was a young, tall, good-looking man with brown, tousled hair and a few days' worth of stubble on his unmarked face. He had the lean, lanky build and confident moves of a former high school quarterback not yet run to fat. This was not exactly a guess on Stone's part, because the kid was wearing his high school varsity jacket dripping with medals, letters and ribbons. The year stitched on the jacket told Stone that the kid had been out of high school for a few years. Long time to be holding on to the glory days, Stone thought, but maybe that was all the kid had.

To Stone's eye the young man also had the look of someone who was certain that the world owed him everything and had never bothered paying its bill. As Stone watched, he rose, climbed over the cheeseburger man and headed to the rear of the car and through the door into the next train car.

Stone reached over and gently touched the baby's fist, receiving a barely audible coo in return. While the infant's life was all in front of him, Stone's was drawing closer to the end.

Well, they would have to find him first. He owed that to an authority that was often callous to the people who served it with the greatest loyalty, with the most quietly suffered sacrifice.

He leaned back in his seat and watched Washington disappear as the train rattled on.

CHAPTER

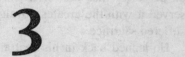

CHAPTER

3

J OE KNOX HAD BEEN READING in the small library of his town house in northern Virginia when the phone rang. The speaker was economical with his words and Knox, from long experience, did not interrupt. He hung up the phone, laid aside his novel, pulled on his raincoat and boots, grabbed the keys to his scuffed up ten-year-old Range Rover and headed out into the foul weather for an equally foul task.

An inch over six feet with the thick, muscular build of the undersized linebacker he had once been in college, Knox was in his fifties with thinning hair that he still had barber-shop cut and then slicked back. He also possessed a pair of pale green eyes that were the human equivalent of an MRI: they missed nothing. He gripped the wheel of the Rover with long fingers that had pulled just about every trigger there was while in service to his country.

From his secluded, forested neighborhood he turned on to Chain Bridge Road in McLean, Virginia. The traffic would still be heavy on the Beltway this time of morning. Actually, there was really no longer a time when the asphalt noose around the capital city's neck *wasn't* strangled with cars. He pointed his SUV toward the District and backtracked his way to eastern Maryland from there. Eventually he smelled the sea, and with it he envisioned the murder scene. All in a day's work.

Three hours later he was walking around the truck as fat raindrops pelted down. Carter Gray still sat in his seatbelt harness, his head destroyed and his life ended by what appeared to be a long-range rifle round, although the postmortem would confirm that. While police, FBI and forensic teams buzzed everywhere like bluebottle flies, looking for some place to land and do their business, Joe Knox squatted in front of the white grave marker and small American flag planted in front of it by the side of the road. It was on a curve. The motorcade would have slowed here. A curious Gray had obviously seen these two items and rolled down his window—a fatal mistake.

Grave marker and American flag. Just like at Arlington National. An interesting and perhaps telling choice.

The fact that the windows rolled down showed Knox that the vehicle wasn't armored. Such vehicles' windows were phone-book thick and did not move. Gray had made his second mistake there.

Should've asked for the armor, Carter. You were important enough.

This wasn't baseball, Knox knew. In his business, it never took more than *two* strikes to finish you.

Knox looked off into the distance, tracing in his mind

the trajectory of the lethal round. None of the protection detail had seen any sign of a shooter, so he had to cast the potential flight path out farther where the optic and muzzle signatures would be nearly invisible to the naked eye.

Thousand yards? Fifteen hundred? To a target inside a vehicle revealed only through a barely two-by-two-foot opening in the dark and drizzle. And planted the bullet right in the brain.

Remarkable shot any way you look at it. No luck there. A pro.

Revealing again.

He rose and nodded at one of the uniforms. Knox wore his ID badge on a lanyard around his neck. When everyone had seen what his official ties were they had been deferential and also given him a wide berth, like he had an incurable and contagious disease.

And maybe I do.

The cop opened the door of the Escalade and Knox peered inside. The shot had hit dead center of the right temple. There was no exit wound. The round was still in the brain. The postmortem would dig it out. Not that he needed the autopsy report to tell him what had killed the man. Blood and bits of flesh and skull had embedded in parts of the SUV's interior. Knox doubted the government would be reusing this ride. It would probably go the way of JFK's limo. It was bad luck, bad karma, call it what you would, but no other VIP would want to rest his butt in the dead man's seat, sterilized or not.

Gray didn't appear as though he were sleeping. He simply looked dead. No one had bothered to close the man's eyes. His glasses had been blown off on impact from the kinetically energized round. The result had Gray perpetually staring at whoever looked back at him.

Knox lifted one of his gloved hands and shut the eyelids. It was out of respect. He'd known Gray well. He hadn't always agreed with the man or his methods, but he'd respected him. If their positions were reversed, he hoped Gray would've done the same for him.

The briefing papers Gray had been reading had been collected already by the CIA. National security trumped even homicide. Knox highly doubted that whatever the CIA chief had been reading at the moment of his death would be connected to his murder, but one never knew.

Yet if they could have read the man's mind in his last moments of life? When he stared out at that grave marker and that flag?

Knox's gut was telling him that Gray knew exactly who had killed him. And maybe others at the Agency did too. If so, they were letting him go through the motions on his own. He wondered why for a second and then stopped. It was tricky business trying to figure out what the hell went on behind closed doors at Langley. The only thing you could count on as the real truth was as convoluted as anything you'd find in popular fiction.

He left the corpse and mentally processed the facts as he stared off toward the Atlantic.

Gray's home had been blown up over six months ago, the man barely escaping with his life. Knox had been briefed via secure phone on the drive over. Any suspects involved in that matter were not to be considered to be involved in Gray's murder, he'd been told. This directive had come from the highest levels and he had no choice but to defer to it. Yet, still, he filed that away in the back of his head. For him the truth should not come with qualifiers or conditions, if for no other reason than that he might need it as ammo to cover his own ass at some point.

He drove to Gray's home, made a brief inspection of the interior, found nothing of interest there, and then walked toward the cliff at the rear of the property. He stared down at the thrashing water of the bay below before glancing out at the fully formed storm front that was not making the nearby murder investigation any easier. Knox eyed the fringe of woods that ran by the right side of the house. He walked through the trees and quickly calculated that a path through here would take one up to the gravel road that Gray's motorcade had used.

He looked back at the cliffs.

And wondered if it was possible.

With the right man there was only one answer to that question.

Yes.

He climbed back in his Rover and headed to the second murder scene.

Roger Simpson.

The great state of Alabama was suddenly one senator short.

And without even seeing the circumstances of Simpson's death, Knox instinctively knew he was looking for only one killer.

Just one.

CHAPTER

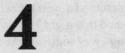

4

As soon as Annabelle stepped on the front porch she saw it. Alex Ford did too. They'd just gotten back from dinner at Nathan's in Georgetown. It had become a favorite haunt of theirs.

She pulled the knife free, unfolded the letter and then glanced around, as though she expected the person who'd delivered it to still be nearby.

She and Alex sat in front of the empty fireplace while she read it. She finished and passed it across to him, waiting in silence while he read it through.

"He says for you to pack up and move. That people would be coming to ask questions. You can stay at my place, if you want."

"I guess we knew it was him, didn't we?" she added.

Alex looked at the letter. "'I've had many regrets in my life,'" he said, reading from it. "'And I've lived with them all. But Milton's death was my fault alone. I did what I had to do. To punish those who needed to be. But I will never be able to punish myself enough. At least John Carr is finally dead. And good riddance.'" He looked up. "Sounds like a man who did what he believed needed to be done."

"He asked us to tell Reuben and Caleb."

"I'll do it."

"They deserved it, you know. From all that Finn told us that happened that night."

"Nothing gives someone the right to murder someone, Annabelle," he said firmly. "That's vigilantism. That's wrong."

"Under any circumstances?"

"One exception destroys that rule for good."

"So you say."

"Burn the letter, Annabelle," Alex said suddenly.

"What?"

"Burn it now, before I change my mind."

"Why?"

"It's not a confession but it's still evidence. And I can't believe I'm saying this. Burn it. Now!"

She grabbed a match, lit the paper and tossed it into the fireplace. They watched the letter curl and blacken.

"Oliver saved my life, more than once," he said. "He was the most decent, reliable person I've ever met."

"I wish he'd stayed to talk to us."

"I'm glad he didn't."

"Why?" Annabelle said brusquely.

"Because I might have had to arrest him."

"You're kidding. You just said he was the most decent person you'd ever met."

"I'm a lawman, Annabelle. I swore an oath, friend or not."

"But you knew he killed people before. And you didn't seem to have a problem with it then."

"Right, but he did that on orders from the U.S. government."

"So that makes it okay in your eyes? Because some politician said it was?"

"Oliver was a soldier. He was trained to follow orders."

"But even he felt guilt for that. Because some of the people he was 'ordered' to kill were innocent. You saw how that crushed him."

"I respect his morals. But that wasn't his call."

Annabelle rose and looked down at him.

"So he kills two people who *did* deserve it, but because he didn't have 'government authorization' you're suddenly prepared to arrest him?"

"It's not that simple, Annabelle."

She flicked her long hair out of her face. "Sure it is," she snapped.

"Look—"

She walked over to the door and opened it. "Let's call it a night before we say something we'll regret. Or at least I do. Besides, I have to pack."

"Where are you going to go?"

"I'll let you know," she said in a tone that left much doubt whether she meant it.

Alex started to say something but instead rose and walked out, his features clouded and his lips set in an uncompromising line.

Annabelle slammed the door behind him. She sat down cross-legged in front of the fireplace and studied the blackened bits of Stone's final message to them. Tears trickled down her cheeks as in her mind she went through the letter's contents again.

She glanced toward the door. Alex and she had become very close over the last several months. When they had heard of Gray's and Simpson's murders they both had instantly suspected the truth. Yet they hadn't said anything about their feelings, afraid perhaps that if they did acknowledge that they believed Stone had killed the two men it would make that suspicion an intractable truth. Now their two very different interpretations of the man's perceived actions had just driven a wall right between them.

Annabelle packed her few belongings, locked up the cottage for what she was sure would be the last time, climbed in her car and drove to a nearby hotel. She got undressed and climbed into bed. She would be moving on now. There was nothing to keep her here any longer. With Oliver gone, her father dead and Alex revealed to be something other than what she thought, she was alone once more.

It seemed to be her natural state.

Good luck, Oliver Stone.

Annabelle was very sure of one thing. He would need all the luck he could get.

Maybe they all would.

CHAPTER

5

JOE KNOX WOULD HAVE preferred to have been back at his town house drinking a beer or maybe even a couple digits' width of Glenlivet while sitting in front of a toasty fire and finishing reading his novel. Yet here he was. The chair was uncomfortable, the room cold and ill-lighted, the waiting unpleasant. He eyed the opposite wall but his thoughts were far from this place.

His tour through Roger Simpson's murder scene hadn't taken all that long. Like his former boss at CIA, Simpson had still been sitting in death, only with him instead of a car seat it was a ladder-back chair in the kitchen that was now all mottled with the dead man's blood. The shot had come from the unfinished chunk of construction across the street. The hour of execution—for Knox was certain that's what this was all about—had been an early one. And eyewitnesses had been in damn short supply.

The only item of interest, really, had been the newspaper. Simpson had been shot right through that morning's edition of the venerable *Washington Post*, taking the round smack in the chest. As had been the case with Gray, most snipers aimed for the brain as the gold standard of all possible killing shots. Sure, you pack the right ordnance and a torso hit would also likely be fatal, but the head shot was like a faithful dog in a professional killer's world because it just never let you down.

So Gray in the head; Simpson in the chest. Why?

And why through *the newspaper?*

That had really bothered Knox. Not that having to penetrate the few pages would've screwed the shot, but the shooter would've had to more or less guess where his round would impact. And what if Simpson had had a thick book on his chest, or a cigarette lighter in his breast pocket that the paper had concealed? That *could've* fouled the shot. Most snipers Knox had known didn't like to guess about anything other than who they'd kill next.

Yet when he'd examined the paper he understood quite clearly why the chest shot had been used. A snapshot of someone had been taped to the inside of the newspaper. The shot had taken the person's head in the photo right off. As Knox looked more closely, the remaining part of the picture showed the torso to be that of a woman. There were no marks or writing on what was left of the photo to help him figure out who it was. He'd talked to the paper carrier to see if he'd seen anything suspicious, but he hadn't. And Simpson's building didn't have a doorman. Yet the killer *had* put that photo in the paper, Knox was certain of it.

And that meant only one thing. This hit had been personal. And the killer had wanted Simpson to know exactly why he was going to die and also who was doing the deed. Just like the flag and grave marker with Gray. His grudging admiration for the assassin increased even more. Gauging the shot accurately enough to take out that picture required remarkable skill, planning and simply a level of confidence that not even most professional sharpshooters possessed.

He'd instructed the medical examiner to let him know if anything showed up in the wound that was out of the ordinary. They almost certainly wouldn't be able to reconstruct the burned bits of photo now plastered into the senator's chest cavity by a high-velocity rifle round. But one never knew. Knox understood from experience that it was the little shit that brought most criminals down.

He straightened up and stopped thinking about gunshots and dead men as the sounds of the footfalls trickled down the narrow hall toward him. There were two men, both in suits, and both carried equally grim expressions. One of them held what looked like a large safety deposit box. He set it down on the table with a loud clunk. It gave added gravitas to a situation that didn't really need any more, at least to Knox's thinking.

The older man was very tall and broad with a crown of thick white hair. Yet he was also weathered and beaten down by innumerable crises spread over decades. There were no safe harbors here; the hitch in his step, every wrinkle on his face and the bow in his shoulders bespoke that essential truth. His name was Macklin Hayes, a former army three-star who'd matriculated to the intelligence side a long time ago, though his ties to military intelligence, Knox understood, were still strong. He had never heard anyone refer to the gentleman as Mack. It was just not something you'd ever consider doing.

Hayes nodded at him. "Knox. Thanks for coming in."

"Didn't really have a choice, did I, General?"

"Do any of us?"

Knox waited, choosing to say nothing in reply to this.

"You understand the situation?" Hayes said.

"As much as possible considering the short time I've been on this sucker."

Hayes tapped the lid of the box. "The rest is in here. Read it, absorb it, memorize it. When it's all over, you are to forget every last bit of it. Understood?"

Knox slowly nodded. *That part I always understand.*

"Any preliminary thoughts?" the younger man asked.

Knox didn't know this gent and wondered why he was even here. Perhaps just to carry Hayes' goody box. Yet he'd asked a question and probably expected an answer.

"Two executions performed by one sniper who knew his business, probably ex-military with some kind of grudge and he wanted Gray and Simpson to know it. He left the grave marker and flag for Gray and a photo of a woman taped to a newspaper for Simpson. He shot the senator first and then came to Maryland to nail Gray, probably before word of Simpson's murder got out and Gray was forewarned."

"You're sure not two shooters?" queried the younger man. "And you're certain of the sequence?"

"I can't be *sure* of anything right now. You asked for my prelim, there it is."

"Escape? He couldn't have left by any road. He would've been seen."

Knox hesitated. "Off the cliff."

Hayes spoke up. "Apparently you're not the only person to suggest that."

"Who was the first?"

"Read the file."

A burn developed in Knox's gut but he held his tongue on that command. "Did Gray say anything in the days leading up to his death?"

"He was involved in something about six months before he was killed. What exactly is so classified even I haven't been allowed a full briefing. Gray, as you well know, was a man who kept things very close to the vest. And he was in the private sector at the time, so that also limits what we know. It's a bit muddled to say the least."

Knox nodded. Gray and secrecy just naturally went together. "Is that connected to the usual suspects who have now been taken off the table? I have to say that revelation was a little out there."

The younger man answered. "But not all of us agree with that decision."

Knox looked from young man to old. "So what exactly does that mean? Are they off-limits or not?"

Hayes cast off a smile that was impossible to read. The man could have made a fortune with chips and cards in Vegas, thought Knox.

"Hard to say. As my colleague here mentioned, there's a split decision about that in the corridors that matter."

"So where does that leave me?"

"Treading cautiously, Knox, treading very damn cautiously." He tapped the box. "I was able to collect some things that I've placed in here. Including a few off-the-record items."

"You mean things that technically I'm not supposed to be privy to?" Knox was now missing his book and cozy town house even more.

"We'll just assume that's the case."

"I'm not looking to take a slug in the back of my head over this."

"I would add that neither am I."

"That doesn't give me a lot of comfort, sir, because if *you're* watching your back, I'm probably already dead."

"I want you to read everything, leave here, go home and think. Then call me."

"With questions or answers?"

"I would hope both."

"The guy's probably long gone by now." *Real pros exit as well as they kill.*

Hayes lightly tapped the tabletop with his long, bony fingers. To Knox they looked like miniature Medusas in the dim light. "Perhaps."

"Look, I can spin my wheels and report back zip. You tell me the parameters, General. I've played this game too long to get the rookie runaround."

Hayes rose, as did his companion; the master and his puppet. "Read, think, call. Good night, Knox. And best of luck."

Knox glared after the pair until they disappeared

down the hall, the aircraft carrier and its faithful destroyer chugging through the storm-tossed seas of American intelligence. He lifted the lid of the box, pulled out a fistful of documents and started to read.

Best of luck said the cobra before it struck.

These were precisely the sorts of days where Knox wished he'd followed his old man into the plumbing business.

CHAPTER

6

STONE'S BRIEF SLEEP was suddenly disturbed by what sounded very much like a fight. He blinked awake and looked around. The woman next to him was comforting her crying baby. Stone stared over several rows of seats at the cause of the ruckus.

It looked to be three against one, all in their twenties, where the testosterone surge frequently overrode all safety valves. Two held one while the third pounded away. Some of the passengers were making halfhearted calls for the men to stop, but no one had climbed from their seats to really do anything. Stone looked around for the conductor but didn't see anyone in uniform.

The kid being held was the one Stone had seen before, the former high school quarterback who held an angry chit against the world. His handsome face was taking another right cross to his already swollen left cheek. Blood ran down his nose as he struggled to free himself. He kicked and spit and lunged, but couldn't break loose as the third fellow laughed and landed a kick to the gut that doubled over Mr. Quarterback.

Okay, that's enough.

Stone sprang up from his seat, and when the hitter swung back to let fly with another blow, he grabbed the fist and pulled hard, almost knocking the fellow off his feet. He jerked around and stared at Stone, his anger dissolving to amusement.

The kid was at least five inches shorter than the six-two Stone, but nearly forty years younger and fifty pounds heavier.

"You want some of it, old man?" the kid mocked, raising his fists. "You want some of this?" He danced and juked around, his belly jiggling, his meaty arms flapping and the bling on them jingling. It was all Stone could do to keep from laughing.

"Just let him go and we call it square."

"He's a card cheater!" yelled one of the other punks as he gripped the quarterback's hair and ripped his head upward. "He cheated at poker."

"And I think you taught him a real tough lesson. So why don't you let him go."

"Who the hell are you giving orders?" the beefy kid with the cocked fists said.

"Let's just call it a day, fellows. You made your point. He's banged up pretty bad."

"Yeah, but you're not."

"Just trying to make the peace." Stone looked at the other passengers, many of whom were elderly. "You've scared everybody pretty bad."

"You think we give a shit?" He pointed at Stone. "Now, what *you're* gonna do, old man, is say you're sorry for bothering us and you're gonna turn yourself around and go sit down if you know what's good for you. Otherwise I'm gonna have to kick your ass too. Hell, I just might do it anyway 'cause I feel like it. How 'bout that?"

It had been a long day and Stone was already pissed that he couldn't even get ten minutes of sleep, so he said, "Just you? Or with your two buddies there helping?"

The kid smiled. "Oh, just me, granddad. But I tell you what, just so's my kicking your ass won't be over too fast, I'll only use one hand." He gave a little jab and Stone darted his head out of the way.

"Oh, looky here, pops can dance. You a good dancer, pops?" The kid suddenly kicked at Stone, who seized the leg and held on to it with an iron grip.

Beefy's face now turned scarlet as he hopped around on one leg. "Let me go, or I'm gonna hurt you bad. Let me go!"

"You get one more chance," Stone said.

The kid swung a fist out. And missed.

Stone's elbow to the side of his head didn't. Neither did the blow to the nose, with the kid's bone breaking on impact. The punk crumpled to the floor moaning and twitching.

The other two dropped the quarterback and started forward. One fell like he'd been axe-cleaved when Stone's foot smashed his crotch and then collided with his head. The other never saw the fist slam into his gut and then shoot up and crush his chin. He ended up on the floor of the train car next to his friends, holding his stomach and his face.

"What the hell's going on here?"

Stone turned to see the rotund conductor racing down the aisle, walkie-talkie and ticket puncher in hand and his Amtrak cap bouncing on his head.

Before Stone could say anything one of the punks he'd laid out yelled, "He attacked us."

The other passengers immediately started talking, telling their version of what had happened, but it all came out pretty garbled.

The harried train conductor looked over the mess of bodies on the floor, then turned to Stone and said, "You're the only one left standing. So did you hit these men?"

"After they attacked me. They said they caught that one cheating at cards," Stone said, pointing to the "glory days" kid who sat on the floor holding his bloody nose. "They wouldn't stop pounding the crap out of him and then they came after me." He pointed to the crowded floor. "You can see it didn't turn out the way they probably intended."

"Okay, let me see some ID," the conductor said.

"What about their IDs? I'm just the Good Samaritan. Ask any of these folks."

"That may well be. But I'm starting with you and I'll work my way through all of them. How's that for a plan?"

Stone didn't want to give the man his ID, because he knew if he did it would end up in an official record somewhere that the folks coming for him might be able to find and use. Besides it was a fake ID and wouldn't pass muster under a database check.

"Why don't you start and *end* with them while I just take my seat? I wasn't really part of any of this."

"Either give me some ID or I radio ahead for the cops who'll be waiting at the next stop." He pointed to the young men. "You too."

The quarterback gave a groan and spit up some blood.

"He needs some medical attention," Stone said quickly. He knelt next to the young man and put a hand on his shoulder, only to have it thrown off.

"I don't need any damn help from the likes of you!"

Stone rose and said to the conductor, "I think we need to call in a doctor."

"If he wants medical attention, we'll get it, but I'm still waiting for your ID, sir," the Amtrak man said stubbornly.

He just isn't going to give up, is he?

"I'm getting off this damn train at the next stop," said the quarterback. He rose on shaky legs.

"That's fine. You can all get off as far as I'm concerned," the conductor said.

"What is the next stop?" said Stone.

The man told him. "And you either show me some ID or I radio for the police."

Stone thought for a moment. "How about I get off the train at the next stop too?"

"Works for me," said the conductor, staring at him intently. Stone did not like the look on the man's face; it was full of suspicion.

The conductor pointed at the young men lying on the floor. "Now all you get back in your damn seats and stay there or else you're going to jail, and I mean what I say."

The beefy kid Stone had pounded first wailed, "What if I want to press charges against this son of a bitch?" He pointed at Stone.

The conductor said, "Fine, and then that feller"—he

pointed at the quarterback—"can press charges against you. And this man," he added, indicating Stone, "can press charges against you too and your buddies, because what I'm hearing from all the other passengers is that you came after him first. So what's it gonna be, mister bloody nose?"

Beefy's cheeks quivered. "Screw it, just forget it."

"Smartest thing to come out of your mouth yet. And next time you want to brawl just make sure it's not on my train. You don't want to mess with Amtrak, sonny boy." The conductor turned and stalked off.

Stone retook his seat, inwardly fuming. Why the hell had he gotten involved? Now he'd lost his ride.

The woman next to him leaned over and said, "You sure were brave to do what you did. Where'd you learn to fight like that?"

"Boy Scouts," Stone said absently.

Her eyes widened. "Boy Scouts? You're kidding?"

"The Scouts were a lot tougher in my day, ma'am."

But then he grinned weakly and she laughed. "That was a good one," she said.

Stone stopped smiling.

Not really. Because now I'm screwed.

CHAPTER

7

CALEB SHAW and Reuben Rhodes had been depressed before Alex Ford came to Caleb's high-rise condo and dropped the latest news on them. Now their attitudes sank right through the floor.

Caleb poured himself a sherry and started popping greasy potato chips in his mouth as fast as possible, a longtime nervous habit of his, and he was the possessor of many. "How much more tragedy are we expected to endure?" he exclaimed.

Reuben said, "So he killed Simpson and Gray?"

"He didn't come right out and say it in the letter, but that looks to be the case," Alex said.

"Pricks deserved it," Reuben said staunchly.

"It was still murder, Reuben," Alex pointed out.

"And look what they did to him. Anybody get one day in jail for that? Hell no."

Alex looked ready to debate the point as he had with Annabelle but then seemed to think better of it.

"Where do you believe he is?" asked Caleb.

"Running," answered Alex. "And don't be surprised if the FBI shows up on your doorstep asking questions."

"If they do, I don't know nothing," Reuben stated firmly.

"Be careful on that score," Alex warned. "A perjury charge can get you a few years in a federal lockup."

"I'm not saying anything that'll get these bastards caught up with Oliver, Alex. And I'd expect you to do the same."

"My situation is a little different," Alex said defensively.

"Are you Oliver's friend? Didn't he save your life?"

"Yes. And I returned the favor, unless you've forgotten."

"And isn't he the reason you got that special commendation for busting that spy ring?"

"I get the point, Reuben."

"No, obviously you don't," the big man said, rising up to stand next to the tall Secret Service agent. "Because if you say anything to help them find Oliver, you're a traitor, plain and simple."

"There's nothing simple about it, Reuben. I'm still a federal agent. I took an oath to uphold the law."

"What does Annabelle think about that?" Reuben demanded.

"What the hell business is that of yours?"

"She thought it sucked too, didn't she?"

"Please," Caleb pleaded. "I'm sure Oliver would not have wanted this to drive a wedge between us."

"There's no wedge, Caleb. There's just the right way to be a friend and a wrong way," Reuben pointed out. "And I just want supercop here to be real clear on which side he needs to come down."

Alex did an eyeball-to-eyeball with Reuben. "Is that some sort of threat?"

"Oliver has been through hell and back because of Simpson and Gray. I'm glad they're dead. I would've put a round in their heads myself."

"Then you would've gone to prison."

"Right, under your way of thinking I guess Hitler deserved a trial."

"What the hell is your problem? You're making it seem like I'm against Oliver."

"It sounds to me like you are!"

"Alex, maybe you should leave, before things get out of hand," Caleb said. "Please."

Alex looked from the red-eyed Reuben to the distressed Caleb and walked out the door.

So much for the Camel Club, he thought. That was over. Done. Dead. And he was reasonably certain he would never see Annabelle again.

So preoccupied was he that Alex never saw the two men watching him from their car. When he drove off they followed. Meanwhile, another pair waited outside Caleb's apartment. The hunt apparently had already started.

CHAPTER

8

As the train pulled out of the station that was basically a few planks thrown together and poorly lighted at that, Stone looked at the quarterback. Then he eyed the three punks, who were staring at them both with looks of unfinished business they wanted to jump right on.

Stone heaved up his duffel bag and grabbed the young man's arm. "Let's go."

He jerked back. "I ain't going nowhere with you."

"Then you can stay here and let them finish what they started," Stone said, nodding at Beefy and his boys.

"They'll wanta jump you mor'n me. You kicked their ass."

"*Your* ass, on the other hand, they were kicking pretty easy. So which road do you think they're going to pick?"

For the first time Stone saw some element of reason slide across the young man's features.

"Okay, now that I seem to have your attention, why don't you start by telling me where you're coming from?"

"Home. Just getting away. Make my own life."

"I know the feeling. But as things stand right now it might make more sense to go back home, get patched up and then start your trip over. You got parents?"

"Got a mom."

"Where's home?"

The kid looked angrily over at the gang of three, who hadn't moved a muscle.

"I don't want to go back there. I just got away from that damn place."

Stone ran his gaze over the kid's jacket. "Looks like you were some athlete."

"Best ever to come out of that little shithole, and look what good it did me."

"Not many people make it in professional sports. That doesn't mean it wasn't worth it, or that you're some kind of failure."

"Thanks for the pep talk, changed my whole life," the kid said scornfully.

Stone let out a heavy sigh. "Look, son, I've got my own problems, so I'm about five seconds from leaving your ass to the hyenas over there unless we get an attitude adjustment real fast."

"What do you want me to do?" he snapped.

"Tell me your name and where you're from."

"Danny. Danny Riker," he said grudgingly. "Satisfied? And what's *your* name?"

Stone didn't hesitate. "Ben." That had been his father's name. "From where, Danny Riker?"

"*Divine*, Virginia. Little coal-mining town just this side of hell."

"How far from here?"

"About here to the moon."

Stone sighed again. "Is your mother still there?"

"That's right."

"So you just left her in the little hellhole all by herself?"

"She's not alone, trust me."

"You got money to get back home?"

"Maybe."

"You sure, or did you lose it all in the poker game? They say you were cheating."

"They just said that because they can't play cards worth shit." He glanced over at Beefy and cracked a smile. "Ain't that right, fat boy?"

"Where were you headed to on the train?" Stone asked.

"Where there ain't no coal to mine."

"You worked in the mines?"

Danny looked around. "I'm hungry."

He walked off toward a greasy spoon visible about a block away. It had a neon sign spelling out "restaurant" in cursive, with only the final "T" still lighted. In his head Stone instantly dubbed it the "One T."

Stone glanced back at Beefy and his battered goons. Beefy had a knife in his hand. If Stone left Danny alone now he was certain the men would finish him off. He'd killed many men over the years. Perhaps it was worth a bit of a detour from his plans to save one.

They ate at the counter with Stone occasionally looking over his shoulder to stare at Beefy and his boys sitting

at a booth gobbling up their burgers and fries and shooting nasty glances at them from over their beer mugs.

When Stone went to pay the check Danny dropped the
cash on the bill and rose.

"Thanks for helping me out back there," he said, without a trace of an attitude.

"You're welcome."

"You fight pretty good for a geezer." Somehow this
statement did not come out as an insult.

"I might not be as old as you think. I've just had a
tough life."

"Ain't we all."

"So where to now?"

"Gotta keep rolling or else you die. Think somebody
important said that once."

Not bad advice to live by, Stone thought. *I'm a rolling
stone right now.*

As they left the One T Beefy confronted them outside
the door, his two mates right behind him.

"Where the hell you two think you're going?"

"You know, I can set your nose back in place if you
want," Stone said amiably.

"You lay another hand on me, you son of a bitch, I'll
cut you bad." He brandished a knife. Well, it was technically a knife, but it was so small and the guy was handling
it so awkwardly that Stone had trouble thinking of it as
actually being a weapon.

"Okay. Good luck then."

He and Danny started to walk past when Beefy slashed
at them with the blade.

A second later he dropped to his knees holding his belly.
Danny rubbed his fist and looked down at his attacker.

"Not nearly as much fun when it's just one-on-one, is it, chunko?"

Beefy weakly threw a punch at Danny, catching him lightly on the knee. Danny wound up to nail him again, but then just pushed him away. He grinned at Stone. "Can't hit a man when he's down. Ain't sporting."

Stone glanced sharply at Beefy's two friends, who seemed to be deciding whether to attack or run. He said, "I'm done with you guys. So if you don't take your friend here and get the hell out of my life right now I'm going to beat both of you into a coma."

He knelt down, picked up the knife, and with a flick of his wrist tossed it ten feet where it embedded neatly in the wooden façade of the One T. Seconds later his two side-kicks were helping Beefy down the street as fast as they could go.

Danny was staring at the knife stuck in the wood, his mouth agape. He pulled it out and tossed it in a trash can. "Where'd you learn to throw like that?"

"Summer camp. So what's it going to be, Danny? Home to get patched up, or running around on that gimpy leg watching your back for those a-holes?"

"Home. Couple days. No more."

"Sounds like a plan."

"What about you?"

"Flop here for one night. Wait for the next train south. Tired of the cold." *Just tired.*

The men started walking down the street.

"I wasn't cheating at cards."

"I believe you."

"How come?"

"You don't seem dumb enough to cheat when it's three

against one. How you getting to Divine? The train go there?"

Danny laughed. "Hell, nothing *goes* to Divine. Bus goes near it. Walk or thumb it from there. Won't be the first time for me."

Stone's gaze caught on a black sedan that pulled slowly down the street. It stopped next to a police car and the driver of the sedan rolled down his window and started talking to the cop. Stone's eyes dropped to the white government plate on the sedan.

Bureau car? Here? Did the train conductor suspect something and make a call?

Stone turned to face Danny. "Divine a pretty isolated place?"

Danny's gaze drifted to the twin cars and then back to Stone. He'd clearly noted Stone's reaction to the police car. "Isolated? Let me put it like this. Divine's the sort of place you got to really want to get to if you want to find it. Although why anyone would beats me. And once you do find it then the only thing you want to do is get the hell out of there."

"Sounds good."

"What?"

"Let's go."

"You're kidding, right? I'm telling you, man, it's hell."

"I don't think so, Danny."

"What makes you a damn expert?"

Because I've actually seen hell. And it wasn't in Virginia.

CHAPTER

9

JOE KNOX CLIMBED IN his Range Rover and drove slowly home, deep in thought. He'd gone over every scrap of paper in that box and each held a startling revelation. Yet while the sum total of information was considerable, the investigative leads flowing from this intelligence were negligible. The CIA was exemplary in covering its tracks, and the Agency had outdone itself here. However, Knox had been able to piece a few things together.

The reason that Gray's home had been blown up six months ago seemed tied to an unauthorized CIA operation targeting the Soviets back in the 1980s. Exact details were not available and probably never would be. The connection in between was anything but clear. No names were available. One page in the box had stunned even the veteran Knox. There apparently had been a gun battle at the unfinished Capitol Visitor Center around the same time that Carter Gray's home had been destroyed. An unknown number of CIA paramilitary personnel had been killed, the real circumstances of their deaths hidden from public view by the Agency's very efficient disinformation machine. It seemed that Gray, then technically out of government, had been behind this mission. Who had killed the agents and why they were there in the first place remained a mystery.

A shoot-out in the middle of the Capitol? Gray must've been insane.

There was an indication in the file that Gray had met with the current CIA director, a man Knox considered a useless political appointee who had started at the Agency but had been brain-drained by his later years in the Congress. Whether Knox could get in to see the man was not a given. As Macklin Hayes had made clear, there was a difference of opinion at the Agency as to how this matter should proceed. Or *not* proceed.

Gray had also been given a secret audience with the president at Camp David. Knox suspected this piece of information was one of the ones Macklin Hayes had gotten hold of that he wasn't supposed to know about. Knox realized that the odds of his interrogating the president of the United States about this meeting were about the same as his spontaneously combusting while in the shower.

One of the most interesting pieces of information he'd gleaned from the file had to do with the now defunct Triple Six Division of the CIA, or its "political destabilization" arm as it unofficially had been known to the CIA rank and file. The less polite term of course was "government assassin." Triple Six was one of the CIA's most closely guarded secrets. Officially the CIA did not kill, torture or falsely imprison. Or, for that matter lie, cheat or steal. Unfortunately, the media had made some inroads into the Agency's past, resulting in some embarrassing revelations. Officially, Knox had followed the company line and been upset that the press had ferreted out some of this skullduggery. Personally, he'd never had much use for that side of the Agency. While it was true that the United States was better off with certain people dead, Knox had felt the CIA's best use of resources was in intelligence gathering, not authorized murder or stringing people up by their toes or making them believe they were drowning to induce them to talk. His experience had been that tortured people would tell you anything to make the pain stop. There were far more effective ways to get to the truth.

Gray had apparently concluded that several retired Triple Six assassins had been murdered. Whether these deaths were tied to the unauthorized mission in the former Soviet Union he had no way of knowing. According to one of Gray's bodyguards, the former intelligence head had met with a man at Gray's home on the very night it had been blown up. That man worked in a cemetery in Washington, D.C., and had been questioned by the FBI in connection with Gray's believed murder. And it was this man—the one Macklin Hayes had alluded to—who had suggested the bomber of Gray's home might've jumped off the cliff into the Chesapeake Bay.

Knox smiled grimly as he thought of the name the man had given the FBI agents.

Oliver Stone.

Was he a lunatic or something else? Since Carter Gray was not known to summon mentally unstable people to his home, Knox opted for the latter. Oliver Stone had been accompanied by a Secret Service agent when he'd visited Gray's demolished house. That too was interesting. He would have to get acquainted with Agent Alex Ford.

The last bit of interesting information had to do with a recent disinterment at Arlington National Cemetery. The grave of a man named John Carr had been dug up on orders from Gray. The coffin had been taken to CIA headquarters. Knox did not know the results of that action or actually who had ended up being in the coffin. He had seen some of Carr's confidential military record, and it was an exemplary one. Yet then the man had simply disappeared.

Knox's instincts told him that a man like Carr, with proven killing skills, would've made a productive member of Triple Six. Many of their members had come from the military. And right around the time Carr had vanished from public record was when Triple Six had been at the height of its activity. That had raised more questions than answers.

He reached his house and pulled into the garage. A moment later his daughter, Melanie, opened the door to the kitchen. She'd earlier phoned him to say she was coming over to take him to dinner. After he'd gotten the summons from Macklin Hayes he'd called her back saying he couldn't make it, so he was surprised to see her.

The aroma of a cooked meal reached him from the kitchen. She gave him a hug and ushered him in, taking off his coat and hanging it up.

He said, "I didn't think busy lawyers in private practice had time to cook for themselves, much less anybody else."

"Reserve your judgment until after you've eaten it. I don't watch the Food Network and I don't hold myself out as any sort of cook. But the intent was honorable."

Melanie had taken more after Knox's deceased wife, Patty, than she had her father. She was tall and lithe with reddish hair that she usually wore pulled back. She was a graduate of UVA Law School and a rapidly rising young star at a D.C. powerhouse legal firm. The older of his two children—his son, Kenny, was currently in Iraq with his fellow Marines—Melanie had taken it on herself to make sure her father did not starve or wallow in pity over the recent death of her mother and his wife of thirty years.

The meal was eaten in the sunroom where they shared a bottle of Amarone and Melanie filled him in on the latest case she was handling. Over the years his children had quickly learned that their father never discussed his work with them, or anyone else. They knew he traveled the world, often on very little notice, and was gone for long periods of time. This was explained as him serving his country in a minor capacity with the State Department.

He had once told Melanie, "I'm unimportant enough to where they can call on me whenever they like, and I just go."

That line had worked all the way through middle school. But once his precocious daughter had reached high school Knox could tell she no longer believed it, though she never tried to uncover the truth. His son had just accepted his father disappearing from time to time as the way life was. Now, as a Marine lance corporal serving overseas and trying to stay alive day by day, Kenny Knox had more on his mind, his father hoped, than worrying about what his old man did for a living.

"When you called to cancel," Melanie began, "I was sure you'd be on a plane somewhere. I got the idea of cooking dinner when you said you'd be back home tonight."

Knox simply nodded at this, while he sipped his wine and stared out at the trees in his backyard as they were whipsawed by yet another approaching storm.

"So everything going okay at work?" she asked tentatively.

"Just looking over some old papers. Not that enlightening actually."

It was hard, he knew, for her. Most kids knew exactly what their parents did for a living and consequently could have cared less. While his children were growing up Knox had declined all invitations to parents' career day at school. After all, what would he have said?

"Given any more thought to retiring?"

"I pretty much already am. One foot in the professional grave."

"I'm surprised the *State Department* can function without you."

Father and daughter exchanged a brief glance and then each looked away, focused on their wine and last bites of roast beef and potatoes.

As she was leaving Melanie let her hug linger around her father's broad shoulders. She whispered in his ear, "Take care of yourself, Dad. Don't push the envelope too hard. Dangerous times out there."

He watched her walk to the cab she'd called to take her home to her condo in D.C. As it drove way, she waved to him.

He waved back, fleeting images of the last thirty years

racing through his mind and ending with the image of Macklin Hayes telling him to tread carefully.

His brilliant daughter was right. It *was* dangerous times out there.

He would call Hayes in the morning. Early. The general was on rooster time. And like the rooster, he believed the sun rose because he did too. He had no answers and many questions. How the general would react to that he didn't know. In the military Macklin had the rep of always getting the job done, by any means possible, which often included excessive losses. After becoming a battalion commander in Vietnam, Hayes still held the record, Knox believed, of having the highest casualty count of any field officer in the war. Yet because those losses often came with victories, at least victories measured in the taking of small hills or even yards of turf, sometimes only for hours, Hayes had swiftly moved up the command chain. Still, Knox did not intend on becoming one of the man's statistics on his way to yet another triumph. The best he could hope for was to thread his way through the minefield, keeping his eye firmly on the target and watching his back at the same time. Macklin was a superb infighter, connected in all the right ways, and a man who excelled at putting other people's necks at risk while protecting his own flanks with skillful dexterity. Competitive past all reason, he reportedly thrashed men half his age in racquetball at the Pentagon's courts. What he lacked in speed, quickness and stamina he more than made up for with sheer guile and peerless vision.

His exact title in America's intelligence empire was unknown to Knox. The man performed a curious—and as far as Knox was aware an unprecedented—straddle between military- and civilian-sector intelligence factions. It was a powerful position and anyone under his control had to play by his rules or risk the consequences. He had been a close friend and protégé of Carter Gray, and no one could have had a better mentor. Knox would do his best to gauge the general's true intentions and then hope to fulfill them. Any way one looked at the task it was a formidable challenge.

He closed the door, stoked up the fireplace and picked up his novel with the intent of finishing it tonight. He might not get another chance for a very long time. When the wheels started to spin in his profession, they tended to spin very fast.

And from what Knox had seen in that box of secrets tonight, this time things could easily spin right out of control.

CHAPTER

10

KNOX WATCHED the earth disappear from underneath him as the tri-engine Falcon Dassault jet shot skyward with enormous thrust. The luxurious, wood-paneled interior of the plane only held three occupants, other than the two pilots up front—Knox, Macklin Hayes and a uniformed steward who'd discreetly disappeared as soon as the plane leveled off and the coffee and continental breakfast was served. When Knox had called Macklin at seven a.m. he'd been told to report to a private airstrip near Front Royal, Virginia, that he had no idea even existed. Five minutes after he'd pulled up in his Rover, the plane had lifted from the tarmac.

Hayes had an office in some building in some undisclosed part of Washington, Knox knew, but the man obviously preferred conducting his meetings at thirty-five thousand feet, as though the altitude made for better decision-making, or at least fewer opportunities to be spied on. Knox knew that just the fuel burn for this flight would have paid for some really nice digs in the heart of D.C. Yet it should have come as no surprise that some high-up government folks treated the U.S. Treasury as though it would never run out of dollars. At least it kept gainfully employed the feds who sold T-bills to the Chinese and the Saudis to keep America running.

The former general was dressed in civilian government standard issue, namely a boring suit and an equally boring tie and black wingtips on the feet. His socks were too short, Knox noted, and revealed pale ankles and the bottom of a hairless calf. The man had definitely not scaled the walls of power based on his fashion sense. He'd done it, Knox was well aware, on nerve and brains. The only sign of his former illustrious military career were the three stars on his tie clip.

They made casual conversation while munching an overabundance of carbs, and then the white-haired Hayes took a final sip of coffee and sat back in his leather seat looking expectant.

"Impressions from your reading session?"

"Many. None of them crystallized. I have to say the record is about as garbled as any I've seen. There're enough holes to fly a jet five times the size of this one right through it without even nicking a wingtip."

Hayes nodded approvingly. "I had the same *initial* reaction."

Knox didn't bother asking about the significance of the emphasized word because he knew from past dealings with Macklin that he would get zip for his troubles. "And

I have to say I'm still not clear on the agenda. Where do you want this to go?"

Hayes spread his long, bony arms. "Where? To the truth. I suppose."

"You don't sound convinced of that," Knox said warily.

"But that could change, depending on what you find out. You know how this drill works, Knox."

"Gray and Simpson are dead. Do we let sleeping dogs lie?"

"We need to know. What we do after we know? Now that's another question entirely and one that does *not* involve *you*."

The man has always been subtle about putting subordinates in their place.

"So I go full-bore on this? Is that what you're telling me, sir?"

Hayes simply nodded. It struck Knox that the former general might have suspected Knox was somehow taping this conversation.

If only I had the balls to.

Knox decided not to press the man on actually verbalizing his answer. For all he knew there was government muscle hidden on the jet somewhere who might be summoned to relieve him of his ride at nearly eight miles up if he pushed Macklin too far. Far-fetched? Perhaps. But Knox didn't want to find out.

"Tell me how you'll proceed."

"I've got some leads I can follow up. I take it DCI is off-limits," he said, referring to the director of Central Intelligence.

"I doubt he'd be much good to you anyway. Intelligence begins at home and his house is unfortunately empty."

Okay, he definitely knows I'm not taping this.

"Then the FBI agents who investigated the bombing at Gray's house. The Secret Service agent Ford. What about Triple Six?"

"What about it? Officially it never existed."

Knox had tired of the word games. Even his natural deference to the man had its limits. "There were subtle references in the papers intimating that somebody was popping retirees from the division and that Gray was aware of it."

"You can run that down if you want, but a dead end is what you'll find."

"How about the unauthorized Soviet op from decades ago?"

"History not worth repeating or dredging up. None of us would look good."

"You're not making this easy, General."

A smile eased across Hayes' face. "If it were easy why would we call you in, Knox?"

"I'm not a magician. I can't make things just appear or disappear."

"We have the disappearing end quite well covered. All we need to find is what we need to make vanish. How about the man Gray met with on the night his home blew up?"

"The famous film director, Oliver Stone?" Knox could not hold back his smile.

"He used to have a little tent in Lafayette Park. Was there longer than anyone else. I believe his sign read, 'I want the truth.'"

"Looking for the truth right across from the White

House? Sort of like hunting for Nazis in a synagogue. You consider him important?"

"The fact that he is no longer where he used to be, yes, I consider him important."

"What else do you know about him?"

"Not nearly enough. That's also why I consider him somewhat important."

"The grave being dug up at Arlington?"

"I was actually in the office on the day Carter Gray ordered that."

"Did he say why he wanted it done?"

"He was always better at giving orders than explaining them."

"So who was in the coffin? John Carr? Another body?"

"Neither. In fact there was nothing in the coffin."

"So Carr might still be alive?"

"He might."

"Was he a Triple Six? I read part of his military record. He would've fit the bill."

"Take that as your working hypothesis."

"So that would be the connection to Gray. Do you have reason to believe that Carr and Stone are one and the same?"

"I have no reason to believe that they're not."

"So why would Carr kill Gray and possibly Simpson?"

"Not all Triple Six personnel ended their deployment there on good terms. Carr may have been one such."

"If so, he waited a long time to pull the trigger. And he had just been to Gray's house. Did he have anything to do with blowing it up?"

"We don't think so."

"He could've killed Gray when he met with him."

"Maybe he didn't have the motivation then."

"So what changed?"

"That's for you to find out, Knox. There was the flag and grave marker. A clear sign, I think, that it's connected to this John Carr and his grave being dug up."

Knox marveled at how Hayes had gone from knowing very little and letting him find his own way in the investigation to, in a few short moments, shepherding him down the path he wanted. "I don't disagree. The man just seemed to have done it ass-backwards."

"Maybe he had his reasons. Regular reports, usual channels. But check back in with me tonight. If you need support, don't hesitate. We'll do what we can. Within limits, of course. As I said, not everyone is on the same page over this. Nothing I can do about that. Consensus in intelligence circles these days is as elusive as sectarian peace in Iraq."

That's reassuring. The right hand tells me to charge ahead while the left hand uses a knife to slit my throat.

Macklin pressed a button on the armrest of his seat and Knox felt the plane begin a tight bank to the right. Apparently, the flight and discussion were over.

To bolster that deduction Macklin rose without a word and made his way down the aisle to a door at the back of the plane. It clicked shut behind him.

Knox watched the clouds pass by as the plane began its descent through the Virginia sky. A half hour later he was tearing east on Interstate 66 in his Rover.

He would begin with Alex Ford and work his way through the usual suspects. But from what Hayes was both saying and leaving unarticulated, it seemed that all roads might lead right to a man named Oliver Stone.

If Stone had been a Triple Six and was good enough to take out both Simpson and Gray all these years later, Knox wasn't sure he wanted to run into the gent. Yet those sorts of encounters just came with the territory. And Knox was still standing.

But so, apparently, was Oliver Stone.

Dangerous times indeed.

Retirement was looking better and better. If only he could survive that long.

CHAPTER

11

GREYHOUND DIDN'T TRAVEL to the vicinity of Divine, Virginia. Yet a rusting bus on wobbly wheels with the name "Larry's Tours" crudely hand-stenciled on the side did. Stone and Danny sat in the back, next to a man who had a chicken in a crate on which he was resting his bare, swollen feet, and a woman who gave Stone far more attention than he would have liked, which included telling him her life story, all seventy-odd years of it. Fortunately, she got off before they did and was picked up by a man driving an ancient station wagon that was missing two of its doors.

They were finally let out at what Stone could only describe as the side of the road in the middle of nowhere. It made the one-horse stop Amtrak had dropped them at resemble a glittery metropolis on full throttle.

"Now what?" said Stone, shouldering his duffel while Danny clutched his small suitcase.

"Now we walk and thumb. Maybe we get lucky, maybe we don't."

Though it was not yet two in the morning they did get lucky and rode into Divine in the back of a pickup truck, with what the driver told them was a prizewinning hog named Luther who kept pushing his pink snout in Stone's crotch.

In the distance Stone saw the silhouette of some massive facility. Narrow towers and three-story buildings rose into the dark sky. In the weak moonlight something glinted along the perimeter of the place.

"What's that?" he said, pointing.

"Some place you never want to end up. Dead Rock. Supermax prison."

"Why do they call it Dead Rock?"

"It's built on the site of an old coal mine where about thirty years ago twenty-eight miners lost their lives in a cave-in. Their bodies are still in there somewhere 'cause they could never get to them. So they just sealed it up. They send the scum of the scum to Dead Rock. Least that's the official story. Hell on earth."

"You know somebody in that place?"

Danny looked away without answering.

Stone continued to stare at the complex until they rounded a curve and it disappeared from his view. He realized that the glint he'd seen must've come from the moonlight bouncing off the slash-your-ass wire that surrounded the place.

After the truck dropped them off their transportation became their own feet. Divine was still mostly dark at this hour, but Stone could see lights here and there as they trudged down the street. A truck passed them going east. And then another followed. And then another. Stone saw eight in all. Through the dirty truck windows Stone spied lean silhouettes of the drivers as they hunched over their steering wheels, cigarettes dangling between fingers, the windows cracked to let the white cancer-causing vapor escape into the frosty air. All around him he could sense the shadows of the nearby mountains, darker even than the night.

He checked his watch. It was barely two a.m. "Folks get an early start here?" Stone asked, nodding at the mini-caravan of dirty Fords and Chevys.

"They're miners."

"Going to work?"

"Nope. Next shift starts at seven. Those boys are heading to the clinic to get their methadone pop for thirteen bucks. Then they go to work."

"Methadone?"

"Some folks have cereal for breakfast, miners have methadone mixed with OJ in a cup. Just the way it is around here. Lot cheaper than snorting oxy up your nose or banging it into your feet. And that way you don't get dinged for dirty urine and lose your miner's license." Danny pointed up ahead to a small storefront set next to a clothing shop on one side and a hardware store on the other. Apparently Home Depot and Wal-Mart had not yet seen an opportunity in the isolated hamlet of Divine.

"That's my mom's place."

Stone eyed the sign. "Rita's Restaurant and Bar. So your mom's name is Rita?"

Danny wagged his head and grinned. "Nope. Rita ran

the place before her. My mom never had enough money to switch the sign out. Then when she got some cash she figured why bother changing it. Everybody already knew it was her place. Her name's Abigail, but everybody calls her Abby."

Danny put a key in the front door of the restaurant and motioned Stone to follow him in.

"Does your mother live here?"

"Nope, but there's an apartment above the restaurant. You can crash there for what's left of tonight."

"What about you?"

"I got things to do, people to see. Get myself patched up." He touched his face and his leg.

"A doctor at this hour?"

"Don't need no doctor. Hell, just feels like Friday night after a football game. Can't let it screw up your life. I got the quick fix all right."

"You sure it's okay that I stay here for the night?"

"Oh, yeah. I'll be back about the time Mom opens up for breakfast. Get it all straight with her."

Stone looked around the interior of the place. A long, polished mahogany bar with stools in front that was set at one end, with a deuce of pool tables and a 1950s-era jukebox anchoring the other end. In between were tables with checkered tablecloths and wheel-back chairs. The place didn't smell like a bar; it smelled like lemons and fresh air. From the looks of things Abigail Riker kept her place of business orderly and clean.

"Danny, is there any place around town I can do some work? I'm a little short on cash."

"I'll see what I can do."

Danny led him upstairs and a few minutes later an exhausted Stone was asleep on the small bed there.

A few hours later he woke up when he felt something hard touch his cheek.

It got his full attention.

Twelve-gauge shotgun muzzles usually did.

CHAPTER

12

"WHO IN THE HELL are you?"

Stone didn't move. Swift motion in the face of a big-bore weapon was never advisable.

"Are you Abigail Riker?"

"I'm asking the questions."

Stone saw her finger slide to the trigger.

"My name's Ben. Danny Riker said I could sleep here."

Stone saw her finger slide to the trigger as her scowl deepened. "You're lying. Danny's gone."

"Well, he's back now. I met him on the train. He got in a fight with some guys. I helped him out. He's a little beat up so he decided to come back here for a bit. I just came along."

The woman was in her early forties, petite, five-three, with narrow hips and the lean body of someone to whom food was not of much interest. Her braided hair was long and dark with hints of silver. Her cheekbones were high and tight. Her face was lovely but her wide green eyes flashed at Stone as she snapped, "How beat up is he?"

"Not that bad, mostly bruises. Can you get the shotgun out of my face? An accidental discharge would do a little more damage to me than that."

She stepped back but kept the muzzle pointed halfway between the floor and Stone's head.

"You said you helped him? Why?"

"It was three on one. Didn't seem all that fair. You mind if I stand up? My back is really starting to ache."

She took another step back as Stone stood and stretched. They heard feet on the stairs and a moment later Danny Riker appeared, his handsome face with the swollen cheek grinning as he sized up the situation.

"See you two already got acquainted."

"Yeah," Stone said tersely, eyeing the gun. "It was a nice way to wake up."

His mother had seemed dumbstruck to see her son. She found her voice and said, "What the hell's going on, Danny? You talked and talked about getting out, broke my heart, I did my crying and now you're back?" She swung the shotgun in Stone's direction. "And this man says only for a little bit."

"Took a detour, Ma. Shit happens."

"Yeah, well, shit seems to happen a lot to you." She lowered the shotgun and looked at Stone. "This man says he helped you in a fight. And from the looks of your face he's telling the truth."

"He did. Took three guys out all by himself. And he throws a knife like I've never seen."

She now seemed to appraise Stone in a different light. "You look a little old to be running around like Rambo."

"Trust me, I feel it this morning," said Stone. "I take it you are Abigail Riker?"

Instead of answering she said, "Guess you two are hungry. Come on, coffee's hot and so are the eggs."

They followed her downstairs where Stone could see the restaurant was already mostly full. Many of the customers were middle-aged men with coal dust rings under their eyes dressed in coveralls with reflective stripes on them.

"Miners off the night shift," Danny explained.

If Stone hadn't known better he would've thought he'd just walked into a hospital ward. Most of the men sat bent over, in obvious pain. Their hands, arms, legs, backs were all wrapped with something. Butchered fingers were curled tight around mugs of coffee. Cracked plastic safety helmets were on the floor next to feet that were encased in steel-toed boots. The men's eyes were red and unfocused. Lung-shattering coughs filled the room.

"Hell of a way to make a living," said Abby in a low voice as she led them to an empty table near the counter. She'd obviously observed Stone's amazed look.

She made plates for them and a famished Stone took the next ten minutes to devour two helpings and drink down three cups of piping hot coffee.

Abby drew a chair up next to them. She eyed her son and waited until he bit into a fourth piece of toast before cuffing him on the ear.

"What was that for?"

"You left and now you're back."

"Don't worry, I'll be heading out before you know it. Nobody needs to get pissed off."

"I didn't say I was pissed off."

"Well, are you?"

"Yes!"

Stone observed this exchange and then, simply to break the tension, said, "Where are you headed to?"

"Don't know. See where it takes me."

"Where what takes you?" Stone asked.

He shrugged. "Dreams. Everybody's got dreams. Might end up in California. Maybe in the movies. I'm tall and good-looking enough. Maybe I'll be a stuntman."

Abby shook her head. "How about college? That dream ever flit inside that big head of yours?"

"Ma, we've had that talk."

"No, *I've* had that talk and you decided not to enter the discussion."

"If my knee had held up, I'd be playing ball for Virginia Tech right now. But it didn't. So what good is college gonna do me? It's not like I was such a great student in high school."

"You're not stupid!"

"Never said I was. Just not book smart."

She looked over at Stone. "Did you go to college?"

He shook his head. "Wanted to but I ended up going to war instead."

She said, "Vietnam?" He nodded.

"So that's why you fight so good. You ain't one of them crazy vets with a metal plate in your head, are you?" said Danny, grinning. "A walking time bomb?"

"The man fought for his country, Danny, don't make that into a joke," scolded his mother.

"I made it home without any metal plates," Stone said.

"Ever get shot?" Danny asked eagerly.

Stone said, "I agree with your mother. College should be on your radar."

"Well, I'll just go sign up right now. Just give me a check for a hundred grand for Harvard, Ma, and I'm out of here."

Abby started to say something when the door opened. Stone could sense the quiet chatter in the restaurant fading away. When he looked up he saw the big man standing in the doorway, his uniform sparkling and his Stetson perched at an angle on his head. His skin was leathery and lined from wind and sun. But it was a handsome face, its jaw tight and jutting like the lower half of a medieval helmet. The curly fringes of his dark hair stuck out from under the rim of the Stetson. His right hand rested over the top of his holstered pistol like a road scavenger's claw over its kill.

His gaze swung around Rita's until it came to rest on Abby Riker. He smiled. Then he saw Stone sitting next to her. And the big man stopped smiling.

CHAPTER

13

Alex Ford was heading out to grab some lunch when the man approached him on the street outside of the Secret Service's Washington Field Office.

"Got a minute?" the fellow asked, flashing his creds.

Alex flinched when he saw the Agency insignia.

Great, here we go.

"What's this about, Agent Knox?" But he really already knew of course.

"We need to talk."

"Now?"

"Now."

The two men started off and soon they reached a small park where Knox sat on a bench and motioned for Alex to join him.

Knox spoke for some minutes, mostly telling Alex things he already knew.

"Your friend's not at home," Knox said.

"Really? I haven't been by to see him lately."

"But according to my sources you have been by to see the lady that was staying there. Funny, she's gone too. What can you tell me about her?"

"Not much."

"Let's start with a name."

Alex drew a shallow breath. *This could get real complicated real fast.* "What's her involvement? Or my friend's?"

"That's what we're trying to figure out. Her name?"

"Susan. Susan Hunter."

"Do you know where she is?"

"No." *At least that's the truth.*

"What's your relationship with her?"

"Just friends."

"And why is your friend gone now?"

"Who knows? Here today, gone tomorrow. She's just that sort of person."

"Your other *friend* Oliver Stone received a commendation from none other than the FBI director for helping to break up a spy ring here in D.C."

"That's right. I was involved in that at the end. But he deserves the credit."

"And he used to have a tent in Lafayette Park. A White House protestor. And he was caretaker at a cemetery. And he helps break up spy rings. Interesting career choices."

"He's an interesting guy."

"What else can you tell me about this interesting guy? Like his connection to Carter Gray?"

"Carter Gray?" Alex did his best to appear baffled even as the sweat gathered under his armpits. By lying to a federal officer he'd already committed several felonies. He was digging his professional grave deeper with each word.

"Yeah. Carter Gray. Stone went to see him on the night his house was blown up. You came out the next day with him to the crime scene. I've talked to the FBI agents who were out there with both of you."

"Right, right. Well, I knew that Oliver had gone to see Gray because he told me he had. I don't know why. He asked me to come with him to meet the FBI agents. So I did. As far as I know that's where it was left."

"How'd you two meet?"

"Anybody who's pulled White House Protection Detail knows about Oliver Stone. He was a fixture in Lafayette Park for a long time."

"You happen to know his real name, or is the famous film director moonlighting?"

"I don't know his real name."

"I thought Secret Service agents were more inquisitive than that. Guy was right across from the White House and you don't even know his real name?"

"It's a free country. He never did anything threatening. Just exercising his right to protest. We just thought he was an eccentric."

"So the name John Carr ring any bells?"

Alex had been expecting that follow-up question. "No, but it sounds familiar for some reason."

"It was the name of a soldier whose grave was dug up at Arlington Cemetery. On Gray's orders."

"That's right. I read about it in the papers. I wonder what the hell that was about?"

Knox just stared at him.

Finally Alex broke the silence. "I don't know what to tell you, Agent Knox."

"The truth would be helpful."

The migraine started in the center of Alex's forehead. "I'm *telling* you the truth."

Knox looked down and shook his head slowly. When he glanced back up his features were sad. "You aiming to scuttle your career over this guy, Ford?"

"I know him as Oliver Stone. That's it."

"You know his buddies. Reuben Rhodes and Caleb Shaw?"

"Yes. They're my friends too."

"And one recently died." Knox looked at a little notebook he held. "Milton Farb. Killed in his house over six months ago."

"That's right. We were all really upset about that."

"I'm sure. Police never solved the crime?"

"That's right, they didn't."

"And you were also working with the feds on nailing the casino king Jerry Bagger. Only he ended up blown to pieces in the Potomac River."

"I almost ended up there myself."

"You're a busy man. And your friend too, what did you call her, Susan Hunter?"

"I called her that because it's her name. And that's right, she was there too."

"And how did you get involved with a guy like Bagger? Through the lady?"

"It's pretty complicated and I'm not at liberty to divulge what happened. But the FBI can probably fill you in. And really I was just helping out a friend again."

"Man, you got lots of friends."

"Better than lots of enemies," Alex shot back.

"Oh, I think you got a few of those too." Knox rose and handed Alex a card. "You think about any more bullshit you want to tell me, give me a buzz. Meantime, I'll check everything you just told me out seven ways from Sunday. And just to show my good faith, I'll give you a two-minute heads-up before they serve you with the arrest warrant for obstruction of justice. How's that sound, Ford? You have a good one now." Knox walked off.

Alex just sat there on the bench because his legs, at that moment, didn't have the strength to support his body.

Thanks, Oliver, Thanks a lot.

CHAPTER

14

Kɴᴏx's ɴᴇxᴛ sᴛᴏᴘ was the Library of Congress' Rare
Book Reading Room where he found Caleb Shaw placing
some priceless tomes on a rolling cart. Five minutes later
they were sitting in the same small room where Caleb had
been interrogated by casino owner Jerry Bagger. On seeing Knox's credentials Caleb said coolly, "And you want
to see me about what?"

"Your friend, Oliver Stone?"

"You call him a friend. I call him an acquaintance."

"That's just semantics."

"I'm a librarian. Semantics are my life. Besides, I
haven't seen him in a long time. I'm afraid I don't know
anything that could help you."

"Well, sometimes people know more than they think."

"If I knew more than I thought, then I'd know it."

His patience clearly exhausted, Knox said, "Okay, let's

cut to the chase, Shaw. I don't have all day to pull this story together so just answer my questions. Who is Oliver Stone really? And where is he now?"

"Oliver is Oliver. He used to have a tent in Lafayette Park. He's the caretaker at Mt. Zion Cemetery. But I don't know where he is. I haven't seen him for over six months. You can water-dunk me and I'd tell you the same thing."

"You mean *waterboarding*, and we don't do that to people," Knox said firmly. "Because that constitutes torture."

"Oh, really?" Caleb replied with both eyebrows tilted to the ceiling. "Then you might want to let your friends in the government know. There seems to be some confusion on that particular topic."

Ignoring this, Knox said, "Does the name John Carr mean anything to you?"

"Yes, it absolutely does."

Knox perked up. "Tell me about him."

"John Dickson Carr is a very famous mystery writer. Well, he's dead now, but I can recommend several of his works to you. Good stuff."

"I'm talking about John Carr the soldier, not the writer," Knox snapped.

"I don't know anyone by that name. There is of course John le Carré, but he's also a writer, though he did work in British intelligence at one point. And le Carré is only a nom de plume. His real name is David Cornwell. I could recommend some of his works as well."

Knox ground his teeth together and reminded himself that beating to death a public servant was not in the best interests of either his investigation or a future peaceful retirement. "This soldier was an *American*. Very distinguished record in Nam. He died. He was buried. This was over thirty years ago. Then they dug up his grave at Arlington and there was no body in it."

"Good Lord! I don't like to disparage my employer, but the federal government really has become so sloppy recently. But to lose an entire *body*? That really is outrageous."

Knox stared at him for a moment, then said, "Maybe the body was never in the grave, Shaw. How does that theory grab you?"

"Interesting, but what does that have to do with me?"

"Maybe John Carr and Oliver Stone are one and the same?"

"Well, I don't really see how that could be. But then again, Oliver never talked about his past and I respected his privacy. He's a good man, though, one of the most loyal friends anyone could ask for."

"You sound pretty sure for him just being an *acquaintance.*"

"I'm a quick and accurate judge of people."

"How about your buddy, Milton Farb? Was Stone loyal to him?"

"Milton's dead," Caleb said firmly.

"I know. I'd like to know how he died."

"He was murdered."

"I know that too. Any idea who might've killed him?"

"If I did, the police would know, I can assure you."

"He dies and your buddy Oliver disappears?"

"If you're thinking that Oliver had anything to do with it, you're sadly mistaken. He loved Milton like a brother."

"Right. Anything else you can tell me?"

"Not unless it has to do with rare books."

He handed Caleb a card. "Call me if you *don't* think of anything else."

He left the room.

At another time in his life Caleb probably would've have fainted dead away after such an encounter. However, he was a different person now, especially after Milton's death.

He simply rose and went back to work, tucking the card into his pocket.

Knox drove to the warehouse where Reuben Rhodes worked, but the big man was not there, nor had anyone seen him for some days. They also did not have an address for him.

"How do you pay the man without a home address?" he asked the foreman.

"He picks up his check in person. I never mail it. That's the way he likes it."

"How about his year-end tax documents?"

"I give him that too. In person."

"I take it the man doesn't want people to know where he lives?"

"I'm not putting words in Reuben's mouth but I'd say that was a fair assessment."

"What can you tell me about him?"

"Good worker, nice sense of humor. Doesn't like rules too much. Likes the government even less."

"Did you know he worked in military intelligence for years?"

"He never mentioned that. I knew he was in the army. Helluva soldier, I bet. Man's strong enough to strangle a bear. Wouldn't want to get on the bad side of him."

"I'll try to keep that in mind."

"Mister, if I were you, I sure would. Four fellows jumped him leaving work one night. Three of them ended up in the hospital and the fourth fellow would've too, but he ran too fast for Reuben to catch him."

Knox climbed back in his truck and headed off. A moment later he received a text message from Macklin Hayes. They had just tracked down the woman who'd been staying at Stone's cottage. She was at a hotel in downtown D.C.

Knox floored it. Right now he had one lying Secret Service agent and one federal librarian who acted clueless but wasn't and an AWOL loading dock worker with a grudge against the U.S. government who could probably break Knox's neck with ease.

Knox could only hope the lady would tell him what he needed to know. Yet he doubted it would be that easy. If he'd learned nothing else about this Oliver Stone character it was that he commanded a great deal of loyalty from his friends.

Knox would just have to see how long that loyalty would endure. He was very good at pushing such things to their limits. And beyond.

CHAPTER

15

THE BIG MAN swept off his hat and ambled forward to the table where Stone, Danny and Abby were sitting. He had the smooth gait and perfect build of the natural athlete. Along the way he shook the gnarled hands of some of the customers and patted many a back like a politician scavenging for votes.

"Hello, Abby," he said as he stopped at their table. He eyed Danny. "Thought you were heading out to make your way in the world, young man."

"Got sidetracked, Sheriff. You know me, short attention span."

The policeman gave him an easy grin. "That include getting your face busted up? Girl or guy?"

"If it'd been a girl I'd have a little bit of lipstick on me," Danny said slyly. "Before she got pissed and slugged me."

"He'll be heading back out soon," Abby said. "So he says."

The sheriff turned his attention to Stone. "Who we got here?"

"New friend of mine," said Danny quickly. "Ben, this here is Sheriff Lincoln Tyree."

Tyree put out a big hand. "Just call me Tyree, everybody does, Ben. Got a bunch of Lincolns in my family. Like most folks round here the Tyrees fought for the Union. Pleased to meet you."

Stone shook his hand. There was great strength in the man's fingers, he noted. But he didn't attempt to crush Stone's hand. The grip was measured, confident but not aggressive.

Tyree pulled up an empty chair and sat down, laid his hat on the table and motioned to the waitress to bring him a cup of coffee.

"When'd you get back, Danny?"

"Late last night or early this morning, depending on how you want to call it. Got in a little tussle on the train. Some fellers jumped me. And Ben helped me out. In fact, he laid all three of them out without any help from me."

Tyree nodded at Stone, a new level of respect on his features. "Thank you for that. We were all worried when Danny told us he was leaving. We're pretty insulated here. Outside world's different from our little town."

"Places are different and also the same," Stone said. "Some bad and some good everywhere you go."

Tyree chuckled. "Well, I hope we've got more good in Divine than bad, right, Abby?"

She fingered her coffee and nodded absently. "Nice town, good place to raise a family," she said.

"Hell, yeah," exclaimed Danny. "I mean, look how I turned out."

Abby's face flushed and Tyree silently drank his coffee that the waitress put down in front of him.

"You gonna be staying around, Ben?" Tyree finally asked. "We don't get many visitors up here. Most people here have been here all their lives. Unlike Danny here, they tend to stay in Divine till they die."

Danny snorted at this comment.

Stone shook his head. "Just wanted to see that Danny got home okay. I'll be heading on soon."

"You're welcome to stay," Danny said. This comment made both Abby and Tyree stare uneasily at him, something Stone was quick to note.

"I doubt he'd find much to keep him here," Abby said.

"You never know, Ma. Ben here might be looking for a little peace and quiet."

Stone stared at Danny for a moment. Was the kid a mind reader? "Thanks, but I'll be moving on soon." Stone wasn't going to stay and he didn't like sitting next to a lawman, small-town or otherwise.

"I do appreciate what you did for Danny. And you can stay in the room upstairs tonight, if you want," Abby said.

"You've done enough for me," Stone said. "Bed and a good breakfast."

"Ben needs some work to do," Danny said. "Needs some cash because he got thrown off that train along with my sorry ass."

"I'm sure I can find something for you to do, Ben," Abby said.

"I appreciate it."

The sheriff said, "You know, you're welcome to stay over at the jail."

"Behind bars?" Danny said, laughing.

"On the cot in the back," said Tyree with slight annoyance. "Probably keep you okay for *one* night. Real quiet. No prisoners in lockup now."

"Yeah, they're all up at old Dead Rock," said Danny. "We passed it coming up. Looks real pretty at night," he added sarcastically.

Tyree nodded. "Put it on a mountaintop in the middle of nowhere, and for good reason. City folks don't want supermaxes in their backyard. But they'll dump them here. Not complaining, it brings jobs to folks, and Lord knows we need them." He motioned to the door where two burly young men in blue uniforms walked in and sat down at a table. "There're two of them right there. Probably be heading up to the prison after they fill their bellies."

"If you ain't working in the mines or the prisons, you ain't making a living 'round here," said Danny. "Because everything else is for shit."

Tyree scowled at him. "Now, Danny, you know that's not true. We got us a whole line of shops up and down that street outside that are doing real good. Folks can earn a decent living in Divine, hold their heads up and take care of each other. It's not like that in most places."

"I can vouch for that," Stone said.

As there was a pause in the conversation the picture on the TV hanging on a wall behind the counter caught their attention; Stone's more than anyone else's. It was about the murders in Washington. The FBI had leads they were running down. Several persons of interest were being questioned. And though no one at the Bureau would be specific, apparently there was a theory tying together the killings of Simpson and Gray.

Tyree said, "Hope that they catch the bastard. I think it's some terrorist plot."

"Towelheads on the run," said Danny, chuckling. "Well, if they come here they'll be pretty easy to spot."

"No laughing matter, Danny. These crazies are trying to take over the world." He touched his gun. "But I tell you what, if they do show up in Divine, they can expect some good old American justice."

Stone turned to Abby. "What sort of work do you need done?"

Tyree stood, the rubbed leather of his gun belt squeaking slightly. "Danny, come see me later, boy, okay?"

It really wasn't a question.

Danny grinned, nodded and went back to his over-easy eggs and grease-fried bacon.

"Supplies need to be brought in from the back," Abby told Stone. "Storage room picked up. Windows washed, floor mopped. One of my dishwashers called in sick so you can pitch in there too."

Stone nodded, wiped his mouth with his napkin and rose. "Just give me a quick walkthrough and I'll get to it."

"Don't you want to know your pay scale?"

"I'll leave it up to you."

"You're a trusting man," chuckled Tyree before he left.

No, I'm not.

As Stone followed Abby to the back room Danny's grin eased off his face as he looked at the dirty, tired men staring back at him. He finished eating, slurped down his coffee, jumped up from the table and made his way to the door. Before he got there, a lanky man rose from his table and blocked his way. He had greasy hair, three days of beard, a coal-dusted face, and eyes that were just begging for trouble.

"Hey, Lonnie," said Danny. "You're looking like shit just like always."

"What you doing back here? Heard you bought yourself a ticket on the train. Had enough of Divine. Ain't that right, Danny boy? Had enough of us?"

"Didn't you know? Got the FBI on my ass for robbing that damn train. Came here to hide out. You'll cover for me, right?"

"You think any of that's funny?" said Lonnie as he slipped a wedge of chew into his mouth, pushing his fingers so far in it was a wonder he didn't gag.

"I try to find the humor in everything, Lonnie. Makes life a lot more bearable."

"You staying this time or not?"

"Why, you gonna miss me if I leave again? Best watch out. People might think you got a weird-ass thing for me, dude."

Some of the men at the other tables laughed at this. Lonnie's hands balled to fists, but Danny gripped his bony shoulder. "Just joking around, man. Ain't made up my mind whether I'm going or not. Soon as I do you'll be one of the first I tell. Now, I got to go. While I'm standing here flapping my jaw with you, I could be making millions of bucks out there in the big city of Divine."

He skirted around Lonnie, who suddenly became aware that all eyes were now on him. As the door slammed shut behind Danny, Lonnie quickly sat back down and with a defiant look shot a wad of chew into an old coffee can sitting on the floor.

Behind the bar, Stone set down a load of boxes. He had heard most of this exchange. Divine was turning out to be quite a peculiar town.

Get the cash and hit the road. Before twitchy trigger finger Tyree finds out I'm the towelhead.

CHAPTER

16

SIX HOURS LATER Stone had finished his work and Abby pronounced herself satisfied with what he'd done.

"You've got a lot of energy," she said. "And you don't waste time. I like that in a person." She smiled and for the first time Stone registered on how lovely she actually was.

"What now?"

"There're some more chores to be done at my house. All outside work. You interested? It's a dirty job."

"Just tell me how to get there. And what you want done."

He grabbed his duffel bag and a few minutes later left the restaurant. For the first time Stone got a good look at Divine in daylight. It surprised him.

Right out of Andy Griffith's Mayberry but with a Hollywood veneer, something the Disney people might have put together, he concluded. The storefronts were all freshly painted and the wood new-looking; the windows were clean, the brick sidewalks smooth and swept, the roads recently laid with black asphalt. Folks walked past waving at each other, friendly "hellos" floated all around him, though none were directed at Stone, apparently the only stranger here.

He passed what looked to be a new brick building that was the town's library. He peered through the glass doors and saw shelves of books and rows of shiny computers. It occurred to Stone that he couldn't even get a library card. He walked on.

The cars and trucks that passed by him as he made his way through the downtown area were all relatively new. He gazed up at the two-story jail, constructed of red brick with white columns out front and tubs of pansies guarding the entrance, and Coke and snack machines set against the wall. It was the most inviting entrance to the shackled life Stone had ever seen, though. Next door was a larger building, built of red brick too, with a clock tower and "Court House" stenciled on the outside.

A jail and a courthouse in such a little hamlet? With a supermax prison not that far away? But the supermax was for the deadliest of the deadly, not small-town criminals who probably stole car batteries and hit their bar mate while shit-faced.

As he was thinking this a small man with snowy white hair came out of the courthouse, perched a soft felt driving cap on his head and ambled down the street away from Stone.

"Want me to introduce you to the judge?"

Stone turned around and saw Tyree standing behind

him. He must have come out of the jail. The big man moved quietly. Stone didn't like that stealth.

"The judge?" *A lawman and a judge.* Just what he needed. They could both arrest and try him for murder right now.

Tyree nodded and called out, "Dwight, got somebody here you might want to meet."

The small man glanced around, saw Tyree and smiled. He headed back toward them.

"This here is Ben," Tyree said. "You got a last name, Ben?"

"Thomas," Stone said quickly.

"Okay, this is the Honorable Dwight Mosley."

Up close Stone had the impression that he was talking to a smaller version of Santa Claus with a trim beard in place of the bushy one.

Mosley chuckled. "I'm not sure how honorable I am or ever was, but it does indeed come with the title of a judge."

"Ben was the one who saved Danny Riker's butt when he got into some trouble on a train."

"I heard Danny was back. Well, thank you, Ben. Danny can be, well . . ."

"Hotheaded?" suggested Stone.

"Impetuous."

"A nicer word, but means the same thing," Tyree pointed out with a laugh.

"Fine-looking courthouse you have there," said Stone, glancing away from the judge. "I guess you have a lot going on?"

"You wouldn't think a small town like this would have need of a courthouse or a judge," Mosley said, apparently reading Stone's mind. "But the fact is it does because my jurisdiction covers a large geographic area in addition to Divine. It's not just litigation, though we have a fair amount of that, mostly over mineral rights and such and mining accidents resulting in personal injury. And federal law just changed a few months ago that required coal-mining companies to file what are termed recertifications for all their property and operational aspects. Unfortunately for me, I'm the judge who has to review all of it." He pointed at a delivery truck pulling into the small alleyway that led to a parking area behind the courthouse.

"Unless I'm much mistaken that's another load of boxes filled with said recertifications. It's been a boondoggle for mining lawyers, but I get paid the same regardless."

"Monotonous work, I imagine," said Stone.

"You imagine correctly. We're also the repository for land deeds, surveys, rights-of-way, easements and the like, which also come to the court boxes at a time. But on a more personal level folks come to me with legal questions or counseling from time to time and I try to do the best I can."

"Being neighborly," said Tyree.

"That's right. It is a small town after all. For example I helped Abby Riker get the restaurant and other property put into her name after Sam died."

"Sounds like you keep pretty busy."

"Yes, but I find time to do some hunting and fishing. And I like my walks. My walks take me all over. Beautiful countryside here."

They paused for a moment as a mother and two kids walked by. Tyree tipped his hat to her and rubbed the heads of the kids while the judge gave them all a gracious smile.

After the family had passed Stone said, "Well, I better be going."

But Mosley said, "Where are you from, Ben?"

Stone's gut clenched. It wasn't what Mosley had said, it was the way he'd said it. Or had he just become overly paranoid? "Here and there. Never had much inclination to put down roots."

"I was the opposite of that, at least for a while. I called Brooklyn home for the first thirty years of my life. After that I spent time in South America and then Texas, near the border. But I've never seen any place as pretty as this."

"How'd you end up here?" Stone asked, resigned at least for the moment to play the casual conversation game so as not to make the judge suspicious.

"Complete coincidence. Drove through on my way back to New York after my wife died, and my car broke down. By the time it was fixed a few days later, I'd fallen in love with the place."

"And lucky for us he did," said Tyree.

"The town has reciprocated," said Mosley. "It certainly helped me get over my poor wife's passing." He added, "Are you going for a walk too?"

"To Abby's actually. She has some work out at her house she wants me to do."

"A beautiful place that is, A Midsummer's Farm."

"Is that what she calls it?" Stone asked.

Mosley nodded. "A variation on the Shakespeare play. A dream, you see. I guess in a way all of us up here are living a dream, isolated as we are from the rest of society."

"Not such a bad thing," Tyree noted. "The rest of society isn't all that great. Divine is just what it sounds like, at least it is for me."

Mosley passed by them and continued on down the street.

Tyree took off his hat and swiped his hair. "Well, you have a good one, Ben. Don't work too hard."

Tyree went inside the jailhouse and Stone continued on his way to Abby's.

Or A Midsummer's Farm.

Or a dream.

Or a nightmare.

CHAPTER

17

As Stone passed down the main street of Divine, he quickly observed that the shops seemed prosperous and the customers happy-looking. It was hard for him to reconcile this image with that of broken-backed, gnarled-handed, dirty-faced miners with the coal-caked lungs having breakfast in Rita's Restaurant. And then his thoughts refocused on what he'd seen on the TV.

Leads. People of interest. Ties between the two murders.

As he glanced through one storefront window he saw it. Ubiquitous for so many decades, it was now rare to find one anywhere, at least one that worked. Yet Divine apparently was a bit slow in following the rest of the country's lead.

He slipped inside and looked at the payphone on the wall and then at the sign behind the front counter:

"Appalachian Crafts." The store's shelves bulged with sculptures made from wood, stone and clay. On the walls were paintings and photos of mountains, valleys and little tin-roofed shacks clinging to the sides of hills. Behind the counter a large, red-faced woman was pecking keys on her computer.

She looked up and smiled. "Can I help you?"

"I just wanted to use the phone. Do you have change for a five?"

She gave him the money and he retreated to the rear of the store and loaded the quarters in the phone's slots. He dialed the one person he knew had a truly untraceable phone number: Reuben. This was because he didn't have a phone in his own account but rather used minutes of piggybacked phone time from hundreds of different people. Stone had always assumed it had been something Milton had shown him how to do.

The big man answered on the second ring. He nearly shouted when he heard it was Stone. After telling Reuben that he was fine and that he would not under any circumstances tell him where he was, Stone asked him about the investigation.

"Guy named Joe Knox from CIA has talked to everybody but me. Real bulldog apparently. He knows you and Carr are one and the same. He knows you're on the run. If they find you you're not going to trial, Oliver."

"That had already occurred to me, Reuben. How is everyone holding up?"

"Okay. Alex is being a shit about all this, though."

"He's a federal agent, Reuben. He's caught right in the middle."

"Well, he did tell Annabelle to burn the letter you left behind. I guess I should give him some points for that."

"Tell him I appreciate that. I really do."

There was a brief pause and then Reuben said, "Oliver . . ."

"I'm not going to tell you that I did it, Reuben. That would do no good at all. I just want you to know that you were a better friend than I deserved. All of you were. And I'll be watching the news. If it even looks like any of you will be harmed because of this, I'll turn myself in."

"Listen to me, we can take care of ourselves. They can't touch us. But if you turn yourself in to the cops, CIA will swoop in, scream national security, and your ass will disappear."

"Let me worry about that. And I know it doesn't do you justice, but thanks for everything."

Reuben started to speak but Stone had already hung up, replacing the receiver with a smack of finality. *It's like I just cut off my right arm. Good-bye, Reuben.*

He glanced up to see the shopkeeper staring curiously at him. He had been speaking so low that there was no risk of being overheard.

"Call go through okay?" she said pleasantly.

"Just fine. Thanks." She kept staring at him so he finally said, "You have some nice pieces." Pointing to a painting on one wall, he added, "Who did that one?"

The woman's face fell. "Oh, that would be Debby Randolph."

"She's talented."

"Yes." She added quickly, "I'm Wanda. Haven't seen you around here before."

"I just got here. Came in late last night with Danny Riker."

"Danny?" she said, startled. "Heard he'd left town."

"Well, he's back, but I think it's just temporary. So how's business?"

"Really good, especially on our Web site. Lot of folks like the Appalachian stuff. Takes 'em back to a simpler time, I suppose."

"I think we could all use a bit of that. Well, thank you."

"Hope you come back. Got a sale on black bear cubs sculpted from chunks of coal. Makes a right fine paperweight."

"I'm sure."

Stone walked out of the "feel-good" shop feeling like he was navigating the last few yards to his own death. He really was all alone again.

CHAPTER

18

THE ASPHALT ROAD gave way about a half mile out to macadam. Stone passed by a stone church that had a small steeple with a dry-stack stone wall encircling the property. Next to this house of worship was a graveyard. The former graveyard caretaker Stone took a moment to walk through the burial plots. The same family names kept popping up on the headstones. Stone saw the grave of Samuel Riker. He'd died five years ago at the age of forty-one.

There were many Tyrees also sprinkled around. One tombstone, darkened by age, was the resting place of Lincoln Q. Tyree. He'd died in 1901. Stone thought it must be a bit disconcerting to pass by a graveyard with a marker already bearing your name, but perhaps the good sheriff didn't come this way often.

Two graves still had fresh flowers on them and the

mounds of dirt looked new. Rory Peterson had died a week ago. The name on the other grave made Stone do a double take. Debby Randolph had gone to her Lord a day after Peterson had died. That's apparently why the woman at the shop had acted a little strangely. Peterson was forty-eight while Debby had only been twenty-three.

Stone walked on, turning left at a fat oak with thick sprawling branches that resembled more Atlas holding up the world than a mere tree. Hanging from one of the branches was a sign that read "A Midsummer's Farm" with an arrow pointing to the left. He went on for another hundred yards down a crushed gravel path until he came to the house, although that term clearly didn't do it justice. He wasn't sure exactly what he had been expecting, but it wasn't this.

"Antebellum" was the first word that jumped to mind. It was large, constructed of white clapboard and sections of stone with black doors and shutters and no fewer than four stone chimneystacks. A broad front overhang supported by rows of elaborately milled columns offered up a fine porch with rocking chairs, sturdy tables, hanging plants and an upholstered swing anchoring one end. The landscaped yard stretched on and on with the perimeter bordered by stacked stone walls. In a cobblestone-paved motor court was parked a muddy pickup truck along with a Mini Cooper in racing green with a white top.

All this from the revenue produced by a restaurant with ten tables, eight barstools, two pool tables and a jukebox?

The work to be done was in the stables that were almost out of sight from the house. He spent the next several hours mucking out stalls and sorting bridles and reins and other equipment as several horses whinnied and stamped their hooves in other stalls.

Stone was rubbing his aching back when he heard the horse's hooves pounding his way. The fifteen-hand-high chestnut drew up next to him and Danny jumped down. He pulled two beers from his jacket pocket and handed one to Stone. "Heard from Ma you were out here."

He popped the can lid and a bit of the liquid spewed out. "Horse riding and beer delivery ain't a good fit," he said.

"Knee looks to be okay," Stone noted.

"I'm a fast healer. What are you doing?"

"Mucking stalls among other things."

"I'll help you."

"You sure?"

"Got nothing else to do right now."

They went into the stables and Danny grabbed a shovel after tethering his horse to an iron ring stuck in cement in the ground.

Stone eyed a bruise on the side of the man's face. "It was the other side that fellow nailed on the train, wasn't it?"

"Duke was too fast for me in the stall this morning. Clocked me in the face when I was trying to bridle him. Damn horse."

"But a beautiful one."

"You ride?"

"Not if I can help it. You call this place a hellhole? Which part—the pool, the mansion or the cool car parked in front?"

"I'm the exaggerating type."

"Seriously, why would you want to leave something like this?"

"It's hers, not mine." Danny slung horse manure into a wheelbarrow.

"You're her son. You'll inherit someday."

Danny stripped off his shirt, revealing a lean, muscled physique. "Who says I want it?"

"Okay, fair enough. You an only child?"

"That's right."

"I saw your father's grave coming up here."

"That's why we got all this stuff."

"How so?"

"Lawsuit against the damn coal company that killed my old man. See, coal companies almost always win those things, or else settle for pennies on the dollar 'cause they got all the good lawyers wrapped around their little finger. But Mom held on, proved her case. Coal company appealed but in the end she kicked their ass, they caved and she got her blood money. And the only thing it cost us was her husband and my dad." Danny tipped another shovelful of horse manure into a large wheelbarrow and banged his tool against the metal side as if in exclamation.

"And your mom still runs the restaurant?"

"She likes to keep busy, and people need to eat."

"The whole town looks pretty prosperous."

"Coal prices highest in decades and there ain't enough miners to do the job. When demand's higher than supply, wages go up. About doubled in fact over the last five years. High wages, low cost of living equals prosperity for the common man. Simple."

"You sound like an economics major."

"Nah, just a dumb ex-jock, but I got eyes, ears and a little bit of common sense. Where you bunking tonight?"

"Must be a motel or something around here?"

"Back in town, couple blocks from my ma's place and around the corner from the courthouse, there's a place that has rooms to let. Cheap but clean. Bernie Sandusky runs it." He laughed. "Tell old Bernie that Danny sent you."

"Why, that'll get me a reduced rate?"

"Nope, more likely get your butt kicked out the door."

"Why's that?"

"Bernie has a real cute granddaughter named Dottie. Few years ago he caught me and Dottie in one of his rooms working on our *biology* homework." He laughed and pitched a big load of manure into the wheelbarrow. "Okay, I'm done shoveling shit. You're on your own, dude."

Stone watched until Danny and his ride disappeared from sight. He finished his work and later idly followed a path that wound around a small hill covered with scrub pines. Abby's property seemed to have no end. He reached another gravel road that headed back out another way. As his eye followed its path he reckoned it would go back out to the main road at some point, on the other side from where he'd come to the farm.

A few minutes later Stone followed a dirt path that was worn black and finally led to an old barn that looked close to falling down. Inside was an old gray pickup truck, bales of rotted hay, and rusted tractors and other farm equipment.

He perched on the bumper of the pickup and counted his meager cash. An act of kindness on his part to help Danny had really cost him. The train ticket hadn't been cheap and the bus ride just to the vicinity of Divine had cost him still more precious dollars. Danny had offered to pay but Stone had refused. And he still had to rent a room in town. He prayed that rich Abby would be generous with her payment for the day's work so he could move on.

Yet should he even still be thinking of escape? Maybe when he'd jumped off the damn cliff, he should have just sucked in a chest of water and ended it. What did he have to live for anyway?

What do I have to live for?

He heard a vehicle skid to a stop outside. He hopped off the bumper and walked outside in time to see Abby step from the truck cab.

"Taking a stroll around the place?" she said, not smiling.

"I finished up at the stables. Beautiful property you have here."

"Okay," she said, her features unreadable.

"Doesn't look like this place gets much use anymore," he said, looking toward the barn.

"This was my momma and daddy's place for fifty years. They ran it as a farm, but we haven't done any farming here for thirty years. Their house was just down there," she said, pointing to the left. "Burned down a long time ago. Only thing left is the chimneystack. I oughta just knock it down, but I can't do it. I mean, it's really the only thing I have left of them."

"I can understand that."

"You can, huh?"

"The past is hard to let go of, particularly when the future is a little uncertain."

"You're wasting your talents mucking stalls, Ben. You ought to be a philosophy teacher."

"I was just heading back to town."

"I need to pay you. Why don't you ride with me back to the house? You can get some supper and your money."

"You don't have to do that."

"I know I don't." Her tone did not seem to invite dissent.

A few minutes later they pulled into the driveway.

"Beautiful house."

"Came at a damn steep price."

"Danny told me a little about that."

"Expect you want to take a shower and change your clothes. Mucking stalls isn't the cleanest job in the world."

"Thanks. I'm sorry about your husband."

"Uh-huh," she said.

She slammed the truck door behind her and headed up the steps.

Stone slowly got out and trudged after her.

He could have landed in any town in the country. And it had to be Divine, Virginia.

Damn, I can really pick 'em.

CHAPTER

19

Knox collared Annabelle Conroy as she was leaving her hotel. He flashed his creds and asked her to go with him.

"I don't think so," she said.

"Excuse me?"

"Those creds could be faked and you could be a rapist. Go call a cop and I'll go with both of you if he's satisfied you are who you say you are. But until then, get the hell away from me."

"How about a cup of coffee in the restaurant over there? If I put my hand up your skirt, you can start screaming and kick me in the balls."

"Just so you know, I kick really hard."

"I have no doubt."

"Will this take long? I'm sort of busy."

"As long or as short as you want to make it."

Over two cups of strong coffee Knox explained what he wanted.

"I don't know where Oliver is," she said truthfully. "We became friends, and I stayed at his cottage, but now he's gone and he didn't tell anybody where he was going."

"How did you become friends and why were you staying at his cottage?"

"Simple enough. He helped me with a problem I had and after he left I wanted to keep his home going for him in case he came back."

"So your problem was with Jerry Bagger, now deceased?"

"I see you do your homework."

"Wasn't that hard actually. What exactly was your beef with Bagger, Ms. Hunter?" Knox didn't believe for a moment that that was her name but he was willing to play along, for now.

"What's it to you?"

"Humor me."

"Why the hell should I?"

He pointed to the cup she was holding. "How about I take the prints off that and run them through a database. Would I pull up the name Susan Hunter?"

"There's no law against changing your name."

"Right, but the *reason* for changing your name, now that might be illegal."

"Bagger hurt someone I cared about and I wanted to nail him for it and I did."

"With Alex Ford and Oliver Stone's help?"

"Yeah. Bagger was a crook and a sociopath. The FBI and Justice Department had been after him for a long time. He got what he deserved. So what's wrong with that?"

"I don't really give a crap about Jerry Bagger. I want Oliver Stone. Or John Carr. I don't know which name you refer to him as."

"I only know him as Oliver Stone. I have no idea who John Carr is."

"When was the last time you saw him?"

"About six months ago."

"You heard about Carter Gray's and Senator Simpson's murders?"

"I watch the news."

"Stone had a relationship with Gray."

"Didn't know that."

"Alex Ford never bothered to tell you? Because he knew all about it."

"We're just friends, and friends don't share everything."

"Why'd you leave the cottage?"

"Got tired of living with dead people."

"You wouldn't have happened to have heard from Stone? Maybe he told you to take it underground?"

"Why would he do that?"

"You tell me."

"How can I tell you about something that didn't happen?"

"I think your buddy's on the run."

"From what?"

Knox stood. "Okay, my BS alarm is clanging so hard it's hurting my ears. So like I told your friend, Ford, I'll be in touch. And don't try to leave the city. That would not make me happy." He walked off.

CHAPTER

20

MACKLIN HAYES did not seem particularly pleased. He and Knox were sitting in front of a fire in the library of a luxurious late-nineteenth-century brownstone in the heart of D.C. that Hayes had access to 24/7. Spy kings, it seemed, had gold-plated perks.

"So you've run around interviewing all the usual suspects today and have *no* progress to show for it."

"I'm not just going through the motions, General. I did my little dog-and-pony show with all of them except for the Reuben Rhodes character, and I'll catch up to him at some point. They're all lying. They all know more than they'll admit. That's progress right there as far as I'm concerned. At some point they'll make a slip and then we move in."

"I seriously doubt the man left them a copy of his travel itinerary."

"I doubt that too, but Carr is a loyal guy. If we can nail

his friends on something, put them at risk for prison time, then that may flush him out."

"Meaning he'll come running back here to save his friends? You really believe that will happen, Knox?"

"I've studied the man, gone over his career, talked to his friends. Yeah, I think that might happen. And what's the downside if it doesn't work?"

Hayes finished off his glass of wine and stared into the fire. "Let me speak frankly, Knox. Hopefully it will be instructive and won't bore you too much."

"I doubt anything you have to say would bore me, sir. And you know I'm a sucker for *truthful* information."

Hayes ignored the barb. "Carr is a killer, clearly. He was at the Capitol Visitor Center that night. We know he murdered Gray and Simpson. That part is simple, the rest is not."

"And do I finally get to hear the rest?"

Hayes rose and poured himself another glass, this time of scotch, and sipped it while standing in front of the fire. Gazing at this tall patrician figure dressed in a three-piece suit with his beautiful snowy hair, square jaw and twinkling eyes and holding his cut-crystal snifter made Knox fantasize he was in a Hollywood spy film.

Let's see, how does that story go again? Oh, yeah, bright, refined, patriotic people recruited from Ivy League schools doing their noble best to keep their country safe while nattily attired in their Brooks Brothers suits, bedding all the beautiful women, sucking thoughtfully on their sweet-smelling pipes and remaining high above the riff and the raff. Like me. And John Carr. The riff and the raff.

Knox had quickly found that that notion was indeed a

fantasy. Intelligence was a nasty, dirty business and necessitated each side to get as filthy as the other. The only rule was there never had been any rules at all. No, actually he was wrong. There was one rule. People like Macklin Hayes did remain above it all. Untouchable. And yet that rule was not absolute. Look at Carter Gray. John Carr had pulled him right down into the trench shit with him.

You go, John.

Hayes said, "Unfortunately, Carr is also probably in possession of certain information, perhaps even proofs of actions taken by this country at sensitive times, that might, in unforgiving hindsight, mind you, place us in an awkward situation. I'm sure Gray was aware of that as well. I believe he attempted to get to Carr, but as we know, Carr got him first."

"So in other words he has the goods on us so this is not a case for the law courts?"

Hayes smiled. "I've always loved your perspicacity, Knox. Saves so much time."

"I'm not a hired killer, sir. You ordered me to find him. I will do my best to do so. But that's it."

"And that's all you need do. Others will take over from there."

"If Carr is as smart as I think he is, he knows all this. He might have devised a way that his violent death will trigger the very disclosure you don't want. A packet of information to the *New York Times* perhaps in the event a bullet slams into his brain?"

"Find him, Knox, and I believe we can persuade him that such action would not be advisable."

"What leverage would you have over him at that point?"

"As you said, he's a very loyal man."

Knox considered this for a moment. "So his friends are his Achilles' heel? Only in your version instead of coming back and going to jail he takes the bullet, he falls on the sword *silently* so his friends can what, live?"

"That's certainly one scenario."

"One or the *only* one?"

"Just find him, Knox, that's all you have to do. Any leads of interest?"

"The *friends* have given me squat, and if we have to do this outside the law now it comes back to following the physical evidence as far as it takes me."

"Back out to the crime scenes then?"

"Yes."

"Time is not on our side."

"It never is. This information would have been helpful earlier, sir, in all candor."

"I'm sure it would have. But there you are."

"So I'm competing with the cops on this one too? What if they get there first?"

"We've taken certain actions that will preclude that from happening."

"And if some detective gets lucky?"

"That's highly doubtful because they know nothing of John Carr or his ties to Gray and Simpson. So you have a tremendous advantage there. But if the police get to him first, we will make sure that he will disappear from their custody. National security trumps all, Knox."

"Of course. Can I inquire as to what the chain of command is on this, sir?"

"You report to me, no one else," he said sharply.

"No, I mean who do *you* report to, General?"

Hayes finished off his drink and carefully put the glass down on an antique side table. "I'll pretend I didn't hear that. Good luck. Regular reports."

"Absolutely," Knox said, with more edge to his voice than he would have liked. One could push Macklin Hayes only so far, but Knox was getting sorely tempted to push as hard as possible. Like off a cliff.

"One more thing. John Carr is probably the best assassin this country has ever produced. The fact that he was able to single-handedly kill a dozen of our best paramilitary field agents thirty years after he left Triple Six speaks volumes. God, he must have been something else indeed in his prime. What an honor to have commanded such a killing machine. Gray was lucky in that regard. The meteoric rise of his career was tied, in no small way, to Carr's ability to hit the bull's-eye time after time."

"And you're telling me this why?"

"Just want you to understand the playing field. We need him alive, Knox. We need to know what he has before the sword falls. Never forget that. There may need to be sacrifices, of course."

As Hayes left the room Knox did indeed understand the playing field. They clearly needed Carr alive.

Sacrifices? But they didn't necessarily need Joe Knox still breathing when the dust settled, did they?

Knox left the brownstone, climbed back in his Rover, and drove off in pursuit of apparently the greatest assassin his country had ever produced, while a cagey former general who had no problem allowing his foot soldiers to die to achieve his goals was crowding his rear flank.

Whoopie.

CHAPTER

21

V<small>ERY EARLY THE NEXT MORNING</small>, Knox started with the caretaker's cottage at Mt. Zion Cemetery. He went over every square inch of it, pulling up loose floorboards, emptying every drawer, checking inside the fireplace, and poring over the books Stone kept there, many in different languages.

"If the guy can speak all these languages, he might have already left the country," Knox told himself. Other than that, the cottage was a bust. The guy had obviously cleaned it out before fleeing. He next set about searching the cemetery. Here he was a bit more fortunate, though it ultimately turned out to be nothing. His sharp eye discerned that one tombstone had been recently moved. He yanked it over and found the small compartment carved in the earth. Whatever had been there, though, was now gone.

The "dirt" Macklin Hayes had hinted at?

Two hours later found him standing in the rear grounds of Carter Gray's former home. Knox had decided not to go by Simpson's murder scene. The vacant construction site had not given up any clues on the first go-round and he'd wisely decided that it was probably not going to give up any simply because he went back.

He stared out at the bay. Stone had told the FBI agents that the person who'd blown up Gray's house might have escaped by jumping off the cliff. He walked to the edge and peered down. Hell of a long dive, but probably easy for someone like Oliver Stone/John Carr.

Okay, he tosses his rifle into the water and jumps. Then where did he go?

He did not for a second believe that Stone had committed suicide. One did not plan hits so meticulously to merely end it all with a plunge off a cliff. He had lived. Knox was sure of that.

Carrying a knapsack over his shoulder, Knox walked along the cliff's edge, following on land what might have been Stone's journey in the water. He passed through woods, open fields, and then more woods, all the while keeping his eye on the shore below. Finally, he stopped. There was a bit of a beach down there. Stone had shot Gray before seven a.m. Knox had checked the tide charts. That time of morning would largely mirror the tide he was looking at right now. He eyed the boulders, then spotted the cleft in the rock, the trail coming up. He followed it to where it reached the top of the cliff. There was a path there. He took it. A half hour later he came to the series of shacks.

"Can I help you?"

Knox looked over at the short, squat man in the Green Bay Packers knit cap and greasy coat who was staring at him from beside an ancient tractor with one wheel off.

Knox approached. "I was over at Carter Gray's house." He held up his creds. "I'm Agent Knox."

"Good for you. They call me Leroy because that's my name. Gray, huh? The important fellow what got himself shot?"

"That's right. I take it someone's been by to see you."

"Hell, yeah. But like I told them, I don't know nuthin' 'bout nuthin'."

"You live here by yourself?"

"That's right, ever since my Lottie went to meet her Lord four years ago."

"Sorry to hear that. Nobody to help you around here? What is it that you do, by the way?"

"Anything I can to make a little money. Had me a helper but he went on."

"When was that?"

"Same day that man got shot."

Knox looked anxious but Leroy held up his hand. "Don't get yourself excited. He was here when them FBI folks come by. You can ask them. He's old, bum leg, bad eyes and feller couldn't even talk, just grunted."

"Tall, short? Fat, thin?"

"Skinny, though with the bad leg it was hard to tell how tall he was. Lot taller'n me, that's for sure. Big beard and thick glasses."

"Why'd he leave?"

"Who the hell knows? Been with me about four months. Then he just went moving on. It's not like I had him locked into no million-dollar long-term contract." Leroy laughed and shot a glob of spit at the ground.

Knox looked around. "Did he stay in one of those buildings?"

Leroy nodded and pointed at the one closest to the path.

"Mind if I take a look through it?"

"What agency you with again?"

"Federal."

"I know that. But which one?"

Knox held up his "public" creds close to the man's face. "*That* one."

Leroy took a step back. "Go on ahead then."

Knox inwardly smiled. That was at least one perk you got doing what he did. There weren't many others.

The search of the shack turned up only one significant fact. There wasn't a single fingerprint in the place and Knox had brought equipment with him that would show if there were. That alone told Knox that he was probably on the right track. Most people, including gimp-legged, nearly blind mutes, were not known to be so meticulous about wiping away such identifiers.

He left the shack and found Leroy puttering around.

Knox said, "I'm going to have an artist come up here and he's going to do a composite drawing based on your description of the guy."

"I'll do my best."

"I know you will."

CHAPTER

22

THE DINNER WAS DELICIOUS, mostly fried and filling. Abby had cooked it herself and Stone had helped her serve it. It was only the two of them. He'd taken a shower in an upstairs bathroom decorated like something out of a design magazine. The coal company must've really paid through the nose.

"So you're a fan of Shakespeare?" Stone said.

"I read his plays in high school. I could never relate to them before."

"And now you can?"

"Maybe. He's got all of what life has to offer, especially the negatives, but I've lived the real thing too much to be impressed anymore by a fiction of it."

Danny came in halfway through the meal, took one look at Stone and his mother in the dining room with their linen napkins and fancy plates, and turned back around without a word. Then a door slammed. Loudly.

Stone glanced after him and then turned back to Abby. "I'm sure he keeps you busy."

"That's one way of putting it. You have children?"

"I did. She's not alive anymore."

"Sorry to hear that. Danny's used up about seven of his nine lives and I feel like he took mine right along with his."

"Were you against him going away? You said you cried a lot."

"What mother wouldn't with her only child saying good-bye?"

"Then you're glad he's back?"

"I wouldn't go that far. Besides, it's more likely than not that he'll be gone again before too many more suns come up. Won't break my heart again, at least I keep telling myself that."

"Has he left before?"

"Talked about it a lot, but never pulled the trigger. I guess I'd made up my mind it always would be talk. Then he threw me a curve." Her voice shook a little as she said this last part.

"Any particular reason he decided to do it this time?"

"It's hard to tell why Danny does anything. Bullheaded, just like his father."

"Danny said he died in the mines."

Abby took her time putting the last forkful of pie into her mouth. "He did. You said you lost a child. How about your wife?"

"Died too. Long time ago."

"What've you been doing with yourself since?"

"This and that. Never stayed in one place too long."

"Did you get out of the army right after Nam?"

"I hung around for a while. Nothing too exciting."

"No pension from Uncle Sam?"

"Didn't stay long enough."

Their conversation trailed off and a while later Stone took his leave, resisting her invitation to drive him back to town. There was sorrow in that house, despite the luxury and designer touches, for one simple reason: the source of the wealth was death.

"I guess you'll be heading on soon," she said as she stood by the front door.

"I'm a lot older than Danny and I still haven't made up my mind what to do with the rest of my life. So I think I better get to it."

"Thanks for helping my son."

"He seems like a good young man, Abby. Just needs a little direction."

"It would've been real good if the direction had taken him out of here and kept him there."

She closed the door, leaving Stone standing there puzzled. Telling himself again that this was not his business, he walked out to the road and made his way back to town. The sky was lit with stars, which was the only light there was. As he drew closer to town, he heard something. At first it seemed to be the moan of an animal and it occurred to him that in this part of the country it would not be unheard of to run into a black bear or maybe even a mountain lion. As he continued to walk along the moan became more recognizable.

Stone picked up his pace. The church and the graveyard were just ahead.

He cut across the road, entered the churchyard, made a beeline for the graveyard, and then stopped when he saw it. Or rather him.

The sobs racking him, Danny was lying sprawled on top of the fresh grave of Debby Randolph.

CHAPTER

23

THE TALL MAN SLIPPED inside the building, hung a left, grabbed an elevator, rode it down, entered the tunnel, skimmed along underneath the streets of Washington, D.C., arrived at another building and turned down a long hall. When he passed one door, it opened and a big hand grabbed him and yanked him inside, slamming the door behind him.

Reuben Rhodes let Alex Ford go. The agent smoothed down his jacket collar and turned to scowl at the others there arranged on busted-up government-issued furniture and packing crates.

"You said the second door on the *left*," Alex snapped.

"Brother Caleb got it wrong," Reuben said. "He meant the first door on the right and we didn't want to call you on your cell in case they put a trace on it."

"They need a court order for that," Annabelle said.

"Like hell they do," Reuben shot back.

Alex looked at Annabelle. "He's actually right about that. As a federal agent my life and cell phone are not my own."

"Sorry about the mix-up, Alex," Caleb said shame-facedly. "I was a little nervous. I'm not really sure why, though." He glared furiously at Reuben. "Oh, now I remember. It was when Reuben called and screamed that I had to find a place for us to meet ASAP or we were all going to die and it would be my fault!"

Reuben shrugged. "I didn't say die. I said we were all going to go to prison for the rest of our lives. And I just said it would be *mostly* your fault."

"How do you figure that?" asked Annabelle.

"This Joe Knox character already met with Caleb."

"So? How do you know I told him anything?"

"Caleb, you'd spill your guts if a Girl Scout got the drop on you."

Annabelle stood. "Okay, we don't have much time. It seems Knox has grilled me, Alex and Caleb."

"And I know he went to the loading dock, but luckily I took a few days off," Reuben added.

"Reuben, I understand that Oliver called you," said Alex. "Did he tell you where he was?"

"He wouldn't tell me where he was calling from." Reuben went on to tell them about his conversation with Stone. "And he did want me to tell you that he appreciated your burning the letter."

Alex nodded slowly but said nothing.

Caleb said, "Is there any way to trace the call he made to Reuben?"

Reuben shook his head. "I sort of have an unusual cell phone arrangement. A little convoluted."

"You mean you steal other people's minutes," declared Caleb.

"Anyway, I had a buddy I trust try and do it for me. He's a real pro with that stuff and it went nowhere."

"Well, let's compare notes on what Knox said and see where we stand," Annabelle suggested.

Alex went first, followed by Annabelle and then Caleb. When they'd finished, Reuben said, "Caleb, I apologize. It looks like you stood your ground pretty well."

"Apology accepted," snapped the federal librarian.

Alex said, "Okay, Knox knows Oliver is John Carr. He knows what he did at CIA. He knows that he killed Simpson and Gray. And he wants him badly."

"And he thinks we can lead him right to Oliver," Caleb replied. "But we can't. Thank God."

"Don't be thanking God yet, Caleb. He knows where we are and our connection to Oliver. They'll use that."

"How?"

Annabelle answered. "Leverage. To reel Oliver in."

Caleb exclaimed, "What do you mean? Use us as bait? That's preposterous. We are United States citizens. Knox is a public servant."

"That line didn't even work in the fifties," said Alex. "He's a public servant with a job to do. Nail Oliver. And while he's on the run, we're left as targets."

"So should we all go into hiding?" Annabelle asked.

Alex said, "That's pretty much impossible for me to do. But Annabelle, you definitely should dig a deep hole and get in it. Reuben too. Caleb, how about you?"

"Why would Oliver have left us in this impossible situation?" Caleb groused.

"He didn't have much choice," Reuben answered. "If we're right, he popped two giant VIPs on the same day. You don't go have coffee after that and wait for the SWAT team to tap on your door with a battering ram."

Caleb shook his head. "Even if Oliver did kill them—and despite the letter he left behind, I bet he didn't leave any evidence for them to find."

"Damn it, what point aren't you getting, Caleb?" Reuben exclaimed. "These guys don't care about prosecuting his ass. They just want him. They'll squeeze whatever useful information he has out of him and then put a round in his brain. He was a former government hit man who had to go on the run because Gray and Simpson screwed him over and tried to kill him." Reuben said this last part while staring at Alex. "Oliver's been on the run for thirty years. And then they killed Milton. And don't forget, Harry Finn told us that Simpson admitted that he was the one who ordered the hit on Oliver and his family way back when. If ever a man had a reason to kill somebody it's Oliver, to hell with what the law says."

"So they might be afraid of what Oliver might know about past government missions," Caleb said. "And they'd want to silence him?"

"Now you're thinking like a librarian," noted Reuben wryly.

Annabelle said, "But there might be another way, I mean instead of us going underground."

Alex leaned against the wall. "What do you have in mind?"

"We find Oliver and help him really get away."

"Forget it, Annabelle. We'd be leading these guys right to him," protested Alex.

"And besides," added Reuben, "I'm sure Oliver had a nifty escape plan."

"Really? No ID. No money. I gave him a credit card. I checked on it. It hasn't been used in months. He can't get on a plane. He can only run so far."

"Before they catch him," said Reuben quietly.

"Maybe that's what he wants," stated Alex. The other three stared at him. "He got Simpson and Gray. He felt terrible guilt for Milton. He may feel he has nothing else to live for. He runs, but not that hard. He knows they'll catch up to him and he's prepared for what that means."

Annabelle said, "I'm not going to let his life end that way."

"Annabelle, stonewalling the CIA is one thing, but you get mixed up in actively helping Oliver elude the authorities then you're looking at prison time too. A big chunk of it."

"I don't care, Alex. Look what he did for me. He risked everything to help me."

"He's done that for all of us," added Reuben.

"You wouldn't be here either, Alex," Annabelle said, eyeing the man. "Except for Oliver."

Alex sat down on an old desk. "Guys, I hear you, but I'm a federal agent. I can only go so far."

"We don't want to get you in trouble, so you don't have to do anything," said Annabelle, though her tone was less gracious than her words.

"Except look the other way," added Reuben.

"How would you even go about finding him?" said Alex.

"That's for *us* to figure out," said Reuben coldly. He glanced over at Caleb. "You're a *federal* employee too, but are you in?"

Caleb nodded. "I'm in."

Alex, his features grim, rose. "Well, I guess this is where we part company. Good luck."

"Alex—" Annabelle began, but the door had already closed behind him.

The three remaining members of the Camel Club simply looked at each other.

"Screw him," exclaimed Reuben. "So how do we find Oliver?"

She gazed at him. "The fox is on the hunt, right?"

"Right. So?"

"So we follow the fox."

"You have a plan?"

"I always have a plan."

"Annabelle, girl, I love you."

CHAPTER

24

STONE WAS ABOUT TO APPROACH Danny Riker when someone else appeared from the other side of the graveyard. Stone shrank down behind the stone wall as the man stepped clear of the shadows and into the moonlight. At first, Stone thought the big fellow was going to attack Danny, so stealthy was his approach. Indeed, Stone was preparing to spring out when the other man gently touched Danny on the shoulder.

"Come on, boy, no good you being here."

Danny looked up into the face of Sheriff Tyree, who bent down to help him up.

"Not right. Ain't right," Danny sputtered, as he leaned against the large frame of the lawman.

"A lot in life isn't fair, Danny. But you can't let it eat you up, boy."

"I want to die."

Tyree slapped Danny across the face. "Don't let me never hear you say that again, Danny. The girl's dead. Nothing you can do will bring her back."

He pointed at the dirt. "You call that fair?"

"You get your head on straight. She had a choice. She killed herself. This ain't doing nobody any good. Now you want me to give you a ride home?"

Danny wiped his face and shook his head. "You're a stupid man if you think that," he snapped.

Tyree studied him. "You know something I don't?"

"I know lots you don't. So what? Ain't worth shit what I know."

"I mean about Debby?"

Danny dropped his head and his defiant tone. "No. I don't know nothing. Just talking is all. Talking and saying nothing, really."

"You said I was stupid if I believed that. What, that she killed herself?"

"You putting words in my mouth now, Sheriff," Danny said, his face whitening a bit.

"I just want to hear what you have to say."

In response, Danny turned and walked off.

"Danny, you come back here."

"Stop yelling, Sheriff, you'll wake the dead."

"Right now, boy."

"I'm not a boy, Tyree, in case you hadn't noticed." Danny turned to look at him. "And unless you want to put a bullet in my back, I'm going home."

Tyree laid a hand on top of his pistol as Stone stooped as low as he could. He didn't want to give either man a chance to spot him.

He waited for Danny to disappear down the road and

then watched as Tyree stalked back to his patrol car parked nearby and drove back toward town.

Should I just leave now? Why wait until morning?

Yet Stone walked to town and got a room at the tiny house Danny had recommended. He climbed the stairs, put his bag away and sat on the soft bed and stared out the window toward the main street of Divine.

What he'd seen at the graveyard had puzzled him. Had Danny been in love with Debby Randolph? Had she killed herself? Why had Danny left and then come back?

"It's not my problem," Stone finally said aloud, surprising himself with the force of the words. He checked his watch. It was nearly ten o'clock. He had a small transistor radio in his bag. He pulled it out and turned it on. It took some twisting of the tuner knob, but he finally found a station that had a national news roundup program at the top of the hour. He sat back on his bed. The murders weren't the lead story, but they were a close second to another salmonella outbreak in some vegetables.

The announcer's voice seemed breathless as he recounted the latest on the high-level D.C. killings.

"The FBI and Homeland Security have combined their efforts in this investigation. The murders of Senator Roger Simpson and intelligence head Carter Gray are definitely connected and are apparently tied to events from decades ago when both men worked at the CIA. The killer is reportedly a former colleague of the two men and was believed to have died years ago. Authorities are watching all airports, train and bus stations and border crossings. We will bring you more developments as they break in what is shaping up to be the manhunt of the decade."

Stone turned off the radio, rose and stared out the window once more. They hadn't announced the name of the killer, but they might as well have.

They know it was John Carr and they know what I look like and they have every escape route bottled up.

He had never really dwelled on his eventual capture. He even imagined that he might make it to New Orleans, start a new life and live out the rest of his years in peaceful obscurity. But that was apparently not to be. The one thing that bothered him was that everyone would believe him to be a criminal. Was revenge always wrong? Was righting an injustice outside the law never condonable? He knew the answer to those questions. He would never have the luxury of facing a judge and jury. They would never let him because then he could tell his side of the story. No, that could never be allowed.

Stone put on his jacket. He needed air. He needed to think. Could he even leave Divine now? He should call Reuben, but he would have to wait until tomorrow. Now he just wanted to walk in the darkness and peace of Divine. And think.

He reached the main street, turned right and walked at a brisk pace. He soon left the little downtown area behind. The trees grew thicker and the lights of the small houses that dotted the perimeter of Divine finally disappeared.

Five minutes later Stone had decided to turn back when the scream reached him. It was from up ahead. It was a man. And he sounded beyond terrified.

Stone started to run.

CHAPTER

25

AFTER LEAVING Leroy's place in Maryland Knox did not drive home. One question had been bothering him so badly that he had to have an answer. He headed not for Langley, but for a nondescript building in the heart of Washington. He'd called ahead and was admitted without issue, what with his military background and government credentials.

He entered a vast room filled with long, scarred tables where gray-haired men, probably grizzled vets of past wars, along with some bow-tied historians, sat reading through piles of yellowed documents. It was windowless and seemed nearly airless as well. As Knox looked around, the one emotion he sensed was misery. This place contained the recorded and too brief lives and violent deaths of far more people than one would ever want to think about.

The main collection center for U.S. Army records was in St. Louis. Unless you were next of kin, to get access to an enlisted person's complete service record there required either that person's permission or a court order. However, Knox had learned something unknown to most people: The St. Louis facility didn't have *all* the records. There were some in D.C.—and, indeed, copies of some of the ones housed in St. Louis. And they weren't simply records of enlisted personnel. Here were housed documents chronicling America's wars. That was why many historians came here to do research, many with FOIA requests in hand, since the military only reluctantly revealed anything about itself.

Many of the records he wanted to look at had not been computerized yet, but some had. Still, after Knox showed his creds, the attendant was able to pull the boxes he wanted very quickly and showed him how to access the computerized files. His butt parked in front of a PC, Knox started with the digital ones first, flicking from screen to screen. He had a hunch and he wanted to see if it was true. What had been bugging him was why Macklin Hayes would want to get to John Carr so badly. If Carr had killed Simpson and Gray, he was now on the run. He was not going to hold a press conference and start blabbing about secrets from the past. Knox could understand Hayes wanting him to nail Carr before the police did. If the cops caught up to Carr he might start talking in exchange for a deal. But Hayes had also said that the cops had been put on a short leash on this investigation, giving Knox, in essence, a clear field in which to operate. And even if the police somehow got to Carr first, the CIA could, like Hayes had said, just swoop in and take him away under cover of national security interests. Carr would never even reach a press conference or make a phone call to his lawyer.

So why the all-out necessity to get this guy? Aside from the moral issue of letting a killer escape justice, in some ways letting him go away and die peacefully made the most sense strategically. The bottom line was, Hayes was acting somewhat irrationally and he was not an irrational man. There had to be another reason.

Knox stared at the screen, reading the military records of the men and women who had served in Vietnam. He exhausted the digital trail and had to resort to the boxes after consulting with another attendant who helped him narrow his area of search. He went through thirty of the boxes without success. He was about to call it a day when his hand gripped a sheaf of papers, the top page getting his immediate attention.

As Knox leaned forward, the rest of the room seemed to slowly disappear around him. He was reading the official history of a soldier named John Carr, an enlisted man who'd quickly risen to the rank of sergeant. The account Knox was enthralled with was Carr's heroic actions during one five-hour period nearly forty years ago.

Outnumbered dozens to one, Carr had almost single-handedly turned back an attack by the enemy, saving his company and carrying several of his wounded comrades to safety on his back. He'd killed at least ten enemy soldiers, several in hand-to-hand fighting. Then he'd manned a machine-gun nest to hold back the North Vietnamese while mortar and rifle rounds hit all around him. He'd left that post to radio in air support to allow his men to retreat safely. Only then had he walked off the battlefield drenched in his own blood and permanently scarred by bullet and machete wounds. Knox had experienced combat in those jungles and knew the confusion and horror that such confrontations almost always held. He'd been wounded. He'd been scarred. He'd been routed in action thinking this was surely his last day on earth. And he'd been part of successful attacks in the last days of America's participation in that war in Southeast Asia, although by that time little victories in the field meant nothing. If they ever did.

Yet Knox had never read or heard of any soldier doing what Carr had done that day. It was beyond miraculous. It was beyond human, in fact. His respect, along with his fear of the man, notched upward even more.

With such heroism there must've been reward. The military was often slow in many ways, but it was quick at awarding bravery and selflessness in the field if for no other reason than to inspire other soldiers. And such accounts also made for great PR. The extraordinary heroism and extreme gallantry Carr had demonstrated that day not only *easily* qualified him for the Distinguished Service Cross, the second highest award the army could bestow, but, in Knox's judgment, it should have earned him the country's highest award for military heroism, the Medal of Honor. John Carr a Medal of Honor winner? Hayes had not mentioned any of that in his briefing. Nor had that piece of background made its way into press accounts when the man's grave had been dug up at Arlington.

Knox flipped through page after page and explored several more boxes before he was able to piece the story together.

Carr's Purple Hearts could not be denied him because

the wounds alone were proof enough. All told, he received four of them, counting injuries received in other battles. Then there had been talk of awarding him a Bronze Star, but the date of this document was long after the fact of Carr's miraculous actions in the field. And the Bronze Star—while certainly prestigious—didn't come close to recognizing what the man had done, Knox felt. The Bronze was a bit of a hybrid in Knox's mind. It could be given out for bravery in battle with a Valor device attached, but also for acts of merit or meritorious service. The Silver Star, Distinguished Service Cross, and Medal of Honor, the acknowledged triumvirate of recognition for the fighting soldier, were for bravery and heroism *in combat*, pure and simple.

He finally found a sheaf of documents showing that Carr's immediate superior *had* recommended Stone for the Medal of Honor. The man had filled out all the requisite documents and assembled all the required proofs and eyewitness accounts. He'd then sent it up the chain of command. The date on the documents showed it to be shortly after Carr's actions in the field, long before the documents talking about awarding him the Bronze Star. What the hell was going on?

And nothing had happened. It apparently had stalled out at that point. Knox could find no other documents that touched on it. But why? It was a perfect story. The man was a hero. Instead Carr had disappeared from the ranks shortly thereafter. Knox thought he knew why. That's when he'd been enlisted by the CIA for its Triple Six Division. The spooks, Knox was aware, often trolled for their assassins in the ranks of the military's best.

He put the documents back in the box. And that's when

he noticed it. Two pieces of paper stapled together that had slid down in between the interior flap of the box and the exterior cardboard wall. Knox almost didn't read it, so disgusted was he at the military's injustice to a man who should have been one of the most legendary recipients of its highest award.

But Knox did reach for the papers.

It was an order, a simple one. It shut off any further consideration of John Carr receiving the Medal of Honor or any other commendation. As Knox read through the document it was filled with official mumbo jumbo about unreliable evidence and inconsistent eyewitness accounts and conflicting background documentation. It made no sense at all until Knox's gaze reached the signature line where the name of the officer appeared.

Major Macklin D. Hayes.

CHAPTER

26

KNOX SLOWLY DROVE his Range Rover into the garage of his town house. Before he hit the button on his remote to close the door, he scanned the street in his rearview mirror. They were out there, he was pretty sure, watching him. Hayes typically covered all the bases.

The former general trusts me about as much as I trust him.

There might come a time when Knox would have to give those boys the slip, and when and if the time came, he hoped he was up for the challenge.

It might seem bizarre to ordinary citizens that a government agent like Knox would be nearly as fearful of his employer as he was his quarry. Yet Knox was only called in when things had gone to hell and people were already pointing fingers at each other and essentially building their "blame" strategies. He sometimes compared his job to that of an internal affairs officer in a police department. No matter what you did, someone was going to be pissed at you. And being pissed off and taking somebody's life as payback did not require a great leap of thought. Sometimes, it simply needed a walk across the street, a decisive trigger pull and a good cover strategy.

And from what Knox had learned about John Carr's military past, Hayes was definitely playing his own agenda on this one. He had clearly lied to Knox already. He'd commented on what an honor it would have been to command a killing machine like Carr. Well, the man *had* commanded him. In his murderous prime. And denied him the honor that was surely his. What had Carr done to tick the man off? Hayes was known to hold grudges for decades, and it seemed like that reputation was proving true here.

Knox had spent several more hours in the records room trying to find an answer to that question, but had come away with nothing more than speculation.

The dark thoughts going through his mind right now were nearly as numbing as what he'd experienced in his last nights in a Vietnam jungle before his country had called it a war and gone home. Knox's battalion had been one of the last to be sent to Southeast Asia. He'd been there all of eleven months and it had felt like eleven years. When he'd gotten back with a piece of shrapnel in his left thigh and a truck load of recurring nightmares as reminders of his time there, he'd decided that war was not a particularly smart way to decide global issues, especially when politicians rather than the grunts on the ground were calling the shots. That's when he'd worked his way to the Defense Intelligence Agency and from there to the civilian side and CIA.

Now his official home was a specialized piece of that agency that John Q. Public had never heard of and never would. He had two sets of creds: one for the public that showed him to be with Homeland Security and was suitably intimidating; and another set that he showed only to certain fellow federal agents. That evidenced his association with OSM, the Office of Special Matters. It was made up of personnel from five of the major intelligence agencies, though it was controlled by a handful of folks at Langley. "Office of Special Matters" sounded a little hokey, Knox thought, but what they did was far from it. Knox had been up to his ass in "special matters" for years, often handling six crises of international meltdown range at once.

In fact he'd been involved in every major op OSM had been handed over the last decade, including some paramilitary action that had gotten him back into the field with a gun and lives to take care of, and others simply to take. He'd narrowly avoided the "WMDs that never were" fiasco and then had spent six years in the Middle East doing things he would never write down and had done his best to forget about since.

He'd been thousands of miles away when his wife had died from a brain hemorrhage. He got back just in time for the funeral to say a hurried, mumbled good-bye to his life partner, the only woman he'd ever loved. To this day he felt like he had cheated her.

Twenty-four hours after burying her, he was back in Iraq trying to figure out where the next suicide blast was coming from and paying yesterday's enemies with good

American cash so they'd kill extremists instead of U.S. troops. When the money eventually ran out Knox knew he didn't want to be within five time zones of the place. Then he'd gone back to his safe room in the Green Zone and wept for the love of his life in the privacy of his own nightmares.

It had been more than a challenge and in the last year Knox had seriously contemplated retirement after talking his way out of the Middle East where no Muslim trusted anyone with light skin who held a firm belief in the supreme holiness of the Lord Jesus Christ. He'd pulled enough time. He could go out on his terms. He was actually on a short sabbatical when Hayes had called. And now look at him. And the same old question had raised its ugly head once more:

Will the sun come up for me tomorrow?

He walked into his kitchen, tossed his keys on the counter, opened the fridge and popped a beer. He sat down in his small study and considered what he did and didn't know, the latter unfortunately being far more voluminous than the former. He slipped the pages from his pocket. He'd taken the two-page order with Macklin Hayes' signature on it. It was probably a felony stealing government property, but Knox really didn't care at this point. He looked at the precise signature of the man.

What were you thinking when you signed that order, General?

He now had a connection between Hayes and Carr. That changed the dynamic of his mission, Knox just wasn't sure how. Yet it did explain one thing.

He was told he'd been ordered to track down Carr because the former Triple Six held secrets that would embarrass the U.S. government, or at the very least the CIA. Sometimes, for Knox, it was hard to tell the two apart. Hayes had said that Carter Gray had been concerned about that too. And that he'd been after Carr, but Carr had evidently gotten to him first.

That's what hadn't made sense. Carr had *been* at Gray's house the night it was blown up. So he'd evidently already known where Carr was. And on top of that Carr hadn't opened his mouth these last thirty years. So why would Gray or Hayes and the CIA be worried that the man was going to open it now?

Perhaps Gray had been after Carr for some reason, but not to kill the man. Ordering his grave to be dug up? Was he trying to flush him out, make him run? But why? Knox had a hunch the answer lay in the area he was prohibited from looking into. But he'd been "ordered" from doing things before. And he'd still gone ahead and done them.

And Hayes too had some strong reason for getting Carr out of the way. He must've thought Carr was dead all these years. Reading the man's face, Knox could tell he'd been out of the loop when the grave was dug up. And then to have no body in the coffin? All these years Hayes had probably felt safe. Now he didn't, and he was using Knox to take care of the problem for him.

And what exactly had happened at the Capitol Visitor Center? Had Carr really killed all those men? If so, why? Were they trying to kill him? Knox thought back to the notes he'd read about someone dispatching retired Triple Sixes. Had Stone been on that list? Had they gone after him for some reason? That was part of the puzzle that he apparently was not going to be allowed access to. Well, he would see about that.

If Carr had something on Hayes? Something personal? Now, that might be an interesting line to hunt down, if only to cover his backside when the time came. But he'd have to straddle the fence. If Hayes found out—

He'd turned the radio on in his study while he'd been thinking, and the news story caught his attention. Authorities knew who the killer was. They were closing in. All escape routes blocked.

What the hell?

He made the call. Hayes picked up on the second ring.

"I just heard the news," Knox said. "I thought the feds were being left off this one. If I've got an FBI posse breathing down my neck I'd like to know it."

"Not to worry, Knox, I had that story planted. It would be inconceivable for a man like Carr not to be listening to the news carefully. I want him to think he's trapped. Trapped men do stupid things. Then we move in. Just making your job easier."

Hayes clicked off.

"My ass you are," Knox said to the dead line.

The buzzing phone cut off his thoughts on what Hayes had just told him. He didn't recognize the number.

"Hello?"

"Mr. Knox, this is Susan Hunter. I'd like to meet with you, about Oliver."

Knox sat up. "Can we do it over the phone?"

"No. You never know who might be listening."

He couldn't argue with her about that. Someone probably was listening.

"Fair enough. When do you want to do it?"

"Right now."

CHAPTER

27

Annabelle was standing on the street corner in Georgetown when Knox pulled up thirty minutes later. He popped open the passenger door and she climbed in. He drove off, heading east toward the downtown area.

Knox glanced at her. The woman's face was flushed, her eyes red. He couldn't know it was from a little rouge and a little eye irritant deliberately applied.

"You okay?" he finally said.

She wiped her eyes. "Not really."

"So let's talk about it."

"I don't want to get in trouble."

"I don't want that either."

"Yeah, but can you guarantee it?"

"If you've done nothing wrong, I can. And even if you have screwed up, depending on what you tell me, you might very well get a walk."

Annabelle started twisting her fingers. "It's complicated."

"Trust me, my job never involves anything remotely simple."

"What exactly is your job?" she said bluntly.

He pulled over and parked on the street and turned off the truck. "Let's get one thing straight. This is not an information exchange. You talk, I listen. If it's good, I help you. If you're screwing me over, well, just don't."

She drew a long breath and plunged in. "Oliver was very secretive. Nobody really knew anything concrete about his past. But we could all tell he was special, different. You probably saw the books in his cottage. He spoke different languages. He just carried himself in a different way."

"His past I'm reasonably well-informed on. It's his current location that I'm most interested in."

"I don't know that."

"So why'd you call me?"

"Oliver had some information on Carter Gray. That was why Gray resigned when he did."

"What kind of information?"

Annabelle shook her head. "He never said, but he visited Gray and the next day Gray resigned, so it must've been pretty incriminating."

"But then Gray got his old position back."

"That's because he got the evidence that Oliver had back."

"The Capitol Visitor Center?" Knox said sharply.

"I think so. It wasn't like I was there. It's just something Oliver said right before he vanished."

"What else did he say?"

"That it's better no one ever finds out the real truth. That it could hurt this country and he would never want that."

Knox smiled. "You'd make a great witness for the defense."

"Do you know about his military service?"

"Guy was a helluva soldier. So what about Senator Simpson? What's the connection there?"

"Oliver said he worked for the CIA before he got into politics."

"That's right, he did. So Oliver knew him back then?"

"I guess. If he did work for the CIA, I mean. I have no proof that Oliver ever did."

"Let me worry about the proof. Does the term Triple Six mean anything to you?"

"I heard Oliver mention it once, but he never explained what it was."

"I bet he didn't."

"He was a good man. He helped break up a spy ring. He got a commendation letter from the FBI director."

"Good for him. So why do you think he killed Gray and Simpson?"

"I have no reason to believe that he did."

"Come on, Susan, or whatever your real name is, you're obviously not stupid. You know Carr and Stone are the same person. He's been hiding out for thirty years."

"If that's so, why do you think he's been hiding out?"

"You tell me."

"Maybe people were after him."

"What people?"

"People looking to kill him, I think."

"Is that what he said?"

"He told me once that with some agencies, even if you want to leave, they won't let you. They'd rather you'd be dead than not working for them."

This remark hit Knox like a hard slap but he didn't show it. *That one I can believe.*

"So let's assume for the moment he was a Triple Six who wanted out. They didn't want him to leave?"

"I know he was married and had a daughter. But he said they were both dead now."

Knox sat back against the seat, his fingers still gripping the steering wheel. "Suggesting that whoever was after him killed them?"

"I don't know. Maybe."

Knox let go of the steering wheel and stared out at the traffic whipping by down Pennsylvania Avenue. His thoughts turned momentarily to his own son and daughter. Maybe his son was safer in Iraq than his daughter was in Washington. *That* was a brutally numbing thought.

"Do you have a family?" she asked.

Knox snapped back. "What else can you tell me? His last few days with you? Anything that might show where he went?"

"If he did kill Gray and Simpson they probably deserved it."

"That's not what I asked, and, by the way, talk like that could wind you up in jail."

"I owe Oliver my life."

"That's you, not me."

"So when you find him are you going to kill him?"

"I work for the federal government. I'm not a hired killer."

"So you're telling me that if you do catch him he'll end up being tried, in a court of law?"

Knox hesitated. "That's not my call. A lot of it depends on him."

"Yeah, I thought that might be what you'd say."

"We're talking about a killer, Ms. Hunter."

"No, we're talking about my friend who was pushed past all human limits."

"You know that to be a fact?"

"I know him. That's how he's built. Was he capable of violence, of killing? Sure. Was he a cold-blooded killer? No."

"I have information that says otherwise."

"Then your information is wrong."

"What makes you so sure?"

"My gut."

"Your gut? That's it?"

"Yeah, the same gut that's telling me you really don't want any part of this job. I'm betting you have a family and a dream of being retired. But you got called into this shit and now you don't know which side is playing you for a fool."

It was a testament to Knox's iron-hard nerves that he didn't even blink in the face of this spot-on observation.

"Unless you have anything to add, I'll drop you back off."

"So am I in trouble?"

"You'll be the first to know."

Back in Georgetown she climbed out of the Rover. Before she closed the door he said, "With something like this, Ms. Hunter, everybody needs to watch his back."

He drove off.

Annabelle pulled her coat tighter around her and watched, stone-faced, as Reuben's truck edged past her and took up the tail on Joe Knox.

The fox had now become the hunted.

A minute later an ancient Chevy with a stuttering tailpipe stopped at the curb, Caleb at the wheel. Annabelle climbed in and they drove off in the opposite direction.

Annabelle glanced at Caleb and he looked at her.

"We're being followed too, you know," Annabelle said.

"Story of my life," Caleb replied without a trace of a whine.

CHAPTER

28

Stone hustled down a clay-packed path, really no more than two truck tire tracks wide, as he followed the cries. From out of the darkness loomed a long shape. The double-wide trailer was no longer "mobile" since it had a cinderblock undercarriage. The hulks of old cars and trucks, like the skeletons from faded battlefields, flew past as Stone hurried to the trailer. It had long strips of vinyl siding dangling off and the front steps were blackened railroad ties nailed together. Stone went from the bottom to the top step in one leap as the screams picked up.

The door was locked. He pounded on it.

"Hello, what's going on? Do you need help?" He suddenly wondered if the frantic calls were coming from a TV set turned up far too loud.

A moment later the door was thrown open and an old

man stood there, his body trembling as though he was in the throes of a Parkinson's meltdown.

"What's going on?" Stone exclaimed.

The next moment Stone was knocked aside as a young man burst past his trailer mate and sprang into the air, landing hard on the ground. Stone recovered his balance and stared after him.

Aside from the fellow's obvious agitation, he was remarkable for having no clothes on. He stopped next to one old wreck in the yard, moaned and fell to the ground, writhing in the dirt like he was being Tasered.

The old man grabbed Stone's arm.

"Help him, please!"

"What's wrong with him?"

"He's got the DTs. Coming off the pills or something. Went crazy. Ripped off his clothes. Tearing up the place."

Stone raced to the fallen man's side. His breathing was shallow, his eyes unfocused. His skin was cold and clammy.

Stone yelled over his shoulder, "Call the ambulance."

"Ain't none up here."

"Where's the hospital?"

"Hour drive."

"Is there a doctor around?" Stone was holding on to the stricken man, trying to calm him.

"Doc Warner's place is on the other side of town."

"You have a car?"

"Truck right there." The old man pointed to a battered old Dodge. "Is he going to be okay?"

"I don't know. Who are you?"

"His grandpa. Come to check on him. Then this happened."

"Can you help me get him in the truck?"

Together they lifted the young man into the cab and Stone covered him with a blanket. The old man was still shaking so badly he couldn't drive. Stone took the wheel and followed his directions to the doctor's place.

"What's your grandson's name?"

"Willie Coombs. I'm Bob Coombs."

"Where are his parents?"

"My son—his daddy—is dead. His momma ain't much good."

Stone glanced at Willie. He'd stopped thrashing and screaming and was now lying quite still. Stone again checked his pulse, slammed on the brakes and grabbed a flashlight off the dash to look at his pupils. They were pinpoints.

"Shit!"

"What is it?"

"He's not in withdrawal. He overdosed. And his heart's stopped."

Stone pulled Willie out of the cab, set him on the ground and started doing CPR. He checked his pulse and then looked desperately around while he continued to push down on the man's chest. There was nothing but woods here, not even the wink of a house light in the distance.

"Come on, Willie. Come on! Don't die on me. Breathe."

Stone checked his pulse.

Bob Coombs looked at him. "Is he okay?"

"No, he's not. He's technically dead. And we've got maybe sixty seconds before there's brain damage."

Stone ran to the truck and threw open the hood. The battery didn't throw off the juice he would need, but something else in the engine did. He ran to the cargo bed and started tossing items around there. His hands seized around a set of battery cables, masking tape and a nail.

He turned to see Bob staring at him anxiously. "Whatcha gonna do with that stuff?"

"I'm trying to get his heart restarted."

Stone ripped out a spark plug wire leading from the distributor cap and jammed the nail in the end of it, securing it there with the tape. He attached the positive end of the battery cables to the nail while he grounded the negative clamp onto a metal part of the engine. He knelt next to Willie and placed the other ends of the battery cables onto his right and left fingers respectively.

He called out, "Bob, fire the truck up!"

Bob looked at the cables leading from the truck to his grandson. "You gonna fry him!"

"We're out of time, Bob. This is our only shot. Just do it! Now! Or he's dead."

Bob jumped in the truck.

Stone looked down at Willie, reached over and made sure the connections were solid. The young man was already turning blue. They only had seconds left.

Stone had done this once in Nam with a fellow soldier who'd gone into cardiac arrest when a massive round had sheared a chunk of his torso off. Stone had gotten his heart going again, but the man had bled to death on the way to the field hospital.

The truck started.

"Rev the engine," Stone screamed out.

Bob smashed the gas to the floor and the engine roared.

Even though he wasn't touching Willie, Stone could

feel the surge of current. The effect on the young man was far more intense.

His legs and arms came off the ground and Willie sucked in an enormous breath. He sat up and then fell back, choking and coughing.

"Cut the engine," Stone yelled and Bob instantly did so. The only sound now was a miraculous one. A dead man was breathing.

Stone ripped the cables off and checked the pulse. Pretty strong and steady.

Bob and he lifted Willie into the truck. Stone put the spark plug wire minus the nail back in place, threw the battery cables in the back, and drove off. They made it to the doctor's home office five minutes later and carried him inside. Warner worked on Willie after Stone told him what he'd done. Warner was not Stone's image of a rustic country doctor. He was barely forty, trim, with a clean-shaven face and wide, intelligent-looking eyes behind a pair of wire-rimmed glasses. He gave Willie an injection and made a phone call.

He said, "That injection should stabilize him for now. But can you get him to the hospital quick as you can? I called ahead and I'll follow in my car."

Stone nodded. "But if his heart stops again on the way? I don't want to rely on the truck's juice again."

Warner opened a cabinet and pulled out a portable de-fibrillator. "If it happens again, pull off the road and we'll use this."

As they were loading Willie back in the truck the doctor said, "You saved his life, you know."

Bob placed a hand on Stone's shoulder. "I can't thank you enough, Mr. . . . ?"

"Just call me Ben. And he's not out of the woods yet. Let's go."

They arrived at the hospital less than an hour later. Stone went in with them, but after Willie was checked in, he came back outside and leaned against the truck, sucking in the crisp, cool mountain air.

The hospital was big. It probably had to be since it was probably the only one for a few hundred square miles.

He walked around the parking lot trying to push back the adrenaline rush. He spotted the squat one-story cinderblock building next to the hospital and walked in that direction.

When he saw the sign on the building Stone realized this was the methadone clinic, where the truck parade came every morning. As he watched he noted the armed security guard patrolling in front of the building. When the man saw Stone standing there, Stone smiled and waved. The man neither smiled nor waved back. Instead he put a hand on his holstered gun. Stone turned and walked back to the hospital. He assumed the presence of the guard meant that the clinic was a target for either drug dealers or druggies. Stone knew that liquid methadone on its own couldn't deliver a high, that's why it was used to wean addicts off drugs. But when combined with other drugs, like anti-anxiety pills, it could produce an often deadly cocktail.

About an hour later Bob came back out and explained that Willie was out of danger and was being admitted.

"So what did they find out?" Stone asked.

"They said he overdosed on something."

"That I knew. You have any idea what?"

"The emergency room doctor asked that too. I saw a

crack pipe in Willie's hand when I came in the trailer. He tried to hide it from me, but I still saw it."

Stone shook his head. "Crack's a stimulant. His eyes would've been dilated, not pinpoints. He overdosed, but on a depressant, not a stimulant."

"Well, I guess I could be wrong about what he took," Bob said hesitantly.

Stone looked at him curiously but the old man didn't seem inclined to add anything to what he'd already said. Stone drove Bob back to Willie's trailer where he'd left his truck. He tried to pay Stone for his help but Stone refused.

Bob dropped an exhausted Stone off at the rooming house. As Stone slowly walked up the stairs he figured that despite the massive manhunt after him he would have to get out of Divine pretty soon, just to get some rest.

CHAPTER

29

By THE NEXT MORNING nearly everyone in Divine had heard of Stone's heroics. Apparently Bob Coombs had told everyone he encountered of the stunning rescue, and the story had quickly spread.

"Cool a hand as I ever seen," he repeated over and over, referring to Stone.

"Heard he was in Nam," another man said. "Good under pressure."

"A true American hero," said one lady. She added in a lower tone while talking with a girlfriend of hers, "Too bad it was wasted on Willie Coombs."

Sheriff Tyree came to Stone's room that morning to congratulate and thank him. "Willie's a good young man except for the pills."

"He's a coal miner, right?" said Stone.

"How'd you know?"

"Scars and banged-up hands. And he had coal dust embedded in his skin. Does his mother know?"

"Shirley? Doubt she'd care."

Stone chose not to ask about that. "Bob Coombs said his son, Willie's father, was dead."

"Yep. Hunting accident. Didn't have his orange slicker on and somebody thought he was a deer. Abby told me to tell you she's got some more work you can do. Same pay scale."

"I'll head over there right now." After the news on the radio last night he was even more uncomfortable being around the lawman.

When Stone arrived at Rita's Restaurant Abby had breakfast waiting for him. When he walked in customers smiled and waved at him. A few miners came over and clapped him on the back, thanking him for helping their fellow miner.

"How's it feel to be a hero?" Abby asked, pouring him a cup of coffee.

"I'm just glad he's okay. But he's got a long road ahead of him. Apparently he has a drug problem."

"Most miners do. Willie Coombs is actually a good young man. He and Danny played ball in high school together. Best of friends but then they had a falling-out."

"Over what?"

"When we were all poor, that was one thing. Then when we got the settlement money Willie seemed to think Danny owed him. We gave him some money, sure, but most of it went up his nose so we stopped."

A tall, thin man came over to them. He was the only man in the place dressed in a suit and tie. His gray hair was neatly parted and fashionably cut. His eyes were gray and alert and his face was deeply lined, carrying the gravitas one usually found in scholars.

Abby said, "Ben, this is Charlie Trimble. He runs the *Divine Eagle*, the local newspaper."

It was all Stone could do not to leap up and run out of the place.

A smiling Trimble said, "I would love to interview you about your experience with Willie, Ben. Not only because it's an amazing story but it shows why we need to reinstate the volunteer rescue squad program here."

Abby looked at Stone. "Is that okay?"

Stone said slowly, "What I did wasn't all that special. And I'm not looking to get any publicity just because I helped someone."

Trimble smiled more broadly. "And modest too. That will work well in the story angle. It's just a few questions, Ben. We can even do it here or back at my office."

Stone stood. "Abby, if you have some more work for me to do that would be great." He looked at Trimble. "I'm sorry, Mr. Trimble. I'm sure Bob would love to talk to you. He helped as much as I did. Maybe more."

Trimble looked put off. "Just a couple of questions?"

"No, I'm sorry."

Abby gave him a list of jobs to do while Trimble sat at his table, drinking a cup of coffee and staring at Stone. And Stone could feel the burn of the man's gaze.

Stone worked half the day at the restaurant and the other half at Abby's home. And every minute he was desperately trying to think of some way out. If he left Divine he would probably be caught. If he stayed in Divine someone might put two and two together and one morning the feds would rumble into town. For one of the few times in his life, Stone did not know what to do.

On his way back to his rooming house that evening he saw Bob Coombs standing in front of it. The old man looked nervous, rocking back and forth on his heels, hands shoved in his pockets as he studied the pavement. Stone crossed the street.

"Hey, Bob, is Willie okay?"

Bob looked nervously around. "Can we talk somewhere private?"

Stone led him up to his room. "What's up?"

"Talked to Willie this morning and the docs over at the hospital and some things don't make sense."

"Like what?"

"It was sort of like you said. Drugs Willie said he took don't add up to what happened to him."

"Was it crack?"

"That's what Willie said he was on."

"He might have made a mistake."

Bob was shaking his head. "I know some folks think Willie's nothing but a pillhead, but he's not. He's a smart boy but killing himself in the mines. Started there right out of high school and looks like he's been there thirty years, just the way it is. But if he said it was crack, it was crack, you can count on it."

Stone studied him, not really sure why the man was telling him this. "Well, if you think something's wrong, Bob, you should let Sheriff Tyree know."

"I was wondering, sort of, if you could maybe step in."

"Me? Step in what exactly?" Stone said cautiously.

"You saved Willie's life. Easy to see you been around,

know stuff. I was just hoping maybe you could talk to Willie, get his side of things and see what you can find out."

"I'm not a PI."

"Lost my son, see. Willie's the only thing I got left. Can't lose him too. Well, that's all I got to say. If you go see Willie, I thank you. And if you don't I still thank you for all you done."

"Has that fellow Trimble from the paper been by to see you?"

"Yep. Had some questions. Told him what you did. He said he's writing up the story. Said you wouldn't talk to him."

"I'm not much into tooting my horn. Is he from Divine?"

"Oh, no, he retired here. Got a little place up near the river and then took over running the newspaper here."

"Was he into journalism before?"

"Oh, yeah."

"Where?"

"Somebody told me once. The *Washington Post*."

Oh, shit.

"Look, Ben, I can pay you if you'd look into it."

"Bob, go see the sheriff. That's his job. Not mine."

"But—"

"I'm sorry, Bob. I can't."

30

LATER, Stone walked to the craft shop and did something he really didn't want to, but he was out of options. He called Reuben.

"Oliver, tell me where you are," he said immediately.

"Just listen, Reuben. I need some information."

Another voice came on the line. It was Annabelle.

"Oliver, we want to help you. But you've got to tell us where you are."

"I'm not getting you involved in this, Annabelle. So stop trying to help me. I don't deserve it anyway."

"I don't care if you killed those men. What I care about is you."

Stone took a deep breath. "I appreciate that, Annabelle, I really do." Stone glanced up to see Wanda, the shopkeeper, eyeing him from across the room. He smiled and turned away from her.

"Oliver, are you there!"

"Look, it means a lot to me that you want to help, it really does. But if I'm going to go down, it's going to be just me, not all of you."

"But—"

He cut her off. "If you really want to help me, put Reuben back on."

He could hear her accelerated breathing for a few seconds and then Reuben said, "What do you need?"

"Has Knox or anyone else been back?"

"No." Technically Reuben wasn't lying since Annabelle had gone to see Knox, not the other way around. In fact, they were parked out on Knox's street right now watching and waiting for the man's next move.

"The news said that they have all the airports, train and bus stations under watch."

"I heard that too."

"That's a lot of ground to cover, even for the FBI."

"They're working with Homeland Security on this, which has opened up all local resources as well. Lot of street cops out there looking."

"You said Knox knew it was John Carr, and that he and I were one and the same."

"That's right. Though nothing in the press has said anything about John Carr now being Oliver Stone."

"Have any photos of me been circulated?"

"Not to my knowledge. At least publicly. But who knows what's going on behind the scenes."

Stone leaned against the wall and studied a miniature black bear formed from a lump of coal. *Coal is king. Stone is dead.* "Any idea if they think I'm still in the area?"

"Are you?"

"Reuben!"

"Okay, slit my throat for caring. Nothing specific, but you can count on the fact that any place within a few hundred miles of D.C. will be under close watch."

Stone sighed. "Thanks for the info, Reuben. I hope I won't have to call you again."

"Oliver, wait—"

Stone hung up the phone and walked toward the front of the shop, managing a smile at Wanda as he passed her.

She said, "Heard about Willie. That sure was real smart of you."

"I'm just glad I could help."

"I told my husband about it. He was in the army. I told him I heard you were too. He wanted to know which part."

"The part that fought in Vietnam," Stone said as he closed the door behind him.

He went back to the rooming house and packed his few belongings. The bus ride to the vicinity of Divine had taken three hours from where they had gotten off the train. He remembered the general direction they'd come, but the corkscrew roads and hairpin curves were impossible to recall with any specificity. He thought back to the night he and Danny had come here via hog truck. He remembered the towers of Dead Rock prison. The main street of Divine. The warm bed above Rita's. The shotgun in his face the next morning. Abby Riker's scowl that had somehow turned to a smile.

He waited until it was well dark and then headed out of town. His route carried him past the road leading to Willie's place. A few minutes later he saw the burn of car headlights coming his way and he quickly stepped off the main road and onto the dirt one leading to Willie's trailer. He quickly retreated into some bushes lining the dirt drive as he waited for the car to pass. He only got a glimpse at the driver as it sped by and continued to watch as the car kept on going before it rounded a curve and its rear lights vanished.

Stone looked back at the main road and then glanced the other way. He was on his way again when yet another car came along the main drag, forcing him to scurry once more back down the road to Willie's place. He obviously hadn't waited until it was late enough. Right now, for him, every car could be a state trooper with his digital picture painted on the laptop computer in the cruiser.

He hustled down the dirt road and stopped. The car was parked in front of Willie's trailer and there was a light on inside. He glanced at the car; it was a small red two-door Infiniti. He looked inside. There was a purse on the front seat and the smell of cigarette smoke was heavy. He peered around at the trailer. The front screen door was partially open. He heard a small crash from inside.

He quickly moved up the steps and said, "You okay?"

"Who is it? Who's there?" It was a woman and her voice trembled.

She appeared at the door a moment later; a tall bleached blonde with a spare tire wedged into slim jeans and spiky heels. A cigarette dangled from her left hand. She looked to be in her late forties, although the amount of makeup she had on made it difficult to tell.

"I'm Ben, the man who helped Willie last night." Her features looked familiar. "Are you Willie's mom, Shirley Coombs?"

She took a drag on her cigarette and nodded absently, but the suspicious look only deepened. "How'd you know that?"

"You look like each other." Stone glanced over her shoulder into the trailer. She followed his gaze and said hurriedly, "I came over to check on things when I heard 'bout Willie. Got folks round here that might take advantage of him being laid up in the hospital. Messing with his stuff and all."

It occurred to Stone that Mom might've been messing with her son's stuff too.

"Have you seen Willie yet?"

"Planning to get over there soon. Long drive. And my car's not too dependable."

Stone glanced back at her car. "Looks to be pretty new."

"Yeah, well, it's a piece of crap. Keeps stalling out on me."

"Everything look okay in there?" he asked.

"Willie's not the neatest person in town, so it's hard to tell, really. Looks okay, I guess."

"You need any help?"

"No," she said quickly, a beat too quickly actually. "I mean, you've helped enough. Willie would be dead except for you. I thank you for that."

"I'm glad I was around. But Bob helped with Willie too."

Her features turned dark. "Yeah, old Bob is real good about helping folks. At least ones he likes."

"He doesn't include you in that group?"

"You could say the whole town doesn't include me in that group."

Okay. "I was sorry to hear about your husband."

She stiffened. "Who told you about him? Bob?"

"No, Sheriff Tyree. He mentioned the hunting accident. Pretty tragic."

"Yeah, real tragic."

Stone looked at her quizzically. "I hope Willie will be okay," he said, after an awkward silence.

"Hell, he'll be fine. He's got four shotguns, a deer rifle, two hunting bows, a pickup truck, his own double-wide, cable TV and propane to keep warm, a camp stove to cook on and folding money from the mine. What's not to come home to? My boy aimed high in life, didn't he?" She smiled. But then it quickly faded. "Look, I got to go," she said. "Thanks again for saving my baby."

She closed the door behind her and moved past Stone. He watched as she got in her car and drove off.

He hoisted his bag and walked back to the main road.

Five minutes later the truck almost hit him as it flew by. He dodged out of the way, rolled and came up in time to see a man throw himself out of the truck cab and land hard in the road. Stone raced toward him and turned him over.

It was Danny. He was badly beaten but still breathing. And then Stone looked up. The truck had stopped. As he watched it turned and headed toward him, stopping a few feet from where he knelt next to Danny. Three men climbed out and each one carried a baseball bat.

CHAPTER

31

JOE KNOX SAT in his town house having a cup of coffee and pondering his next move. The idiot Agency artist he'd requested to do a composite had gotten lost on the way to Leroy's place. And when he'd gotten there Leroy had gone off on his damn boat. Leroy didn't have a phone so the best Knox could do was send another agent up there to try and pin the man down. Until he had a picture to show around, Knox was at a standstill in his investigation. And if Leroy had been involved and was now on the run after Knox had conveniently warned him?

There will be no way to explain such a junior mistake to Hayes.

He decided to run through again what he'd learned at the military records center, in case it might suggest something. A half hour later he was no further along. Maybe he should go back to the records center and go through some more documents. The attendant had been able to easily find the other boxes for him. It probably wouldn't take—

Knox slowly set down his coffee cup. The next moment he was racing to the phone. He got the number for the records center and punched it in. A minute later, after being forwarded along to several extensions, he heard the voice of the man who'd helped him before. Knox identified himself and then asked the question.

"How did you find what I wanted so easily? It was like the boxes were already out."

"Well, actually they were," the man replied a bit sheepishly. "I mean, they'd been checked out some months back. Maybe six months or so, and I'm a little embarrassed to say that no one had filed them away yet. And we've been a bit shorthanded as of late," he added quickly, as though suspecting that Knox might actually be some sort of military archives inspector trying to pull a slick one.

"So someone else was looking at those records?" Knox said slowly. "Can you tell me who?"

The man excused himself for a minute. When he came back on the line he said, "Guy named Harry Finn. Says here on the sign-in log he used to be with the Navy SEALs. He had the credentials and top secret clearances to get access to the boxes you looked at. That help you any?"

"That helps me a lot, thanks." Knox clicked off and spent the next hour tracking down Harry Finn, former SEAL.

An hour later he pulled his truck to a stop, got out, walked up to the steps and rang the doorbell. A few moments later it opened and he was staring across at a tall young man whose gaze burned back into his.

"Harry Finn?"

Finn didn't answer. His gaze instinctively checked behind Knox.

"I'm alone. Well, as alone as is probably possible on something like this."

"Something like what?"

"Can I come in?"

"Who in the hell are you?"

Knox flipped open his creds. "I'm here to talk about Oliver Stone. Or you might know him as John Carr."

"I've got nothing to say."

"I'm not sure why you were looking up the guy's military record, or whether you're his friend or not. But he's on the run and somebody's going to get to him at some point. And when they do." Knox simply shrugged.

Finn was about to say something when Knox's cell phone rang. He'd been half expecting it actually, even as he glanced over his shoulder and saw the black sedan parked down the road. His expert gaze, however, did not pick up the nondescript white van parked farther down. It was Macklin Hayes on the phone, and as usual he got right to the point.

"What the hell are you doing there, Knox?"

"Where?"

"Harry Finn is off-limits."

Knox backed down the steps and turned away from Finn. "Nobody told me that."

"I'm telling you now. How did you get on to him? Anything to do with your visit to the military records center?"

"And why do you find need to follow me, sir?" Knox turned and waved to the men in the black sedan.

"What did you find?"

"Not much. He fought in Vietnam. He was a good soldier. Then he just disappeared. Probably when he was recruited for"—Knox glanced at Finn and smiled—"for that thing that doesn't exist."

"You are to leave that house now and never go back."

The phone went dead. Knox put it back in his pocket and turned to Finn.

"You'll be happy to know that you're officially off-limits, or so my boss just told me. But just keep in mind that something really screwy is going on with Carr. I've already gabbed with his friends, including the lady who calls herself Susan Hunter. She told me Carr had the goods on Carter Gray but that Gray got it back probably at the Capitol Visitor Center. You probably already know that from your suitably blank expression. Maybe you were even there. All I can tell you is I've been assigned to track Carr down. That's all. But when I do track him down, and rest assured I will, other people will show up and take over. And I doubt they'll have his best interests at heart. Whether you give a shit or not, I don't know and really don't care."

He put out a hand for Finn to shake. When he did, Finn came away with a business card with Knox's contact information on it.

"You have a good day, Mr. Finn."

Knox walked back to his truck while Finn stared after him.

Knox didn't know exactly why he'd done that. Well, maybe he did. John Carr had gotten his ass shot up for his country and they'd screwed him. Whatever else the man had done, that just wasn't right.

* * *

In the white van, Annabelle punched in the number. A moment later Harry Finn answered. He relayed to her what Knox had told him and she in turn filled him in.

"Do we trust this guy, Annabelle?" Finn asked.

"I didn't at first, but now I'm not so sure. He seems to be caught right in the middle."

"So what do we do?"

"Sit tight. I may need your help later. Or more to the point, Oliver will."

"I owe Oliver everything. So I'll be there if you need me."

CHAPTER

32

STONE ROSE, his right hand undoing his belt as he did so. He slipped it off and held it by the buckle. The silver pointed end dangled a few inches from the road.

The men circled him, holding their bats ready.

"Odds don't look too good for you, pops," said one of them.

An instant later he was on the ground, his face covered in blood from where the belt point had bitten into his eye.

As he writhed and screamed with his hands over his face, one of his buddies took a step toward Stone and swung his bat with all his strength. Stone ducked under the blow and snapped his belt against the side of the man's face, gouging it. The fellow yelled in fury and came at Stone again, his bat whipping back and forth. Stone dodged out of the way, but one of the wild blows caught him squarely on the arm. He dropped his belt, rolled and snatched up the fallen man's Louisville Slugger with his good arm. One smack to the man's knees brought him down; the second to the base of his neck kept him there.

The remaining attacker dropped his bat and ran. Stone turned and threw the bat he was holding. It whipsawed through the air and nailed the guy in the back. He screamed, dropped to the road, picked himself up and kept going. Stone started to go after him but stopped when Danny moaned. He raced back to his side even as the truck sped off.

"Danny, Danny, can you hear me? Can you get up?"

Stone looked around. One man unconscious. The other still rolling around on the ground. He was worried the third attacker would go get reinforcements. And his arm was killing him.

"Danny, can you walk?"

Danny finally focused on Stone and nodded. Stone heaved him to his feet, the pain shooting across his injured limb. He was still able to support Danny as they made their way down the road. They reached Willie's trailer. Stone loaded Danny into the truck and raced into the trailer. He found Willie's truck keys, ran back out, fired up the truck and pulled off.

He drove first to Doc Warner's office but no one was there. He changed direction and headed to the hospital.

Danny lay against him in the front seat. His face was bloody and one arm hung limp. "Hold on, Danny, we're going to the hospital."

Danny mumbled something.

"What?"

"Call my mom."

Stone watched as Danny slowly dug his hand in one pocket and drew out his phone. Steering with his knees, Stone flipped it open, found the number on the speed dial and hit the key.

It took a few rings but she finally answered. "Hello?"

"Abby, it's Ben. I've got Danny. He's been attacked by some guys with baseball bats. I'm taking him to the hospital. Meet us there."

To her credit the woman didn't scream or start crying. All she said was, "I'm on my way."

Less than an hour later Stone once more pulled into the hospital parking lot. He half carried Danny into the emergency room entrance. While they were working on him Abby screeched to a stop in the parking lot, jumped out of the Mini Cooper and rushed in. Stone met her at the door and took her to Danny, who was lying on a gurney in the triage room.

Tears gathered in the corners of her eyes as she held her son's hand. "Danny, what the hell happened? Who did this to you?"

He murmured, "Just an accident, Ma. Don't worry. I'll be good to go. Took better hits on Friday game nights."

Abby looked at Stone. "An accident?"

He shook his head.

The doctor said, "We need to get him admitted and have some tests run. He seems stable now, but he may have internal bleeding."

"Will he be okay?" Abby said anxiously.

"Ma'am, we need to run some tests. We'll take good care of him. And we'll let you know how he is."

A moment later they whisked him away.

Abby stood there, teetering a bit. Stone put an arm

around her shoulders and led her to a chair in the waiting area.

"He said it was an accident."

"It was no accident. Three men. Big and mean with baseball bats."

"How do you know that?"

Stone didn't answer her immediately. Something had just occurred to him. One of the men he'd beaten up had looked familiar. He tried to think where he'd seen him, but couldn't place him.

"Ben?"

"What? Oh, because they came after me when they were done with Danny."

"How'd you get away?"

Stone touched his waistline. "It cost me my belt, but I hurt two of them pretty bad. One of them got away. I need to call Tyree and report it. Do you have his number?"

She handed him her phone and he made the call.

After he explained things to the sheriff and described the men and their truck, he nodded at something Tyree said. "Right, we'll be here," he replied.

Stone handed the phone back to Abby. "He's going to come here to get a statement after he checks out the crime scene."

"I can't believe this is happening." But there was a hollow ring to her words that puzzled Stone.

"When I called you didn't sound all that surprised that someone had attacked Danny."

She didn't look at him.

"Abby, I know I'm a stranger here, but I saw those guys up close and personal. If Danny hadn't managed to throw himself out of the truck, he'd be dead. And they might come back to finish the job."

She touched her eyes with one of her hands, brushing away the tears. "There's some things been going on in Divine. Strange things."

"Like what? Was that why Danny left? And now some-one's upset he's back?"

"I don't know why he left. He wouldn't tell me."

"Abby, I saw Danny crying his heart out over the top of Debby Randolph's grave."

She looked at him strangely. "Debby Randolph?"

"Yes. Did he know her? Did he love her?"

"They dated a couple times in high school. But she was Willie's girl now."

"How did she die?"

"Committed suicide. With a shotgun in a little shed behind her parents' house."

"Why would she have killed herself?"

"I don't know. I guess she was depressed. Tyree's look-ing into it."

"But right after she died, Danny left Divine?" Abby balled a tissue between her fingers and nodded slowly. "Did he ever mention Debby to you recently?"

"No." She dabbed at her eyes again.

"So what strange things are you talking about?"

"Just things."

"Abby, can't you be more specific?"

"There was a murder right before Danny left."

"Murder? Who?"

"Fellow named Rory Peterson."

"I saw his grave too. Who murdered him?"

"Don't know. Tyree's still looking at that one too."

"Who was Peterson?"

"An accountant. He also helped run the town fund."

"Town fund?"

"Divine has been through enough booms and busts so we decided to try a different approach. Everybody kicked in some money, businesses, regular folks. I put in more than most because I had more money. We put it all in an investment account and it's done real well. Rory did the books. The fund pays out quarterly dividends. It's been a godsend to folks around town. Kept businesses going that otherwise wouldn't be able to make a go of it. Allowed folks to keep their houses, pay off their debt, survive the lean times."

"You said Peterson did the books. Was he maybe skimming and somebody didn't like that?"

"I don't know. I know Rory had some contacts in New York. That was where he was from originally. That was another reason the fund was doing so well. He got us piggybacked on some of those private equity people's investments up there. At least that's what he said. Hitting stuff out of the park, at least according to the dividends I get."

"Would Danny be mixed up in that somehow? Or Debby?"

"Don't see how. Danny's never been what you'd call financially savvy. His interests are a lot more basic. Debby was an artist. She had nothing to do with the fund."

"Well, those guys tonight didn't seem like the Wall Street types either."

Abby's phone buzzed. She answered it and then passed it across to Stone. "It's Tyree," she said.

The sheriff said, "Ben, I went to the place you said.

Nobody was there. Didn't find nothing. No bats, no blood, no belt."

"They must've come back and cleaned it all up."

"How's Danny?"

"Getting some tests run."

"Did you ask him who did it?"

"He said it was an accident."

"And you're sure it wasn't?"

"Not unless you categorize three guys with baseball bats doing you bodily harm an accident."

"I'm heading over to talk to Danny. How's Abby?"

Stone glanced at her. "She's holding up."

Stone passed back the phone. "I'm going to get a cup of coffee, you want one?"

She shook her head and tried to smile. "No thanks. I'm just going to stay planted here until they tell me Danny's going to be okay."

Stone walked off looking for a vending machine, stretching out his sore arm as he did so. Then the rather obvious occurred to him. Willie Coombs was still here.

Crack and pinpoint pupils. And now Danny beaten nearly to death. And a dead woman in the middle of it all.

The coffee could wait. He needed to talk to Willie.

CHAPTER

33

Knox's cell phone buzzed. The caller ID came up as blocked. He hesitated and then answered it.

"Hello?"

It took a second for Knox to place the caller's voice. "Finn?"

"I thought about what you said and I thought you might want to know something."

Knox snatched a small notebook off the kitchen island and uncapped a pen. "I'm listening."

"I *was* at the Visitor Center with Stone. That won't come as a surprise to the folks at CIA. Carter Gray was there too, as was Senator Simpson."

"What were you all doing there? Having a pre-opening party?"

"We were doing an exchange. My son for Senator Simpson."

Knox caught a breath. "CIA snatched your kid?"

"And we grabbed a U.S. senator in return."

"Why Simpson?"

"He, Gray and Stone have a history. Not a good one."

"I didn't think they were all best buds."

"Anyway, we did the exchange, gave Gray all he wanted, including a cell phone with a recording on it that Stone had."

"What was the recording of?"

"Don't know. But whatever it was, it's the reason Gray resigned his post as intelligence czar."

"Some dirt?"

"Seems to be."

"I take it after the exchange was made they weren't going to let you walk away?"

"You could say that Gray had a different idea as to how we were going to leave the place."

Knox was writing fast and scribbling questions in the margins. "Let me ask something. Was Milton Farb a casualty in this little skirmish?"

"He's dead, isn't he? Stone was getting us all out on a prearranged route. He knew Gray would try and screw him so he had a backup plan. But while we were getting out of there, Milton was killed by one of Gray's men. Stone didn't leave after that. He went back in." Finn paused. "I went with him."

"Why?"

"He saved my son. He saved me along with everyone I cared about. I owed him."

"Okay. I can see that." Knox clenched the top of the pen between his teeth.

"One more thing. Before Simpson left the building he called out something to Stone."

"What was that?"

"He told him that he'd been the one to order the hit on Stone and his family when Stone was with Triple Six and Simpson was with CIA. His wife was killed and his daughter just disappeared during the hit. Stone got away and he's been on the run ever since. They took everything he had, Knox. Everything."

"Why would they want to torpedo one of their own?"

"He wanted out. He'd had enough. Only they didn't want him to leave," Finn said simply.

Knox settled down in a chair and peered out the window into his small front yard as he digested this. "Why are you telling me all this?"

"Two reasons. Owing to something that happened a long time ago involving Gray and Simpson, my family and I are bulletproof so far as the U.S. government is concerned. They're not coming after us no matter what I say or don't say."

"Yeah, I got that impression. And the second reason?"

"I've still got contacts on the inside and I checked you out. I peg you as a good guy in a tough spot. You may need a lifeline more than anybody before this is all over."

"I hope you're wrong but I appreciate the assist."

"Here's another one. If you are trying to find Oliver Stone, I'm not going to wish you luck."

"I can understand that."

"It's not just for the reason you think."

"Come again?"

"That night at the Capitol Visitor Center he had a

thirty-year-old sniper rifle and a shitty scope. There was a seasoned CIA paramilitary force on the other side loaded for bear with a six-to-one advantage over us. We walked out, they didn't. I've never seen anything like it, Knox, and I was a SEAL who pulled time in just about every flame point there is in the world. Oliver Stone is the most stand-up guy you'll ever meet. He'll never let you down. He's a man of his word and he'll lay down his life for his friends without hesitation. But with a gun or knife in his hand the guy's no longer human. He knows ways to kill people I've never even heard of. So if you do run into him the chances are pretty high that you won't be the one walking away. Just thought you ought to know."

Finn clicked off and Knox sat there looking out his window, his pen now making nonsensical doodles on the paper.

This intelligence from Finn, while compelling and interesting, should not have made a difference to Knox insofar as his mission was concerned.

But it did.

It had come as no shock to Knox that his agency had less than clean hands. That was just the nature of the business. But though Knox was a veteran of the intelligence world, there was something in his gut—perhaps as deep as his soul—that had recoiled in anger with every fact that Finn had revealed about John Carr and how his country had repeatedly ripped the man's life apart.

There was right and wrong, although those lines got blurred all the time. Justice and injustice too were often all over the place, he knew. There were no easy answers and whatever road you took, be it the high, low or more likely somewhere in between, half the people would hate the result and half would applaud. And the hell of the thing was in a way they'd both be right.

However, as Knox dwelled on all this, it seemed to him that John Carr, no matter what he might have done on that rainy, gray morning a few days ago, deserved to live out his life as a free man, but that was not Knox's decision to make. His investigator mind told him to verify what he'd been told. Then he would just have to see.

CHAPTER

34

VISITING HOURS at the hospital were long over, but Stone found a sympathetic nurse who let him into the ward after he explained his connection.

"That's right," the nurse said. "Doc Warner mentioned that. Who would've thought to use a car engine to start somebody's heart?"

Somebody who's been in a war.

Willie was propped up in the bed and hooked up to an IV drip. Other cables connected to his body ran to a monitor where lines and numbers darted across.

When Stone walked in Willie opened his eyes and said, "Who the hell are you?"

"Ben. I helped your grandfather get you here."

Willie put out a hand. "Gramps told me about that. I guess I owe you my life."

"You look like you're doing better."

"Don't feel all that much better."

"Did they tell you how long you'll be in here?"

"No. I still don't know what the hell happened."

"You overdosed."

"I know I did. I just don't know *how* I did it."

"So what'd they find in your bloodstream?"

"Docs said oxycodone along with some other stuff."

"That would do it."

"But I didn't have any. That shit is expensive unless you got a prescription. You're talking a couple hundred bucks a pill on the street."

Stone pulled up a chair and sat next to the bed. Willie Coombs had longish brown hair and a good-looking face though tiny lines were already massing around his eyes and lips. He looked like Danny Riker, only more worn. "All right, what did you have and what did you take?"

"Hey, you some kind of undercover cop?"

"Well, if I were it'd be a pretty clear case of entrapment."

Willie let out a long sigh. "I'm too tired to give a shit. What I usually do is get me some fentanyl patches, shuck 'em in two, squeeze out the juice, cook it up and inject it in my feet. Gives you a nice pop, like heroin."

"Fentanyl? China white, right?" Stone said.

"You sound like you know your drugs."

"You said that's what you *usually* do?"

"Prescription ran out. So I just got me some run-of-the-mill street crack. Never had no trouble like this."

"Bob told me it was crack."

Willie looked surprised. "Well, if he told you, why the hell ask me?"

"I always like to confirm things with a corroborating source."

"You sure you ain't a cop?"

"Not even close. But crack is a stimulant. Your pupils would have been seven or eight millimeters, not pinpoints."

"I don't know what to tell you."

"How can you take crack and then go to work in the mines?"

"Had a couple days off. Sick leave," Willie added hastily.

"You sure you didn't take any oxycodone that night?"

"I wouldn't have taken any even if I had it."

"Why not?"

"Doc Warner put me on it when I busted up my arm in the mines couple years ago. Got some kind of reaction to it so I don't use the damn stuff."

"Did you take anything else? Anything you can remember? Eating or drinking?"

"Had a couple beers. Picked up some takeout at Rita's."

Stone perked up. "What sort of takeout?"

"Burger and fries and a platter of grilled nachos."

"So you ate, drank and then did the crack?"

"Yep. Started acting jumpy and shit and rambling on, but I was by myself, so that was okay. Before I was going to bed I took some Tylenol. I always take Tylenol anyway, every night. Just turned twenty-three, but I feel like I'm sixty some days."

"Tylenol?"

"Then I remember Gramps showing up. Then things really started getting weird."

"Who knew you took Tylenol every night?"

"Ain't like I kept it a secret. Lot of folks take pills up here."

"Yeah, I'm starting to see that," Stone said dryly. "So anybody really could've known?"

"What the hell are you getting at, mister?"

"If somebody replaced your Tylenol with oxycodone pills, that could explain how it got in your system. How many did you take?"

"A couple, least I think."

"Were there any left in the bottle?"

"A few."

"Do you remember if they looked like Tylenol pills?"

Willie sat up, pulling the IV lines and cables taut. "You saying somebody's trying to kill me? Who the hell would wanta do that?"

"You'd know that better than me, Willie."

"I doubt somebody's coming after me for my double-wide, guns and hunting bows. Other than that, I ain't got much."

"Forget the money factor. Anybody have a grudge against you?"

"'Bout what?"

"Did you tick somebody off? Steal somebody's girl?"

"I had a girl," Willie snapped. "But she's dead."

"Debby Randolph?"

"How did you know that?"

"Small town. I heard she committed suicide."

"Yeah, that's what they say."

"You think different?"

"What the hell reason did she have to commit suicide? Tell me that."

"I saw some of her work at the craft shop. She was talented."

Willie's face assumed a proud look. "She could draw and paint. And make stuff out of clay. She had a studio set up in a storage shed behind her parents' house. That's where her momma found her," he added quietly. "That's why I took some sick leave. I went back to work after the funeral, but, man, my head was all messed up."

"I can understand that, Willie. I really can."

"You wanta see a picture of her?"

Stone nodded and Willie reached into the drawer of his nightstand and pulled out his wallet. He slid a photo out and passed it over to Stone.

Willie and Debby were standing next to each other. The tall Willie towered over the petite Debby. She had dirty blonde hair and an infectious smile with eyes full of warmth.

"You can tell from her face she's just a really nice person."

Willie slowly nodded as he stared down at the dead woman's face.

As Stone gazed at the picture, an obvious point clicked in his head. "She doesn't look like someone who would kill herself."

"I'd asked her to marry me and she said yes. Happy as can be. Then the next thing I know she's dead." His face trembled and the tears started to slide down his thin, pale cheeks. "That's why I got back on the drugs after she died. I had nothing left."

"Did you tell people she and you were getting married?"

"No, I asked her not to till I had time to get a ring. I

wanted to show her momma and daddy that I was serious. I'd saved up 'bout all I needed. Then I'd just come off the shift at the mine when I heard. Couldn't believe it."

"What time was she found?"

"Early in the morning. She'd been dead awhile they say."

"And no one heard the shot."

"They live in a little holler, nobody close."

"But you said it was in a building behind the house."

"Her momma didn't hear nothing 'cause she's about deaf without her hearing aids in. Her daddy Toby's a trucker and he was on the road in Kansas when Debby died. So unless he's got himself elephant ears, he didn't hear a damn thing either."

"Whose gun was used?"

"Toby's ten-gauge."

"Did you tell Sheriff Tyree about your doubts?"

"Till I was blue in the damn face. He just kept saying, 'Where's the evidence, son?' Her prints and her daddy's prints were the only ones on the gun. She was all alone. Nobody had no reason to kill her so they decided she must've done it herself. Real damn smart."

"Can you think of any reason why someone would want to kill Debby?"

"She never hurt nobody. Sweetest thing under the sun. And she's all I had."

"Before she died, was she upset or nervous about anything?"

He shrugged. "No, not that I could tell."

"When's the last time you talked to her?"

"Around eleven that night. She sounded fine."

"Would it surprise you if I told you that Danny Riker was really upset that she was dead?"

Willie wiped his eyes with some tissues, balled them up, and threw them in the wastebasket. "I guess not."

"You guess not?"

"Danny and her even dated before we got together. But Danny dated every girl in the high school so there wasn't nothing there really."

"Danny's here in the hospital too."

"What! What happened?"

"Some guys busted him up, bad. Any ideas there?"

"No. Danny and me weren't that close anymore."

"But you two *were* friends."

"Best friends." He paused. "He came to see me here."

"When was that?"

"Yesterday afternoon. We had a good talk. High school football and all."

"You two were teammates."

Willie grinned and Stone could suddenly see the young man under the coal dust. "Man, we *were* the team. He threw thirty-seven touchdown passes his senior year and twenty-eight of them were to me. We both could've played for Virginia Tech. But I got a damn DUI and they rescinded my scholarship and Danny hurt his knee. Glory days all right." His grin disappeared and the young man was gone as quickly as he'd appeared.

"So Danny didn't say anything that might explain why he got attacked?"

"No, nothing like that. He said he was real sorry about Debby. And he told me to keep off the pills. Said he was thinking about heading out again and he wanted me to come with him. We'd go west and start over."

"Were you interested?"

"Maybe. Ain't nothing keeping me here now."

"I understand things changed between you two when the Rikers came into all that money?"

"I got my head turned around over that. I mean, they had a lot and I ain't got nothing. But I should've just sucked it up. They didn't owe me nothing. And he lost his daddy over that and all. I know how that feels."

"I heard your father was killed in a hunting accident. Did he work in the mines too?"

"No, he was a guard up at Blue Spruce Prison. It was one of his best friends that accidentally shot him."

"Who was that?"

"Rory Peterson."

"Peterson? And then he ended up being murdered."

"Yeah, but that was just recent. My daddy got killed over two years ago."

Stone checked his watch and rose. "I need to get going."

"Is Danny going to be okay?"

"I don't know. They got him pretty bad. But you need to worry about yourself."

"What are you talking about?"

"If somebody tried to kill you by switching those pills, they're likely to try again."

CHAPTER

35

KNOX MADE a late-night trip to Langley to talk to some folks he'd known for a long time. He trusted these people as much as he trusted anyone these days. And, more important, they had no love lost for Macklin Hayes. He asked the questions he needed to ask and got the answers. Some surprised him, some didn't. It was only a start, but it was more than he'd had a few hours before.

The CIA had lost a human asset about the time that John Carr was disappearing. Nicknamed "Einstein" by his colleagues, Max Himmerling had been nearing retirement when he'd died in an overseas chopper accident, his body burned so badly it had been identified through dental records. The reason this interested Knox was because that sounded like a typical Carter Gray maneuver in disposing of an agent who had committed an unforgivable act. Himmerling was nearing seventy, with the physical ability of a cow and who'd been assigned stateside at Langley for the last thirty years. So his turning up in a flamed-out chopper somewhere in the Middle East did not make sense. Yet no one at CIA or the U.S. government dared question the circumstances of the man's death. What Himmerling had done must have been particularly egregious because he'd been a valuable asset for the CIA and Carter Gray. And though no one would say it out loud, from what Knox was able to find out, that *something* might have to do with John Carr. And he'd found something else out. The records of the Triple Six Division hadn't been destroyed, like he'd thought. The CIA, apparently loath to part with any documented part of its past, no matter how politically incorrect it might seem in hindsight, had moved those records somewhere.

And that led Knox to the next phase of his "parallel" investigation.

It took him to several different locations and he was aware that Hayes' men were following him every step of the way. Yet he had pretty decent cover, he *was* conducting an investigation on the man's behalf. After many twists and turns along the investigative trail, he reached his final destination. The fairly new and ultra-secret CIA underground records complex was in the middle of three hundred bucolic acres twenty miles west of Thomas Jefferson's Monticello near Charlottesville, Virginia. The CIA had purchased the property over two decades ago for an exceptionally good price that set the American taxpayer back a mere eleven million dollars. That had been, by far, the cheapest part of the project.

The property had barns, stables, paddocks and even a stately brick colonial manor house that was *ostensibly* owned by a multinational corporation headquartered in Belgium that *ostensibly* used it for corporate retreats. Indeed, several times a year, long convoys of limos and SUVs with camera-toting, Flemish-speaking executives could be seen heading to the estate along the winding gravel path. The CIA spent about one million bucks a year to perpetuate this myth and considered every dollar well spent.

High-speed elevators inside the manor house and two of the barns allowed access to an elaborate underground labyrinth of concrete tunnels, bunkers and rooms that were protected against any type of eavesdropping. It sounded very James Bond–like, and yet the reality was there were several facilities like this across the country. On two occasions curious souls had managed to open the doors of these structures—one in the Pacific Northwest and one in Nevada—and seen what was actually going on inside. Knox had never known what had happened to those unfortunate folks. Abducted by aliens was probably the myth spread by Agency disinformation teams. It was just the cost of doing business and keeping Americans safe. Well, except for folks who unfortunately opened doors they shouldn't have.

When complete the underground labyrinth had only set the American people back over one billion dollars, not a cent of it acknowledged in any budget of the U.S. government. The construction workers were relocated, without really ever knowing exactly where they'd been. Yet keeping secrets was an expensive proposition and the CIA had more secrets than most. And governments had hundreds of billions of dollars to spend on projects like this. For that level of coin one did not rent space at Storage

Town USA; one built cement cities underneath crappy barns.

As Knox rode the elevator down he carefully went over for the hundredth time his next step. He had pretty much every security clearance one could have, but he did not have the necessary authorizations to get to where he believed he needed to go right now. One person who could give him that authority was Macklin Hayes. To get the man to cooperate entailed Knox both tricking the spy chief and outthinking him. The sweat under his armpits continued to spread even as the elevator hurtled him downward to where the temperature was a constant sixty-one degrees.

A few seconds later, Knox was walking steadily toward his destination. Along the way he endured increasing scrutiny as stern-faced men checked him out from every angle before reluctantly passing him along. Apparently, spies didn't even like fellow spies coming to visit them and going through their stuff. Knox had one advantage. He had a friend who worked here, Marshall Saunders. Knox sat in this man's office a half hour after going through the identification gauntlet.

"Been awhile, Joe," Saunders said, rising from his desk and shaking his visitor's hand. Everyone down here wore sweaters, and indeed Knox felt himself shivering despite his jacket.

"You've gussied up the place from the last time I was here, Marsh," Knox said.

"Budget cuts have yet to come our way. Just lucky. I guess."

It was far more than a matter of mere luck, both men knew. You couldn't cut what you never saw.

"I won't waste your time. I'm doing some under-the-radar work for Macklin Hayes."

"So I've been informed. How is the general by the way?"

"The same." Knox left his friend to interpret that remark however he wanted. Marshall, whom everyone called Marsh, had served three years directly under Hayes' command. That meant if he ended up going to hell when he died, he would have a pretty good idea of how it would be.

Knox told him what he wanted to look at and his friend's features turned uncomfortable. "That'll take a phone call to the man."

"I'm aware of that," said Knox. "I actually just thought of it on the way over, or else I would've gotten the okay already. I don't think it'll be a problem." He added with as big a smile as he could manage, "On the other hand, if I end up disappearing you'll know I was wrong about that."

Marsh didn't even grin at this crude joke and Knox felt his ass suddenly clinch.

The call was made and the man passed the phone over to Knox.

As though a distant rumble of thunder heralding the approaching storm, he heard Hayes bark, "What's going on, Knox?"

"Just thought of this new angle, sir, but I need to check out a couple more pieces."

"Explain this new angle. But tell Marsh to leave first."

Knox glanced at his friend who got the sign immediately, rose and left. If he felt any anger for being kicked out of his own office, the savvy agent was too smart to show it.

Knox hunkered down, gripping the phone tightly. "I turned a lead that got me thinking about something in Carr's past."

"Where *exactly* in his past?"

Knox didn't hesitate. "Triple Six days."

"Knox—"

"I know what you said before, but here's my theory. If Carr was with Triple Six and colleagues from his past were being killed—"

"That's out of bounds."

Knox said, "I know Finn and his back story are off-limits, but if I'm going to track Carr down, I need to understand where this guy came from."

"I don't think that's relevant—"

Knox had anticipated this question and broke in. "With all due respect, if you're deciding what's relevant or not on this case, get somebody else to tackle it for you."

"I'm not trying—"

"If you want results, General, then I need some control over *my* investigation. You called me in to do a job. Then let me do it!"

Knox waited for the man's response, trying to breathe normally. He was betting the farm that Hayes would react one way, but the truth was, Knox could just as easily go down hard for this insubordination. *Real hard.* As in his butt being catapulted to Afghanistan, where he could spend a little quality time in the mountains with Osama's boys on the Pakistani border.

"I'm listening."

Knox went on autopilot. "Carr knows we're going to

be on him. He's been on the run for a long time now. He's loyal to his friends like you said. He'd want to keep as far away from them as possible. But he still needs cover. He still needs help." Knox paused here to allow the bait to sink in. He wanted Hayes to say it. The man had to say it.

"You think he might turn to some old Triple Sixer for help?"

Thank you, God. "Well, General, look at it from his point of view. He pops Gray and Simpson and makes his initial escape. He can't go near his civilian friends. He knows the machine is on his ass, so he has to look somewhere for cover. These Triple Six guys would be retired by now and deep underground. If I can get a lead on any that Carr was close to and either shadow them or beat it out of them, we might turn this guy. It's a shortcut, but it might just work. I know you don't care how we get there, so long as we get there. You know as well as I do the longer Carr is out there, the greater the odds that he does something that will hurt *us*."

When Knox said *us* he of course meant *you*.

He waited again. He could almost hear the former military man's synapses firing off, weighing from virtually every conceivable angle what Knox had just proposed.

Virtually every conceivable angle. Just hopefully not the real one.

"It might be worth checking," Hayes said finally.

"And just so we're clear, this will only be a tangential line of inquiry." Knox wanted to feed the man a comfort bone, however disingenuous. "I'll be following up other leads at the same time. We can only hope that one of them will pop for us."

"Put Marsh on the phone so I can give him the necessary authorizations."

"Thank you, General." *You bastard.*

Hayes did his thing with Marshall and twenty minutes later Knox was being led into one of the most secure areas of one of the most clandestine facilities the United States of America had.

CHAPTER

36

STONE HAD REJOINED Abby when Tyree burst into the emergency room.

"How's Danny?" he said when he spotted them.

"Doctor just came out and said the x-rays look okay," Abby said shakily. "And they don't think there's internal bleeding."

Tyree knelt down and held her hand. "Well, thank God for that. Have you talked to him any more?"

"No."

Tyree looked over at Stone. "You seem to always be in the right place at the right time. First Willie and now Danny."

"Any leads on the guys who attacked him?"

"I'm hoping to cut to the chase and get Danny to tell me. Any chance of me talking to him?"

Stone pointed at a man in a white coat. "There's the doctor over there."

Tyree hurried over to the man while Stone turned to Abby. "Do you want me to drive you home?"

"No. I'm going to stay here. I'd just worry myself sick if I left."

"Then I'll stay with you."

"You've done enough. You saved Danny's life. Again. I really don't know how to thank you."

"Abby, I talked to Willie a few minutes ago. He said Danny came to visit him yesterday. He talked about him and Willie heading out of town together. Going west."

"Did Willie know why anybody would want to hurt Danny?"

"No, but I asked him about Debby Randolph. He said she and Danny dated some in high school, but it wasn't serious."

"I'm not sure Danny can get serious with a girl. It's all fun and games for him."

"But Willie doesn't think that Debby committed suicide. You see, he'd asked her to marry him. And she'd said yes. He talked to her around eleven the night before she was found dead. She was in good spirits."

"I didn't know he'd proposed."

"I guess they were keeping it secret. So we have Willie in the hospital with an overdose of a drug he didn't take. Debby killing herself for no reason, and now Danny nearly died. There has to be a connection."

"I can't see one."

"Willie also said that his father was accidentally shot by Rory Peterson."

"But that was over two years ago."

"It could still be important."

"Can we go outside for a few minutes? I need some air."

They walked out in time to hear the *thump-thump* of the aircraft going over. Stone looked up.

"Chopper?"

She nodded, staring up too. "Going to Dead Rock. Prisoner transport."

"Why not just drive them?"

"Most of the prisoners spending the rest of their lives up there come from pretty far away, lot of urban areas. Roads are pretty crappy around here and lots of places for ambush. Hard to bust your buddy out of jail thousands of feet up there."

"I can see that."

She turned to face him. "So what were you doing when you ran into Danny?"

Stone stared over at Willie's pickup truck where his bag was in the back. "I was heading out of town," he said a bit guiltily.

"Okay. Does this have something to do with Trimble wanting to write a story about you?"

Stone tried hard to look surprised. "What are you talking about?"

"Danny told me that you came along with him because a government car pulled into the town where you two got off the train."

"I think he made a mistake."

"If you're in some kind of trouble—"

"I'm in no trouble, Abby."

"I was going to say if you are in trouble, I want to help you."

"Why? You barely know me."

"You saved my son. And I can't explain exactly why, but I feel like I've known you all my life."

Stone looked down, stubbed the sidewalk with the toe of his shoe. "I appreciate the offer, Abby, I really do."

"But you're leaving anyway?"

He shot her a glance. "I didn't say that."

"But you didn't *not* say it either. Everybody's got problems. You have no obligation to stay here and help us. Hell, it's not your battle."

"Why don't you just leave here? You've got plenty of money."

"Run out of my hometown? No thank you. I'm not built that way."

"But Danny left."

"He didn't want to go. I made him."

Stone looked stunned. "What, why?"

"This is no place for him. What's he got here? Work in the mines or the prison?"

"Is that all? Or how about the strange things happening here you mentioned?"

"It's not your fight, Ben. If you need to move on, you move on." She hesitated. Stone thought she was going to say something else. "I better go back and check on Danny. And I'll look in on Willie too."

She left him there. Stone sat down on a low brick wall. An hour later he was still there, trying desperately to make sense of what he should do.

As he watched, the miner brigade began pulling in for their methadone pop. He checked his watch. Not even five in the morning yet. He continued to watch as the bone-thin men climbed out of their rides and straggled into the clinic before leaving to pull twelve hours in the pits of hell, contorting their bodies way past all sane levels. That only led to more pain, and more painkillers, and the cycle just kept on spinning.

All so the lights remain on in this country.

He looked on a few minutes later as the zombie-eyed men headed out in their dusty Chevys and Fords.

I'm going to start using candles and cook my food over a fire.

He was still sitting there when Tyree came out and reported that Danny had refused to say anything about who had attacked him.

"Sheriff, I think I've seen one of the men before. But I just can't remember where."

"Soon as you do remember, call me."

An hour after Tyree left, Abby finally came out, bleary-eyed and hunched over.

"Danny's going to be fine. They're moving him to a room pretty soon. I think the one next to Willie's."

"That's great, Abby."

"He said you beat those men up pretty good."

"I got lucky."

"Lucky once, maybe. Lucky twice, I don't think so."

"I guess the army did teach me a thing or two. Do you want me to drive you home?"

"No, but you can follow me there. I'll make us both some breakfast."

"Abby, you've been up all night. You don't have to do that."

"Just follow me home, Ben, unless you want to head on out of town right now."

They eyed one another.

Stone finally said, "I'll be staying, at least for now."

CHAPTER

37

AFTER HE FINISHED UP in Charlottesville Knox made a quick trip to downtown D.C., his mind spinning from all that he'd learned. John Carr *had* been a member of Triple Six. Three members of his team had been killed about six months ago. The case had not only remained unsolved but apparently abandoned too. Knox wondered if Harry Finn's immunity was connected to that outcome somehow. However, he didn't wonder about that for long. It was not his problem. He had enough of his own.

There was nothing in the official record about Carr wanting out of Triple Six. Knox didn't expect that there would be. Personal feelings, and certainly hostile personal feelings, would never be officially acknowledged. Carr had had a family, though. That sort of information had been duly noted in the records, if only for security and threat assessment purposes. Carr had been techni-

cally listed as MIA on a certain date over thirty years ago.
Cross-referencing these records with other info he'd collected previously, Knox was able to piece together that
only a few days later Sergeant John Carr somehow mi-
raculously reenlisted in the army. He then quickly died
under mysterious circumstances and had been laid to rest
at Arlington Cemetery. It was amazing, really, how history could be effectively rewritten on both large and
personal scales.

Stone and Carr were one and the same. Long suspected, it was nice to have confirmation. Stone had fled
Triple Six. A short time later an empty coffin had been
put into the ground at Arlington with Carr's name on the
white marker.

Later that morning Knox poured himself a cup of
coffee and drank it at his kitchen counter as his gaze ran
over the personal items in the room that had been his
wife's. He hadn't changed it much after her death. The
home had been both of theirs, but it had really been Patty's. Knox had spent more time in other countries than
he had his own. It just came with the job. This was her
space. In a sense, after her passing, Knox felt he was
merely renting it.

The place he'd gone to in downtown D.C. was a news
archive center maintained by the federal government. The
feds burned a lot of money, without doubt, but some of
what they purchased was actually useful. In his last days
at Triple Six Carr had been assigned to a post in the
Brunswick, Georgia, area with his official cover being
that of an instructor at the then relatively new FLETC, or
the Federal Law Enforcement Training Center. From the
daily logs that Knox had found, Carr was gone a lot from

his post. On several occasions Knox had discovered that when Carr had been missing from FLETC, somewhere else in the world, a person of interest to the United States had died or disappeared.

Knox had canvassed the archives looking for one item in particular. After an hours-long search, but aided by his knowing the week span he was looking for, he found it. An obscure item in the local Brunswick paper detailed the disappearance of a local couple and their two-year-old daughter. A grainy photo of a woman was identified as Claire Michaels. Her husband, John, and their daughter, Elizabeth, had also vanished. John Michaels had been employed as an instructor at FLETC, the article said. There were rumors that some local federal cop-haters might have been involved and had targeted the Michaelses because of John's occupation. Knox searched for additional stories or any possible break in the case, but found none. The CIA had effectively buried it all, deflecting suspicion onto a logical if bogus source.

Knox stared at the old black-and-white image of Claire Michaels that he had taken a copy of from the archives. He wondered if the fragments of another picture of the woman currently resided inside the ballistics entry in the chest of a senator from Alabama. If he were a betting man, he would've laid down a stack of hundred-dollar chips that the photo taped to Senator Simpson's newspaper the morning he died was of Claire, John Carr's wife.

Okay, Finn had been telling the truth. They'd killed the man's family because he wanted out. Knox didn't want to believe that his government would treat a man who'd served them faithfully for many years in such a way, but the reality was it certainly could've gone down like that.

Knox walked to his book-lined study. He was chasing a man who'd been betrayed by his own government. True, the evidence was compelling that Carr had killed Gray and Simpson. Knox stared over at a photo of his wife on one wall. Yet what would he have done if he'd found out the two men had killed Patty? He sat down in a chair and stared at the floor. He couldn't say he wouldn't have done the very same thing.

And if that wasn't enough, Carr had been screwed in Vietnam by the very man Knox was working for. The war hero had never gotten his just due. The military man in Knox took great umbrage at that. It was hard enough to fight. It was hard enough to survive without some prick denying you something you'd earned fair and square. And Knox still didn't know why Hayes had cheated Carr out of his medal. Yet if he had to guess, he would have concluded that the fault rested with Hayes and not the heroic enlisted man.

The real question became: what did Knox do now? He had to keep looking for the man. But maybe what he did when he got there might change. And that meant he was now basically a traitor to his own agency. Helping the enemy. It could tank his career, ruin his retirement, perhaps cost him his freedom or maybe even his life.

For a man he'd never even met, but one whom he felt he probably knew better than many he'd called a friend.

Was John Carr worth it?

He didn't have the answer to that. At least not yet.

CHAPTER

38

ABBY AND STONE had just finished breakfast. Stone
had been famished while Abby barely touched her food.

He looked at her nearly full plate and said, "Remember
that Danny is going to be okay."

"For now, yeah. He never should have come back
here."

"And you're saying you only wanted him to go because
there were no decent jobs here? You've got plenty of
money."

"It's not the money! He hated how I got it anyway."

"They killed your husband, Abby. What other way was
there for you to get justice? You can't exactly imprison a
company."

"For what they did to my husband somebody should've
gone to jail."

She rose, poured another cup of coffee and sat down next to him.

"You know much about digging coal out of the mountains?"

"Only that I probably wouldn't want to do it for a living."

"My husband worked at a dog hole mine. I guess you don't know what that is?"

"No."

"Small-scale shops, usually only a single shift crew and a foreman. Doesn't pay as well as the big shops and you get no health insurance. But if you've failed enough drug tests the dog holes tend to be more forgiving than the big outfits. Nice fallback."

"So your husband had a drug problem too?"

"The men are beat to hell from digging in the earth on their hands and knees. Sam had three back surgeries before he was forty. Got a hand caught in a grinder machine that they use to chew up coal seams. Even after a bunch of surgeries his hand was still a mess. Out of his mind with pain and the meds the clinic gave him didn't do anything after a while. He was snorting six hundred dollars' worth of crushed-up oxycodone up his nose every day."

"Can't they get help for their addiction? Other than the methadone juice?"

"I kept begging until Sam tried. Tore my heart to see him all wormed over after a few days in withdrawal. But he could never hold it."

"I'm sorry, Abby."

"The mining companies don't care so long as you pass your pee test and show up for work. They make their money and America stays warm."

"Abby, how did your husband die?"

She put down her cup and gazed past Stone, perhaps all the way to the past when her husband's life had abruptly ended. "Lot of things to worry about when you're sitting a thousand feet under rock, but there are two big things to keep in mind besides the earth falling on top of you. One is carbon dioxide and the other is methane gas. The first one will suffocate you and the second one will blow you up. The methane got Sam because the meter the company gave him to use to check out a new seam line was faulty. And they knew it. Explosion caused a cave-in. That was it."

Stone didn't know what to say, so he just stared down at his hands.

"Yeah, we're going through a real boom right now, coal and natural gas just pouring out of the mountains. Funny thing, though."

"What's that?"

"Most folks around here use propane or wood to warm themselves and cook with, *not* coal or natural gas. Maybe nobody else knows the real cost of digging that stuff out of the rock, but we sure as hell do, you hear what I'm saying?"

"Yes."

"A young man right out of high school with clean urine can start in the coal mines at twenty dollars an hour. Never get that kind of money anywhere else. But by the time they're thirty-five they'll be broke-backed and worn out, looking closer to seventy with lungs full of shit."

She finally looked over at him and her eyes seemed to refocus. One large tear was perched at the corner of her right eye.

"So you staying or going?"

"I'm not going to leave you like this, Abby." If Stone was startled by his words he didn't show it.

She reached over and squeezed his arm. He involuntarily grunted in pain.

"What's the matter?" she said in an alarmed tone.

"Nothing, just . . . it's nothing."

"Ben, what is it?"

"One of the guys with the bat got me a little bit on the arm."

"Oh good Lord, why didn't you say anything?"

"Abby, it's nothing."

"Take off your shirt."

"What?"

"Take it off."

He slowly peeled it off and she exclaimed, "Oh my God."

There was a lumpy black bruise the size of a walnut on his left upper arm and the discoloration had spread down to his forearm.

She ran to the freezer and grabbed an ice pack and placed it over the bruise. "You're a hero, okay, you don't have to be stupid," she scolded. "And if—"

She was staring at his chest and other arm. Stone followed her gaze to the old knife slashes and bullet pocks.

She looked up inquiringly.

"Coal miners aren't the only ones with scars," he said quietly.

A half hour later, she came back into the room. He noticed that she'd changed her clothes and the scent in the air spoke of a shower and shampoo. She gave him an unfathomable look as she checked his arm. "Does it feel better?"

"Yeah, it's fine."

"Good." She leaned down and kissed him. In the same motion her arms slid around his middle and he felt her nails dig lightly into his back. Before he realized it, Stone felt himself kiss her in return. Abby's lips tasted sweet.

Stone felt his hand slide to her back and squeeze but then he pulled back.

"Abby, I don't think—"

She put a hand against his mouth. "That's right. You don't have to think at all. Come on."

Abby took his hand and led him up the stairs to her bedroom. She closed the door and motioned for him to sit on the bed. She stood in front of him and undressed.

She was fit and fleshy in all the right places and Stone felt a small gasp jump from his throat as he took all of her in. He noted that she had a small tattoo of a cross near her left hip bone. She pressed against him, her warm breasts pushed flat against his own hard chest; her hands began massaging his shoulders and back even as she made soft moaning sounds in his ear. She nimbly worked his pants off. A minute later he lay down beside her on the bed.

Later, they lay back, side to side, her hand clasping his arm, lightly rubbing the hairs.

"I haven't been with anyone since Sam died." She rolled over on her stomach, her arms supporting her chin. "Not once."

"There must've been opportunities, Abby. You're . . . beautiful."

She kissed him on the cheek and smiled. "Opportunities, yes, desire on my part, no."

"Not even Tyree?"

"It's not like that with us. We've known each other since we were little kids. Went on exactly one date in high school and we didn't really click. I think he might want more now. He never married, but I don't feel the same way."

"It's been a long time for me too. A long time." He wondered if Claire would have disapproved of what he had just done. After decades of loneliness for him, perhaps she would have understood.

"Opportunities or desire lacking?"

"Both."

He rolled over on his side and rubbed her back. She stretched and smiled and Stone smiled back as he watched her do this. The braids in her hair had come out and several tresses dangled in her eyes. He carefully moved one away, revealing a green pupil looking at him.

"You ever think about leaving Divine?" he said.

"All the time."

"Why'd you never do it?"

"Scared, I guess. Divine's a little pond but I know it well. Hard to prove yourself all over in a new place."

"I suppose."

He rolled onto his back.

She curled next to him and slid her leg up and down his. "You ever think about settling down somewhere?"

"Lots of times. In fact I thought I had the place to do it, but it turned out it wasn't."

"What happened?"

"It just wasn't."

The phone rang. Abby looked at the clock. "Who could that be at this hour?"

"The hospital?"

"I just talked to them before we had breakfast. And to Danny. He was okay."

"Maybe it's the restaurant. People want their breakfast at Rita's." Stone was glad of the change in the conversation's direction.

"I already called there too. I got my helpers opening the place."

She climbed over Stone and snatched up the phone. Stone put a hand on her butt and gave her a gentle squeeze. She smiled, grabbed his hand and gave her backside a hard slap with it. Then she let go.

"What? Um." She glanced at Stone. "No, he's not here. Right. If I see him I could ask him, sure. Okay, right."

She put the phone back in the cradle, pulled a pillow into her lap and sat cross-legged facing him.

"Who was that?"

"Charlie Trimble. He heard about Danny and what you did. He wants to ask you some questions. And he seemed very determined."

"Great, well, my position hasn't changed. I'm not answering any questions."

"Ben, listen to me. If you don't want to do it, fine. But if you keep saying no to Charlie he's going to start digging. And unless you've got nothing you care about him finding, it might be smart to just talk to him. That way he can focus on what happened here instead of on you."

Stone opened his mouth and then closed it. "How come you're beautiful *and* smart? That's hardly fair."

"Just the luck of the draw, I guess."

"You have his number?"

"Yes, or you can just go to the newspaper. It's around the block from the restaurant. Can't miss it."

"Call him and tell him I'll be there sometime this afternoon."

He rose to get dressed.

"This afternoon? We can do a lot in that amount of time," she said playfully.

"As great as that sounds, I've got something I really need to do."

"What's that?" she said, sounding a little hurt.

"I'll let you know if I find it."

He finished dressing and drove Willie's truck back to the trailer. A few minutes later, after a thorough search, he found the bottle of Tylenol. It was empty. Had Willie taken the last few pills but forgotten? *Were* they oxycodone tablets? But why leave an empty medicine bottle in the drawer? As he looked around at the mess Willie Coombs called home, he concluded an empty bottle left in a drawer in this pigsty was hardly compelling evidence of anything. But still, it might be important. Maybe this was what Shirley Coombs had been looking for.

He pocketed the bottle, left the trailer and started to climb in the truck.

The next instant Stone lay unconscious on the ground, blood seeping from the wound in his head.

CHAPTER

39

STONE ROSE SLOWLY to a sitting position, his limbs shaky, his head throbbing and his belly queasy. He touched the knot on his head. The blood was dried solid over the wound. He'd been out for a while, apparently. He sat on his haunches for a bit, breathing slowly, trying to keep from puking.

He finally staggered to his feet and looked around. Or tried to. He could move his hand a foot in front of him and be unable to see it. He put a hand up and it nicked the hard, low ceiling.

He was in a cave. He breathed in and nearly gagged. No, he was in a mine. A coal mine. He took a few tentative steps forward and then stopped.

Rattle-rattle.

Stone took a slow step back from the sound. It seemed like more than one snake actually. Standing in the pitch black with rattlesnakes within striking distance probably constituted a pretty decent nightmare. Most people would have been frozen to the spot, waiting to be bitten and die. Stone was not stupid, so he was scared. But he wasn't paralyzed. He moved both arms out from his sides. One hand brushed wall, his left nothing but air. He leaned toward the left and his fingers now grazed the rough side of the mine. That the mineshaft was not very wide was not much help since he couldn't exactly walk on walls. He reached up again and his hand hit the low ceiling. Rattlers could not see very well in the dark, he knew. But they could register his body heat and also sense any movement he made from the vibrations on the ground.

He was in grave danger of being fanged repeatedly with no way to get out. How long before they found his body? Or his bones? And then it dawned on him. That's why they hadn't just killed him and left his carcass to be found. Here he would die and never be discovered. People would just assume he had left town. No explanation or cover-up required. And yet there was more to it, he sensed. Whoever had done this could have just left him in the mineshaft with no way out; they didn't have to use snakes too. Or they could have just shot him and left him here. There was a desire here to cause not only death, but terror as well. They wanted him to die horribly, and alone, and in the dark. Then the panic did hit him. But not for the obvious reason.

Abby.

He'd been with her. They might know that. They might think he had told her things. What things he wasn't sure. But they might go after her just in case.

Stone felt around the ceiling until his fingers touched

what he deduced was a support beam. The beams helped hold up the ceiling, preventing tons of rock from raining down and crushing him, for which Stone was understandably grateful. Yet more important, there was a light cage attached to the beam by a sturdy metal plate. The light obviously wasn't working. Yet he didn't need light, just the cage.

He moved backward, away from the rattles, holding his arm up to the ceiling. Roughly four feet later his hand grazed another beam and another caged light. Four feet later, another.

Figuring that the snakes would've been placed between him and the exit to the mine, Stone slowly moved back toward the sounds. A rattler was deaf so it couldn't even hear its own rattles, but it was an instinctive signal to prey or predator that the snake was there, coiled and ready to strike. With each hesitant step he took Stone braced for the venom shooting into his legs. When he reached the first ceiling beam he'd touched, he reached up and gripped the metal light cage. Praying that it would be strong enough to hold his weight he lifted himself into the air, his legs bent and raised to chest-high. His injured arm ached badly, but he simply focused on what he was doing and willed the pain away. The Triple Six Division had been great at beating that technique into him at the Murder Mountain training facility, because they'd been expert at inflicting all types of agony, both physical and mental.

He swung back and forth and then lunged forward in the air, his hand outstretched like he was working the monkey bars, as he had in basic training. His hand closed around the next metal cage. Keeping his knees high, he let go of the first cage and kept moving. He had no idea if a rattler would strike upward and nail him in the ass, but he also didn't want to find out.

Four beams later, and after he missed one cage and almost fell, he stopped and listened, dangling there, his knees still bent to his chest. The rattles had stopped. But he didn't want to drop to the ground just yet. He kept swinging until his lead hand went out and touched nothing but rock wall.

Shit!

Had he actually gone the wrong way? Or had the snakes perhaps moved past him while he'd lain unconscious? Or had whoever put him here out thought Stone and placed the snakes on the side opposite the exit? Or was this actually a nightmare and he would wake up any moment now?

His arms growing heavy, Stone cautiously lowered his legs and stood on firm ground. He put out his arms again, trying to gauge the width of the shaft here. He touched what he believed was the dead-end wall, but nothing was on the other side. He kept moving to that side, but nothing was there. Puzzled for a moment, the truth finally struck him.

Idiot.

This was a turn or bend in the mineshaft. He got his bearings, walked his fingers along the wall and moved forward, listening carefully for more rattles. Ten minutes later he ran smack into wood.

The mine entrance must've been boarded up, because he could see a thin line of light at the bottom edge of the wood. He considered his options. That was relatively easy, because he had none. He took a few steps back and ran full tilt at the wall. All that did was land him on his butt with a bruised shoulder. He started to rise and then froze. His fingers had grazed against something metallic half-buried in the dirt. It was long and slender. As his hand closed around it, Stone could tell it was a pole with a flat end, like the shaft of a screwdriver.

He worked the bottom edge of the pole into one side of the wooden wall and started to lever. He felt the nails in the frame start to give a bit. He probed at another spot and pushed his weight against the pole, his feet slipping and sliding with the effort. Twenty minutes and much sweat later, the top right edge of the wooden wall gave way and a big shaft of light lit the mine. Encouraged by this break-through, Stone really put his shoulder to the effort and only another twenty minutes passed before he was able to force the board enough away from the frame to squeeze out and fall on his back in the dirt.

Free.

He let out a deep, relieved breath. Then, blinking rapidly, he looked around to see if he recognized where he might be. He didn't. There was a dirt road here that was actually colored black. It took him a moment to realize why. Years of coal trucks carrying the stuff away. Their tires had ground the black dust and bits of rock into the red clay and the black had won out. He looked down at his clothes. The black had won out on him too. He brushed himself off and walked down the road, keeping alert in case whoever had sucker-punched him was still watching to see if he escaped the snake party.

A mile later he cleared the trees and turned onto a gravel street. As soon as the stuff crunched under his feet something occurred to him and he put his hand in his jacket pocket. The empty bottle of Tylenol was gone.

Great. His skull felt like it was cracked, and now he'd lost the only real clue he'd found in pounding the increasingly dangerous streets of Divine.

He hitched a ride on a truck to Rita's and went in through the back but found out that Abby wasn't there. Then he called her house from the restaurant but there was no answer. He ran to Willie's trailer, grabbed his truck, drove pell-mell to Midsummer's Farm and caught her as she was walking out to her car.

When she saw him she said, "What the hell happened to you?"

When he told her, she simply stared at him. "Oh my God, Ben," she finally managed to stammer. "What is going on?"

"Have you talked to Danny?"

"Just a bit ago. I was just now going to see him."

"I tried calling you from Rita's."

"I thought I heard the phone ringing, but I was drying my hair. What are you going to do?"

Stone thought about that. What *was* he going to do? "I'm going to see Trimble. And then I'm going to hook up with Tyree to see what he found out." He took her by the arm. "Abby, I want you to be careful. I know you have the shotgun. How about a pistol?"

"Sam had a couple. They're upstairs in the closet."

"You know how to fire one?"

"You're asking a girl from the mountains if she knows how to fire a gun?"

"Okay, I'll take that as a yes. You said you had a couple of guns. Mind if I borrow one?"

"I can't think of anybody right now who needs it more."

They went in the house and Stone got the pistols. He loaded them both and handed one to Abby.

"I'd like to keep in close contact with you, but I don't have a cell phone."

"You can use Danny's. I brought it home from the hospital." She looked at his filthy clothes. "You can't go see Charlie like that. You can shower here and change your clothes."

Stone looked toward the truck. He hadn't thought to check. He looked in the cargo bed. His duffel was gone.

"I, uh, I don't have any clothes to change into."

"Come on. You're about the same size as Danny."

She led him to Danny's room and picked out some clothes for him. When he came out of the shower they were all neatly packed in a bag except for a pair of pants, shirt, socks and skivvies.

Dressed with phone and gun in hand, Stone gave Abby a hug. "Thanks, I'll meet you at the hospital later," he said.

He watched her drive off. Then he sped off in the opposite direction to keep his appointment with Trimble. Then he would go see Tyree. He had to play this just right. Or the only future he'd have would be either six feet under or else making calendar scratches on the walls of a federal prison.

CHAPTER

40

A TRUCK DROVE UP and a man got out and sprinted to Knox's front door. He answered and the man handed him a package and left.

Knox sat in his office, put the DVD into his computer, and the images spread over the screen. The artist and Leroy had finally hooked up. The digital sketches of presumably a bushy-bearded John Carr looked back at him. The artist had also, on Knox's instructions, done images where the beard and glasses were removed. Knox compared these to old photos of John Carr from his military days along with more recent pictures that he had obtained from CIA files. They looked like the same guy to him. He printed out multiple color copies and hustled out the door.

The wheels squealing on his Rover, Knox sped out of his driveway.

From down the street, Caleb started the van and followed.

"Looks like our hound might have a lead," Annabelle said as she lowered her binoculars.

Knox went to National Airport first and Annabelle followed him in. An hour or so later he got back in his truck and drove off.

Annabelle jumped back in the Chrysler.

"Looks like he got zilch at the airport, though. Let's see where he goes next."

Knox's next stop was Union Station. Normally he would've flooded the area with the images of the altered John Carr, putting them on the metro database, with all the airlines and law enforcement agencies, but he couldn't do that here. If the FBI recognized the bushy-bearded man as one they'd allowed to slip through their fingers, they would wonder about CIA's interest in him. And despite Hayes' assurances that he could keep the FBI at bay, you never knew.

Inside the station Knox hit what might have been the jackpot. A ticket clerk believed she recognized the composite drawing of Stone with the bushy beard and glasses. He'd paid in cash for a coach fare but the clerk couldn't remember what name was on his ID.

"Do you remember which train he took?"

"Yep. Don't have many people who pay in cash. He booked the Crescent. To New Orleans."

"How can I get in touch with somebody who was on that train? A conductor, maybe?"

The woman picked up a phone. Minutes later Knox relayed his request to a supervisor in his office. The man made some calls and told Knox he was in luck. One of the conductors who'd been on that train had just gotten back to town. He came in an hour later to the station after the supervisor phoned him. He was shown the picture but didn't recognize the man. Knox handed him another composite with the beard and glasses removed.

"Yeah, this could be the guy who got in the fight."

"Fight?"

"Laid out three guys a lot younger than him on the train."

"Is that right?"

The conductor went on to explain what had happened, ending with Stone and the other men getting off at the next station. He told Knox the name of the town.

"He wouldn't give me any ID. Offered to get off the train instead. Little suspicious, I thought."

"Did you get the names of the other guys?"

"Nope. They said they'd get off the train too and they did. No skin off my nose. Saved me from filing a police report. Damn punks."

"Give me descriptions of all of them."

After Knox finished writing this information down he glanced at the supervisor. "Can you pull the ticket records for that train trip?"

"Yeah, but we can't match them to faces on that train."

"I'll take a list of the names anyway. Something might turn up."

The manager printed out this information and gave it to Knox.

"So is this something big?" the conductor asked eagerly.

"So big you'll probably never hear anything about it

ever again. And I'd strongly suggest that you two gents forget I was ever here."

Knox hustled out of the station with Annabelle following. His truck rumbled off from the parking lot and the van eased after it.

The Rover picked up its pace and threatened to leave Caleb and Annabelle behind. When Caleb started cutting in and out of traffic in an effort to keep up, Annabelle told him there was no need.

"But we'll lose him."

"No we won't." She pulled a small device from her bag. "When I was in his truck in Georgetown, I placed a transmitter under the seat. It has a range of about twenty miles."

"Why didn't you tell me that before?"

"I'm sorry. I've had a lot on my mind."

Caleb grumbled for a bit but then said, "That was a pretty good idea. Putting that in his truck."

"And that way we can hang back a little just in case he's checking."

"He strikes me as a man who checks and often."

"Me too."

"So Oliver took a train?"

"Appears to be."

Knox's Rover turned on to Interstate 66 heading west. After traveling out past Gainesville, the Rover exited off the highway.

"I don't believe the train goes this way," Caleb said.

"Let's just see where he's headed."

Twenty minutes later Annabelle said, "Shit! There goes my perfect record."

They watched as Knox climbed into a chopper and it rose from the ground in a whirl of power.

"Now what?" Caleb asked.

"Back to Union Station, just as fast as you can." She glanced at Caleb with a quizzical look. "Wait a minute." She grabbed her camera. "Take off your ball cap and that sweater."

"Why?"

"I need to take your photo."

She snapped his picture. "We'll stop on the way into town at a photo place. And then I'll need to grab a laminator and some other supplies."

"What are you going to do?" Caleb said as he put the van in drive.

"You're about to change careers."

CHAPTER

41

THE CHOPPER DROPPED Knox off about thirty miles from the town where Stone had detrained. A truck was waiting for him there. The aircraft had come courtesy of Macklin Hayes, who had sounded heartened over the phone that Knox finally had grabbed hold of a solid lead.

His instructions to Knox had been clear. Locate Carr but do not move in.

"Phone me and I'll take it from there."

I'm sure you will, General.

When Knox pulled into the town he decided he'd better hit the first place that looked promising. His prayers were almost immediately answered. The sign of the One T restaurant loomed ahead. He parked, went in, settled himself at the counter and ordered some food. There weren't many people in the place, but still, Knox figured

if Carr had come by to eat after ditching the train someone could remember seeing him. He showed his composite and asked his questions and thirty minutes later
he walked out, not knowing much more than when he'd
gone in.

Neither the people behind the counter nor the customers were the observant type apparently, or else didn't
like to volunteer any information about anybody. All he
got in response to the artist's comp were dull shakes of
the head. Even the flash of Knox's creds had not helped
matters. In fact, it might have hurt. Knox had to keep in
mind that around here the federal government was probably only a bit more popular than Osama bin Laden.

There was a bus station, he found, though it was now
closed and wouldn't reopen for a while. Apparently folks
up here didn't need to travel every day.

Knox sat in his truck and studied his map. The terrain
around here was rugged and the towns few and far between with the roads connecting them two-lane and ser-
pentine. He decided to find a place to sleep and start
anew in the morning. He would have to come back to the
bus station when it reopened. He'd asked around about
the people that worked there, but they operated on some
sort of circuit basis and wouldn't be back in town for a
couple days. Yet Knox was counting on the bus station
to pop for him if nothing else turned up in the meantime. There were probably limited ways out of this
dump, and a bus was at least one of the more promising
ones. Carr might have taken one after losing his ride on
the train.

The motel was yellow-painted concrete and crummy,
the rates so low they were easily covered by his

government per diem. Crackers and a soda constituted room service that he grabbed out of the vending machine outside the tiny office. He showed the artist's comp to the manager but the man shook his head and went back to his TV and can of Bud. Knox spent another hour roaming the streets, showing the picture to passersby and shop owners. Either no one had seen the man or else they wouldn't confess to it.

Knox sat fully clothed on the bed in his room, crunching his miniature cheese and peanut butter sandwiches and sipping his diet Coke. He channel-hopped from wars to natural disasters to corruption scandals to ESPN, NASCAR, and finally settled on the TV Land channel watching, of all things, a decades-old episode of *Happy Days*.

Carr was the hunted and Knox the hunter. Those were the official roles anyway. In reality those identities could be switched at any time, and with Carr's skill level, the odds that they would reverse at some point were pretty good. And after what he had learned, Knox had quite the misgivings about his exposed rear flank, because there lurked the master of the ambush and blame game, Macklin Hayes.

He pulled out his phone and punched in the number.

"Hello?"

"Melanie, it's Dad."

"Hey, I was just thinking of you. Do you want to get together tomorrow night? I've got center orchestra seats. *Wicked* is playing."

"I'm sorry, sweetie, I can't. I'm out of town."

"Where are you? Paris? Amsterdam? Kabul? Tikrit?" Her tone sounded light and upbeat, but Knox knew his daughter well enough to sense the anxiety behind the casual words.

"I'm a little west of you. And a little rural."

"Terrorists hiding out in the hollers, Dad?"

"You never know, honey. Have you heard from your brother lately?"

"I got an e-mail from him this morning. He sounds good. He sent some pictures. There was some bad news, though. His deployment was supposed to be up in four weeks but they just got notice of extension for another six months. Apparently the Taliban is really coming back with a vengeance. Mark said they're pulling twenty thousand troops from Iraq to send to Afghanistan and he might end up there."

Knox swore under his breath. "I know he can't say exactly where he is, but is he in the line of fire at his current position?"

"He only said he was keeping his head down and trying to do his job."

Knox slumped back on the bed. "Look, what do you say we all plan to do something together when he gets back? Go away somewhere. Maybe the Mediterranean. Just the three of us. Wind down and take a breather. My dime."

"That sounds great. But the Med is expensive and I probably make more money than you. How about I chip in too? Mark's the poor one. Serving his country doesn't even get him minimum wage."

"Nope, *my* dime. And you need to save your dollars."

"Why?"

"To take care of me in my old age. I won't be doing this crap forever."

There was a change in his tone when he said this and his daughter was quick to pick up on it.

"Dad, is everything okay?"

"Fine, sweetie. And a piece of advice, you don't waste premium theater tickets on old farts like me. You get a nice young man to join you in seeing *Wicked*. I want grandchildren, okay? I'm not getting any younger here."

"Okay, sure."

"I'll talk to you soon, honey."

"Good-bye, Dad. And . . . take care of yourself."

"Always."

"Dad?"

"Yeah?"

"Are you sure you're okay?"

Knox didn't want to hesitate, but for some reason he did. "Everything will be fine, Mel."

Knox clicked off and dropped the phone on the bed. Now he felt worse than he did before he'd called. He knew he'd frightened his daughter and there was nothing he could do about it now. Maybe he wanted to scare her. Or at least prepare her for when he didn't come back home, or even for when she might have to come and ID his body.

He looked around the dismal interior of his room. How many crappy hole-in-the-walls, how many effed-up towns, how many shitty countries had he spent the majority of his life in? The answer was clear: way too many.

He lay back on the bed feeling lonelier than he ever had.

Wicked? Yeah, I can tell you all about wicked, honey.

But then I'm afraid you'd hate your old man, and I'd rather eat a machine-gun round.

His cell phone buzzed.

It was Hayes. He knew without even looking. He didn't want to answer it but he had to. Official protocol, meaning he didn't want to be transferred to undercover duty in, say, Tehran or Pyongyang.

"Joe Knox."

Hayes snapped, "Where are you?"

"On the hunt."

"On the hunt precisely where?"

"Southwest Virginia."

"That's not precise enough."

"To tell you the truth, I'm not even sure where I am and the reception up here is lousy, sir, I can barely hear you."

Hayes raised his voice a few notches. "Have you sighted him yet?"

"If I had I would've already called you. I'm just trying to run some leads down and get a more pinpoint location."

"Why didn't you have the chopper take you all the way in?"

Because then you'd know exactly where I was. "A bird dropping a fed in the middle of this place would've aroused a little bit of suspicion. If Carr was around he wouldn't have been much longer. I'm going to poke around and then get back to you."

"I'm not exactly on board with how you're handling this, Knox."

"Flying by the seat of my pants, sir. Doing the best I

can, what with all the *prohibitions* on what I can look at or the roads I can go down."

"The minute you know anything, Knox. The very minute!" He clicked off.

Knox looked up in time to see the Fonz deliver his trademark line on TV.

"Sit on it, asshole," Knox said in his best Arthur Fonzarelli voice.

CHAPTER

42

ANNABELLE AND CALEB marched into Union Station and went straight up to the clerk that Knox had talked to. Annabelle flashed her fake FBI badge.

"Agents Hunter and Kelso. Was there a man in here earlier asking questions and showing you a photo? He would've identified himself as Joe Knox? Said he was with Homeland Security?"

"Yes, that's right," the woman said nervously.

Annabelle let out an audible sigh. "Then we have a big problem."

The woman looked anxiously at her. "What was the problem? We helped Agent Knox as best we could."

Caleb spoke up. "The problem is his name isn't Knox and he isn't with Homeland Security."

The woman blanched. "Omigod."

Annabelle said, "Omigod is right. I need to speak to everybody he talked to, right now!"

A few minutes later Annabelle and Caleb were seated in the supervisor's office. The train attendant was there too, having stayed behind at the station to catch up on some paperwork and been summoned when Annabelle had made her demand of the manager.

"We thought he was a fed."

"I'm sure. He probably told you not to say anything to anyone about what he'd told you, right?" said Annabelle.

"That's right, he did."

"Standard operating bullshit, I'm afraid."

"But his credentials looked authentic," the Amtrak supervisor said.

Caleb held out his creds so they could look at them closely. They were still a bit warm from Annabelle having just created them in the van on the way over. "*I'm* with Homeland Security. Did you note that in the upper-right-hand corner of the picture there's a small 'e' done in reverse like there is in mine?"

The train men looked at each other and shook their heads. The supervisor said, "I didn't know to look for that."

"That's because it's a secret," Annabelle chimed in. "To prevent people from successfully duplicating our creds. It's a double-edged sword, I know. It's a secret so the public isn't supposed to know. But I thought a notice had gone out to certain levels of the federal government about it. You're a federal agency, right?"

"Quasi-governmental," the supervisor replied. He added, "And let me tell you, nobody from the federal government tells us shit about anything. Hell, a lot of them question why the country needs trains at all. What with the highways suffocated and the skies filled to overflowing and every civilized country in the world building trains and rails at record paces, you'd think they could figure it out for themselves."

"We'll put in a good word for Amtrak at the next budget meeting," Caleb said sarcastically. "But right now we need to find this jerk-off, fast."

"Wait a minute, aren't you guys supposed to wear jackets with your acronym on the back?" the train conductor said.

"Yeah," Annabelle said impatiently. "When we're knocking down somebody's freaking door to make an arrest! Not when we're undercover trying to nail a spy."

Caleb gave her a sharp and totally choreographed glance along with a quick shake of the head.

"He's a spy?" exclaimed the supervisor.

"Yeah, he is," she admitted. "Now, I need to know exactly what you told him."

The two men filled her in while Caleb took notes. When they were done, she said, "I don't blame you for what happened. And hopefully we'll be able to run him down with the intel you just gave us."

"Wish us luck," Caleb said sourly. "We're going to need it because he's got quite a head start."

The pair quickly left and returned to the van.

"Nice job in there, Caleb," Annabelle said admiringly.

"I was in the thespian club in college. I had dreams, you know. Not Hollywood, God forbid. The stage."

"So you wanted to be on Broadway but ended up a librarian? How come?"

"I loved acting but there was a downside I could never get over."

"What was that?"

"Stage fright. I was sick for hours before every performance. I lost so much weight and went through so many costumes I finally had to give it up."

"Well, today you were a star."

CHAPTER

43

THE INTERVIEW with Charlie Trimble was going better than Stone had expected. His questions were polite but prepared. And then it began to change. The reporter sat in his old swivel chair, a piercing expression in his gaze, one that was making Stone extremely uncomfortable.

"You seem familiar to me, Ben. Have we met before?"

"I don't see how."

"You ever been in Washington?"

"Never."

Trimble sat back and drummed his fingers on his desk. "Why'd you come here?"

"Just making sure Danny was okay."

"That's all?"

"Why not?"

Before Trimble could launch another question, Stone

pounced. "What do you know about Debby Randolph's and Rory Peterson's deaths?"

At first, Trimble seemed taken aback by this, but his expression became bemused. "Why do you want to know?"

"Some people tried to kill Danny. I think somebody tried to OD Willie."

"I talked to Bob Coombs about that. Do you have any proof?"

"Just what Willie told me and what the doctors found in his system."

"Willie's a drug user, not the most reliable people in the world."

"Have you talked to him about that?" Stone asked sharply. Trimble shook his head. "Then you're not really in a position to gauge his credibility, are you?"

Trimble's face flushed but then he smiled. "You make a good point. I do need to talk to him."

"So getting back to my question. Danny and Willie both are targets. They both knew Debby. Willie was engaged to marry her."

"I didn't know that."

"No one apparently did. Debby supposedly commits suicide. Willie thinks that's impossible. He talked to her the night before she was found dead. She sounded great."

"Sheriff Tyree looked into all that. It did seem crazy that Debby would do that, but all the evidence pointed to suicide."

"It's pretty easy to make murder seem like suicide if you know what you're doing."

Trimble shot him a penetrating look. "You know about such things?"

"I'm just trying to get to the truth, Mr. Trimble."

"Call me Charlie. And why are you so set on doing that? You've only been here a short while."

Stone rubbed his shoulder and then his head. "Let's put it this way, I don't like being pushed around." *And then there's Abby.* "How was Peterson killed?" he asked.

"Gunshot. Probably during a robbery. There was a safe in his office that had been forced. Cash, some files, and his computer were stolen. Tyree's been working that one too, but he's not come up with much, at least that he's confided in me. He's the entire police force, you know."

"He could call in the state police."

"He might do that." Trimble smiled. "Or maybe his brother."

"His brother?"

"Howard Tyree. He's the warden up at Blue Spruce Prison."

"He never mentioned that."

"Well, I'm not sure the two get along all that well. So my suggestion of him calling in his brother to help was a poor attempt at a joke. Tyree's on his own."

A few minutes later Stone left the *Divine Eagle* office and headed to see the sheriff.

He found him in the jail building going over some papers.

When he told Tyree what had happened to him in the mineshaft, the lawman nearly came out of his chair. As Stone continued explaining, Tyree started to nod.

When Stone finished he said, "The hospital confirmed that Willie had oxycodone in his system. Willie *was* allergic to it. He never would've voluntarily taken it. Plus it's pretty expensive without a prescription."

"So somebody did try to kill him," Stone said.

"Looks that way. And a smart way to do it, actually. Prescription drug abuse is rampant around here. I spend a lot of my time with that crap. Black stain on what is otherwise a nice place to live. But you can't lock everybody up who's addicted. Hell, there wouldn't be any miners left to work. You try to rehab them, get their methadone pop every day, but it's not enough. Every cop up and down the Appalachian mining country knows we're fighting a losing battle. But we don't have enough resources. We're overwhelmed."

"This area is pretty remote. Where do they get all the drugs? It's not like there's a pharmacy on every corner."

"They can get it from any number of sources. Sham pharmacies on the Internet, pipeline from the Mex border. Many a miner has sucked away his life savings and his marriage over that crap. Old saying up here is, 'Methamphetamines keep you awake and oxy keeps you high.'"

"Sheriff, I believe there's a connection between Danny, Willie and Debby Randolph's death." Stone went on to tell him about Willie proposing and then him talking to Debby the night before she was found.

"I didn't know about the engagement, but I knew Willie was convinced she hadn't killed herself. He was all over me about that. But all the evidence pointed to suicide."

"Who performed the autopsy?"

"Doc Warner. He's not a full-time pathologist, but he's a qualified medical examiner. And it seemed straightforward. She put a shotgun in her mouth and pulled the trigger."

Tyree didn't look at Stone when he said this last part. Stone noticed this and said, "I'm not telling you how to do your job, but it's rare for a woman to kill herself with a gun. And with so many drugs around here, you'd think she would've just popped some pills and gone quietly."

"I know. That's been bugging me too."

Stone began cautiously, "I saw Danny lying on top of Debby's grave that night."

Tyree looked surprised. "Where were you?"

"Behind the stone wall. I heard something and came to see what. I was going to go to Danny when I saw you walk up."

Tyree looked uncomfortable. "Craziest thing I ever saw. I didn't understand what he was even doing there. I just put it down to Danny being Danny."

"Meaning what exactly?"

"Meaning unpredictable."

"Abby made him leave town."

Tyree sat back in his chair and scowled at Stone. "She never bothered telling me that," he said in a hurt tone. "And she told you?"

"She was afraid for him, I guess. And from what happened to him once he got back, it seems she was right. And maybe she was afraid to tell you."

"Why?"

"You're the law. Maybe Danny was mixed up in something not quite legal."

Tyree's anger faded away. "I guess I can understand that. By the way, that description you gave me of the men, I'm sending it around to the state police and to sheriff's offices in other towns. But they didn't ring a bell with me and I know just about everybody around here."

"Well, it was dark and things were happening pretty fast. I didn't get that good of a look at them so my description wasn't all that great. But I caught Shirley Coombs snooping around Willie's trailer right before Danny was attacked. I think she was looking for something."

"Like what?"

Stone told him about the Tylenol bottle. "And Josh Coombs was shot by his friend, Rory Peterson. Quite a coincidence."

Tyree nodded dumbly.

"Those are a lot of pieces dangling out there," noted Stone.

"But how do you tie it all together? That's the thing."

Stone stood up. "I'm heading over to the hospital to see Danny and Willie."

"Well, you tell Danny he needs to start telling me the truth. He's the way we get to the bottom of all this. I'm convinced of that. And once his story comes out, those boys won't go after him again."

"I'll tell him."

As he was walking out, Stone noticed a long-barreled shotgun resting on a table with a tag on it.

"What's that?"

"The shotgun Debby was killed with."

"Do you mind?"

"Go ahead."

Stone picked up the gun, first holding it by the stock and then by the muzzle. When he laid it back down his face was puzzled.

"What?" asked Tyree curiously.

"Not sure. I'll let you know."

Actually Stone was sure. He was six-two with exceptionally long arms. He had gauged that with the muzzle perched in his mouth he could have managed to pull the trigger. Barely. He thought back to the photo of Debby that Willie had shown him. There was no way the petite Debby could have done it.

Someone *had* killed her.

Stone walked outside. That's when he noticed the sign on the one-story building across the street.

Peterson's Accounting Service.

He crossed the street and peered in one of the windows. He saw a desk, file cabinets and shelves and a dead corn plant. Other than that the place looked to have been cleared out. There wasn't a computer, printer or fax machine in sight. He noticed some people passing by on the street who were staring at him. He smiled at them and ambled off. Crossing back to the other side of the street, he pretended to be window-shopping. He passed by the bakery and decided to go inside when he saw Bob Coombs standing at the counter.

"Hey, Bob, how's Willie doing?"

Bob smiled and said, "Docs say he'll be coming home real soon."

"I'm going over to see him today. I've been using his truck. Hope it's okay."

"After what you did, you can use anything of his you want."

Bob bought a cup of coffee and some donuts while Stone admired the half-finished mural of a country meadow scene on the wall behind the cash register. Bob offered to buy Stone a coffee but he declined.

The two men walked outside where Stone said, "I ran into your daughter-in-law the other night. She told me that the whole town blames her for something. Any idea what?"

Bob's features turned dark as he bit into his donut. "It was because of Josh's death. He wasn't even supposed to be hunting that damn day. Shirley had been nagging him about not killing any deer that season. Now, Josh was a good hunter, but the truth was Shirley didn't give a crap about eating venison. Couldn't cook it worth nothing, all gamey. It was just her way of cutting Josh down. Well, she wouldn't stop nagging and Josh finally headed out that morning by himself. He was real upset."

"How'd you learn all that?"

"Josh called me when he was driving over to the woods and told me what had happened. Hour later my boy was dead."

As the two men parted company, Stone glanced over at the courthouse. There was a white Cadillac parked in front with the license plate HCDJ. Then Stone froze when he saw her.

Why was Shirley Coombs going into the courthouse?

CHAPTER

44

AFTER A LONG DRIVE Annabelle and Caleb had arrived in the town where Stone had gotten off with Danny. Annabelle had done a quick recon of the small downtown area and then settled herself at the counter of the venerable One T. A few other butts were parked next to hers, all of them male. She got more than one look from some of the younger men at the counter. She shot back a smile here, a nod there to keep the interest stoked in case it came in handy later.

"Where you coming from?" the waitress asked her as she poured coffee into Annabelle's mug.

"Winchester, Virginia." To Annabelle, mentioning that area was good enough to give her a bit of rural cred.

"Got a cousin lives up that way. Horse farm."

"It's pretty country," Annabelle agreed, sipping her

coffee and ordering off the menu. "Kind of reminds me of around here, only a little flatter."

The man next to her chuckled. He was big and broad and wore a checkered shirt, jean jacket with Dale Earnhardt Sr.'s image on it and boots with all the shine worn off. "Just about anything's flatter than 'round here."

"You been out to see the Rockies?" Annabelle said.

"No, ma'am, can't say I have."

"They're a lot bigger than these mountains, but not nearly as pretty. Just chunky and brown with a top hat of snow. Not many trees. These mountains are green."

"You just passing through or looking to mark yourself out a piece of green?" said the waitress, coming back to them after placing Annabelle's order.

"Neither, really. I'm looking for somebody. Maybe you've seen him?"

The waitress and Annabelle's stool mate glanced at each other.

"Who might that be?" said the man warily.

"Son of a bitch ex-husband who skipped town owing a year's worth of child support for our two kids."

"Prick," said the man. "What's he look like?"

Annabelle gave them a description of Knox.

"Sounds like the feller who was in here asking questions right before I finished my shift," said the waitress as she made doodles on her order form. "He was a fed. Least he said he was. Asking questions. Didn't like that."

Annabelle said, "He *is* a fed. And I know Uncle Sam's paying him enough to keep his kids clothed, with food on the table. Got a tip he was working on something up this way. That's why I'm here. Tired of the man coming and going when he pleases. You think he gives a crap I can't even afford proper meds for our son? He's got really bad asthma. Almost died once."

"Prick," the jean jacket man said again as he pushed a forkful of biscuits and gravy in his mouth, and chewed with a force to match his choice of words.

"If you see him, don't say anything," Annabelle warned. "He's armed and prepared to use it. Don't get him pissed. Believe me, I've been on the receiving end of that."

"Are you telling me the asshole struck you?" the jean man asked as he swallowed his mouthful and partially lifted his wide butt from his narrow seat.

Annabelle said, "Just be real careful around him, you hear me?" Every time she spoke her voice picked up more of a drawl, as though she was absorbing their twang whenever they opened their mouths. She edged him back on his stool with her hand.

"So what's your plan?" said the waitress, obviously taking an avid interest in this little drama.

"I'm going to find his ass." Annabelle handed her a slip of paper. "You see him, call me on this number please."

The waitress nodded. "My old man did that crap to me too. Took me eight years but I got my money."

"Hope I'm as lucky. Any place to stay around here?"

"Don't go to Skip's Motel down the street," said the waitress, a smile playing across her lips.

"Why not?"

"'Cause that's where he's staying, honey. Or at least he asked for a place to crash and I told him about that one. Try Lucy's at the other end of town. She's got a couple nice rooms for let."

"Thank you. Skip's, huh?"

"You got it, sweetie."

The waitress grabbed Annabelle's plate off the pass-through counter and put it down in front of her. "So what's your plan to nail the scumball, honey?"

"I brought someone with me," Annabelle said. "He works for the government too and he specializes in bagging other feds who pull crap like this."

"Shit," said jean jacket man. "They got a department for that too? No wonder our taxes are so damn high."

"Hush up, Herky," said the waitress. "Can't you tell this young lady's distressed?"

"Sorry, ma'am," said Herky, his gaze downcast as he stuffed a whole sausage patty in his mouth.

"So you gonna nail the little weasel good?" said the waitress eagerly.

"Something like that. Just give me a call if you see him and meantime I'll check out Skip's too. Thanks for the tip."

Annabelle finished eating and ordered some takeout for Caleb.

She walked out of the diner, looking cautiously around for Knox. She made it back to the van and told Caleb what had happened.

"Apparently he's staying at this Skip's Motel. We can ease down there and see if we pick up his trail. If not, I've got friends in high places here now."

Caleb looked at the platter of food. "It's all fried," he said in dismay.

"I'm sorry, Caleb, that's all they had."

"Not even any yogurt? Or fruit? Do you have any idea what my LDL cholesterol count is? And my triglycerides are off the charts. I could literally drop dead at any moment, Annabelle."

"It's a *diner,* Caleb. There're enormous men in there eating entire sides of beef without a fruit cup in sight, okay? Besides, what happened to the new, old Caleb? The dangerous come-at-me-with-both-guns-blazing Caleb?"

Caleb stared darkly at her. "Oh, what the hell. We're probably going to end up dead anyway." He made a face and then crunched down on a thick slice of sugar-cured bacon.

CHAPTER

45

THERE WAS NO ONE in the front office of the court-house when Stone walked in. He waited a moment and then eyed the stacks of boxes against one wall. He slipped over to them, pulled one off the top, and looked inside it. It was filled with legal documents. This must be one of the shipments of mining recertification documents Judge Mosley had told him about. He picked up what looked to be a shipping manifest. Eighty large boxes. Stone looked at the cardboard towers and wondered how Mosley had any sanity left after going through that mind-numbing mountain of legalese.

He heard someone coming, dropped the manifest on top of one of the boxes and hurried back to the front of the large desk in the middle of the room. A moment later Shirley Coombs walked through an interior door, her gaze on a mess of papers in her hand. She looked up and gave a little cry when she saw Stone standing there.

"You work here?" he said.

She nodded, one hand on her chest. "You startled me."

Stone glanced around the space. "Are you the court secretary?"

"The court *clerk*. Have been for years. Why? Don't I look like a court clerk?" she said icily. "Or do I just look like a secretary?"

"I went to see Willie. He's doing okay."

Shirley busied herself with some papers on her desk. "I'm going over to see him soon."

Sure you are. "There's a Caddy parked out front with a vanity plate."

"HCDJ?"

"Yep."

"That's Judge Mosley's car."

"What does HCDJ stand for?"

"Here comes da judge." She said this as though Stone were an idiot for not having figured it out on his own.

"By the way, did you get everything you needed at Willie's trailer?"

"Excuse me?"

Stone said, "I think you left a bottle of Tylenol at Willie's trailer. I had it with me, but then I lost it." He stared at her pointedly and then rubbed the back of his head. *Why be subtle at this point?*

Shirley looked like Stone was pointing a gun at her. "I didn't leave anything behind."

"You sure?"

"Sure I'm sure. And I use Advil. Have ever since they had that pill scare with Tylenol."

"Willie thought there were pills left in the bottle, but when I found it, it was empty. And now it's gone. Maybe someone wanted it."

"Wanted an empty bottle? What for?"

"Well, there might have been some residue in there."

"Residue of what?"

Stone could tell she was lying. It was in every twitch of her face and shake of her voice. It had been her. She'd tried to kill her own son.

Now, who threw me into the snake pit, because it wasn't Miss Court Clerk with her stilettos and Pall Malls.

"You can't believe anything Willie says. Boy's always high."

"He was high on a stimulant, not a depressant. But the hospital said he had oxycodone in his system. That's a depressant."

"Willie doesn't know half the crap he's on. Probably forgot he took it."

"Or somebody wanted it to look that way."

She looked at him sharply. "What's that supposed to mean?"

"Just that somebody might have wanted to make it look like he'd OD'd accidentally."

She scoffed, "Why would anybody waste time trying to kill Willie? I mean, what'd be the point. It's not like he's got any money."

"That's not the only reason to kill somebody."

"What then?" She said this almost fearfully.

"Willie told me he'd asked Debby Randolph to marry him. Did you know about that?"

Shirley flushed at this information. She fumbled in her purse and pulled out a cigarette and a lighter. "No, I guess Willie didn't see fit to tell me that, his own mother."

"I take it you knew Debby?"

"Everybody in Divine knows everybody else," she said resignedly as she lit up.

"Would anybody in town have a problem with that happening?"

She blew smoke out and stared up at him. "What the hell does it matter to you? You're not from here. You don't know us. And just because you helped Willie doesn't mean I have to answer your damn questions."

"I thought you might want to help me, in case someone *is* trying to kill your son."

"Mister, no one is trying to kill Willie."

"But seeing as how he almost died and he says the drug that almost did him in he didn't take. Well, it does make you wonder."

She glanced at the wall of large boxes stacked a half dozen high and ten across. "I got a lot of work to do."

"Right. You want some help? I hire out cheap."

"I think you need to leave. Right now."

Stone turned and walked out.

As soon as he'd left another door opened and Judge Dwight Mosley walked slowly into the room. His tie was undone and his shirtsleeves were rolled up.

"Shirley, was someone here? I thought I heard you talking."

"Just to myself, Judge. Just to myself. You know how I get sometimes."

"Yes, I know." He smiled and went back through the door.

Shirley puffed on her cigarette, staring thoughtfully at the wall.

CHAPTER

46

JOE KNOX LAY in his underwear on a thin piece of puffed-up nylon masquerading as a mattress while he tried to connect the dots. Carr had killed a deuce, a mighty prominent deuce, and hit the road after slipping past the feds disguised as a bushy-bearded, gimp-legged village idiot. He'd gotten sidetracked on the train and ended up in this cluster of shacks. Where he was now, Knox had no clue. By asking around he'd discovered that the bus had headed out the very night the man had gotten to town, lucky, lucky him. By now, he could be pretty damn far away.

He sat up, jerked on his pants, socks and his Timber-lands. He washed his face, finger-brushed his teeth and smoothed down his hair with the palm of his hand. If he was going to be on the chase much longer, he'd grab some clothes and toiletries other than the small travel bag he always carried with him. He slipped on his shirt and checked his cell. No messages, though the bars were looking a little jumpy at this altitude in the middle of nowhere.

Hayes was the show-runner on this dramatic piece; Knox his faithful attack dog. Well, the "faithful" part was in serious doubt right now. Knox chewed some gum and stared out the window of Skip's Motel. Checking in last night he'd actually run into said Skip, an ancient man who said little, but his hand had shot out for the cash that was required to stay here with the jab speed of a welterweight in his prime. Old Skip apparently did not believe in the merits of consumer plastic.

Hayes had a hard-on for Carr for reasons he had not bothered to share with Knox, but which were growing a little clearer each time Knox thought about the possibilities. If Hayes had his way when Knox caught up to Carr, the man would not be read his rights, have his call to a lawyer or his day in court. But why kill the Medal of Honor man? It would have been a feather in the cap of then Major Macklin Hayes' career to have had such a soldier in his ranks. Carr had certainly pissed off his leader somehow. The paper trail had demonstrated that the lower chain of command had had no issue with Carr getting the mother of all American medals pinned to his chest. It had stopped at Hayes. What had Carr done to merit that sort of stonewall; a grudge that had apparently lasted over thirty years?

Now Knox's dilemma was obvious. If he did his job successfully and found Carr, he would, in essence, be delivering him to his executioner. A part of Knox said that was neither his business nor his battle to fight. Turn him over, be done with it and start collecting your pension. Rome in summer, his kids, sailing in the Med, the wine, the food. His kids.

If only that damn aneurysm in Patty's head hadn't popped—

The other part of Knox fell down on this theory like a four-hundred-pound WWE monster coming off a wrestling-ring rope. If Carr had killed the men, he would have to be proven guilty of those charges and then punishment could be meted out. Once you let way too smug and smart men like Hayes call those kinds of shots, play God for all seasons and all reasons, it was over. You might as well pull the democratic tent poles and phone in for Joe Stalin to make a comeback. The old US of A was finished. And Knox would not be a party to that. Twenty years ago the answer might have been different. But not today, not now. It was funny and a little ass-backwards, but he believed in the principles that made America what it was more strongly now than when he'd first started out in this line of work. Back then he was a raw, snot-nosed kid fresh from the military grunt side itching to carve out a credible rep as an intelligence op. He did anything and all to accomplish that goal, many things just over the line and a few that obliterated it. Looking back, he was not particularly proud of those moments, but he also took some solace in the fact that his work had saved lives and also that he'd eventually come around to the good side again. He knew many others who had never accomplished that last step. Hayes was clearly one of them.

It wasn't that he wasn't cynical. You couldn't do this job as long as he had and not cross that line a long time back. Experience without cynicism was a sure sign your brain had dry-rotted and you hadn't bothered to notice. He went into every high-level meeting these days knowing there were at least three agendas and also knowing he'd only be told one of them.

He put on his jacket and fingered his wallet with one hand, his rental truck keys with the other. He could also run, head for the hills, let Hayes find another lackey to do this job. There were plenty waiting in line. And truth be known, Knox was finding his enthusiasm for locating Carr waning the more he learned about the man and the more he found out about Hayes' probable reasons for taking down a war hero who'd never gotten his due.

He went down to his truck and debated whether to go to the One T and give it another whirl. He decided that might be worth it but he would do it later. First, he wanted to take a drive around and see what the night had hidden from him. He highly doubted one of those things would be John Carr. He had started out wanting no more than to find the man. Now a part of him was hoping it would never happen. And not just because a run-in with Carr, the grizzly bear of government assassins, would probably not end well for Knox.

It had something to do with justice, a concept Knox had not entirely forgotten, even if his boss apparently had.

CHAPTER

47

"THERE HE GOES," said Annabelle. They watched from inside their van parked at the corner as Knox drove off.

"What do we do?" Caleb asked.

"Follow him." She held up a device. "I've got another tracker I can put in that truck."

Caleb put the van in gear. "You come prepared, I'll give you that."

"Just wait till you see what Reuben's bringing."

They followed from a discreet distance as Knox did a sweep of the area before parking at the One T and going inside.

"This should be interesting," said Annabelle with a grin.

* * *

Knox sat down at the counter. Herky, who was two seats down and working on his third plate of food, looked up, scowled and moved over next to Knox as the same waitress hurried over to take his order.

"Back again?" said the waitress.

"Thought the night might have refreshed your memory," Knox said.

"Only thing it refreshed was me knowing I was right to tell you to blow it out your butt."

Knox dialed back his natural anger and tried his best to keep it light. "Hey, give Uncle Sam's guy a little more respect than that, will ya?"

Herky moved slightly and bumped Knox in the arm. He glanced over at the big man. "Is there a problem?"

"No problem," said Herky, whose menacing features clearly said otherwise.

The waitress moved away to make a phone call.

"So you got any kids?" said Herky.

Knox looked surprised, but said, "Yeah, two, why?"

"So why don't you take care of 'em?" Herky snapped, stuffing a biscuit in his mouth.

"What the hell are you talking about? My kids are grown and gone. They should be taking care of me."

"Asshole," said Herky between bites.

"What?"

"You leave your wife and kids with nothing. Asshole," he said again.

"Herky!" the waitress said as she rejoined them. "Shut up!"

"Doris, this man is letting his wife and kids starve."

"Starve! My wife's dead. Who the hell have you been—"

Herky bumped him again. "I got a mind to take you out back and teach you some manners, mister."

"I wouldn't advise that."

"Advise this!"

Herky swung a big fist. Knox caught it, twisted it around Herky's back and then slammed the man's face into his grits and eggs.

"Hey!" the waitress screamed as other men in the One T started rising from their chairs to help their friend.

Knox pulled his badge and his gun. "Everybody sit their butts back down in their chairs unless they want to spend some quality time in a federal prison a long way from here."

The men froze, all except Herky, who was snorting out grits and egg yolks.

Knox looked at the waitress. "Who the hell told you that I—"

The waitress committed the mistake of glancing toward the door.

Knox burst outside, his gaze sweeping up and down the street.

Annabelle peered back from inside the van, the front of which was just barely in Knox's line of sight. She was still holding her phone from when the waitress had called her. "Damn it, they must have tipped him off somehow. Caleb, put the van in reverse and very slowly back up."

Caleb did so, and then once out of Knox's sight he backed into a parking lot, shifted to drive and sped off.

"That was close, but at least I got the tracker on his truck while he was in the One T." She looked at a small device in her lap. "He's on the move. Let's go, but take it slow."

Knox knew that someone was on his trail, but he wasn't sure who. Hayes would have most likely taken a direct route. Was it one of Carr's friends? The chick with the fast tongue? The Secret Service agent? But how could they have possibly followed him here? He kept gazing in the rearview mirror as he drove to the bus station. It wasn't due to be open for another day, but Knox was done waiting. He didn't like the sensation of people creeping up behind him. He would tear up this whole town and find somebody who could tell him something.

He banged on the door of the bus station long and loud enough till a middle-aged man looking very put off came into view. Knox plastered his creds against the glass. When the man saw them he paled and quickly unlocked the door.

"Can I help you?" he said in a trembling voice.

"You better hope to hell you can."

Twenty minutes later he had his answer and was rushing back out to his truck.

The man had recognized Carr. He'd been traveling with another man, younger. They'd taken a bus heading even farther southwest. The man had gotten hold of the driver at home. He'd remembered where he'd dropped the pair. Basically in the middle of nowhere, but it was a start.

Knox floored it.

He was coming to realize that maybe the only way he was going to survive this was to find John Carr.

CHAPTER

48

KNOX WAS MOTORING DOWN the road trying to fathom how somebody had been able to follow him up here. Not even Macklin Hayes with all his support had been able to accomplish it. It was like they knew exactly where—

He nearly swerved off the road. He cut the wheel hard and turned off into a dark path. He put the truck in park, threw off his seat belt and went over the interior of the cab meticulously. He found nothing. But his examination of the truck's exterior was far more productive. He held up the small tracking device with the magnetized side. It had been placed inside one of the rear wheel wells. As he held the tracker, a smile crept across his face.

Annabelle was driving and Caleb was staring at the tiny screen.

"How we doing?" she asked.

"He's up there about a mile ahead, going straight." They had a vertical slab of mountain on one side of them and on the other a drop of nearly a half mile with not a guardrail in sight. "Seems like Oliver took a bus."

"Judging from the way Knox ran out of the bus station, I'd say that was a pretty safe bet."

He glanced over at her. "What about Reuben?"

"I talked to him. He's back there somewhere," she said. "He'll eventually catch up to us the next time Knox stops."

Caleb stared out the windshield. "Pretty isolated place."

"What, did you expect Oliver to take up residence in the suburbs?"

"Sometimes the best place to hide is with a lot of people."

"Yeah, and sometimes it's not. For all we know he could be up in those mountains somewhere. It worked for that abortion clinic bomber in North Carolina."

"But they finally caught him," Caleb pointed out.

"Okay, but—"

"Oh, damn!"

"What?"

Caleb was staring at the tiny screen that registered the movements of Knox's truck.

"He's turned around. He's coming right at us."

Annabelle glanced at the screen and, sure enough, the red blob of light representing Knox was flying right at them.

"Quick, pull off," Caleb cried out.

"Where? Into the side of the mountain or over the edge and two thousand feet down?"

"There!" Caleb stabbed his finger in the direction of a tiny sliver of dirt that ran between a stand of trees on the left where the mountain slab receded a bit.

Annabelle zipped into that crevice. They both turned around and watched the road. A minute later an Exxon tanker truck flashed by.

Caleb stared down at the screen. "We're in trouble."

Annabelle followed his gaze. "He found the tracker and put it on the fuel truck. Shit!"

Caleb nodded absently before tossing the useless contraption down on the seat. "Now what do we do?"

Annabelle put the van in gear and backed out onto the road and floored it. "We drive and we watch. And with any luck we'll pick up his trail again."

"I don't think I'm that lucky."

"Well, I am."

"Why?"

"I'm Irish. We always keep some reserve in the tank."

CHAPTER

49

JOE KNOX WAS FEELING GOOD for the first time in a long time. He'd ditched the tail and could now move on. He looked at the map on the seat next to him. The guy at the bus company had given him fairly precise directions to where the bus had dropped Carr and his friend off. Knox did a rough estimate in his head. He was probably an hour or so away.

When he got there he slowed the truck and looked around. It really was the middle of nowhere. Yet maybe not. He punched in some buttons on his navigation system and on the screen sprang up a number of different locations in the relative vicinity. "Tazburg, Mise, Divine, South Ridge." He read the names off the screen. All these places were scattered in different directions. So which should he take? And what should he do when he got there? His experience in the last tiny town had not been good.

He swore he would not flash his federal badge, for one thing. And he was a stranger, so they would be suspicious anyway. If Carr were still in one of these places he might have already ingratiated himself with the townsfolk. Knox could be walking into something he would end up not liking. And the bus driver had said that Carr had a young guy with him. Was he from one of these towns? If so, he hadn't told the driver which one.

Knox pulled off the road and left the engine running as he stared at the navigation screen. He sighed. Hell, even for intelligence experts it sometimes came down to something as simple as this.

He closed his eyes and stabbed the screen with his finger. When he opened his eyes and pulled his finger back the town's name was revealed. He had a twenty-five percent chance that it was right.

Tazburg, Virginia, here I come.

He put the truck in gear and pulled back on the road.

While Joe Knox was enjoying a rare moment of exuberance Annabelle was slamming her hands down on the steering wheel. They'd been driving round and round trying to pick up the scent, but when they pulled past the same gas station for the third time, she'd driven into the parking lot, ripped the van into park and was now scowling at a dog that was sunning itself next to the air pump, only rising every few seconds to investigate its private parts.

"This isn't working, is it?" said Caleb.

"You think!" snapped Annabelle.

"Do you have another idea?"

She glared over at him. "Why do *I* always have to come up with the ideas, Mr. Librarian of Congress?"

Caleb said imperturbably, "I only asked because I happen to have one, an idea I mean."

She drummed her fingers on the steering wheel and looked at him expectantly.

"Do you want to hear it?" Caleb said tersely.

"Yes!" she shouted at him.

"I don't appreciate being yelled at."

She leaned into him. "Will you appreciate it more if I pull you out of this hunk of junk and kick the shit out of you instead?"

Caleb put one hand on the door lever and looked ready to sprint for it. "How about I just tell you my idea?"

Annabelle gripped the wheel so hard her forearms quivered. "That would please me very much," she said between clenched teeth.

"You see, civility is really not that difficult." She gave him such a ferocious look that he hurried on. "Okay, we go back to that town where they serve heart attacks instead of meals. You go to the bus station, do your usual bushelful of lies routine, maybe show some leg, buy a ticket and get the driver to drop you off at the exact same spot he did Oliver. He might have even overheard where they were headed. I'll follow in the van, and when you get there I'll pick you up and we go from there. At the very least it'll put us in the general vicinity of where Oliver was. How does that sound?"

Actually it sounded pretty good, Annabelle had to admit. She put the van in gear and pulled onto the road, setting a course back to the town.

Caleb's cell phone buzzed. It was Reuben. He spoke for a few minutes and then clicked off.

"Well?" said Annabelle.

"He's about two hours away, he said. I filled him in on the plan and he'll meet us there."

"Good."

"So you like my idea?"

"I'm doing it, so I must think it has *some* merit," she snapped.

"Annabelle, can I make a personal comment?"

She took a deep breath. "Go ahead."

"You really need to do something about your anger issues."

She stared over at him with an incredulous look. "I've been in this van so long I can't even remember when I haven't been in this van. I'm tired, I'm filthy, I'm worried and I'm frustrated. Okay? I don't have anger *issues*."

Caleb smiled knowingly. "That was a good first step to getting your feelings out. Only then can you achieve real progress."

"Can I share another feeling with you?" she said pleasantly.

"Of course."

"Either go back to being the mildly amusing testosterone Caleb, or else your ass can walk back to D.C."

Predictably, they drove on in silence.

CHAPTER

50

KNOX CRUISED INTO TAZBURG and passed the local police station. He parked the truck and watched uniformed officers come and go, some on foot, others climbing into old mud-splattered Ford LTDs and speeding off to somewhere. The downtown area consisted of brick and clapboard buildings, a few leaning into each other, with old telephone lines running to them, while cars were parked slantwise in front of them. He'd passed through a long tunnel cut straight through a section of mountain on his way here. It felt like a border crossing.

What country am *I in?*

He pulled out the photos of Carr and mentally absorbed them one more time. He put the truck in gear and slowly pulled off. He would grid the downtown area street by street. From the look of the place that would take all of five minutes. Then he would get something to eat at the local place. He wouldn't pull his badge or show his photos. He would just watch. He had one big advantage. He knew relatively well what Carr looked like, while Carr had no idea who he was. He would press that to his full advantage. If that didn't pay off, he would eventually go to the police and work through them. It was a plan at least.

Three hours later and after having sat his butt down in four hole-in-the-walls and downed more cups of coffee than his stomach or bladder cared for, he concluded that he had struck out.

He parked in front of the police station, went in, flashed his creds, explained his mission to the extent he could, meaning it was mostly refined by-the-spook-book gobble-dygook, and got zip for his troubles from the lawmen who were understandably excited that a dangerous desperado might be in their midst, but not very helpful. No one had seen anyone remotely resembling the man in the photo. Although one young deputy did mention that a fellow that looked just like that had lived in Tazburg for sixty-three years and happened to be his daddy. Knox thanked them politely and nearly sprinted back to his truck.

Before he'd gotten the door of his truck closed, his cell phone rang.

It was Hayes. The spy chief was not happy. But then again, Knox had never known the man to be really happy about anything. Knox had been with him when the Berlin Wall had come down. While everyone else had been raising their champagne flutes and making victory toasts, Hayes had only sipped on club soda and grumbled, "About damn time."

"Yes, sir?"

"Have you ever known me to give an idle command?"

"Can't say that I have."

Hayes bellowed, "When I ordered you to give me regular updates, I didn't mean at such wide intervals that obviously seem to appeal to you."

Knox punched the gas and rapidly left the good hamlet of Tazburg behind. He didn't want the megaton blast that he sensed was coming from Hayes to flatten the place.

"Well, General, you're a busy man and if I'd had something of substance to report you'd be the first to know." Before Hayes could send off another broadside he added, "But in fact I was just going to call you. I've narrowed the search area to four places. I just cleared one and I'm heading on to the second one now."

"Give me the locations."

Knox knew that one was coming. "With all due respect, sir, can I ask why?"

"Why *I* want to know where your investigative search is going on? Are you on drugs, Knox?"

"Stone cold sober, I can assure you. But if your plan is to flood the area with agents, that would definitely be a bad move in my opinion. We're looked on with suspicion here, and for all I know Carr has already gotten cozy with some folks around here and they may provide him with cover."

"Why would they do that?"

"Big bad government coming after a persecuted Vietnam vet. He could've made up any lie about his background. Believe me, sir, I've passed enough pickup trucks with shotguns and deer rifles in the window rack and bumper stickers that read, 'Thanks for visiting, now get the hell out,' to know an unfriendly atmosphere when I see it. There was even a ten-foot-tall graffiti sign on a train overpass that said, 'The Feds Suck!' I couldn't fail but note by the faded paint that it had been there apparently a long time without a single attempt to wash it off."

"Where are you, Knox? Now!"

Okay, here comes Plan B. Knox sped up, rolled down the window and stuck the phone out so it was blasted by the wind. He leaned out the window and spoke into the phone. "General . . . mile . . . border . . . hour . . . berg."

"Knox!" Hayes roared. "You're breaking up."

Knox pretended not to hear. In for a dime, in for a dollar. Maybe his lawyer daughter could represent him in his criminal insubordination trial. Although Hayes probably wouldn't bother with a trial. Knox would simply just disappear.

"Next . . . then . . . report. . . . investigation . . . west . . . lead." This was so absurd he had to work hard to keep from laughing his guts out, he really did.

"Damn it, Knox!"

Knox turned the phone off, wound the window back up, patting his hair back into place. With any luck Hayes was so apoplectic they would find him facedown on his desk, the unfortunate victim of a Joe Knox–induced fatal cardiac blast.

He pointed his ride to the next town on the list.

CHAPTER

51

As Stone walked down the hospital corridor he heard laughter. When he reached Willie's room he understood why: Danny was in the bed next to his friend and Abby was sitting between them.

They all looked up when Stone walked in.

Danny's head was bandaged and one eye was swollen and there were cuts on his face. When he sat up he moved slowly and stiffly. Still, when he saw Stone he grinned in his usual cocksure manner.

"Looky what the cat dragged in. Dudley Do-Right. Savior of mankind, or at least two sorry-ass mountain boys."

Abby smiled. "The 'boys' seem to be doing a lot better ever since they were put in the same room."

"I can see that." Stone pulled up a chair and sat down next to her. "Danny, how you doing?"

"Thinking better than ever. See, couple knocks on the head straightened my brain out."

Willie piped up, "Too bad it didn't happen when we were playing football. Remember that godawful play you called in the state semis our junior year? I was wide open but you threw it right to the safety. Almost cost us the game."

"Play was fine. Only problem was I was checking out the other team's cheerleaders when I let go of the ball. One of 'em kept bending over. Trying to distract me, I expect."

"Some things never change," said Abby wearily. "Boys never grow up, they just get bigger with more hair and people start calling them men."

Stone said to Danny, "Tyree told me he came by to see you."

Danny's look changed. He glanced toward the window but uncharacteristically kept his mouth shut.

"Those men almost killed you, Danny. They almost killed me."

"I'm sorry about that, Ben. Sure wasn't your fight."

"Who were they?"

"Can't really remember. Docs say I got a concussion." He looked back and his face brightened. "Had a few in high school. Didn't I, Willie?"

"Hell, yeah. He always held on to the ball too long."

"Had to so your sorry butt could get open. If you'd run a little faster my brain would be doing better."

Willie grinned.

"Once we get out of here me and Willie are heading to California. Ain't that right, Willie?"

Willie nodded. "We talked it over last night. Got it all worked out."

"You sure it wasn't the painkillers talking?" said Abby.

"I'm sure. Divine ain't big enough for the two of us, is it, Willie?"

"No way."

"He's getting out of the mines and I'm gonna be a movie star. Willie's going to be my agent."

"What do you two know about any of that?" asked Abby with an incredulous look.

"Actors are just paid liars, far as I can see. They memorize a bunch of lines and then just say 'em. And, Ma, you've always said I could spout the biggest load of crap you've ever heard."

"He's got a point there, Mrs. Riker," said Willie.

"California is a long way away," she said slowly.

Danny looked over at her. "You want me to stay here?"

"No, I mean, I want you to be happy, honey. And safe. So if that means California, then so be it. Maybe I'll come and visit."

"Hell, when I hit it big I'll buy you a place next to Brad Pitt. But you got to let me use it too so I can sneak peeks at Mrs. Pitt."

"Okay, Danny, okay," she said quietly, but looking anxious.

Danny seemed to notice this. He slid a hand out from under the covers and took one of hers.

"Ma, it'll be okay. All right? I promise."

"Sure. I know."

"You can't remember anything about last night?" said Stone persistently.

"No," Danny said firmly. "But you'll be the first to know when and if I do."

Stone was about to say something else when a nurse walked in. "Willie, the doctor's releasing you. We're getting the paperwork done up. You have a way to get home?"

Stone said, "I drove here in your truck. I can take you back."

"Okay, but I'll call Gramps. He'll want to be there when I get home."

"Hey, Willie, don't you forget now. California here we come."

"I'm there, man."

The two did a little knuckle smack to seal the deal.

Stone said to Abby, "How long are you staying here?"

"A few hours. Why don't you come by for dinner tonight?"

Danny said, "Hey, you two got something going on?"

"Look, Mr. Movie Star, you're not the only one with dreams," said Abby, who blushed slightly as she said this.

On the drive back to town, Stone asked Willie something that had been puzzling him.

"You said Debby called you the night before she was found dead. Where from?"

"The bakery. She was doing some work there. They liked her to come after hours. Folks coming in to get muffins and cookies don't want to smell paint. Ain't good for business."

Stone thought of the half-finished mural he'd seen on

the wall there. "And the bakery is right across the street from Rory Peterson's office."

"That's right. So?"

"So he was killed too."

"But in town. And the night before. Debby was out at her folks' house."

"No. Debby's body was *found* the next morning. But you said she'd been dead awhile. Maybe she was killed the night before. The same night Peterson was. His body was probably found that same morning too."

"Okay, but her parents' place is a good fifteen miles from town."

"But at eleven o'clock she called you from the bakery in good spirits. Let's say Peterson was killed around then or a bit later. The mural she was painting was in front of the store, with a good view of the street and the buildings opposite."

Willie sat up straighter. "Are you saying she maybe saw who killed Peterson?"

"At the very least she might have seen someone go in his office. Then she might have gone to investigate or the killers saw her and grabbed her because she was a potential witness. They take her back to her parents' house, kill her, make it look like suicide and no one thinks to connect the two together."

"Damn," Willie said slowly. "That makes a lot of sense. We gotta tell Tyree about this."

"I plan to."

When they pulled into the front yard of Willie's home they saw Bob Coombs' truck parked there. Willie got out as the front door opened and Bob was standing there smiling and waving. Willie hurried up the steps to embrace his grandfather while Stone, who'd been following Willie, turned and walked back to the truck to grab Willie's bag.

He had just closed the truck door when the force of the explosion knocked him off his feet and slammed him facedown into the mud. As debris rained down around him, a dazed Stone lifted up his head. Where the trailer had been there was now nothing. He could see straight through the gap to the trees behind. Something large landed next to his head, smoke rising off its sizzled surface. He didn't recognize it. And one could hardly blame him.

They were the earthly remains of Willie Coombs, what little there was of him left.

Stone's head dropped back into the mud and he lay still.

CHAPTER

52

ANNABELLE AND CALEB had returned to the bus station and discovered that, somewhat ahead of the regular schedule, the same driver was just about to head out with a load of people on the route Stone had taken. Annabelle snagged a seat right behind the driver and peppered him with questions while Caleb followed in the van. A half hour into the ride Annabelle saw the 1924 Indian motorcycle with the rare left-hand sidecar pass the bus, drop back and then fall in behind the van.

She sighed with relief. Big Reuben Rhodes had arrived. They might very well need the man's muscle. She'd told Reuben to bring quite a few things with him that she'd thought they might need. She noted with satisfaction that the sidecar was filled with items.

A few hours later Annabelle climbed off the bus in the middle of a curvy road bracketed by a mountain on one side and a typical sheer drop on the other. This was where Stone and his friend had gotten off, the driver told her.

Before she left the man had added, "Lot of interest in those two. What's going on?"

"Can't talk about it. National security."

"National security, huh? They looked like a couple of bums."

"If you were on the run from the feds, what would you dress like?"

"I guess I see your point."

"And you're sure you don't remember anything they said about where they were actually going?"

"Kid just got up and told me to drop him off here. The older guy got off with him." He paused. "The kid was wearing a varsity jacket. You know, for sports."

"Did you get the name of the school? College? High school?"

"Didn't pay that close of attention."

Annabelle held up a sheet of paper where'd she taken notes during her conversation with the driver. "And these are the towns nearby? All of them? You're sure?"

"Lady, there ain't that many of them. That's it. Happy searching."

He closed the door and the bus pulled away.

Annabelle met up with Caleb and Reuben and filled them in on what she'd learned. "Knox is doing exactly what we are, only he has a head start," she said.

"Yeah, but there are three of us," Reuben said. "We can split up. I'll take two of the four places and you guys hit the others."

"Good idea," said Caleb.

"And you brought everything I told you to?" asked Annabelle.

"Yeah, but I feel like I'm running a damn Hollywood prop department."

"You just never know when something might come in handy. We can load it in the van." After they were done she looked at the sheet. "Caleb and I will do Mize and Tazburg. Reuben, you can hit South Ridge and Divine." She pulled maps from her bag and handed them to Reuben. "I got these from the bus station. The towns look to be anywhere from two to three hours apart. They're not far as the crows fly, but all the roads are back roads and switch backs with chunks of mountain in between."

"Winding roads. Perfect cruising turf for the Indian," Reuben said, affectionately patting the motorcycle's gas tank.

"They just make me queasy," said Caleb. "Not that I'm complaining," he quickly added as Annabelle shot him a look.

"We'll keep in touch via cell phone. Whoever finds something positive, we can hook up within a few hours." She handed a photo to Reuben. "This is a picture of Knox, just in case you run into him."

"Thanks," said Reuben as he climbed on his bike and put his helmet and old-fashioned goggles back on.

"What if we find Oliver at the same time that Knox does?" asked Caleb.

"Then we persuade him to let Oliver go with us," Reuben said.

"He's not going to do that, Reuben."

"He will if we're *really* persuasive."

"We can't take out a fed," Caleb said. "Even new testosterone Caleb draws the line at that."

"Caleb," Annabelle said, "let's worry about that only if we have to. Right now, all I want is to find Oliver. And the longer we stand around here the better the chances are that Knox will find him first."

Reuben kick-started the Indian and the engine roared to life. He gave them a little salute, glanced at one of the maps and took off heading east.

Annabelle started to climb in the driver's seat of the van but Caleb stopped her. "I'll drive," he said, hopping in and putting the keys in the ignition.

"Why?"

"You don't know how to handle curves. Too herky-jerky. That's why I was feeling sick."

"Really? What if the time comes where we need to drive really fast, Caleb?"

"Get in!"

"What?"

Caleb fired up the van and Annabelle had to hustle around and jump in before he roared off. He accelerated so fast she tumbled into the backseat.

"What the hell are you doing?" she cried out as she struggled back up.

"When the time comes, I'm your wheelman."

She managed to clamber into the front seat and quickly buckled up as he took one curve and then the next at almost sixty miles an hour. When she glanced over she noted how professionally he was maneuvering the steering wheel and then realized how smoothly the bulky van, which was clearly not designed for this sort of terrain, was handling the road.

"Caleb, how are you doing that?"

"I can drive, okay? You should have seen me at a guy named Tyler Reinke's house. I took the Nova airborne."

"I can see that you can drive. But how?"

He sighed. "Why do you think I kept that crappy Nova all these years?"

"I don't know. I just thought you were either cheap or had no taste. Or both."

"Well, I am cheap, but I actually do have taste. No, it was about my father."

"What are you talking about?"

"My dad was a stock car driver."

"No way!"

"After he retired from racing he worked on a NASCAR pit crew for Richard Petty."

"King Richard?"

Caleb nodded. "I was his protégé."

"What?"

"You heard me."

"You were Richard Petty's protégé? Get out of here."

"Annabelle, I started racing Go-Karts when I was six. Then I moved up to dirt track racing, and then on to ARCA where I was the top rookie. After that I finished number one in the Late Model Sportsman Series, which is like the junior circuit for NASCAR. I was just about ready to launch my career in the big leagues with Petty's help. I was going to be the number two driver on Billy Nelson's Chevy team out of Charlotte. They'd won the Winston Cup three years in a row and Bobby Mallard, their number one driver and a four-time Daytona 500 winner, was going to be my mentor. It was all set up, and then it all went to hell."

"What happened?"

"I was doing a qualifying lap at Darlington. Some call it the 'paper clip' because it's shaped like one. Others refer to it as the 'Lady in Black.' That's what it was for me."

"Why, what happened?"

Caleb's features turned somber. "The Lady in Black is very unforgiving. I came out of turn number four at 185 miles an hour, let my wheel drift and the car bumped the wall. I left half my paint on the wall, the 'Darlington Stripe' they call it. Then my right front tire blew and I was completely out of control. This was before the roof flaps era so my car flipped over and then went airborne. There are two interior walls at Darlington, the inside and pit walls. I cleared them both and slid right into a pit crew."

"Oh my God."

"*My* pit crew," Caleb said solemnly. "My *personal* pit crew."

Annabelle gasped. "It wasn't your father, was it?"

Caleb turned to look at her, his eyes watery. "I walked away from the crash with a few bumps and bruises, but he was in the hospital for months before finally pulling through. But after that, I couldn't do it anymore. Couldn't shift a gear, couldn't mash an accelerator, couldn't even slide in the car. So I just walked away from it all. Turned my life around. Went from speed to being a librarian. As far away as I could get from that world. But I kept the Nova. It was one of the first cars I ever raced in. I painted it that shitty gray to cover up the numbers and stripes. The number twenty-two car, Double Deuces, they called me. It didn't look like much but under the hood it had muscle, that car. Dual carbs, overhead cam, four hundred–plus horses and a gas pedal that never let me down. Whenever I needed to bring it, it was there. Years ago, late at night, I used to run it on straightaways when Centreville was still cow country. Got it up to 150 more than once. Those were the days."

"Caleb, I'm so sorry." She gently squeezed his shoulder.

A few moments of silence passed.

"Hey, I really got you, didn't I?"

She glanced back over at him. He was smiling broadly.

"Come on, Richard Petty's protégé? Me?"

"You made that all up? You shit!" She smacked him on the shoulder hard. But there was admiration in her features.

"What? You think you're the only one who can lie really well? I've spent my adult life surrounded by stories at the library, Annabelle. I can 'fiction' with the best of them."

"That still doesn't explain how you can drive like this."

"I grew up on the side of a mountain in Pennsylvania. First thing I ever drove was a Bobcat down a dirt road that would make this stretch of gravel look like the Autobahn." He paused. "And I did do some stock car racing when I turned eighteen. Mostly junk on dirt tracks. But after my third near-fatal accident, I decided to go into library science. But I'm still a big NASCAR fan."

"Caleb, I'm seeing a totally new side to you."

"Yes, well, everyone has their secrets."

"The Camel Club more than most, I'm finding."

CHAPTER

53

STONE OPENED HIS EYES and felt rather than saw the people around him.

"Ben?"

He turned to the right and focused on Abby standing there, holding his hand. He gazed over her shoulder and realized he was in a hospital room.

"What the hell happened?" he said, trying to rise up.

Abby and someone else gently pushed him back down.

"Just take it easy, Ben."

This was Tyree, who was standing on the other side of the bed.

Stone leaned back against the pillow. "What happened?" he said again.

"What do you remember?" Abby asked.

"Driving Willie home and then waking up here."

"It blew up," Tyree said quietly. "His trailer, I mean. It blew up."

"Willie? Bob? He was there too."

Abby gripped his hand. "They're both dead." Her voice broke as she said this.

"How did it happen?"

"They think it was his propane tank. Only thing that could've blown like that," Tyree said. "Another few feet and you would've been gone too. You're lucky you were standing on the other side of that truck. It took most of the blast instead of you."

Stone thought for a moment. "I remember something falling right next to me."

Abby and Tyree exchanged glances. "Just some debris," she said quickly.

"How did the gas thing happen?"

"I'm checking that out right now," said Tyree firmly. "He apparently had a cookstove and some propane tanks in his trailer along with a lot of ammo."

"I don't care about that. It can't be an accident," said Stone. "It can't be."

"I'm inclined to agree with you," said the sheriff. "I just need some proof."

Stone managed to sit up a bit. "Wait a minute. On the drive home, Willie and I talked about Debby." He went on to tell Tyree and Abby what he had figured out about Debby seeing who had killed Peterson.

Tyree rubbed his jaw. "I never saw the connection there, but Willie never told me she was at the bakery that night either. But I knew Debby hadn't killed herself."

"How?" asked Stone and Abby together.

"Her arms weren't long enough to put the muzzle in her mouth and still pull the trigger."

Stone looked at him with new respect. "I actually thought of that when I saw the shotgun. Willie had shown me a picture of Debby. I saw how petite she was."

"Tyree, you never mentioned you believed Debby was murdered," said Abby.

"That's because I didn't know who killed her. Or why. Figured it had to be somebody local. Might as well let the murderer think I'm a clueless country bumpkin. He might make a mistake, and it lets me snoop around under the radar too."

"You're clearly no country bumpkin," said Stone, and Tyree gave him an appreciative look.

"Does Danny know about Willie?" asked Stone.

Abby nodded. "He was so upset they had to give him something to calm him down. He was bawling like a baby."

"No more California dreams," said Stone.

"What?" asked Tyree.

"Long story," replied Abby.

"We need to get to work, Tyree, before somebody else gets killed." Stone started to get up again.

Tyree pushed him back down. "Whoa, now. You just got yourself nearly blown up and the doc says you need to stay quiet for a day or two."

"We don't have a day or two."

"I'm going to poke around some. With what you told me I got some new angles I can work."

"Danny and Abby need protection," said Stone.

"Me?" said Abby.

"Look at what happened to Bob. They don't care who they kill."

"I agree," said Tyree. "I got a couple of men I've deputized in the past. I'll have one here with Danny and another with Abby."

"Tyree, you don't have to do that."

"But we're gonna do it, Abby. Anything happens to you, I couldn't live with myself. I mean, well, it's just not going to happen. Understand?"

The strength of his words seemed to surprise even the sheriff. He reddened slightly.

"Okay," she said meekly.

Stone said, "What are you going to do?"

Tyree sat down and drew up a chair. "You said three men beat up Danny. Now, he won't talk to me about it but I think at least one of them was a miner."

"Why?" asked Stone.

"When I came to see Danny at the hospital like I said he zipped his mouth. But that didn't stop me from looking at his clothes. They had coal dust on them. I figure it came off at least one of the boys who jumped him 'cause Danny's never been in a mine that I know of."

"That's true," said Abby. "But why would a miner go after Danny?"

"Damn, I knew I'd seen him before," exclaimed Stone. They both looked at him. "The first day I was at your restaurant. Tyree had left, and Abby, you'd gone in the back. Danny had finished eating and was leaving when this big guy blocked his way. Asked Danny if he was going to stay this time or run out on them again. He's one of the guys with the baseball bats."

"This guy have a name?"

Stone thought for a moment. "Lonnie."

"Lonnie Bruback?"

"Describe him." Tyree did. "That's him," said Stone. "He'll have a wound on his face from my belt."

"Lonnie works a floating shift at the Cinch Valley Number Two Mine. I didn't even know he and Danny hung around with each other."

"They didn't as far as I knew," added Abby. "He's never come to the house. He's not, well . . ."

Tyree said, "Abby's too polite to say that Lonnie is definitely white trash. He's come my way a few times, petty crap, stealing gas, poaching, and then there's the addiction thing of course. Thanks for the tip, Ben. I better go check it out."

"Has anybody told Shirley about Willie and Bob?" Abby said.

"I haven't, but I expect she knows by now. But I'll check in with her too."

"I'd check her real well too, Sheriff," Stone said.

"You think Shirley's involved in this somehow?"

"Let me put it this way, you don't nag your husband about deer hunting only to see him go out and get shot. What are the odds?"

"You think it was premeditated?"

"I wouldn't necessarily except the shooter was Rory Peterson, who ended up murdered."

"Right." Tyree tapped his gun holster with his thumb. "Who'd ever thought the town of Divine would end up like the damn Wild, Wild West?"

He left and Abby pulled her chair closer to Stone and laid a hand on his. "I brought your bag with the clothes I packed for you. It's in the closet."

"Thanks, Abby."

"And I took Danny's cell phone from your pocket and put it in your nightstand."

"Won't Danny need it back?"

"I don't think he wants to talk to anybody right now."

"I'm sorry about everything that's happened to you."

"I think you've suffered a lot more than me."

"It seems so complicated, I wonder if we'll ever get to the bottom of it all."

She looked down as she said this and Stone thought he knew why. "If Danny is involved in something not quite legal, Abby, I'm pretty sure it didn't involve murder."

She looked up. "You're a mind reader too? Sort of unsettling." She sighed. "I know my son, or at least I think I do. But there's also the chance he might be involved in something really crazy."

"Let me tell you something. When those guys on the train came after us again, Danny dropped one of them with a gut shot. The kid was beaten but he punched Danny again. Your son could have landed a haymaker but he didn't. Said it wasn't sporting to hit a man when he was down. That doesn't sound like a cold-blooded killer to me."

"I lost Sam. I can't lose Danny too."

He gripped the woman's arm and pulled her to him. "You won't, Abby. I promise."

CHAPTER

54

REUBEN WAS IN TROUBLE. He'd driven into South Ridge and had nearly run into Joe Knox as the man walked down the streets of the small, plain town. After about an hour, he'd climbed back in his truck and driven off. An excited Reuben had phoned Annabelle and filled her in. Then, on the way out of town while barely keeping Knox in his sights, Reuben had blown a tire on the Indian. He'd pulled off the road and phoned Annabelle again.

"Sit tight, Reuben," she'd said. "We're going to finish up the two towns and then we'll pick you up."

"Why not come now and we can tail Knox?"

"He'll be long gone by the time we get there. And if he didn't find Oliver in South Ridge, we might find him first. What town do you think he's headed to next?"

Reuben checked the map and looked around to gauge things. "If I had to guess, I'd say this Divine place."

"Okay, call back if anything else comes up."

Reuben clicked off, looked sourly at the flat tire and then kicked it. After all these years the Indian had finally let him down. And the thing was he usually carried a spare in the sidecar, but he'd taken it out so he could fit all the crap Annabelle had asked him to bring.

He sat on the side of the road and figured the odds. If this was the first town Knox had cleared, he still had three more to go. So the odds that Oliver was in Divine were one in three. Not great, but not terrible either. He would just have to keep his fingers crossed that Divine didn't turn out to be the jackpot for the federal agent and a probable death sentence for Oliver.

Melanie Knox had tried calling her father several times. The fact that Joe Knox had not answered or called her back wasn't surprising. Yet her last conversation with him had left her feeling disturbed. There had been something, well, fatalistic about his comments. A seize-the-moment sort of thing as though he was doubtful there would be many more tomorrows.

On impulse she took a cab to his town house and asked the driver to wait. When she unlocked the door, she was surprised that she didn't hear the alarm warning sound. Her father was scrupulous about setting the security system when he was away. When she turned on the lights, Melanie had to fight the impulse to scream.

The place had been trashed. Initially she thought it had been broken into and her first inclination was to run out in case the burglars were still here. To be safe she raced back to the cab and explained to the driver what she'd found. She told him that if she wasn't out in five minutes to call the cops. She hurried back in, picked up a heavy vase in the foyer and moved cautiously forward, leaving the front door open just in case.

It took less than five minutes for her to discover that the place was empty. She leaned out the front window of the upstairs bedroom and waved to the cabbie that all was okay. Melanie ducked back inside and started doing a more thorough search. She knew that her father kept two safes in the house. One was in the bedroom and the other was behind a panel in the garage; both had been undisturbed. Nor did it appear that anything of value had been taken.

That left only one possibility. Whoever had broken in had been searching for something other than valuables. And whoever it was had her dad's alarm code.

She went into her dad's study and looked around. She knew this was where he kept items from work, although she was also aware that her father did not routinely leave any important items lying around. She turned on the light, bent down and started going through the piles of papers on the floor. Thirty minutes later she had found only one thing of interest. It was a list with names on it. She didn't recognize any of them, but one did capture her attention.

Alex Ford was a Secret Service agent working out of the WFO. Why he was on a list in her father's house she didn't know. But she did know one thing: she was going to call him and find out if he knew anything about what her father was involved in.

She ran back out to the cab after locking the door and resetting the alarm. As she sat back breathless in the taxi she had the sickening feeling that her father's "job" had finally come back to bite him. Hard.

CHAPTER

55

Alex Ford was sitting in his kitchen working his way slowly through a bowl of soup and a beer. He had been largely going through the motions at work since his last meeting with the Camel Club, or what was left of it. He'd driven past the cottage at Mt. Zion Cemetery in the hopes that Annabelle might have returned. He'd tried to call Reuben several times without success. And Caleb had been absent from the library. Unexpected personal issues, he'd been told when he called for him there.

He knew what they were up to. Working together to try and save Oliver. And a big part of him hoped they were successful.

When the phone rang he groaned. It was probably his boss trying to scrounge up some overtime drones to pull some low-level protection duty. Well, tonight he was busy.

He had TiVo reruns to catch and tomato soup to finish and beers to pour down his throat.

"Hello?"

It *was* his boss, but he wasn't looking for overtime. He told Alex that he would be receiving visitors any moment now. And that he was to cooperate fully with them.

"Who are they?"

But the man had already hung up.

The knock on the door came barely thirty seconds later, which told Alex that his boss was in communication with his "visitors" and had just given them the all-clear. He poured the rest of his beer down the kitchen sink, tucked in his shirt, quickly adjusted his tie and opened the door.

Alex was six-three but the white-haired, bony-faced fellow facing him had him by at least two inches.

"Agent Ford, my name is Macklin Hayes. I'd like to have a word with you."

Alex stepped back and motioned the man in, peering behind him to see if he was alone. There wasn't anybody else, but Alex knew enough about Hayes to understand that the man went nowhere by himself. He closed the door and indicated a chair for Hayes to sit in.

"Thank you."

Alex plopped down across from him and tried to appear nonchalant.

"What can I do for you, sir?"

"I believe that one of my subordinates, Joe Knox, came to see you about a certain matter?"

Alex nodded. "He did. Had some questions about someone I knew."

"John Carr?"

"He asked about Carr, but I don't know anyone by that name."

"Oliver Stone then? You do know the man calling himself Oliver Stone?"

"Most Secret Service agents who've pulled White House protection duty do."

"But you were closer than most?"

Alex shrugged. "I'd call him an acquaintance."

"You were far more than an acquaintance. And you're going to tell me everything that you knew about his plans to assassinate Carter Gray and Senator Simpson. And whether you helped him to escape. At worst that makes you a coconspirator. At best, an accessory before and after. In a matter as grave as this one, either one gets you put away for life."

Well, the man doesn't waste any time, does he? "I don't know what the hell you're talking about."

Hayes drew a slip of paper from his coat and glanced at it. "Nearly twenty years in the Service, good record. You were the one guarding the president in Pennsylvania when he got kidnapped."

"I was the only one left standing."

"So you were there when he disappeared. Did you have anything to do with his reappearance? And more to the point, did your friend Stone?"

"Again, I—"

Hayes didn't let him finish. "Ever heard of Murder Mountain? A vanished CIA agent named Tom Hemingway? A piece of evidence that your friend Stone held over Carter Gray? Or a former Russian spy named Lesya?"

Alex, of course, knew about all of these things, but

stayed silent because what could he possibly say that would do him any good?

"I'll take that as a yes."

"Oliver helped break up a spy ring operating in D.C. It involved one of your employees. Maybe you heard of it? He received a commendation from the FBI director."

"Wonderful for him, but I doubt that will carry much weight when he's caught and prosecuted for two murders."

"What exactly do you want from me?"

"I want to know what Knox asked you, and I want to know what you told him."

"Can't you just ask him yourself? I'm sure he has it down in some nice, neat report and—" Alex stopped. "Do you not know where Agent Knox is?"

"I'm not here to answer questions, merely to ask them. I believe you received a phone call from a superior at the Secret Service telling you to cooperate fully."

Alex spent the next two minutes telling Hayes what he and Knox had discussed.

"That's all?" Hayes said in a clearly disappointed tone. "I must have Knox go through an interrogation refresher course."

"He said he'd be coming back around to ask more questions. I'll be sure to tell him you're looking for him," Alex said, getting in a subtle jab.

Hayes rose. "One piece of advice. If I find that any of what you've told me tonight is untrue, or if I discover that you withheld anything of importance from me, you can catch up on your solitary confinement skills at the Castle."

"The Castle? That's the military prison at Leavenworth. I'm not military."

"Actually, it's also for prisoners convicted of national security crimes. But to more directly answer your question, you're anything I want you to be."

As soon as the door closed behind him, Alex realized he'd been holding his breath. He let it out with a gush and stood up on wobbly legs. He might as well have banded with the Camel Club to help find Oliver since it looked like he was headed to prison anyway.

The phone rang again. It was probably his boss telling him he hadn't been particularly cooperative and how did suspension without pay sound?

But he was wrong. The caller ID readout surprised him.

"Agent Ford? My name is Melanie Knox. My father is Joe Knox. Someone broke into his house and I can't get hold of him. The only thing I found was a list with your name on it."

"When's the last time you heard from him?" She told him. "I spoke to him before that. I haven't heard from him since. It could be a burglary. You should call the cops."

"Nothing of value was stolen. The two safes he had weren't even touched."

"I'm not sure what I can do about it."

"What did he talk to you about?"

"I'm afraid I can't disclose that."

"Agent Ford, I am really worried about my dad. The last time I talked to him he sounded, well, he sounded like maybe he was talking to me for the last time. I really think he might be in trouble."

Maybe that was why he'd gotten the visit from Hayes.

His faithful dog had gone off the scent and the old man was operating blind. "When you talked to him did he give you any indication of where he might be?"

"He said something about being west of here, only a little more rural. I joked about terrorists in the hollers. And he said you just never knew."

"This isn't really my bailiwick, Ms. Knox."

"I'm a lawyer in private practice with lots of connections, and while my dad has never mentioned what he actually does for the government, I know it's not some State Department crap, that's just a cover. Can you at least confirm that? Please?"

Alex hesitated, but the pleading sound in her voice finally got to him. "As best I can figure he was doing investigative work for the CIA, or at least in connection with them somehow."

"Over something critical?"

"Critical enough. He's trying to find somebody who doesn't want to be found."

"Can this person be dangerous?"

"Most people who don't want to be found are dangerous."

He thought he could hear a groan from her. "What should I do?" she said. "My mom's dead. My brother's in the Marines in Iraq. What should I do, Agent Ford? I don't know anybody else to call."

Alex sat there staring off. It was as though his nearly twenty years in the Service had simply disappeared from his memory. If Hayes had had his way, that would be more true than not. So why sit here waiting for the nuke to hit him in the head?

"Give me a number where I can reach you anytime. I'll poke around and see what I can find."

"Oh, God, thank you so much."

"I can't promise that if I find out anything it'll be what you want to hear."

"Agent Ford, I know you don't know my father, but if you were in trouble there wouldn't be anybody else you'd want covering your back more than Joe Knox. He's as straight as they come. I hope that means something to you."

"It does," Alex said quietly.

CHAPTER

56

LATER THAT NIGHT Stone sat up in his hospital bed staring at the wall opposite. He checked his watch and then slipped open the nightstand next to his bed and pulled out Danny's phone. He called Abby first and Tyree next. Abby was working at the restaurant and Tyree was out in the field trying to track down Lonnie Bruback, who, he said, seemed to have disappeared. They had found nothing in Willie's trailer other than a couple of torn-apart propane tanks and the remnants of the cookstove, he told Stone.

"I've got a bomb squad guy from the Virginia State Police coming to examine the scene. I know you don't want to hear this, but it might have been an accident. Willie was gone, maybe the propane was leaking and Bob lit a cigarette when Willie came through the door, and boom."

"If the propane was leaking, it would have exploded

before then. I saw Shirley there like I told you and she *was* smoking a cigarette. And you would think Bob would've smelled the propane. The odor they put into the gas is pretty pungent for that very reason."

"I know. But why would they want to kill Willie so badly?" Tyree asked. "First an overdose and now a bomb?"

"He knew Debby didn't kill herself. He was going to keep making noise until the truth came out. Somebody obviously didn't like that."

"But now that they killed him we know there's something going on," Tyree pointed out.

"But these people are good and we have no proof that a crime's even been committed. So in their eyes it's better."

"Well, I'm not giving up until I get to the bottom of this."

"Tyree, everybody needs to watch their back here, and that includes you."

"I hear you."

Stone clicked off and stared down at the phone. Danny had a late-model Verizon cell phone with all the bells and whistles, including e-mail. Stone had never been into mail that didn't involve pen and paper. He scrolled down Danny's contact list. The names there were mostly female. He'd even made annotations by each entry indicating the lady's strong suits, and each contact also came with a digital photo of the woman. Several of the pictures would have qualified as pornography, at least in Stone's estimation.

He shook his head. Danny needed to seriously upgrade the quality of his female companions.

He looked outside. It was dark. He slowly eased himself from the bed. He was pretty stiff and sore but the more he moved around, the better he felt. His butt was already numb from lying in the damn bed all those hours.

He walked out of the room and over to the nurses' station. After being chastised for being out of bed, he asked and was told where Danny's room was.

He walked down that hall and saw a man sitting outside of Danny's room. When Stone approached the man stood. "Can I help you?"

"You the deputy Tyree put on Danny?"

"That's right. Wait a minute, you're that Ben fellow, aren't you?"

"Yes. I wanted to see Danny?"

"Seeing as how you saved his life, sure, go on in."

When Stone popped his head in, Danny was sitting up in bed, his face red and his eyes puffy slits.

"Danny? Can I come in?"

He looked over at Stone. He didn't say anything but waved him in with a feeble sweep of his hand.

Stone pulled up a chair and sat down. "I'm really sorry about Willie."

Danny didn't look at him but kept his gaze on the pillow he held over his midsection. When he did speak his voice was heavy and slow. The meds, Stone thought.

"He didn't deserve to die that way."

"Nobody does."

Danny glared at him. "Some people do."

"I guess you're right. Maybe some people do."

"He never hurt anybody, you know that?"

"I know."

"And Bob. I mean he's a damn old man. And they blew him up too?"

"Who blew him up, Danny? Who are we talking about?"

Danny glanced at Stone. "Why ask me?"

"Why'd you leave Divine?"

"Fresh start, like I told you."

"And why'd you come back?"

"My business."

"You want to tell me about Debby Randolph?"

"What's to tell? She was Willie's girl. He loved her, man. They were going to get married."

"So you knew about that?"

Danny nodded absently. "I was all over his case to get off the drugs. Mine work was killing him. He was in pain, okay, I get it. But I saw what the shit did to my old man. I didn't want that happening to Willie. And then Debby came along and she got him back on the right track, you know what I mean? He was doing all right. Called me up out of the blue, told me he was thinking about proposing. Asked me what I thought. Part of me wanted to say, 'No man, run the other way, you're too young. We got stuff to do. Girls to bed.' But deep down, I was jealous, man. I got pieces of meat on my plate. He had a woman who loved him."

"So what'd you end up telling him?"

"I told him to go for it. I knew Debby. She was a great gal. And great for him. He asked me to be his best man."

"Sounds like you two had patched up your differences."

"We never had any real differences. It was just crap really."

Danny fell silent and Stone sat back in his chair and watched him for a while as the darkness fell more heavily outside.

"I saw you crying over Debby's grave. You want to tell me about that?"

Danny's head snapped up. "Nothing to tell. I was sorry she was dead. And I knew Willie was all busted up about it."

"You know who killed her, don't you?"

"If I did I would've told Tyree, wouldn't I?"

"Would you?"

"I'm tired, man. Going to sleep."

"You sure you don't want to tell me?"

"Sure as I'm lying here doing nothing."

Stone returned to his room but did not get back in the bed. Something was gnawing at him. Something he'd seen, heard or maybe both. Something that just did not add up.

He absently pulled out Danny's phone. He went through the contact list again, to see if anyone on there would provide him with a clue and explain why Danny refused to tell him what had happened. Yet nothing stuck out.

He continued pressing buttons, pushing the phone's memory into advanced fields of content. Then he stopped as the screen came up with only one name and phone number on it. *Tyree*. Yet the phone number next to the name was not the one Stone knew for the lawman. He punched it in. A few rings later a voice answered.

"Danny?" the man said.

Stone immediately clicked off. It was Tyree. He'd recognized the voice. Why would Danny have the man's name and a different phone number hidden in his phone's memory? And if this number was to be a secret, why not just memorize it? Why input it where someone like Stone could find it? He looked back at the regular contact list. Even on here he saw the numbers for Abby's house, the restaurant, numbers Danny should have easily remembered. On impulse he called Abby and told her about his conversation with Danny, though he didn't tell her about finding Tyree's number on her son's phone.

"Abby, does Danny have trouble remembering numbers?"

"Ever since high school. Doctors said it was from the concussions he got playing ball. I told him to stop playing but he loved it too much. Killed him when his knee wouldn't let him play for Tech. Why do you want to know?"

"Just sitting here with too much time on my hands. Thanks."

He clicked off and then heard a rumbling sound coming from down the hall and glanced over in time to see an orderly passing by with a load of boxes. That ordinary sight produced an extraordinary reaction in Stone.

It came together in a neat little box all its own.

Sixty, not eighty boxes. Black dirt instead of the normal red clay. And miners who left town to get their methadone pop long before the crack of dawn.

It seemed like a spontaneous revelation, but it really wasn't, Stone knew. This stuff had been swirling around in his subconscious for a long time now. And it had finally percolated to the surface.

He grabbed his bag from the closet and quickly changed into clean clothes.

"Come on, let it be there," he said to himself as he

searched the bag some more. He remembered putting it in there.

His hands finally closed around the gun Abby had loaned him. He stuffed it in his waistband and covered the bulge with his shirt. A moment later he peered out the door. When the nurses' station was empty he bolted down the hall. When the nurses came that night to give him his meds they would find his room vacant.

He had no way of knowing that they would find the very same thing in Danny's room. An hour earlier, the young man had juked his guard and made his escape.

CHAPTER

57

KNOX ROLLED INTO DIVINE not really knowing what to expect. It was late and it was dark and hardly a light burned on the town's main street. He drove down the road looking to the left and right, although he doubted he'd see John Carr loitering on the corner awaiting his arrival. He passed a restaurant named Rita's. There was a courthouse and jail, both seemingly deserted at this hour. Knox contemplated whether to wake up the local constabulary to help him in his quest, but he'd found the other town cops to be useless at best. He would try a different approach this time.

He turned off the main drag and headed east, at least according to his vehicle's compass. Knox's own internal direction monitor had long since given up trying to keep track of his heading after meandering through the boxy Appalachians all this time.

He slowed the truck when he saw what looked to be the remains of a trailer home. At first he thought it must have been a tornado passing through that had destroyed the place, but the trees and earth around it had not been disturbed by a twister's route. He stopped the truck, got out and inspected the site.

The blackened and jagged remains and the diameter of the debris field told him that an explosion of some kind was the cause. That was a little unusual. Of course it didn't mean that John Carr was in the vicinity, but it was at least something out of the ordinary.

He did a circle of the downtown area and drove back through. That's when he spotted the little rooming house. He parked down the street from the entrance and did a slow walk up, keeping his gaze alert for any sign of Carr.

He knocked on the door and kept tapping for another five minutes until he heard the steady if unhurried footfalls heading his way.

The door opened and the little old man with tufts of white hair standing on the other side of the threshold looked up crossly at him. "Do you know what time it is, young man?"

Knox hadn't been called a young man in at least twenty years. He hid his smile and said, "I apologize. But I got in a lot later than I thought I would."

"You mean you were *heading* to Divine?" the old man said incredulously.

"Is there a law against that?" Knox said, now smiling broadly and, he hoped, disarmingly.

"What do you want?" the man said gruffly.

So much for disarming. "Right now, a place to sleep, Mr. . . . ?"

"Just call me Bernie. Sorry, but I'm all booked up."

Knox looked over his shoulder. "This the high season in Divine?"

"I've only got two rooms to let."

"I see. Thing is, I was supposed to meet a buddy of mine up here. Maybe you've seen him, tall, lean guy around sixty with close-cropped white hair."

"Oh, you mean Ben? He's got one of the rooms, but he's not there right now."

"Any idea where he is?"

"Over at the hospital?"

"What's he doing there? Did he get hurt?"

"Almost got his butt blown up. Killed Bob and Willie Coombs, and your buddy came real close to meeting his maker."

Knox kept his voice calm and level. "So where is this hospital? I want to go see if he's okay."

"Oh, he's okay. We're all glad of that. Ben's a real hero."

"How's that?"

"Helped a couple of our own. Danny Riker when he got in trouble on the train. And Willie Coombs when he almost died on drugs. Ben saved 'em both. Right good fellow. And then Danny got attacked here in town. And Ben saved him again. Beat up three guys, or so I heard."

"Wow, that sounds like Ben all right. He was always in the middle of all the action. I'll give him your best when I see him at the hospital. And where was that again?"

Bernie told him. "But visiting hours are long over."

"I'll try to talk my way in. But if I can't, anybody else around here that can help me?"

"You can try Abby Riker out at her place, Midsummer's Farm." Bernie gave him directions. "From what I heard she and Ben got real tight."

Knox slipped a twenty into the old gent's hand when they shook.

"You're welcome to sleep in the front room," Bernie said, indicating the space behind him.

"Thanks, I might take you up on that."

He walked back to his truck trying to keep his nerves steady. He climbed in the rig, fired it up and pulled away. As he steered one-handed along the winding country road, he used his free hand to flip open the glove box. He pulled out his nine-millimeter pistol and laid it on the seat next to him.

John Carr here I come.

CHAPTER

58

Annabelle looked down at her vibrating phone. "Who would be calling me in the middle of the night?"

"Maybe it's Reuben?" said Caleb as he drove along.

"No. I don't recognize the number." She flipped open the phone.

"Hello?"

"Annabelle? How's it going?"

She snapped, "What the hell do you want?"

Alex Ford said pleasantly, "It's nice to hear your voice too."

"I'm a little busy, Alex."

"I'm sure you are."

"Wait a minute. Where are you calling from? I didn't recognize the number."

"A payphone."

"Why a payphone?"

"Because I'm pretty sure my home, cell and office phones are being tapped."

"And why is that?" she said slowly. "Is Knox on your case still?"

"That's why I'm calling. I got a frantic phone call from Knox's daughter, Melanie. She's a lawyer in D.C. Her dad's disappeared."

"No he hasn't. He's after Oliver and we're after Knox."

"And where is all this taking place?"

"In the boondocks of southwest Virginia. So you can tell little Melanie that her daddy is just fine. For now at least."

"That's not all. His house was turned over by someone looking for something, and I'm not talking your random burglary. And on top of that I had a visitor, a man named Macklin Hayes."

"Doesn't ring a bell."

"No reason it should. He's a former army three-star who's now on the intelligence side. His rep is like a Carter Gray only more sinister and evil. He's also Knox's boss and he doesn't know where his guy is, which means Knox is roaming free."

"Why would he be doing that?"

"He might if he found out something that made him uncomfortable about what was really going on with all this. I don't think Knox is a killer. He's a tracker, and if Hayes put him on Oliver, he must be the best they have on that score. It seems clear that when Knox finds Oliver, he was to call in Hayes' heavy artillery to finish the job."

"What would Knox have found that would make him start freelancing?"

"No clue. How close are you to finding Oliver?"

"Hard to say. We narrowed it down to four towns up here—at least we think that's the case. We've cleared two of them and we're heading to a third now."

"Caleb and Reuben with you?"

"Of course. We're the Camel Club, remember?"

"Or what's left of it."

"Yeah, we seem to be dropping members like flies in a jar. Of course some chose to leave, others had no choice."

"Annabelle, I'm trying to help here, okay? I'm taking a big risk just talking to you about this."

"Nobody's asking you to take any risk, Alex. Just go back to your nice, safe federal job."

"What is it about you that pisses me off so much?"

"My girlish personality?"

"Well, keep this in mind, *girly*. If Knox is on his own then in Hayes' eyes he's become a target just like Oliver. Hayes will take them both out and anybody else who's standing around."

"The three of us are willing to take that risk."

"I know *you* are, but have you bothered to ask the other two?"

"I don't have to ask. The fact that they're with me right now is all the answer I need. Unlike some people."

Caleb glanced nervously over at Annabelle.

"Okay, just don't say I didn't warn you."

"Yeah, thanks for all your help." She clicked off and threw the phone down.

"I take it the conversation didn't go all that well," Caleb said.

"You can take it that way, yeah."

"So what did he say?"

"Hang on a minute. There's Reuben."

The big fellow was waving to them from the side of the dark road. They pulled over and in a few minutes had loaded the motorcycle into the back of the van. As they resumed driving Annabelle filled them both in on what Alex had told her. At the mention of Hayes' name Reuben's face turned a shade paler.

"Macklin Hayes?"

"Yeah," she said. "Do you know him?"

Reuben nodded. "I served under him at DIA. Also did some fieldwork for him in certain parts of the world, where the good general had a well-deserved reputation of leaving his men out to drown when things went to hell. I happened to be one of his little sacrifices. But no dirt ever splashed on him. Which is why the asshole sits where he does today."

"Well, he's apparently after Oliver *and* Knox now."

"So Hayes' plan *is* to take out Oliver then?" Reuben said slowly.

"But we're ahead of the dude on that score," said Annabelle, noting the nervous look on Reuben's face. "And since he screwed you this would be a perfect way to settle things, Reuben," she added.

"You don't settle things with a guy like Macklin Hayes, Annabelle," he said. "He's got an army behind him and, while the man's heart is as black as they come, he's also smart and cagey as hell. I've never known him to lose at anything."

"Reuben, we can beat this guy."

Caleb said, "But we really don't know if Knox is on the run from Hayes. That's just Alex's opinion. They could still be working this thing together. Maybe Hayes' visit to Alex was a ruse."

"That makes no sense, Caleb," Annabelle snapped.

"It makes as much sense as us running around the country trying to find Oliver while the CIA is too. I mean, do we actually think we can beat them at this? And what if we do find Oliver first? Then what? We just make him disappear without a trace with all those people looking for him? We're not experts at that."

"I am," Annabelle retorted.

"Fine, *you* are. I'm not. So we make Oliver disappear. Then what? I go back to my job at the library after being inexplicably absent? You don't think they won't be all over me?" He looked over at Reuben. "And if they water-board me, I'll spill my guts. I'm not naïve enough to believe that I can withstand that crap. And then I go to prison for the rest of my life. Great!"

"If that's what you thought, why the hell did you even come with me?" Annabelle said hotly.

Reuben answered, "We came because we care about Oliver and we wanted to help him."

"And you've changed your mind?" she said.

"It's not that simple, Annabelle."

She said fiercely, "Sure it is, Reuben. The question hasn't changed. So your answer must have." She looked between him and Caleb. "So what now? You two want to give up? Go back to town? Fine, go! Get the hell out of here. It's not like I need you."

Reuben and Caleb glanced guiltily at each other.

"Pull over the van, Caleb," she said. "I want out of here."

"Annabelle, just calm down," Reuben said in a slightly raised voice.

"No, I won't. I can't believe that you two and Alex are such wimps that—"

Reuben roared, "Shut the hell up!"

Annabelle looked as though he'd popped her in the mouth.

Reuben stared at her, his eyes those of a man barely in control of his anger. "I fought in wars for my country. I got my ass shot up for my country. I've almost died about twelve times following Oliver on his little adventures. I love him like a brother and he was there for me when I didn't have anybody else. I walked into a death chamber called Murder Mountain with him and we almost didn't walk back out alive. And you know who was right there beside us? Alex Ford. He put his career right on the line when he could've just walked. And he also got his ass shot up, stood up to a team of freaking Korean ninjas looking to slit our throats, took a round for the president of the United States and pretty much single-handedly got us out of that hellhole." He glanced over at Caleb. "And this guy's been kidnapped, knocked out, almost asphyxiated, nearly blown up and saved me and Oliver's ass on several different occasions. And we both had to deal with one of our closest friends in the world getting blown away. And all we did was hold up our heads and try to keep going. And now we're out here in the middle of frigging nowhere trying to keep Oliver alive while an asshole that would make Charlie Manson look like a soccer mom is breathing down our backs. So if that's your definition of a wimp, then we're wimps with a capital W, lady."

For the next minute all that could be heard in the

confines of the van was the heavy breathing of Reuben Rhodes.

Annabelle stared at him, a series of emotions competing on her features until one finally won out.

"I'm an idiot, Reuben. I'm sorry. I'm really sorry."

"Yeah, well. Hell." Red-faced, he looked down at the floorboard and punched the seat with one of his massive fists.

Before Annabelle could say anything, Caleb spoke up. "Maybe we should keep going."

A red-eyed Reuben looked over at him and smiled grimly. "Won't be the first time. Or hopefully the last."

Annabelle reached out and took each man's hand in one of hers. "I just realized something," she said.

"What's that?" Caleb asked.

"That I should probably keep my big fat mouth shut. I've been acting like I'm the leader here, but I'm not even a full member of the Camel Club yet. I haven't earned it."

"You're getting there," said Reuben, giving her a quick smile.

She squeezed their hands and gave him a smile back.

Reuben said, "So what's the next town on the list?"

Caleb looked at the sheet. "Divine."

CHAPTER

59

STONE CROUCHED LOW with his pistol out. He didn't like doing this alone, but with Tyree now implicated in whatever was going on here, he didn't have many options for assistance. The trucks were already lining up. The methadone pop brigade. Rusty trucks and rustier miners looking for their joy juice. Only they wouldn't find it here. The men came out of the old barn at the rear of Abby Riker's property carrying large boxes. They were loaded in the back of each truck with a tarp over them. After that, the drivers pulled off.

Stone mentally kicked himself for not realizing the truth sooner. The very first night he'd arrived in town and seen this caravan of miners heading to the methadone clinic, Danny had told him that they got up this early because they had to get back in time to start the seven a.m. shift at the mines. Yet it was only a two-hour round trip from the clinic back here. Stone had made the trip himself to the hospital several times. He'd actually seen the men roll into the methadone clinic at nearly five in the morning.

At the courthouse he'd seen the manifest for the delivery of legal documents. It had listed eighty boxes, but there had only been sixty there. Six high, ten across. That had meant nothing to him until he'd thought of the discrepancy in time with the miners going to and from the clinic. At least three extra hours, missing boxes and one more thing.

He glanced at the grass in front of the barn. He'd seen it while he was here working, yet had really thought nothing of it. The carpet of grass was worn down and blackened, blackened by the filthy tires of the coal miners' trucks as they came here to pick up their cargo. Just like the road in front of the snake-filled mine from which he'd barely escaped. Black dirt, black grass; he should have seen it sooner.

So the big question was, what was in the boxes?

After connecting all the dots Stone thought he knew the answer to this too. But would he get the chance to find out for sure?

There was one truck left. The boxes were put in the cargo bed. Right before he tied the tarp over them, the driver opened one of the boxes and pulled out what looked to be a small black bag. Stone had seen each of the other drivers do the same thing. He closed the box and was about to secure the tarp when one of the other men who'd been helping load the boxes called to him. They went into the barn together.

Stone slid his pistol in his waistband and crept out of

the woods, keeping as low to the ground as he could. There was a bright full moon that had made the night far less dark than usual. He reached the truck, glancing at the barn as he did so. He moved the tarp away and slowly slid a box toward him. Fortunately it wasn't taped shut, just closed up. He opened it and peered in.

He'd been right. Clear baggies filled with what looked to be prescription drugs. Probably in the oxycodone family. Two hundred bucks a pill on the street, Willie had said. Based on that he was looking at millions of dollars in this box alone.

And the *black* baggies the druggie miners had taken were probably their payment for driving the boxes to what was probably the next step in the pipeline, with the final destination being some major urban area on the East Coast. It was pretty powerful leverage when all your employees were addicts. They'd do whatever you told them to get the pain meds they couldn't otherwise afford. It was also pretty damn heartless—not surprising with drug dealers.

With the sixth sense that he possessed, Stone reacted to the presence he suddenly felt behind him. Yet it was still a fraction of a second too late.

The gun muzzle was next to his head and Stone heard the man say, "You move, you die."

Stone could feel the man's other hand expertly pat him. His gun was yanked out of his pants, dropped to the dirt and kicked under the truck.

Stone didn't move. He just stood there with a baggie of pills clutched in one hand.

The man said, "What the hell is that?"

"Illegal prescription drugs," Stone said, confused. "Why, who the hell are you?"

"Joe Knox. Central Intelligence. And you're John Carr."

Stone didn't know whether to feel a bit of relief that it was the CIA who'd caught up to him and not the drug runners. However, the end result might not be all that different. "Well, Mr. Knox, you just walked into a drug transport going down."

"What?"

"I suggest we carry on this conversation somewhere else." Stone pointed to the men coming out of the barn.

"Hey!" one of them screamed when they saw the pair next to the truck. Shotguns and pistols appeared in the men's hands even as other men rushed out of the barn to join them.

"Run, Knox!"

Using the truck as a shield, Knox and Stone sprinted off, hurtling into the woods. The men raced after them, taking aim with their weapons.

Running next to Stone, Knox snapped, "What the hell is going on?"

"Your timing was as bad as my selection of towns to hide out in." Stone glanced behind them. "Look out." He grabbed Knox by the sleeve and pulled him off the path they were on. A moment later a shotgun blast ripped the limb off a tree that Knox had been next to.

Knox pointed his pistol over his head and fired four shots in a wide swath to buy them some time. The only thing it bought was a barrage of bullets, one of which burned a crease in Knox's right arm but didn't go in.

"Damn it!" He clutched his wounded limb but kept running.

In a flash Stone grabbed the pistol from his hand, whirled around and emptied the clip at the men coming for them. He hit one of them and placed his shots so well that the other pursuers were forced to take cover.

Stone said, "This way, quick!"

They cut across a gulley, hit the asphalt road, crossed it in three leaps and plunged into the woods on the other side.

"How's the arm?"

"I've had worse."

"Got another clip?" Stone asked.

Knox dug in his pocket and flipped it to him. "Damn sorry I took your gun now."

"Me too." Stone slapped the ammo clip in and held the gun ready.

"We can't outrun them," Knox said, panting, even as he nervously eyed the gun in Stone's hand.

"No, we can't. They look a lot younger than we are."

"You're a damn good shot."

"I don't think it'll matter this time."

"You are John Carr, aren't you?"

"He's dead."

"I'll take that as a yes."

Another bullet blast came at them, forcing them to turn east. They raced up a slope, both men's breaths coming in gasps now even as they slowed. Stone slipped on some mud and fell down. Knox stooped and helped him up.

They were nearly at the top of the hill.

Stone said, "Get behind that tree, Knox. We've got some high ground here and I don't want to waste it."

Knox took cover and watched as Stone nimbly scaled an oak, shimmied out onto a thick branch, took aim and when the first man appeared out of the brush he opened fire. The man yelled out and went down. Two other men appeared behind him. When they raised their weapons, Stone shot one of them in the leg. A moment later a barrage of gunfire erupted from the woods. Stone returned it, spraying shots all across the front of the tree line. He jumped to the ground, rejoined Knox and handed him back the gun.

Knox looked surprised. "You do understand that I'm here to arrest you for the murders of Carter Gray and Senator Simpson?"

"Yeah, I do."

"So why are you giving me back my gun?"

"Because it's empty."

They ran hard, or as hard as two middle-aged men could manage over hilly terrain.

Knox said, "Shit!"

Up ahead they heard the men coming.

"They outflanked us," Stone gasped.

They stopped running as four men with shotguns broke through the brush and took aim. Behind them four more men stood, panting, guns fixed on them.

Knox held his pistol up in a surrender position. "Would it make a difference if I told you I'm a federal agent with a shitload of backup heading your way?"

One of the men placed a shot that came within an inch of taking off Knox's right ear.

"That answer your question?" the shooter said. "Now put your gun down real slow."

For a number of reasons Stone had half expected to see Tyree standing there, but he didn't recognize this guy.

"I'm just here to take this man into custody," Knox said, indicating Stone. "I don't give a damn what else is going on."

"Right, and then we just go about our business and trust you and your friend to keep quiet. Drop the gun, I ain't asking again."

Knox bent down and placed his pistol on the ground. One of the men stepped forward and pocketed it along with his wallet and cell phone. They did the same with Stone.

The man who'd fired the shot flipped open the wallet and checked the ID. He looked up at Knox and slowly shook his head in disbelief. He spoke into a walkie-talkie.

"We got a big problem down here."

After a minute or so of conversation the man put the walkie-talkie away on a holder on his belt.

"Do we kill 'em here?" one man asked.

"No, we don't kill 'em here," he snapped. "We got to get this figured out." He motioned to his men. "Tie 'em up."

They shot forward and expertly bound Knox and Stone together. They carried the pair back to the road, where they were laid facedown in the cargo bed of a pickup truck. It drove off while the other men piled into other vehicles that had pulled up behind the truck.

Five minutes later the truck raced off the road and into a clearing, where it spun to a stop in a swirl of dirt and ripped-up grass.

Stone heard it before Knox did.

"Chopper."

It landed next to the truck, its prop wash so strong that, roped together as they were, Stone and Knox had a hard time keeping their balance as they were pulled out of the truck and loaded into the aircraft. Two armed men climbed in with them and the chopper lifted off.

"Where are we going?" Knox said.

When the men didn't answer he looked over at Stone. "Any ideas?"

Stone glanced around the interior of the chopper. He'd only seen one other chopper up here before. "I think we're going to Dead Rock."

"What the hell is Dead Rock?"

Stone looked out the window. "That."

Knox crowded next to him and gazed down at the lights of the prison.

"Supermax prison," Stone volunteered.

"Why the hell are drug runners taking us to a super—" Knox broke off, his face ashen. "We're screwed."

"Yes, we are."

CHAPTER

60

AS THE VAN DRIFTED down the street early the next morning, Annabelle, Caleb and Reuben eyed the people walking by on the sidewalks; several of them stared back with suspicion.

"Not a very welcoming lot, are they?" said Caleb.

"Why should they be?" growled Reuben. "They don't know who we are or what we want. All they know is that we're not from here."

Annabelle nodded thoughtfully. "We'll have to tread carefully."

"We may not have time to tread carefully," Reuben pointed out. "Knox had a big head start. He might have already gotten to Oliver for all we know."

"There's an obvious starting place," Caleb pointed out.

The three of them stared at the sheriff's office and jail next to the courthouse.

"Stop the van, Caleb," said Annabelle. "I'll go in."

"You want some backup?" Reuben wanted to know.

"Not now. We need to keep something in reserve in case things go to hell."

"How are you going to play it?" Caleb asked. "FBI or wronged woman?"

"Neither. New angle."

She checked her face and hair in the rearview mirror, slid open the door and climbed out.

"If I'm not back in ten minutes, pull off and I'll meet you at that end of the street."

"What if you don't come out at all?" asked Reuben.

"Then assume I blew it, just start driving and don't stop."

She slid the door closed and walked into the building.

"Hello?" she called out. "Hello?"

A door opened and Lincoln Tyree stepped into the small waiting area.

"Can I help you, ma'am?"

Annabelle stared up at the tall lawman resplendent in his crisply starched uniform and highly polished boots with a leading man's jaw and brooding eyes.

"I sure hope so. I'm looking for someone." She drew a photo out of her pocket and showed it to him. "Have you seen him?"

Tyree studied the photo of Oliver Stone but made no immediate reaction. "Why don't you step on in here?" He held open his office door.

Annabelle hesitated. "I just need to know if you've seen him."

"And I need to know why you're looking for him."

"So you have seen him?"

He indicated the open door.

Annabelle shrugged and walked past him and into the office. There was another man seated there. He was in a seersucker suit with a red bow tie.

"This here is Charlie Trimble, runs the local paper."

Trimble shook Annabelle's hand.

Tyree closed the door and motioned for her to sit. He plopped behind his meticulous desk, still clutching the picture.

"Now why don't you tell me what this is all about," said Tyree.

"This is sort of confidential," she said, looking at Trimble. "No offense, but I'd like to speak to the sheriff in private."

Trimble got up. "We can talk more later, Sheriff." He glanced over at the photo. From this angle he could see it was the man he knew as Ben. "Maybe you and I can talk later too, ma'am."

Once he'd left Annabelle said, "My name is Susan Hunter. Here's my ID." She handed him across a professionally done and totally fake driver's license. "The man in the photo is my father. He might go by Oliver or John, or maybe another name."

"Why so many names?" asked Tyree as he studied the license before handing it back.

"My father worked for the government many years ago. He left under somewhat unusual circumstances. Ever since then he's sort of been on the run."

"Unusual circumstances? Is he a criminal?"

"No, these unusual circumstances are that enemies of this country are looking to kill him because of what he did to them."

"Enemies? Like who?"

"Like governments, the names of which you would recognize. I don't claim to know the whole story, only that between the ages of six and when I started college, we moved fourteen times. Different names, histories, jobs were lined up for my parents, we had handlers."

"Then y'all were sorta like in witness protection?"

"Sort of, yes. My dad was a real American hero who did incredibly dangerous work for his country. That work came with a price, though. We've been paying that price for a long time."

Tyree rubbed his chin. "That might explain a lot."

Annabelle leaned forward eagerly. "So he has been here?"

He leaned back in his chair. "He was, yes. Called himself Ben, Ben Thomas. How'd you track him up here?"

"Something he managed to send me, a coded message. But it hasn't been easy. I've been to just about every small town in the general vicinity. I was running out of hope."

"Well, like I said, he was here, but he's not here now."

"Where did he go?"

"He was in the hospital the last time I saw him."

"Hospital? Was he hurt?"

"Got himself nearly blown up. He was okay, though. I went by the hospital early this morning to see him but he was gone."

"Gone voluntarily?"

"I don't know the answer to that."

"You said he was nearly blown up?"

"We've had some strange things happening here. Haven't gotten my arms around it. Your dad was helping me. And he's not the only one missing. Fellow named

Danny Riker was at that hospital too. Had a guard posted to watch him because some folks tried to kill him. But Danny slipped by my guy and he's gone too."

"And you have no idea where my father might be?"

"No ma'am, I don't. Wish I did. I'm a one-man police force in over my head. But if he was in protection why is he on the run now?"

"A few weeks ago an attempt was made on my father's life. He made sure I was okay and then he left. The way the attempt came I believe he thought it was an inside job."

"Well, if he was looking to hide out here and get a little peace and quiet, he was sorely mistaken."

"What are you talking about?"

Tyree took a few minutes to sketch out what had happened in Divine since Stone arrived there.

Annabelle sat back, thinking fast. She didn't want to get bogged down in whatever was happening in Divine. Yet if these events were connected to Oliver's disappearance it also might be the only way to find him.

She rubbed her hands nervously over the arms of her chair. "Has anybody else been in town, another stranger, asking questions about my father?"

"Not that I know of. He was staying over at Bernie's, that's a little rooming house right around the corner from here. You could check there."

"I will, Sheriff, and thanks." She rose and so did Tyree. "Anybody else in town you think I should talk to?"

"Well, there's Abby Riker. She owns Rita's just down the street. She and Ben seemed to get on right good."

Was it Annabelle's imagination or did she detect a note of jealously there?

"Thanks." She handed him a card. "Here's my phone number in case you think of anything else."

She left Tyree standing in his office looking troubled.

Outside the jail the man had obviously been waiting for her.

Charlie Trimble said, "I couldn't help but see the photo of the man you were looking for. I interviewed him in connection with some of the things occurring in town. Perhaps the sheriff explained that to you?"

"Murders and suicides and people getting blown up, yeah, he filled me in. You say you talked to him? What did he tell you?"

"Well, perhaps we could have a bit of negotiation there."

"Excuse me?"

"I own a newspaper, ma'am. I thought when I moved here and started running the little town paper that the most exciting thing I'd have to report was when someone drove his truck off a mountain road or a mine cave-in. Now with all that's going on I feel like I'm back in Washington."

Annabelle looked impatient and felt more than a little disgusted at his gleeful tone. "What exactly do you want?"

"You tell me things and I tell you things."

"Like what?"

"Like who Ben really is."

"And if I do, what can you tell me?"

"We have to have a bit of good faith there. But I can tell you that he struck me immediately as not being your typical drifter. He was too well-spoken, too cunning. And his physical abilities spoke for themselves. According to what I've learned, he beat up three men on a train, saved a man's life using battery cables and fought off three other men wielding baseball bats. Not your typical wandering soul."

"He had some special skills, yes."

"And your relation to him?"

"My father."

"Excellent. I'd heard he was in the military."

"Vietnam."

"Special Forces."

"Very special."

"And does he make a habit of wandering the country-side?"

"He had a job in the government for a while but got tired of sitting behind a desk."

Trimble gave her a patronizing smile. "I doubt your father ever sat behind a desk. If you don't tell me the truth, I have no reason to accord you any."

"Well, it seems like I've told you a lot already. How about some action on your end?"

"All right, that seems fair actually. Your father has been spending a lot of time with Abby Riker and her son Danny. He's a troubled youth. Sort of the epitome of the high school poster boy who reached his prime when he was eighteen and everything's been downhill since."

"Is he a druggie? A boozer?"

"Not drugs, but he does like his alcohol. His mother won a big lawsuit against a coal company involving an accident that cost her husband his life. So they have a lot of money, live in a big house, but Danny's life has been off track for a while."

"The sheriff says he's missing too."

"Your father struck me as a good man trying to do the

right thing. My advice would be to not assume that anyone else here has those same intentions, including Danny, even though your father saved his life."

"Would that caveat include you too?" she said.

"I'm a fairly recent arrival here. I called Washington home for forty years. I still have a lot of friends there, get regular updates. And—" Trimble broke off, his eyes seeming to look right through Annabelle and on to something of far greater interest.

"Mr. Trimble?" Annabelle did not like that look at all.

He seemed to refocus on her, but his eyes showed his mind was still elsewhere. "Excuse me, I have something I need to check right now." He hurried off.

Annabelle raced down the street to the van and climbed in. She quickly filled them both in on what Tyree had told her and her run-in with the reporter.

"You think he suspects who Oliver really is?" asked Caleb.

"I wouldn't bet against it. And right now our margin of error is zero."

"Damn, Oliver can't buy a break, can he?" exclaimed Reuben. "The one town he picks turns out to be teeming with killers."

"Let's hit the rooming house fast. The clock is running."

A few minutes later Annabelle had charmed the entire story out of Bernie Sandusky.

She got back in the van. "Knox was here. He found out about Oliver. Bernie told him that Oliver was in the hospital or else he could try Abby Riker's place, A Midsummer's Farm. If Knox went to the hospital and found Oliver gone he might have tried Midsummer. Let's roll."

CHAPTER

61

Stone and Knox sat, manacled to metal chairs that were bolted to the slab floor, in a windowless cement block room painted gray. They'd been here for many hours now and the room was so cold that they were both shivering. They jumped when the door banged open and the group moved in. There were five of them, all in blue uniforms and all armed with pistols and billy clubs dangling from thick belts. They formed a semicircle of flesh behind the pair of prisoners, arms folded across their muscular chests.

So fixated were Stone and Knox on this little army that they didn't hear the other man come in until he closed the door.

When Stone turned to look at this new arrival, he flinched.

It was Tyree. Only it wasn't Tyree. Not Lincoln Tyree anyway. It was a shorter, stouter version of the man.

In an instant Stone made the connection—Howard Tyree, the older brother who was also warden of this place. He wore a navy blue polo shirt, pressed khaki pants and tasseled loafers; wire-rimmed glasses covered his clean-shaven face. He didn't look like a rottweiler warden at a supermax. He looked like an insurance salesman on a golf holiday.

"Good morning, gentlemen," said Tyree.

Stone's heart sank with the words. It was the voice he'd heard when he'd made the call on Danny's phone. He and the sheriff sounded nearly identical.

Son of a bitch!

The other men had instantly come to attention when Tyree walked in. He sat down behind a small table opposite Stone and Knox. The warden held a file in his hand, opened it and read through the contents.

A minute later he slipped off his glasses and gazed across at Stone. "Anthony Butcher, triple murderer, fortunate enough to have done it in a state that does not believe in capital punishment. So you received a life sentence without possibility of parole instead of the execution you so well deserved. Transferred out of four different correctional facilities over the last twelve years, including the supermax in Arkansas, because you have an anger issue." He glanced down at the file. "And a problem respecting authority."

Stone glanced at Knox and then back at Tyree, his *anger* at what was being done to them building beyond all hope of containment. Stone knew he shouldn't but he also couldn't stop himself. "How much does one of those scripts cost, Howie? They must come in real handy in your line of work."

The warden tapped his thumb on the table and one of the guards handed him his billy club and a towel along with a bungee cord. Tyree stood, took his time wrapping the towel around the head of the club and secured it there with the cord.

The next instant Stone was slumped sideways in his chair, blood running down his battered face.

Tyree sat back down after dropping the bloody club on the table. He resumed looking at the file after methodically wiping a speck of Stone's blood off his glasses with a handkerchief he pulled from his pants pocket.

"With the towel it doesn't really leave much of a mark," he murmured in a casual tone. "We find that helpful in keeping order here. Prisoners have far too much time to complain about trivial things."

He thumbed through more pages of the file and then pointed at Knox. "You're Richard Prescott, a.k.a. Richie Patterson from the great state of Mississippi. Killed two people in an armed robbery in Newark twenty-one years ago and one more since you came into the correctional system. The Garden State didn't want you anymore so you're now our guest for the rest of your natural life." He said all this as though he were reciting tedious lecture notes to an auditorium full of bored college freshman.

"My name is Joseph P. Knox of the Central Intelligence Agency. And in about twenty-four hours there'll be an army of feds at this place, and the next thing you know, you assholes are the ones who'll be rotting in a super-max."

Tyree hit Knox so hard with the billy club that the chair

tore loose from its underpinning and he fell over unconscious onto the slab floor.

Tyree closed the file. "Get 'em up."

The guards unhooked them from the chair shackles
and pulled the men to their feet.

Tyree looked at the unconscious Knox. He said in a
weary tone, "Wake him up, George. He has to hear this."

A bucket of water was thrown in Knox's face. Gagging, he came to, spitting up water and his own blood.

Tyree waited for Knox to catch his breath and then
paced in front of the two with his hands clasped behind
him.

"This is the Blue Spruce Supermax Prison. It is unlike
any prison you gentlemen may be familiar with. My name
is Howard W. Tyree. I am privileged to be the warden of
this outstanding facility. Here, we receive from all over
prisoners who have problems adjusting to the life of in-
carceration, or simply who have problems in general. Our
sister prisons sent you here because at Blue Spruce we
specialize in being problem solvers. We have never had
any disruptions here or, needless to say, any escapes. We
are a professional organization. So long as you follow the
rules, you will have no reasonable cause for concern for
your personal safety either from your fellow prisoners or
the fine men who guard this place."

Blood from both Stone and Knox dripped onto the
floor as Tyree was talking. He impatiently flicked a finger
at one of his men, who quickly cleaned it up with the billy
club towel.

"Excessive force is only used here when absolutely
necessary. Just so we're clear on the boundaries, I will
demonstrate."

He stopped pacing and faced the two men.

"If a prisoner does not instantly obey a command from a guard, this level of force can and will be utilized."

Tyree took the billy club from the guard and slammed it point first into Stone's gut. Stone bent over, throwing up what little there was in his belly, and then dropped to the floor.

Tyree calmly kept going. "Please keep in mind that at Blue Spruce, unlike other correctional institutions, warnings to inmates of any kind are not required and typically will not be given. Unauthorized action on the part of any inmate will be met with immediate consequences." Tyree paused to let Stone be wrenched back to his feet, still heaving and gasping for air.

Continuing, Tyree said, "If a prisoner in any way verbally abuses a guard, this level of force can and will be utilized."

Tyree slammed into the still dazed Knox, knocking him to the floor. He pushed the billy club against his throat until the man turned blue and his body started to spasm from lack of oxygen.

Tyree got up, tossed the club to one of the guards and a gagging Knox was heaved back to his feet.

Dusting off his pants, Tyree went on. "If a prisoner in any way threatens bodily harm to and/or physically attacks a guard, deadly force can and will be utilized without prior warning."

Tyree nodded at one of his guards, who pulled out his pistol and handed it to the warden. He checked to make sure there was a round in the chamber, popped off the safety, lifted the gun up and aimed at Stone's head.

"For Chrissakes! Don't!" screamed Knox through his busted mouth.

The door opened and a tall black man was hauled in, his face bloody and swollen, and his hands and legs chained together, forcing him into a prisoner shuffle. The guards slammed him up against a section of wall that was paneled in a rubbery material covered in pockmarks and then moved away.

Tyree explained, "This man attacked a guard barely five minutes ago. He felt it violated his civil rights to be beaten for extending his middle finger to one of my men because he'd made a silly little joke about this fellow's mama."

Tyree swung the pistol around and fired a round into the black man's head. He slumped to the floor, an exit crater blown into the back of his head. A part of his brain along with the slug was embedded into the rubber wall behind, leaving another large pockmark.

"And he was shot while trying to escape after taking a hostage, all of which we have duly documented for regulatory review."

Tyree handed the gun back and resumed his pacing. "Those are basically the rules here. We keep them short and simple so that you will have no trouble remembering and thus following them. Please also keep in mind that here you have no privacy, no rights, no dignity and no reasonable expectation of anything except what we say you can have. At the moment you walked into this facility you ceased to be human beings. Indeed, because of the crimes that you have committed against humanity you have forfeited all rights to be considered human beings. No guard at this prison will have any compunction about ending your life at any moment and for any reason. You now will be officially processed into this prison's inmate population. If you give us no trouble, I can reasonably assure that you will live out your lives here in relative peace and security, though I cannot say how long that life will be. Supermax facilities are by their very nature dangerous places. We of course will make all reasonable attempts to ensure your safety, but there are no guarantees." He paused and faced them. "Welcome to Dead Rock, gentlemen. I *can* guarantee that you will not enjoy your stay with us."

CHAPTER

62

ANNABELLE WALKED INTO RITA'S, pausing at the door to survey the landscape. Half the tables were filled, as were all the stools at the counter.

"Can I help you?" A man came around the bar and was looking at her.

"I was looking for Abby Riker?"

"She's not here. She's at home."

"Midsummer's Farm?"

"Who are you?"

"Sheriff Tyree told me to come and see her."

"Oh, well I guess that's okay then. You might want to call out to the house and talk to her."

"Do you have her number?"

Annabelle made the call. When Abby answered it was clear that she had been crying. She didn't want to talk to

Annabelle until she mentioned the man Abby knew as Ben.

"He's my father." Annabelle quickly told her the same story she'd told Tyree.

"He told me his daughter *and* his wife were dead," Abby said coldly.

"My mother *is* dead. Has been for decades. He told you I was dead because that's how he protects me."

"Government spy type? I knew there was something about him. Just different, you know?"

"Yep, that's my dad. Different. Do you have any idea where he might be?"

"He was at the hospital yesterday. Along with my son, Danny. Now they've both disappeared. I'm worried sick for a lot of reasons."

"Sheriff Tyree told me about what's been happening around here. I guess you have good reason to worry. Can I come out to see you?"

"Why?"

"Right now you're the closest lead I have to my dad."

"I told you I don't know where he is. Or my son either."

"But you might remember something if we keep talking about it. Please, it's my only shot."

"All right." Abby told her how to get to the place and a little while later Annabelle was seated across from Abby in her living room. Caleb had parked the van well back and had stayed there with Reuben. Annabelle tried various lines of questioning and Abby answered each of them, but nothing she learned helped her.

"Had you two become friends?"

Choosing her words carefully, Abby said, "He's a good

listener. Not judgmental. I find that a rare combination. I hope he's all right." A tear slid down her cheek. "He had a way about him too. Just made you feel good about yourself."

"Do you think he and your son might have left the hospital together?"

"I don't know. Danny was pretty beat up. If it wasn't for Ben." She stopped and looked at Annabelle. "What's his real name?"

Annabelle hesitated, but Abby appeared to be genuinely concerned about Stone. "Oliver."

"If it hadn't been for Oliver I wouldn't have my son at all, so whatever I can do to help you I will."

"If you think of anything that might be helpful you can reach me at this number." She handed Abby a card, gave her hand a reassuring squeeze and left.

Back in the van, she sat lost in thought in the passenger seat.

"What do we do now, Annabelle?" asked Caleb, while Reuben stared at her curiously.

"You okay?" he asked.

She started and looked at him. "What? Yeah, I'm good."

"Boy, Abby Riker has some big bucks," said Reuben as he glanced back at the enormous house.

"Yeah, only thing it cost her was her husband."

"What do we do now, Annabelle?" Caleb asked again.

Annabelle didn't say anything, because she didn't have an answer.

Where the hell are you, Oliver?

CHAPTER

63

BEING PROCESSED into Dead Rock included standing bent over naked with your butt cheeks spread as painfully as possible while a group of men and one woman looked on. The woman was also videotaping the proceedings, which added considerably to the dignity of the event. The body cavity search completed, their heads were then shaved.

Suspicion of lice, Stone heard one guard say, while another chuckled about a weapon perhaps being concealed in their hair roots.

They sat crouched in a corner naked while men scrubbed them raw with stiff brushes that felt steel-tipped. After this a fire hose blasted them with such force that they were pinned against the wall like ants at the mercy of a berserk garden hose.

Dressed in orange jumpsuits, cuffed and shackled,

they were led down a stone hall to a cell. Guards held stun guns an inch from their prisoners' sides, seemingly just praying for a reason to hit them with a 50,000-volt tickle. The cell door was solid two-inch steel with a food and cuffing slot cut into the bottom half and a small viewing window in the upper half. They were pushed in, the shackles removed, the jagged links stripping at their skin, and then the door slammed shut and was loudly bolted behind them.

Knox and Stone slumped down next to each other as their gazes drifted dully over the eight-by-twelve-foot space. There was a steel toilet and sink unit bolted to the wall with no knobs that could be fashioned into weapons. There was also a steel slab for a desk and two steel slabs on the wall with a thin plastic mattress and pillow on each. A six-inch vertical slit in the thick concrete block and rebar wall constituted the sole window.

For the next half hour each man groaned and moaned and rubbed at innumerable bruises, cuts and bumps on their bodies.

Knox finally sat back against the wall, wiggled a loose tooth in the back of his mouth with his finger and looked over at Stone. "Whatever the hell happened to due process?"

"It seems to be growing less popular these days," Stone replied as he rubbed at a knot the size of a quarter on the side of his head.

"I'm surprised they put us in here together. I'd assumed we'd be segregated."

"They did it because they don't care what we tell each other."

"You mean because we're never getting out?"

"We don't really exist. They can do anything they want. And he murdered a man right in front of us. That shows he doesn't expect us to be a witness anytime soon. You think the cell is bugged?"

"I doubt they care that much, but you never know."

Stone drew closer and lowered his voice to a whisper and tapped his shoes against the walls to disrupt any audio surveillance. "Any chance your agency will find you?"

Knox joined in the wall-tapping. "There's always a chance. Looks like the only one we've got right now. But even if they do, you realize how many places there are to hide us here. Like you said, we don't exist."

"And they can always kill us. Invisible in life, nothing in death. Who sent you after me?"

"I guess it would sound pretty stupid to say that's classified under the present circumstances. Macklin Hayes."

A tiny smile crept across Stone's face. "I guess that makes sense."

"You served under him."

"If you want to call it that."

"What would you call it?"

"I didn't serve under him, I *survived* him."

"You're not the first to tell me that."

"I'd be surprised if I were."

"You earned that medal. Why didn't you get it?"

Stone looked surprised. "How'd you find out about that?"

"Did some digging. You were a slam dunk for the big one."

"Every soldier in my company would've done the same for me."

"That's bullshit and you know it. I was over there too.

All soldiers are not created equal. So why didn't you get it? I looked at the paperwork. It stopped at Hayes."

Stone shrugged. "I haven't given it that much thought over the years."

"You did something to really piss off the man, didn't you?"

"If I did, it doesn't matter now, does it?"

"Tell me."

"No, I'm not going to tell you!"

"Okay, next subject. I know you killed Gray and Simpson."

"Good for you."

"Is that a confession?"

Stone picked up the intensity of the tapping. "Right now we need to come up with a way to get out of here. Because if we don't it won't matter to either of us what I did or didn't do."

"Okay, I'm listening," said Knox.

"And I'm still thinking. But if we do escape, what are you going to do?"

"What do you mean?"

Stone's eyes flashed. "You know what the hell I mean. About me?"

"If I had to answer you now I'd say I was going to complete my assignment and turn your ass in."

Stone took this in and finally nodded. "Okay. Fair enough. Just so we know where we stand."

"So fill me in on the events leading up to us ending up here."

Stone started talking. A half hour later he was finished as both pairs of shoes continued to drum against the wall.

"Damn!" Knox said. "You weren't kidding about picking the wrong town to hide out in." He rubbed at a cut on his face. "I talked to your buddies, by the way."

"Which buddies?"

"You know which."

"Are they okay? Tell me the truth. No bullshit." Stone looked Knox directly in the eye.

"I didn't do anything to them. And as far as I know, they're fine."

"They don't know anything and did nothing. If we manage to get out of here you put that down in your report. This is about me, not them."

"Okay." He leaned close to Stone and whispered in his ear. "But they still managed to follow me up here."

"You're sure? You saw them?"

"Not exactly, but it couldn't have been anyone else. At least the chick is up here. Susan, not that that's her real name. Pretty sure she spun a story at a local diner that almost got my ass handed to me."

"If she did, it was only out of friendship to me, Knox. She's not worth going after. You've got me. That's all Hayes wants anyway."

"But still, you think they might figure out we ended up in here?"

"I'm not sure because even I can't believe we're here."

Knox slapped his hand against the hard wall. "So how do you think they're running a drug op from a supermax prison?"

"Haven't gotten that all figured out yet. But it's not like they have to worry about witnesses. They sort of have a *captive* audience."

"And the prisoners might not even know. But I guess all the guards are in on it."

"That's not necessarily true," said Stone thoughtfully.

"Why?"

"There was one guard who used to work here. He was killed in a deer hunting accident that I don't think was so accidental. His name was Josh Coombs and I believe he stumbled onto what was going on here and paid the price for it."

"Coombs? Also the name of the folks who got blown up."

"Yeah. Willie knew Debby Randolph hadn't killed herself. His mom's in on it, I'm pretty sure. They used her to try and kill him with an overdose. When that didn't work, they went for essentially a homegrown IED."

"Mother killing her own son?"

"In a town called Divine. Yeah."

The door to the cell was hit with a massive blow. Both men staggered to their feet and backed away.

"Shut up in there!" a man screamed through the door.

"Okay, we're shutting up," Knox said.

"I said shut up, assholes."

Knox and Stone said nothing, just stared at the door.

"One more word and we're extracting your asses."

Silence.

"Okay, you asked for it. Walk over to the cuffing slot, turn around and extend your hands through the opening. Now!"

Stone and Knox looked at each other. Stone went first, extending his hands through the slot with his back facing the door. He was cuffed hard, his bony wrists slammed together and cut by the edge of the slot. Then Knox did the same.

"Now move away from the door," the same voice barked.

Knox and Stone retreated to the back of the cell.

The door was opened and what happened next was only a blur.

Five body-armored men with face masks poured in carrying two huge inch-thick Plexiglas shields. They hit Knox and Stone hard, slamming them against the stone wall. Pepper spray hit them both in the eyes, even as Taser shots paralyzed them. They went down, wanting to claw at their eyes, but with limbs electrified stiff as a corpse *and* cuffed hands that wasn't an option. They were stripped of their clothing, lifted into the air and hustled down the corridor. Thrown in a shower, they were hit with blasts of water, which at least helped ease the agony of the eye spray.

Picked up again, they were carried to a room that had two steel slabs covered in what looked to be urine and feces. They were smashed down on these hard cots and put in five-point restraints. Before the guards left they were Tasered once more.

"What the hell was that for?" Knox managed to scream as the current pounded him.

A guard with one stripe on his sleeve hit him in the mouth with his fist. "Not obeying orders. This ain't like other prisons, old man. This is Dead Rock. Don't know what prison you come from but you get no warnings up here, boy. No damn warnings. And just so's you know, I can Taser your ass just for the hell of it. 'Cause my old lady didn't blow me, or 'cause my dog shit on the rug."

"I work for the CIA."

"Sure you do. Hey, fellows, we got us a spy right here. Bet your friend is KGB."

He walked to the next slab and smacked Stone in the face. "You KGB, Grandpa?" The guard reached a gloved hand down to Stone's crotch and squeezed. "I asked you a question, old man."

Stone didn't say anything; he just looked at the guard, remembering every detail of his face through the clear mask. And he suddenly recognized him too. He was one of the men with the baseball bats who'd beaten up Danny and then come after him. This was the third one, the coward who'd run for it, but Stone had still managed to nail him in the back with one of the bats.

"You ever tell your buddies you ran out on them?" he said quietly as the Taser sting wore off.

The guard gave a nervous, hollow laugh under the burn of Stone's gaze, glanced at the other guards and took his hand away. As he was leaving the room with the other guards, Stone managed, despite the restraints, to turn his head just enough to keep his eyes on the fellow. Then the door closed.

"I guess they're trying to break us quick," groaned Knox.

"They'll have to work harder."

"You think so, do you?"

"Yeah, I do."

Something in his voice made Knox glance over at him. "Were you ever a POW?"

"Six months. This place is actually pretty nice compared to what the Viet Cong thought was humane. All I had there was a pit with a sheet over it, beatings whenever they felt like it, along with an interrogation technique that would make waterboarding seem like dunking for apples. And the food they threw down once a day would not be considered edible by any stretch of the imagination."

"But we're not twenty years old anymore, Carr."

"Call me Oliver, Carr is dead."

"Okay, but we're still not twenty."

"It's all in the mind, Knox. It's all in the mind. If we don't believe they can break us they never will."

"Yeah, sure," Knox said, clearly unconvinced of this.

"You got any family?"

"Son and daughter. My boy's in the Marines stationed in the Middle East. My daughter's a lawyer in D.C."

"I had a daughter. But she died. How about your wife?"

"Dead."

"So's mine."

"Brunswick, Georgia? Claire?"

Stone didn't say anything.

"Guy named Harry Finn said that Simpson admitted to having her killed. That he ordered a CIA hit on you and your family."

Stone stared at the ceiling, slowly flexing his limbs against the thick leather bindings. "Harry's a good guy. Knows how to cover your back."

"I'm sorry about your family . . . Oliver," he murmured.

"Get some sleep, Knox. Just get some sleep. You're going to need it."

Stone closed his eyes.

A few minutes later an exhausted Joe Knox did the same.

CHAPTER

64

"WE'RE RUNNING OUT OF TIME," Caleb said.

The three of them were sitting around an old picnic table in a small clearing off the main road to Divine. A meal Annabelle had purchased at Rita's was on the table. Reuben gnawed on a piece of fried chicken while Annabelle glared at Caleb.

"I'm open to suggestions," she said.

"Maybe Alex can help," suggested Caleb as he carefully picked the skin off his piece of chicken.

"Help what, screw things up?"

"We talked about Alex, Annabelle," retorted Reuben. "He's as professional and brave as they make 'em. And I think Caleb's got something."

"What do you expect him to do, come running to help us? It'll mess up his career. You heard him."

"You can always ask."

"Why me?"

"Okay, I'll do it," said Reuben. "*Anything* to help Oliver."

Annabelle stared at each man, sighed and pulled out her phone. "No, I'll do it."

A minute later she said, "Alex?"

"Annabelle? You okay?"

"I—" She stopped. "*We* need a favor."

Five minutes later she clicked off.

"Well?" Reuben and Caleb asked together.

"He's going to help us. He's coming up here, in fact."

Reuben slapped Caleb on the back, almost sending him headfirst into a tub of potato salad.

"I knew it. Friendship *is* thicker than official duty."

"Yeah, well, we'll see, won't we?" she murmured. "But in the meantime we can't just sit on our butts. We need to keep digging away."

Reuben tossed the bones of his chicken breast into the woods, wiped his mouth and balled up his napkin. "I'm ready to roll. I'll do a recon of the area, see if anything hits me."

"And me and Caleb?"

"Talk to some more people in town. And Caleb stays with you. Remember there's a killer on the loose. We'll meet back here later."

"I'm worried about that reporter," said Annabelle. "Even if we find Oliver, that guy could screw it all up. I didn't like his look. It was like he'd just suddenly figured something out."

Caleb said, "Well, maybe we have to convince him it would not be in his best interests to follow any of that up."

Annabelle considered this suggestion. "I think you might be right."

Reuben drove off on his Indian while Caleb and Annabelle headed back into Divine. When they reached the main street Annabelle had Caleb park near the courthouse.

"The sheriff told me that Willie Coombs' mom works at the courthouse as the clerk. I want to see if I can get a word with her."

Caleb looked around and his eyes brightened as his gaze fell on the library.

"I think I see something *I* can do," he said. "But if you need a bodyguard, I can hang with you. Like Reuben said, there is a murderer on the loose."

She gave him a gracious smile. "I appreciate the offer, killer, but I think I'll be fine. The sheriff's office is just right next door."

Caleb headed off and Annabelle went inside the courthouse.

Shirley Coombs looked up from her desk when the door opened. Annabelle introduced herself and said why she was there. Though Annabelle couldn't know it, Shirley Coombs looked as though she'd aged several decades.

"I'm really sorry about your son."

Shirley eyed her suspiciously. "Did you know Willie?"

"No, but Sheriff Tyree told me what happened."

"Parents aren't supposed to outlive their children," she said in a hushed tone and then lit up a cigarette; her fingers shook so badly she was barely able to work the Zippo.

"No, ma'am, they're not."

"Lost my husband too. In an accident," she said quickly. "And my daddy in a mine cave-in."

"God, that's awful."

"Yeah, life is just awful, ain't it?" she said sarcastically. "What can I do for you?"

"I was hoping you could tell me something about my dad."

"I never met him," she said immediately.

Annabelle studied the woman closely without appearing to do so.

Okay, that was a lie.

She looked over at the stack of boxes.

Shirley said, "Got a lot of work to do."

"I'm sure. I'm really worried about my father."

"Somebody told me he was heading out of town."

"Who was that?"

"Don't recall. Probably heard it over at Rita's."

"You're friends with Abby Riker?"

At that moment an interior door opened and Judge Mosley ambled out. He wore a suit and held his driving cap in one hand.

"Shirley, I'm—" He broke off when he saw Annabelle. His smile was instant.

"Well, who is this?"

Annabelle shook his hand and felt his fingers linger just a beat too long on hers. She explained who she was and why she was here.

"Ben seemed to be a very interesting man," said Mosley. "I wish I'd gotten to know him better. I hope you find him. Well, I have to be off."

"Up to the prison, Judge?" said Shirley.

"That's right." He turned to Annabelle. "I go up there once a week and resolve disputes between the prisoners and the guards. And there are many, I'm afraid."

"I'm sure."

"Rehabilitation is the key," he said. "Although not many of the folks at Blue Spruce will ever see the light of day as free men, they still deserve some respect and dignity."

"That's what Josh thought," blurted out Shirley.

They turned to look at her.

She reddened. "My husband. He was a guard up there." She glanced at Annabelle. "He's the one who died in the . . . accident. He thought you should treat folks with respect regardless of what they've done, prisoner or not."

"Exactly," said Mosley. "I would be the first to admit that Howard Tyree is not exactly sold on that concept, but that's why it bears repeating. And my weekly presence I hope lets everyone see that common ground in fact can be reached."

"Howard Tyree?" said Annabelle sharply.

"He's the sheriff's brother," answered Shirley. "The warden up at Dead Rock."

Mosley smiled at Annabelle. "Its official name is Blue Spruce, but folks 'round here call it Dead Rock."

Shirley snapped, "They call it Dead Rock because a bunch of miners got trapped in a cave-in. Never could get to them. Sealed up in there and they built a damn prison on top of them. And one of 'em was my daddy."

Tears smeared Shirley's mascara while Annabelle and Mosley looked politely away. The judge finally said, "Mining is a very dangerous business."

"I can see that," replied Annabelle.

"Well, good day, ladies."

After he'd gone, Annabelle rose. "I guess I'll let you get back to work."

"Sorry I couldn't help you," Shirley said gruffly.

Oh, you already have, lady.

65

STONE AND KNOX were kept in the restraints for nearly six hours and slept the whole time. The guards who came to take the pair back to their cells seemed chagrined that they'd navigated the ordeal so easily.

They were dressed back in orange jumpsuits and hauled back to their cells. Each man had to exercise considerable self-control in the face of the guards' taunts. Knox had to bite the inside of his lip while Stone just stared straight ahead unblinking and telling himself that an opportunity would present itself if he were patient.

An hour later, they were strip-searched again, cuffed and shackled and led to the cafeteria, where the cuffs were taken off so they could eat.

Knox's belly was rumbling as they sat down at an unoccupied table. They stared around at the sea of other prisoners. Quickly counting, Stone arrived at nearly five hundred inmates, with well over three-quarters of them black, while all the guards he could see were white.

Some of the prisoners stared back at them with an array of expressions that ranged from curious to indifferent to hostile. Only a few people were talking. Most focused on their meals. Knox looked down as his food was slid in front of him.

After the attendant walked off he said to Stone, "I wonder if they have a nice cabernet to go with this slop?"

"Humor, Knox, I like that. Helps the time go by. What do you see out there?" He indicated the inmate population.

"Sorry asses just like us, only we haven't committed any crime. Correction, *I* haven't committed any crime."

Stone took a bite of his food with a limp Styrofoam spoon that was the only utensil provided. "You've seen the insides of prisons before, haven't you?"

"Yeah, but not as an inmate."

"So what's different? Think about it."

Knox looked around. "Well, they seem a pretty quiet bunch to be the baddest asses in the land."

"That's right. Subdued, beaten down, scared. Anything else?"

Knox stared at one group closest to them. Four men, all black, who sat there idly prodding their food and not bothering to even look at each other.

Knox squinted at them, following their lethargic movements and glassy eyes. "And drugged?"

"And drugged. We know they have enough pills to do the job."

"Do you think that's where the pill shipments are coming? Here?"

"No. That stuff was all for street sale probably in New York, Philly, Boston, D.C. and other big cities up and down the East Coast. They probably just use a little overflow to knock these guys down."

"Drugging prisoners involuntarily? That's got to violate about a million rights."

Stone suddenly bent down and started shoveling food in his mouth. Sensing why, Knox immediately did the same. The footsteps came up behind them and stopped.

"Manson, are the new prisoners adapting to our routines?" Howard Tyree said to the burly guard standing next to him.

Manson had an eye patch over his right eye. And as he glanced up Stone knew why. Manson was the one he'd hit in the eye with his belt.

This is just getting better and better.

"It's taking some work, but we'll get them where they need to be, sir."

Stone watched as Manson curled and uncurled his fingers as he stared at Stone with his one remaining eye. The man's look was one of unconcealed homicidal intent. He lifted his billy club out of its holster and stuck its end against Stone's jaw and pushed.

"This one here will take a little *extra* work, but we'll get him to understand our ways."

"Good man," said Tyree.

When Manson pulled the club back he did it in such a way that a jagged edge of the wood tore at Stone's face. It started to bleed, but Stone didn't make a move to wipe it away.

Tyree said, "You know, at most supermax prisons the prisoners eat in their cells and recreation time is only done one inmate at a time. But here at Blue Spruce we're a little more liberal than that." He surveyed the deadly quiet room. "Here, we allow our inmates to experience some human touches. A nice meal together, some camaraderie."

Tyree placed a hand on Stone's shoulder and squeezed lightly. Stone would've taken the bite of the rattlers in the mine over this man's repulsive touch. Yet he didn't flinch and Tyree finally released his grip.

"And because of our compassion and understanding on points like that," Tyree continued, "sooner or later they all learn our ways. But I'd be the first to admit that the route can get bumpy at times."

As he walked along with a wall of guards every inmate stared down at his plate, as though it was the most wonderful cooking they'd ever seen.

These guys are not only drugged, they're terrified, thought Stone, *because they know this guy will kill them, and there's nothing they can do about it.*

He can kill me too. And probably will. Unless Manson gets to me first.

Only when Manson and Tyree had left the room did he wipe the blood off his face with his napkin.

CHAPTER

66

AFTER THE MEAL they were allowed thirty minutes outside. Outside being a floor of concrete in the middle of the prison courtyard with a sheet of razor wire as a roof and a lone and netless basketball hoop and patched ball as apparently the sole recreation.

So much for the liberal human touch, thought Stone.

Some of the prisoners slowly jogged in tight circles, one bounced the ball, yet most just stood there staring down at their shoes. Up on the tower walks were the guards, their AK-47s, shotguns, and sniper rifles at the ready and clearly visible to every man down in the pit. Stone noticed that there was a blue line that ran around the concrete field.

"You cross that line, put one toe over it, the man up there shoot you." This came from a small, twitchy inmate with a bristly gray mustache, wild hair and eyes that didn't promise much of anything behind them.

"Thanks for the scoop," Knox said. "They forgot to mention that in the orientation class."

Twitchy looked at Knox and laughed. "Hey, that's a good one. That's a damn good one." He looked at Stone. "You boys ever getting out?"

"Doesn't look that way," Stone answered. "You?"

"Life, life, life," Twitchy said in a singsong voice. "Three life sentences to run consecutively instead of concurrently. That's a big-ass difference. Oh yeah, I found that out. Both begin with the letter 'c' but that's where the similar shit stops, man."

"I can see that." Stone methodically eyed the position of each tower walk, and the shooting angles available to the guards up there. He came away impressed with the design of the place. It wouldn't take great skill to kill any man down here before he even had a chance to piss on the concrete, much less make a break for freedom.

"Is that what most people are here? Lifers?" Knox asked.

"Everybody I know is, and I been here eleven years. Least I think it's been eleven. Used to keep a calendar but I ran out of wall space. It ain't matter. No parole for old Donny boy."

"What'd you do, old Donny boy?" Knox asked, the distaste clear in his tone though Donny boy seemed oblivious to it.

"Killed me three little kids," he said as matter-of-factly as though he were merely giving his date of birth. He blew his nose in his cupped hands and then wiped them on his thighs.

"And why the hell would you do that, Donny boy?" Knox asked as his fingers curled into a fist.

"'Cause the bitch told me to, that's why. They was her kids from her second marriage, man. Insurance money. Least that's what she said. Seduced me. That's right. Gave me some ass. High on shit when I killed 'em too. You'd think that'd be a defense, wouldn't you? But hell no it ain't. I was robbed, man, robbed. I mean, where the hell is the accountability?"

"Accountability?" Knox said incredulously.

"Yeah, man. Lawyers, judges, bitches giving ass to make you do shit. Nobody wants to take responsibility for nuthin' no more. It's a damn disgrace. God bless America but we need to get our shit together in this country."

Knox clenched his teeth. "Did *she* get three life sentences?"

"The bitch? Hell no! Blamed it all on me. And she's married again and sitting pretty with all that insurance money, while my ass rots in here. Called me a *maniac* at my trial. And we had cocktails together, man. I swear to God."

"Sounds like you needed a better lawyer. But then again I think you're right where you need to be, *Donny*. Now why don't you go find another corner to hang out on?" Knox said, taking a menacing step toward the man.

Before Donny could move, Stone hooked him by the arm even as one of the tower guards stared down at them, his hands perched on the trigger guard of the AK.

"Hey, Donny, you been in many prisons?" Stone asked.

"Me? Hell yeah. This here's my fourth one. And my second supermax," he added with pride.

"Why'd you get sent to Dead Rock?"

"Hit a guard. They ain't like it when you hit *them*, but they sure as hell don't mind busting our asses, do they?"

"Yep, life's real unfair," Knox exclaimed.

"I bet you're a guy notices stuff. Notice anything weird around here?" Stone said.

"Notice stuff? Man, we only get one hour out a day. Half for chow, half for this recreation shit. Twenty-three hours and two meals in the old eight-by-twelve after that. Ain't much time to notice *stuff*."

While they were talking the man bouncing the ball let it get away from him. It rolled past the blue line. He went to get it.

"Oh, hell," said Knox, who had just noticed this. "Hey, buddy!"

The man either didn't hear him or didn't care. He crossed the line and the bullet hit him right in the back. He went down, face first. Stone and Knox started to run toward him, but other shots were fired and they pulled up.

As they watched, two guards sauntered over and picked the man up. There was no blood, Stone noted.

Donny said, "They use those damn dummy bullets if it's your first time. Hurt like hell. Knock your ass out, but it ain't kill you. Now, if it's your second time, well, you ain't gonna be around for a third time, get my drift?"

They returned to their corner as the unconscious man was carried away.

Stone continued their previous conversation. "What about the prison library? Classes? Workshop? You notice anything there?"

Donny snorted. "What, you been watching reruns of

Escape from Alcatraz? Look around, man, ain't no Clint Eastwood 'round here. They been promising a library the whole time my ass has been here and I ain't seen one damn book yet. Supposed to have GED classes on TV too, but they say it keeps breaking down. Ain't no workshops. Ain't no nuthin'. Get a shower three times a week for five minutes and they stick a damn poker up your butt every time they do that, like you gonna pull a bazooka out your ass somehow and blow 'em away. I'd rather stay dirty. Ain't like I got nowhere to go."

He popped a piece of gum in his mouth and chewed it hard with the few teeth he had.

"Visitors, phone calls home? Lawyers?"

Donny chuckled. "At Dead Rock you got to earn your visits. Get a max of two a month. You screw up the least little thing, guess what, you ain't getting no visitors. And guess what else? From what I hear ain't been nobody earn a visit at this place in the last five years. I sure as hell ain't. Not like there's many folks lining up to come see me, but still. And you got to call collect if you even get near the damn phone. And not even my damn momma is gonna pay for a collect call from me. And ain't no lawyers coming up here. Ain't no more appeals for these boys. Everybody's forgotten us. We ain't anybody no more. We Dead Rock. Gonna die here, just the way it is. Better get used to it." He swallowed his gum and hacked up some phlegm.

Stone looked around at the other prisoners. "People seem a little mellow here." He eyed Donny. "Little too mellow."

Donny cracked a smile and drew closer. "You noticed that too? Most of these boys ain't never caught on to that crap."

"So what drug do they use?"

"Ain't know, but it's pretty strong."

"Do they put it in the chow?"

Donny nodded.

"Which meal?"

"Lunch or dinner, but that's the thing. You never know which one."

"So why do you seem so chipper?"

Donny's eyes twinkled. "I could let you in on my little secret, but what you gonna gimme me for it? Now that's the sixty-four-zillion-dollar question."

Stone started to say something but Knox broke in. "Tell us and if I ever get out of here, I'll take you away from old Dead Rock."

"Right, shit you will. And besides, you ain't never getting out of here."

"I'm a fed, Donny. Assigned to look into corrupt prisons. You think this place is corrupt?"

"Sure as hell is. But if you a fed why would you be getting *me* out of here?"

"Feds can do anything, Donny. You help me, Uncle Sam helps you."

Stone added, "And it's not like you have a lot to lose by doing it."

Donny considered this. "Okay. Not that I believe you're a fed, but what the hell." His voice sank lower. "Any meal you get, don't eat the damn carrots, just flush 'em down the toilet and then practice your dumbshit look for the boys with the billy clubs."

A guard started to move their way and Donny skittered off.

Knox said, "Well, that was informative but not particularly helpful except for the carrots. You believe him?"

"Maybe." He gazed once more up at the walls. "They designed this place well, Knox. I don't see many weaknesses."

"Day gets better and better."

A horn sounded and the prisoners started shuffling in.

Stone said, "The only way I see—"

The shot hit the cement right next to him, shards of concrete splattering up and slicing Stone and Knox in the lower legs. Both men grabbed at their calves even as another shot hit close to them. These were clearly no dummy bullets.

"Get your hands up!" screamed a tower guard through a bullhorn as the shooter stood next to him, his scope crosshairs dead on Stone's brain.

They both whipped their hands in the air as the blood trickled down their pants and into their shoes.

"What the hell—?" said Knox.

"Ain't walking fast enough, boys," Donny cackled over his shoulder.

"What the hell happened to the dummy bullet for first offense rule?" Knox snapped as they hustled after the group.

"Apparently, that doesn't apply to us."

"Yeah," Knox snarled.

A female nurse came to their cell later. They were stripped, searched and then shackled while she stood and watched surrounded by guards.

Through the open door and into the hallway outside, Stone could see a video camera bolted to the wall. He gauged that whenever a cell extraction was done the camera was perfectly positioned to, at best, capture a nice shot of the guards' backs while they pounded the crap out of the unseen inmate.

Invisible for sure.

The nurse cleaned their injuries and bandaged them up while the guards made snide comments about sissy wounds.

Neither Stone nor Knox said a word.

However, when the nurse was finished Stone did say, "Thank you, ma'am."

He was instantly hit in the mouth with a toweled billy club, the blow felling him. "You don't talk to the lady, asshole," screamed Manson the one-eyed guard as he leaned down into Stone's bleeding face.

The nurse smiled graciously at her defender as they headed out.

Knox helped him to his feet. "We've got to get out of here, Oliver, or we're dead."

"I know. I know," said Stone as he wiped fresh blood off his face, and then he froze.

The guard was looking in at him, his hand curled around the cell door as he was closing it. He wasn't a young punk one-striper. He was older, and gray hair peeked out from under his cap as he stared at Stone. Right before the door clanged shut the guard gave one brief nod at Stone.

CHAPTER

67

WHEN REUBEN hooked back up with Annabelle and Caleb later that day at the campground, the big man didn't have much to report. Yet he did have one observation.

"We been to all these little towns up here, but Divine is different."

"Different how?" asked Caleb.

"There's money here," answered Reuben. "Thriving shops, new cars, renovated buildings, a courthouse and a jail. Went to the church, even did a little praying. I talked to the padre, he said it was all done in the last few years."

"What cover are you using?" Annabelle asked.

"Said I was a writer looking to set a novel in a small mountain town. Everybody seemed to accept it okay. I guess I look like a writer," he added smugly.

Caleb stared up at his giant friend with the long, curly black hair and beard shot with gray. "I'd say you're more bohemian-looking, but that's probably just splitting hairs. But I think I see what you're saying. The library was really beautiful. The librarian said it had been recently redone too. Brand-new media center, computers, the works."

"And who'd you tell 'em you were?" asked Reuben gruffly.

"A wandering bibliophile. I think I fit that role rather well."

"You really told them that?" asked Annabelle.

"No, I actually said I was looking for work as a short order cook and was checking the classifieds. For some reason she accepted that without question, though I hardly look like a Fry Daddy connoisseur," he added stiffly.

"Sure you don't. What'd you find out, Annabelle?" asked Reuben.

She told them of her conversation with Shirley and Judge Mosley.

"The woman knows something, that's for sure. I think we should follow her and see what else we can find out."

"Sounds like a plan."

"When will Alex get here?" Caleb wanted to know.

"Soon, at least I hope."

"Missing the lawman, are we?" Reuben asked.

"No, I'm just tired of doing all the thinking."

"Well, here's another one for you to think about. Where are we going to be crashing?"

"Not in town," she said. "How about we just sleep in the van out here?"

"In the van?" said Caleb with a stricken look. "What about bathroom facilities?"

Annabelle pointed to the woods. "Nature's own."

"Oh, for Chrissakes," began Caleb.

Reuben held up a hand. "Caleb, if a bear can shit in the woods so can a librarian."

"And what about that reporter?" Caleb pointed out.

"I've sort of got a plan, but I need Alex's help." She turned to Reuben. "So why do you think Divine is so prosperous?"

He said, "Maybe if we answer that, we can explain why people keep getting murdered and/or blown up."

"Do you think something's happened to Oliver?" Caleb asked.

"I've never met anyone better able to take care of himself than Oliver," Reuben answered quite truthfully.

At least we can hope, thought Annabelle.

CHAPTER

68

WHEN SHIRLEY COOMBS left the courthouse it was already seven in the evening and the darkness had fallen solidly on mountain-bound Divine. She stopped at one store, and when she came back out she toted a plastic bag full of wine bottles. She put this in her car and then walked into Rita's. When she came back out a couple hours later she climbed in her late-model red two-door Infiniti where it was parked behind the courthouse. Apparently so absorbed was the woman in her thoughts that she never saw the white van behind her as she pulled on to the road and sped off.

She arrived home and went inside, staggering slightly.

Caleb pulled the van to a stop a little ways down from the house. Shirley Coombs lived in a one-story vinyl-sided house with a small front porch decorated with tubs of pansies. A gravel drive led to a detached garage. Twenty yards behind the house was thick forest. In a side yard a vegetable garden had been laid out, though the only things planted in it now were a couple of bare and leaning tomato stakes. A pile of rusted lawn chairs and a stack of firewood dominated the small backyard. The lady had no neighbors; hers was the only house down here.

Reuben hunched forward between the two front seats and stared at the house as lights came on inside.

"Do we wait till she passes out and search the place?"

"Why don't you go and see if you can get a look inside one of the windows," said Annabelle.

"I'll go with him," said Caleb.

"Why?"

"Four eyes are better than two."

They slipped out of the van and headed to the house, keeping to the tree line until they neared the house. Then the two made a beeline for the back porch.

Five minutes later they were back in the van.

"Talk about your diamonds wrapped up in a tin can," said Reuben.

"What do you mean?" asked Annabelle.

"What he means is the inside of Shirley Coombs' humble abode hardly matches the outside. The furniture is all high-end, the paintings on the walls are real oils, a couple by artists I recognized, the rugs are authentic oriental, and she's got at least one sculpture that is museum quality."

"Shirley the small-town court clerk is living high on the hog," added Reuben.

"But not so anyone can see it," said Annabelle. "Crappy on the outside and I bet she doesn't encourage visitors."

"She must just like to be surrounded by nice things," ventured Caleb.

"I'd like to get a look at her bank statement," said Annabelle. "What do you want to bet it shows she's loaded?"

"And still staying in this place," said Reuben. "Why?"

"Greed," said Caleb, and they both stared at him. "She's doing something up here, something at that courthouse, and she's getting paid for it. But she wants more and she won't get it if she leaves."

"I bet you're right, Caleb. Nice deduction. She did strike me as the greedy type."

"The thing is, do we know it's connected to whatever happened to Oliver?" asked Reuben. "We could be wasting time with her and meanwhile Oliver might be in serious trouble."

"I think they are connected, Reuben," said Annabelle. "From what the sheriff told me, Oliver was right in the middle of all this stuff. I can't believe a small town like this would have two completely unconnected major secrets. Whatever Shirley's got going on has to be tied to all the other stuff. It has to. It's the only thread we've got."

An hour went by and then another. Finally, the front door to the house opened and Shirley came out. She was dressed in jeans, a long-sleeved blouse and flats and carried a bag. The way she meandered to her car indicated that at least some of the wine she'd purchased had made its way down her throat.

"She's going to drive like that, up here?" Caleb said worriedly.

When Shirley shot out of her drive, Caleb followed. They headed back to town and through it. Shirley finally turned off and drove up a dirt road, pulling the car to a stop in front of the demolished trailer.

She popped open the car door, grabbed her bag, and staggered up to what was left of the front steps and sat down. She opened the bag, pulled out the bottle of wine and chugged it. It went down badly and she ended up throwing most of it back up. She tossed the bottle down and lit up a cigarette. Then she started to weep, her head resting on her knees.

"Willie! WILLIE!" she sobbed.

"Can I help?"

Shirley jerked up and saw Annabelle standing there. She wiped her face with her sleeve, stared at her suspiciously for a moment and then shook her head wearily. "Nobody can help me, not now." She indicated the destroyed mess behind her.

"Was this where your son . . . ?"

Shirley nodded and dragged on her cigarette. "What the hell are you doing here?" she slurred.

"Just driving around looking for my dad and heard someone crying. I'm sorry, Shirley, I really am. I know how you feel. The loss and everything." Annabelle sat down on the steps next to her.

"Why come here?"

"The sheriff told me my dad had helped Willie. I don't know, I thought there might be some clue here. At this point I'm basically grasping at straws."

With this earnest explanation Shirley's suspicious look faded. She flicked her cigarette away and rubbed at her eyes. "He *was* curious about what happened to Willie," she said slowly. "Came to see me about it."

"He did?" Annabelle said quickly. "I thought you two hadn't spoken."

"I lied to you," Shirley said bluntly. "I didn't know who you were and all," she added vaguely.

"Sure, I understand that."

Shirley's hands nervously slid back and forth over her thighs. She pointed straight ahead. "Lot of things out there in the dark, can't see 'em till it's too late."

"Right. What did he talk to you about?"

"Said somebody had tried to kill Willie. Said they'd put stuff in his Tylenol. I think he thought I did it. But I never would've done that to Willie. I even went to Willie's trailer one night to check on what pills he had there. I was thinking somebody was trying to get some crap in Willie's system that shouldn't be there. That's when I ran into your daddy, and he got all suspicious. But I loved my boy. Never would've done anything to hurt him."

She started sobbing again and Annabelle put a comforting hand on her shoulder. "I'm sure my dad was just trying to help."

Shirley wiped her eyes dry and sucked in some fresh air, calming down. "I know that now. And he was right. Somebody killed Willie, sure as I'm sitting here talking to you."

"Do you have any idea who would've done that?"

"I got ideas, sure." Shirley's cheeks quivered.

"Can you tell me?"

"Why?"

"Shirley, whoever killed your son might have gone after my father because he was trying to help Willie."

"Sure, that makes sense, I guess. Oh, I don't know. Just don't know anymore."

"I'll try to help too. If you can just trust me."

Shirley gripped Annabelle's hand. "Lord, girl, do you have any idea how long it's been since I trusted anybody around this damn place?"

"Trust me and I'll help you. I promise."

Shirley glanced back at what was left of Willie's trailer. "When my daddy got buried up in that mine cave-in, we were all sick in our hearts. People die, sure, but you get to say good-bye, bury 'em proper, at least you're supposed to. But not with cave-ins. You know what you get? A condolence letter from the mining company that some damn lawyer wrote so a company executive wouldn't say anything actionable or that could be used against them. You know, admitting liability? I work for a judge, I know about that crap."

"Absolutely, it's terrible," Annabelle said encouragingly, continuing to hold the older woman's hand tightly.

"Mining company wouldn't do nothing, so the rest of the miners got together and dug a parallel shaft up there with the idea that maybe they could cut over to where the trapped miners were. They worked day and night, borrowing and begging equipment from everybody they could. This was long before the Internet and most folks up here didn't even have TVs or nothing, and there weren't any news trucks with satellite crap or nothing like you see everywhere when some movie star gets drunk and goes to court. So nobody knew what was really going on. My momma and I and all the rest of the women set up a kitchen and laundry and had cots and such for the men while they dug. And God did they dig. Ran a shaft all the way up there and were about to cut over when there was an explosion in the other shaft. Probably methane. Half the mountain dropped on top of my daddy and the others. After that, you couldn't risk it. And we all knew they were dead anyway. Nobody could've survived that blast. So they just sealed it up and built a damn prison on top of it. Some damn grave marker for my daddy that was.

"And when my husband Josh got a job there, I didn't like it one bit. But like he said, it was either the prison or the mines. And I sure as hell didn't want him digging for the same black rock that killed my daddy. So the prison it was. He wanted to get Willie a job up there too, but the boy went into the mines instead. Josh was working hard on him to get him out when he got killed."

"You said it was an accident?"

Shirley snorted. "Accident? Yeah, it was 'bout as much an accident as this was." She pointed to the trailer's remnants.

"You're saying your husband was murdered? Who? Why?"

Shirley stared at her, bleary-eyed. "I shouldn't be telling you this. I shouldn't be telling anybody this. It's been a hole in my heart for two years now."

"I just want to help. I just want to find my father. You've lost your son and your husband. Shirley, it's time the truth came out."

Come on, lady, tell me.

"I know you're right. In my heart I know you are."

"Then you know you should tell me."

Shirley took a deep breath. "I'm just so tired. And this has gotten way out of hand."

"Please, Shirley."

Shirley's red eyes seemed to finally focus as she stared out into the black night. "We get big shipments at the courthouse all the time. Lots of boxes. But the manifest and the boxes never match up."

"How do you mean?"

"I mean if the manifest says fifty boxes, there's only thirty that show up."

"Do you know why?"

"I'm not looking to get into trouble."

"I'm not the police, Shirley. I just want to find my dad."

"I've been poor all my life. You see this town now, it's doing good. Everybody is happy. Why shouldn't I get my piece? You know."

"I know. It's only fair."

"Damn right it is. I wanted to go to college. My brother got to but not old Shirley. We didn't have the money."

"I'm sure," Annabelle said patiently.

Shirley took another swallow of wine. Now she didn't even appear to remember that Annabelle was there. She seemed to be talking to herself. "And was I supposed to know that Josh would get killed when he went hunting deer? Rory just said to make Josh go and then call him. And so that's what I did. How was I to know? You tell me that."

"You certainly couldn't have known. But about those boxes?" prompted Annabelle.

"There's a big drug addiction problem up here. People'll do anything to get their pop."

"Is that what's in the missing boxes. Drugs?"

If Oliver ran into the middle of a major drug ring he's probably already dead. But if he isn't, he might not have much time.

"Prescription pills. Throws off a lot of damn cash."

"How are they transferred? I mean from the missing boxes with the pills to wherever they're going?"

Shirley lit up another cigarette and eyed Annabelle shrewdly. "Missy, we got us a bunch of drug addict miners go to get their methadone pop over at the clinic every morning so they can get back and hit seven a.m. shifts at the mines."

"Okay," Annabelle said. "But how does that tie in with anything?"

"They start out about *two* a.m. I know that because I've seen 'em. It's less than an hour drive each way, and it takes about a minute to get the pop. Anybody sees them and asks why so early, they tell 'em they can't sleep, just go to the clinic and shoot the breeze. But I know for a fact that doesn't happen. What happens is those boxes get driven a good ways from here and are dropped off at designated spots."

"Okay, but where do they pick them up?"

Oliver might have found that out and gone there.

Shirley stood and stumbled down the blackened timbers to her car.

"Shirley, where are you going?"

"Where I'm going is getting the hell out of here. I'm done with Divine. Should've left a long time ago."

Annabelle raced after her, grabbed her shoulder. "Please, Shirley, it's my dad. Please. He's all I've got left."

"I already said way too much. Booze talking."

"Can't you tell me something? Anything? To at least point me the right way?"

Shirley hesitated and then looked at the ruined trailer and then back at Annabelle.

"Okay. But you'll have to think about it real good."

"All right."

"When is a bottom changed into an ass?"

Annabelle immediately looked puzzled. "What?"

Shirley let out a drunken giggle. "Like I said, you think about it. When is a bottom changed into an ass? You want to find your daddy bad enough, you'll come up with it."

She staggered to her car and got in.

"Are you okay to drive?"

Shirley poked her head out the window. "Hell, honey, I been driving drunk since I was thirteen."

Shirley peeled off and Annabelle raced to the van, which was hidden down the road and behind some trees. When she got there she found four men waiting for her instead of just two. And the new pair had guns.

CHAPTER

69

DINNER CAME right at six-thirty; two trays pushed through the slots. Knox and Stone took them, sat down on their cots and started to eat.

Knox pointed at the carrots on the plate. A few moments later the toilet flushed and the vegetables spun down the metal bowl and out of sight.

Stone was cutting his meat, which was a little difficult considering he only had a flimsy spoon to work with, when his eye caught on the edge of white poking out from under his plate. He nudged Knox with his elbow as he slid the piece of paper out. He unfolded it and began to read, while Knox looked anxiously over his shoulder.

I was the guard at the door when the nurse finished with you. I was a friend of Josh Coombs. Tomorrow in the rec yard. Just follow my lead. Flush this note.

Knox and Stone glanced at each other. Knox took the

note, read it once more and then sent it sailing down into the prison's sewer to join the drug-laced carrots.

"What do you think?" Knox said in a low voice as they resumed eating. They both tapped their feet against the floor to cover their conversation.

"I saw him glance at me when he was at the door. And he nodded. Didn't know exactly what was going on, but I was hoping."

"Follow his lead?"

"He'll have to cover himself. And we'll do exactly as he says when the time comes."

Twenty minutes later something hit their door. "Trays," bellowed a voice.

They pushed them through and sat back on their cots.

"Why do you think they're even keeping us alive?" Knox said. "They don't know that folks won't show up for me."

"Anybody comes near this place, they'll know long in advance. Then they either kill us or hide us. Plenty of places to do that here."

"So why not kill us now? Not that I'm glad they're not," he added hastily.

Stone thought about being left in the mine with the snakes. He was certain now that had been Tyree's handiwork. "Killing is fast, a second of pain and then it's over. We're free of this place. That's apparently not good enough for Howard Tyree. He wants to control us, every second of our lives. I'm sure he'll kill us at some point. But in the meantime he's looking forward to making our lives as miserable as they can possibly be."

"Guy sounds like a serial killer."

"He is, only on the wrong side of the bars."

Knox stretched out on his steel cot. "So now we wait?"

"I don't see another option right now, do you?"

Their door was hit with a hard object. "Hands through the cuff door," yelled a voice.

"Aw shit, what now!" moaned Knox.

Stone whispered, "Just remember that we've been drugged, so act punchy."

"I'm so tired I won't have to act."

They were cuffed, stripped, searched and probed. This had quickly become almost as natural as taking a piss. Both men hung their heads and acted as listless as possible without overdoing it.

They were herded down the hall, guards and Tasers on either side while they shackle-shuffled along. They climbed stairs until there were no more stairs to climb. Stone figured they were in the west tower of the prison but he couldn't be sure. His usually reliable internal compass wasn't working all that well in here.

The room they were brought to was circular-shaped with a table and two chairs in the very center. Three-inch-wide slits in the wall revealed the dark outside. A fluorescent light bubbled overhead. They were placed in the chairs and the guards stood back, waiting.

So were Knox and Stone. With apprehension. They didn't know what was coming, only that it would be painful.

The door opened and Tyree walked in followed by four more guards, including the one who'd grabbed Stone by the balls and Manson, the one-eye.

"Gentlemen," said Tyree. "We need to talk."

Stone stared up at him with a dull expression. Knox

kept his gaze on the table as though he hadn't understood the man.

One guard whispered into Tyree's ear. He nodded. "Right. Of course. Give them a pop then, because I need their undivided attention."

A guard pulled a syringe from a black bag he carried. Stone was swabbed and then injected in the upper arm. The needle was cleaned with alcohol and Knox was hit next.

Whatever they'd been given, the effect was immediate. Stone could feel his heart racing and every nerve he possessed was on overdrive. He glanced over at Knox and saw he was having the very same reaction.

"Good," said Tyree. "Now get 'em hooked up."

A duffel bag was opened and out of it came two thick leather belts with black wires attached. They were placed around each man's middle and padlocked down. Tyree was handed a black box with buttons on it.

He depressed one of the buttons and a green light came on. He stood in front of the men and then turned his attention to Knox.

"All right, Mr. CIA. Does anyone know that you came to the town of Divine?"

"Yes."

Tyree depressed the button and Knox stood straight up, screaming as the voltage entered him. Tyree released the button, and like a marionette that had lost its handler, Knox slumped back down in the chair, panting and swaying.

Tyree looked at Stone. "What is your real name?"

"Oliver Stone."

A second later, Stone was involuntarily on his tiptoes,

feeling like both his brain and his heart were going to explode.

Tyree removed his finger and Stone dropped back down, missed the chair and hit the floor. The guards grabbed him and slammed him back in his seat.

Tyree turned back to Knox. "Does anyone know that you came to the town of Divine?"

"NO!"

The blast hit him again. After he was slumped back in his chair, he barked, "What the hell answer do you want?"

"The truth."

"Well, one of those answers *had* to be the truth, you dickhead!"

Tyree held the button down so long that Stone feared Knox would not come back. But he did, sweating and swearing. — —

Tyree turned to Stone. "Oliver Stone?"

Okay, buddy, let's see if you can take it as well as you can dish it out.

Speaking as steadily as was possible after having his organs fried, he said, "My real name is John Carr. I used to be a government assassin, decades ago, tasked to a special division of the CIA so classified not even the president knew about it. I had a falling-out with my superiors. I've been on the run ever since. Agent Knox is one of the best men the intelligence community has. He was assigned by the president of the United States himself to hunt me down because they believed that I murdered Senator Roger Simpson and Carter Gray. I'm sure you heard about that. Well, Knox is as good as his rep, because he found me. Now we're here at Dead Rock being beaten and tortured by a bunch of drug dealers masquerading as prison officials." He glanced around at the guards. "But I'm sure you have nothing to worry about. The president will probably just forget the matter and do no follow-up. I doubt they care what happens to me. Or one of their best agents."

Stone could now see just the reaction he was hoping for. Sweat. Sweat and nervous glances, particularly from the one-striper and Manson, who looked ready to piss all over their Gestapo boots.

The next instant Stone was on his feet, the current thundering through him. When Tyree released the button, Stone took a little while to recover, panting and gasping for air, his muscles twitching uncontrollably.

He gasped, "You can do a polygraph. I'm sure you're set up to do that what with all the electronic gizmos you guys seem to enjoy so much. I can tell you enjoy the pain thing, but it's not getting you what you want. So be smart about it, Warden. Ask me the question again. *Who am I*, while I'm strapped to the meter. Then you'll see what the truth really is. But again I wouldn't worry. I don't see how sixteen intelligence agencies plus the Department of Homeland Security, with thousands of highly trained agents and collective budgets of about a hundred billion dollars, will ever find us here."

Now, finally, Stone could see the twitch in the warden's eyes too. Tyree fingered the box but did not push the button again. He also did not meet Stone's gaze.

Later that night after their hearts and other organs had settled down from the pounding, they were both hooked to polygraphs. Questions were asked and answered. And results were read. The squiggly lines from the polygraph did not appear to please the warden. Stone could see that clearly from the man not looking at him as he ordered them back to their cell.

Let *him* sweat tonight.

They lay there on their cots staring up at the ceiling, recovering from their ordeal by electric shock and each no doubt daydreaming about their strong hands closing around the throat of one Howard Tyree and crushing the life out of him.

"Smart thinking, Oliver," Knox said, finally breaking the silence. "I loved it when he followed your *order* about the polygraph. And you saw the guards' expressions when you hit 'em with the facts?"

"I saw."

"What do you think they'll do now?"

"Snoop around and see if anything might be coming their way. That gives us the one thing we really need."

"Time," answered Knox.

"Time," agreed Stone.

They heard a sound at the door and both men braced for another painful extraction. Yet the only thing coming in was a slip of paper through the cuff slot. It drifted down to the floor. Knox snagged it and passed the note to Stone.

Stone read it. "Next chow, watch out for Manson."

Stone glanced up at Knox. "You thinking what I'm thinking?" he said.

"Absolutely, but they could kill us or at least mess up our chance with this guard."

"Not if we do it the right way."

CHAPTER

70

"Harry, what are you doing here?" Annabelle looked from Harry Finn to Alex Ford as they sat crammed in the back of the van.

"Alex filled me in on what was going on. Sounded like you could use some help."

Harry Finn, while perhaps not as lethal and skilled as Oliver Stone, was worth at least five ordinary men in his ability to fight and think at the same time.

"What did you get from old Shirley?" asked Reuben.

"A lot." She quickly filled Alex and Harry in on all that they'd found out, including her conversation with Shirley.

"How does a bottom turn into an ass?" said Alex. "What the hell kind of clue is that?"

"It's a very clear one," answered Caleb, who was in the driver's seat. Everyone turned to stare at him. "Nick Bottom is a character, a weaver actually, whose head is transformed into an ass's head by Puck the Hobgoblin."

They all stared at Caleb in befuddlement before Reuben said, "Are you on some kind of librarian crack?"

"No, it means that drunk Shirley is actually fairly well-read because that's a scene from Shakespeare's *A Midsummer Night's Dream*."

"Abby Riker's place," exclaimed Annabelle. "A Midsummer's Farm."

"Sounds like a plan," began Alex, but he stopped talking when Harry held up a hand. They all listened.

"There's someone out there," hissed Caleb.

Harry and Alex pulled their weapons. Alex tossed a spare gun to Reuben, who took up position near one of the wide windows.

"Caleb, are you okay driving—"

They were nearly knocked over when Caleb rammed the accelerator and the van crashed through some bushes and hit the road even as bullets pinged against the sides of the vehicle.

Alex shoved Annabelle to the floorboard and then he ducked down.

Reuben slid open the window, took aim and fired behind them. Alex and Harry did the same from the other side.

Caleb hit a straightaway and pushed the van to its max.

"Eighty is all the juice this shit-can has," he barked. "Next time give me a decent ride if you want me to outrun the suckers. I can't make tomato sauce without tomatoes, for godsakes!"

Confused, Alex eyed Harry and then looked down at Annabelle.

She said wearily, "You don't want to know."

Over the next five minutes Caleb took hairpin turns barely on four wheels, cut down this road and that, and ran around one curve where the van's left-side tires were nearly kissing air over a vertical drop. He finally slowed.

"No lights back there for the last two minutes," he said. "Where to now?"

"The farm," answered Alex. "Fast, but without killing us, please."

Keeping alert, they made their way slowly back and drove through downtown Divine. When they reached the other side they saw the red rooftop lights of the cop car that was parked on the side of the road near a long drop-off. Other vehicles, including a fire truck, were parked next to it. Men were milling about, and a fire hose extended down the slope.

Annabelle said, "Stop, Caleb. That's Sheriff Tyree."

Caleb pulled off the road and Annabelle climbed out of the van and hurried over to Tyree, who was standing there, hands in his pockets and seemingly studying his boots with little interest.

"Sheriff, what happened?"

He glanced at her and scowled. "What are you doing around here this time of night?"

"Still looking for my dad." She stared down the steep slope where she could see smoke rising and some men tethered to ropes looking over the remains of a car. Then she noticed where the dirt shoulder had been torn up. "An accident?"

He nodded. "Shirley Coombs, or what's left of her."

Annabelle gave a sharp intake of breath.

He eyed her sternly. "What?"

"I was talking to her not more than an hour ago."

"Where?"

"At her son's trailer, or what's left of it."

"What were you doing there?"

"I was driving by and heard somebody sobbing. It was Shirley. I was trying to comfort her."

"Had she been drinking?"

Annabelle hesitated but then said, "Yes."

"Damn fool woman ran off the road."

Annabelle looked around and saw the tire marks and then a bit of gray metal lying on the road under the glare of lights. She bent down to pick it up.

"Don't touch that!" snapped Tyree.

She stood quickly. "But Shirley's car was red."

Tyree grabbed her by the arm and hustled her away from the accident scene and across the road while several of the men looked on curiously.

She exclaimed, "Sheriff, what is going on? That wasn't an accident. Someone hit her car."

"I know that. I just don't want other folks to."

"But why?"

"Because I said so, that's why! Now, what did Shirley tell you that would get her killed?"

Annabelle nervously licked her lips. Shirley had made it clear that she trusted no one in this place. So how could Annabelle?

"Ma'am, I want to get to the bottom of this whole thing. It's my town and I need to make things right."

Annabelle had a great BS meter and it was making no noise. "Come over here."

She led him to the van and opened the back door, revealing the others inside. She introduced them one by one and said, "Sheriff, you got some time to hear what we know? It's going to take a while."

"Let's get on over to my office then. Too many ears 'round here."

An hour later, sitting in Tyree's office, the lawman rubbed his face, stood and glumly stared out the window. "So he's not your father but he did work for the government and has been underground for years. And you and your friends are FBI agents tasked with bringing him safely back?"

"That's right," said Annabelle. She'd of course made no mention of Joe Knox being after Stone for the murders of Simpson and Gray. Yet she had told the lawman as much of the truth as she could, which for Annabelle was a new way to operate.

"You lied to me once and now I'm just supposed to believe you? How about I call the FBI in D.C. Will they know who you are?"

Alex stood and held out his ID. "I'm not FBI. This is a joint task force. So how about you call my headquarters in D.C. and verify I am who I say I am. We'll wait here while you do. But if you're going to do it, do it now. We need to find him, fast."

Tyree eyed Alex's creds and then shook his head. "I believe you." He stepped back to his desk and perched on the edge while Annabelle shot Alex a grateful look. "And you think it has something to do with Abby Riker's farm?"

"The clue clearly referred to her place," said Caleb.

"But you're not saying Abby has anything to do with it. That's crazy."

Annabelle said, "I'm not accusing anyone of anything. But her son *is* missing."

"A drug ring operating out of Divine," said Tyree. "And if Shirley said the boxes were coming to the courthouse with some missing, the judge must be in on it too. Pretty slick, because who's going to check legal documents going to a courthouse? And using the miners going to get their methadone? Who the hell thought of that?"

There was a knock on the door and a man came in. Charlie Trimble was dressed in khaki pants and a striped button-down shirt.

"I know it's late but I saw your light on, Sheriff—" He broke off when he saw the other people with him.

"I'm sort of busy, Charlie."

Trimble looked keenly at Annabelle. "Ah, the daughter. Still looking for your *father*?"

Annabelle did not like the emphasis the man put on the last word.

"No, he's actually not my father." She turned to Alex. "He's the man I was telling you about. The reporter looking to make a fast scoop."

"I see. At the expense of national security, I don't think so."

"National security?" said Trimble, taken aback. He glanced at Tyree. "What are they talking about?"

"Apparently Ben isn't who we thought he was."

"I know that," said Trimble excitedly. "But I think I do know who he is. I've got the story all ready to go. But I—"

He shut up as Annabelle shoved her ID in his face. Alex did the same. "Trimble," she began, "you're not going to print one syllable of anything having to do with this matter."

Trimble said in a defiant tone, "Don't think you can intimidate me."

"We're not trying to intimidate you, just give you a fair warning," said Alex.

"Warning, about what?"

"If you print your story and something happens to our guy, your butt will end up at the Castle."

"The Castle? What castle?"

"Leavenworth."

"Leavenworth? That's for military crimes. I'm not in the military."

"Actually," said Alex, barely able to conceal a smile, "it's also for national security crimes. And just for the record, you're anything I want you to be."

"What about the first amendment?"

Reuben towered over him. "What about the *second* amendment?" he said menacingly, the pistol in his belt clip clearly visible.

"I . . . I mean, uh, nothing, nothing."

Annabelle hooked him by the arm. "Trimble?"

"Yes?" he said shakily.

"Go home. Now! Before you get hurt."

The journalist nearly shot out of the room.

She turned to Tyree. "I think it's time we go to see where a bottom turns into an ass."

CHAPTER

71

TYREE LED THE WAY in his patrol car with the van behind. About a quarter mile from the farm he pulled off and the van slid in behind him.

Getting out of the car, he said, "We'll make the rest of the way on foot. Don't want to spook anybody. We got time before the miners come."

They threaded their way through the woods until they came to the outskirts of the farm and set up an observation post near the house, which was dark. Abby's pickup truck and the Mini Cooper were parked out front.

Tyree said in a near whisper, "There's another back road into the farm that leads to an old barn. We should probably post some folks there too just in case."

Reuben, Harry and Caleb headed that way following directions Tyree gave them.

Both groups hunkered down and waited. And waited some more.

Finally, Alex checked his watch. "Four in the morning. I don't think it's happening. Maybe they don't transport every night."

Tyree stretched his limbs. "They killed Shirley so maybe they postponed the shipment."

At that moment Harry came hurrying up to them.

"Did you see anything?" Alex asked excitedly.

"Not a person, but we did see something. Come on."

They hurried after him. When they reached the spot where Caleb and Reuben were waiting, Harry pointed to the woods at a spot right across from the entrance to the barn. "You can see somebody's gone crashing through there. Brush and low tree limbs all busted up."

"Let's follow it," said Tyree, taking the lead. He pulled out a flashlight and slipped another off his belt and handed it to Alex.

"Never worked with a fed before."

"It's sort of a first time for me too, Sheriff," Alex said wryly.

They came to a dirt road in the woods.

"Look," said Annabelle.

It was Joe Knox's truck.

They ran to it and looked inside.

"No rental docs," said Tyree. "Any idea who it belongs to?"

Annabelle glanced at the others, her thoughts moving rapidly. *Does this have nothing to do with the drug dealers? Has Knox gotten to Oliver, killed him already? But why would Knox's truck be here then? Has Oliver killed Knox?*

"No," she said.

Tyree saw the bloodstains in the woods a bit later. "There, and there, and over there," he said, making stabbing motions with his light.

"That's not good," Caleb said quite unnecessarily.

Annabelle's spirits sank further. It seemed like one of the men had been hurt or killed. But which one?

They followed the trail across the road and up the slope. There were more bloodstains here. They moved across some more ground and then stopped. There were lots of footprints in the soft mud and more dark stains. Annabelle's gloomy expression changed now and she became more alert. As they followed the marks they came to a spot where it appeared as though the people had marched in lockstep.

"Or carrying something. Or somebody," Alex deduced.

They followed the trail back down to the road but at another spot. There were more dark stains here, and also what looked to be a slick of oil.

"It looks like someone was put in a car or truck," said Harry.

"A truck," noted Tyree. He flashed his light on the asphalt. "Tire ran over some of that oil and left a mark. That's a tire tread from a truck. Maybe we can track it that way."

As the edges of the night began to lift around them they hustled down the road, desperately looking for more clues.

Reuben was the first to see it. "The truck cut across here." He pointed to the smear of oil on the road. "And went into that field."

They rushed into the open space. It was quite easy to

see the ruts the truck had made in the soft earth here. As they got to the middle of the field, Alex swept his light in a wide swath.

Harry said, "Stop. Hold it right there." Alex did so and Harry knelt down and grazed his hand along the top of a long depression in the dirt.

He looked up. "That's a mark from a chopper's skids." He eyed Tyree. "Who has a chopper around here?"

Tyree's light was square on this mark, his features were very grim.

"Tyree, does anybody you know up here have a chopper?" Alex said, tugging at the lawman's arm.

"Yeah," he said slowly. "My damn brother."

There was a buzzing sound. Tyree reached in his pocket and pulled out his phone.

"Tyree?"

The tall lawman's legs buckled. "What? When?"

Annabelle said, "What is it?"

"I'll be right there."

He clicked off and looked at the others.

"What is it?" Annabelle demanded again.

"That was a fellow I deputized to look after Abby Riker. He just came to."

"Just came to?" Alex said uneasily.

Tyree was already rushing back to the road. "They've got Abby," he yelled.

CHAPTER

72

KNOX AND STONE ate their breakfast in silence, doing their best to act as lethargic as the rest of the prison population actually was from their drug dose the day before. Both men's gazes were in fact sweeping the cafeteria.

Near the end of the meal, Knox, who was sitting across from Stone so they could watch both sides of the room and not be surprised from the rear, gave a little rehearsed cough and his gaze darted to nine o'clock. An instant before the blow struck, Stone lifted his tray up and used it as a shield. The shiv glanced off the hard plastic. In the next motion, Stone had hooked Manson's leg with his own, and the big guard's momentum caused him to slide across the table. He crashed through plates and plastic cups until he toppled to the floor on the other side, taking two prisoners next to Knox down with him. In the commotion that followed, Knox edged his plate off the table with his elbow and his uneaten grits plopped directly on Manson's head.

When the other guards came running they found Stone and Knox sitting there calmly, but with bewildered expressions, and staring at the pile of bodies on the floor.

When the guards pulled Manson to his feet, he was still holding the shiv.

"Frank, what the hell are you—" began one of the guards before Manson roughly pushed him away. With an enraged scream he tried to jump over the table at Stone. Only Knox had stood on his foot at that precise moment and his leap turned into an abrupt fall. His chin slammed down on the table in front of where Stone was sitting. As if on cue, Knox stood, blocking the view of the other guards.

"Let me get out of your way so you can deal with the psycho guard," he said politely.

In that instant, Oliver Stone delivered a crushing blow to the back of Manson's neck with his elbow. When the guards finally got around Knox, Stone had slipped to the other end of the table and seemed to be innocently watching the events.

Manson was carried off on a gurney unconscious and barely breathing. Even the most comatose con in the room had a smile on his face at the sight.

Later that morning Stone and Knox were standing in the rec yard. No one had come after them about what had happened to Manson, though Stone had been popped once in the head for apparently chewing too loudly.

"How hard did you hit him?" Knox asked.

"Hard enough."

"I like your style."

Donny boy smiled at them as he passed by. He gave a stupid thumbs-up to Stone. The guards on the pod towers were making their rounds, eyeballing the gaggle of cons with binoculars and scopes on stationary tripods. And the guns. The guns were always front and center. The power. The deterrent. Stone thought this as he leaned against the cement block wall and wondered how the older guard was going to accomplish it, whatever it was.

Knox kept checking the periphery without seeming to do so as he stood next to Stone.

One inmate was bouncing the ball. He made a layup, caught the rebound and went back for a jumper. Like most of the inmates Stone and Knox had seen, he was black, young, tall and muscular. He seemed to have all his wits about him, so maybe Donny had let out his secret to others about the carrots. He missed the jumper and Stone stiffened as the black guy jogged to get the ball that had rolled past the blue line.

Before he could get there though, another inmate crashed into him, knocking the man across the line where he landed on the ball. The two men got up and faced off. A horn sounded. And the riflemen on the towers took aim. A shot was fired, but it didn't come from the tower. The guards looked everywhere for the source of the round.

As if on cue one inmate hit another inmate, sending him down with a bloodied nose. Another shot was fired. Whistles erupted, horns blared and a cluster of cons in the middle of the concrete playground bolted, screaming. Two guards who ran up to stop this human stampede were run over, their caps and billy clubs disappearing beneath the tidal wave of fleeing prisoners.

Hands closed around Stone's and Knox's wrists and they were pulled forward.

"Back to your cells, now!" barked a voice.

Stone's gaze fell on the older guard, the one who'd nodded at him. He was pushing Knox and Stone toward one of the entrances into the prison.

As they passed a throng of prisoners standing there watching the melee, Knox spotted Donny, who was smiling and cheering on the fighters.

Knox sucker-punched him and old Donny boy, the killer of three kids, slid unconscious to the cold concrete lawn of Dead Rock.

"Now, that's what I call accountability," Knox muttered as he followed behind Stone.

Inside the building the guard herded them up a set of stairs and into a small room, where he closed the door.

"Turn around."

They did so, a little hesitantly.

He quickly cuffed and shackled them, then spun them back around to face him.

"We don't have much time. I was Josh Coombs' best friend. I heard you helped Willie."

"I did. He's dead now, I guess you heard. Bob too. Blown up."

The guard nodded. "Any idea what's going on?"

"Drugs." Stone gave him the thirty-second version and ended with, "And Josh was murdered because he'd found out."

"I kind of figured something like that. I've heard things, seen some weird stuff, but nothing I could prove. But I sure as hell know you two weren't prison transfers."

"How many guards think like you?"

"No more than two or three. The rest are in Tyree's pocket."

Knox said, "I'm with the CIA. My name is Joe Knox. I need you to contact a guy named Marshall Saunders and tell him where I am. His phone number is—" He broke off and stared at Stone. "You can tell him I'm alone," Knox finished.

"I'm not going to let you do that," said Stone.

"You don't have a choice. That's why I'm calling my buddy Marsh and not Hayes."

"We both know Hayes. If he finds out you screwed him, your next stop will be a torture center in Afghanistan, and you won't be the one doing the interrogating. So go back to your family. And finish your life on your terms, not his."

"Oliver, do you know what he's—"

Stone broke in, "I've always known. Some things never change."

"Guys," the guard said nervously. "Hurry the hell up."

Knox gazed for another moment at Stone and then gave the phone number to the guard and the fact that he had a man named John Carr with him. "Call Saunders just as soon as you can and tell him where we are."

They were hustled back to their cells as the entire prison was put in lockdown.

As the pair sat shackled in their cell, Knox said, "I'll do all I can do to ensure you get a fair shake. I'm not going to let Hayes make you disappear."

"I've already disappeared. I've been invisible for the last thirty years, in fact."

A few moments of silence passed.

"Why didn't Hayes let you have that damn medal?"

Stone scooted up to a standing position and leaned back against the wall. "It was so many years ago, I don't think I remember anymore."

"Sure you do. That place you never forget. Ever."

Stone glanced at him. "When were you in Nam?"

"Last eighteen months of the war."

"I was more on the front end." Stone gazed down at the floor as he spoke. He had never really told anyone about this before, but he also knew it really didn't matter anymore. They would either die in this place or Stone would die in another prison, if he wasn't executed.

He looked up at Knox. "Macklin Hayes had one way of fighting. Throw as many grunts into the meat grinder as he could find, and see where the chips fell. But regardless of the outcome he saw to it that the reports that went up the line all detailed his brilliance on the battlefield. Although I believe the closest he ever got to actual combat was the occasional dustup in the officers' mess."

"I had some brass just like that. Talked a great game but never wanted to come up to bat."

"Hayes believed that I cost him a fast promotion to lieutenant colonel. And maybe I did."

"How?"

"There were three villages on a patch of dirt that the higher-ups suddenly decided we had to own. I guess so they could make it seem like we were winning the war back home. They gave the assignment to Hayes. A nice little carrot for his next bump up the line to the one-star. He ordered three companies forward, one company to hit each village. The night before we were going in Hayes called a meeting of all the sergeants."

"What about the captains?"

"They were all dead. We ran through captains and second lieutenants like you wouldn't believe. Anyway, he ordered us to flatten the places. Nobody left."

"No soldiers, you mean."

"I mean nobody, Knox, men, women and children. Nobody. Then we were to put a torch to the place and say that the Viet Cong had done it. It was some disinformation bullshit campaign that Hayes had come up with. He was constantly pulling that crap. Guy was like Machiavelli reincarnated. I think he saw it as a career enhancer."

"What happened?"

"Two of the three companies followed orders. One didn't."

"And Hayes came after you?"

"He tried. But I told him if he did I'd tell everybody the truth. It wasn't like he could say I'd disobeyed orders, because the orders he gave should have landed him right in front of a court-martial. See, I knew how he played the game. The brass upstairs might look the other way if the mission went off, but any hiccup that the journalists could get hold of and they'd eat him alive. Anyway, with one village left, the command chain wasn't pleased. So it took old Hayes a little longer to get his cluster of oak leaves."

"But he found another way to hurt you. The medal."

"I really didn't give a shit at that point. I'd been fighting a war that had no end. Every friend I'd ever had over there was dead. I was tired. I was sick of Southeast Asia, the rain, the heat, every minute of every day of my life spent taking and giving up a hundred yards' worth of dirt and jungle, and for what? For what, Knox?"

"Is that when you joined Triple Six?"

Stone hesitated. "I guess you've earned the right to know."

"I promise you it won't go any further. If they convict you it won't come with any help from me."

"Yeah, that's when Triple Six came, although I wouldn't say I joined. They made it clear that was my only option. I just ended up trading one hell for another. I was always lucky that way."

"I'm assuming you were great at your job. So why did the CIA turn on you?"

"The years went by and I married Claire and we had our little girl. Best thing that ever happened to me. Without getting too sappy about it, it was like a whole new world of possibilities opened up for me. And I decided I didn't want to play the game anymore. I just couldn't pull the trigger, Knox. I couldn't stand my own stench. I couldn't fly halfway around the world, pop someone in the brain and come home and hold my little girl and kiss my wife. I couldn't do it anymore."

"And they didn't appreciate that?"

"Men like that think they own you forever. And maybe they do."

Stone slid back down to the floor, tipped his head back and closed his eyes.

"I'll help you, Oliver. I swear it."

"You just help yourself, Knox. It's too late for me. And all I'll be getting is exactly what I deserve."

CHAPTER

73

THEY'D ALL CAUGHT a few hours' sleep at Tyree's home about two miles from downtown Divine. It was a modest-size plank house on a nice piece of land set on a hill with a long meadow behind.

Tyree made a big pot of coffee and put together some breakfast. The big sheriff's eyes were red and puffy.

"I apologize for the sorry state of the vittles. I'm not used to having this much company."

"This is all the *vittles* I need," said Reuben, gulping from a large mug of straight java.

They'd gotten to Abby Riker's place and the scene there had easily told them what had occurred. Front door busted in. Furniture overturned and the deputy sitting in the middle of the floor with blood running down his face. Besides that there was no clue who had taken Abby or where they'd gone. Tyree had put out an APB but they'd heard nothing yet. And every hour that slipped by did not bode well for the woman's safe return.

"I can't believe I didn't think of that," said Tyree guiltily.

"You had a man posted to guard her, Sheriff," Annabelle pointed out.

"Earl isn't much good in situations like that. But he's all I had. I should've been the one to protect her. If anything happens to her—" He broke off and stared down, and a tear fell from his eye onto the kitchen table.

"Why do you think they took her?" Alex asked quietly after an awkward silence.

Tyree wiped his face and looked up, clearing his throat loudly. "Been thinking about that. Danny's out there somewhere. Maybe they were afraid of what he'd do. So they took his mother as insurance. That boy loves his mother."

"Do you think Danny was involved in the drug-running?" asked Annabelle.

"Don't know. Fact that they were using that old barn makes me think the answer to that might be yes."

"But you said he left town."

"After Debby died. Maybe he drew the line at folks murdering his friends."

"Any word on the judge?" asked Alex.

"Surprise, surprise, he's gone too."

"So he must've been in on it and got tipped off," said Harry.

Tyree nodded. "He'd been a judge down in Texas. And he spent time in South America, least that's what he told me."

"They know drug dealing real well there."

Tyree added, "See, I been reading about how easy it is to ship stuff up from Texas that comes over the Mexican border. Seems there's two ways to deal prescription drugs. Steal it or make it."

"*Make* prescription drugs?" said Caleb, looking astonished.

"Drug labs in Colombia in particular have been producing oxycodone knockoffs by the ton and smuggling them in here," Alex explained. "The stuff isn't pure, of course. It's not like a filthy drug lab has the same quality control as a legit pharmaceutical manufacturer. And that's why it's so dangerous."

Tyree nodded. "So maybe our friend the judge had connections down there. Maybe the place was too hot to hold him. And when he stumbled across old Divine he thought he'd found a good place to lie low for a while."

"So the judge has the pipeline connections. Would your brother have big-city connections for distribution purposes?"

"Eighty percent of the prisoners up there are from big cities and most of 'em were in the drug business and killed somebody. That's what got them to Dead Rock. So, yeah, he might have distribution contacts."

"But if your brother is involved in this, how did they get together? Were they friends?"

"Mosley went up to the prison once a month to mediate. I thought that was right funny when I first heard about it."

"Why?"

"My brother's not much into compromise. It was always his way or the highway."

Annabelle said, "You don't seem all that surprised to learn your brother might be a criminal."

Tyree gave a weak smile. "I was the son who won all the sports awards and Howard was the one who got all the academic scholarships. The dumb jock and the smart older brother. But he had another side to him. Cruel, I guess you'd call it. Before I got bigger than him, he would put the hurt on me if I did something he didn't like. That's why him and me have never been that close. And he always liked to live well. And while he's the top dog up there, it's not like wardens make a ton of money, even at a supermax."

"Peterson was an accountant. Maybe he was doing the books for the ring. Maybe he was skimming and they found out," Alex suggested.

Tyree rubbed his hand along his chin. "There might actually be more to it than that."

"What do you mean?"

"We have a town fund here. An investment fund that Peterson was doing the books on too."

"A town fund?" said Annabelle.

"Yeah, people and businesses pooled some money. Abby kicked in quite a bit; she had more than anybody else. It's done real well over the last few years. Paid quite a dividend."

"Which is why Divine is a lot more prosperous than other towns like it," added Reuben.

"But it might not be because of great investments," ventured Harry.

"No," said Alex. "It might be for another reason: they're using the town fund to launder the drug proceeds."

Annabelle said, "And it's a perfect way to do it. Lots of little checks cut. A town in the boonies. Who'd suspect? The cash comes out pure white."

Tyree said, "What if your guy is up at that prison, how do we get to him? It's not like we have enough to get a search warrant."

Annabelle snapped, "Screw a search warrant. What we need to do is just get up to that prison and get him out fast if he's there."

They all stared at her, Tyree looking the most nervous.

"I'm not sure that's such a good idea, ma'am. My brother is a pretty smart guy. And if he is involved in all this, you can bet he won't let us waltz into the place and look around."

"That's okay, Sheriff, I rarely go in the front door. Shirley told me about those miners getting killed and that's why they call the prison Dead Rock. She mentioned a parallel shaft. I wonder where it is and how far it went in?"

Tyree said, "I don't know the particulars."

"I can check at the local library," Caleb offered.

"And find out everything you can on Dead Rock prison," she added. She looked at Tyree. "And I'd appreciate everything you can tell me about the place too."

"I'll be glad to, but there're lots of places to hide folks up there," Tyree pointed out.

"I'm sort of counting on that," said Annabelle.

CHAPTER

74

THERE *WAS* ANOTHER CHOPPER in the vicinity of Divine and it soared along the treetops before landing in the parking lot of Blue Spruce Prison.

Only one man got out of the bird; he walked unhurriedly toward the prison.

It took a few minutes of processing at the front entrance and a phone call. And for such a special visitor, the warden himself came down.

Macklin Hayes shook hands with Howard Tyree.

"What does the CIA want here?" Tyree said in a surly tone.

"I think you have one of my men here," the CIA chief answered pleasantly.

"I have no idea what you're talking about."

"All right, we'll play the game. For now, anyway. His name is Joe Knox. He's about six-one, two-twenty, with slicked back salt-and-pepper hair. He should have another man with him. A little taller, leaner, white hair, cut short. Answers to the name Oliver Stone or John Carr depending on the day and the situation."

"There's no one here who fits that description. Now, I'm going to have to ask you to leave. This is a supermax prison and unauthorized visitors are never welcome even from the CIA." Tyree's men clustered behind him.

Hayes looked slightly alarmed. "You seem to have me outnumbered. My goodness, what was I thinking?" He put the slim briefcase he was carrying down on a table, popped it open and drew out a slim file. From it he took several slips of paper. "Drug-running, was it? Yes, that's right." He gave a mock shiver. "I'm sure you all are suitably tough and dangerous, so I must watch my step." He pressed his long, bony fingers against the pages. "These documents are awaiting signature by the attorney general to authorize a lockdown of this prison and all personnel here."

"On what grounds?"

"On the grounds that your drug-dealing operation is funneling monies to terrorist organizations that have infiltrated the United States."

"That's ridiculous."

"Actually, we already have the proof ready to go. This document," Hayes continued imperturbably, "is an arrest warrant for Joseph Knox, John Carr *and* Howard Tyree. You can see that it's duly signed."

The warden didn't even bother glancing at the papers. He said, "You might be a big deal in Washington, but in case you haven't noticed this isn't Washington. So I'm not going anywhere."

"That's the whole point," said Hayes. "Let me see Knox and Carr and you'll have no more problems."

"Right. If they were here, and I'm not saying they are, how do I know they wouldn't tell you some bullshit story that you'll use to come after me? Tell me that?"

Hayes looked at his watch. When he glanced back up, his smile was gone. "I don't give a shit about your little drug operation. In the grand scheme of things you don't even rise to the level of a hemorrhoid on my *ass*. You have one minute to take me to these men."

"Or what?" snapped Tyree.

"You really are tiresome." Hayes reached slowly in his pocket, lifted out his phone and pushed one button.

A second later there was an explosion in the prison's front parking lot.

Tyree and his men raced to the window and looked out at the smoldering remains of the car. Smoke was still rising off the chopper's side cannon muzzle.

"That was my damn Cadillac," screamed Tyree.

"I know. We checked the registration. I wouldn't have wasted a cannon round that expensive on a mere guard's ride. Let me make this as clear as I possibly can. *This* is a national security issue. Not even the president himself could stand in the way. And *you*, my little friend, are no president. Take me to see them. Now!" He added in a softer tone, "And Uncle Sam will even buy you a new car."

Stone and Knox sat shackled at the table. Everyone in the prison had heard the explosion outside, but no one knew what was going on. When the door opened and he saw the man, Knox cried out, "Oh shit!"

"It's nice to see you too, Knox." Hayes smiled at them both and sat down.

"What the hell are you doing here?"

"I had anyone you might contact on a surveillance list. When Marsh got the call I was ready. And don't waste time wondering if he'll come to your aid. He's already been transferred out of the country. You shouldn't have played me for an idiot, Knox. You really shouldn't have."

He gazed at a stunned Knox for a moment longer and then turned to Stone.

"It's been a long time, John. I can't say the years have been kind to you."

"They've been better to me than they have been to you, *Mack*."

"Tell me, how did it feel to kill our old friends? Did your chest puff with pride when you finished them off?"

"That's right, you wouldn't know how it felt to kill somebody. You always got other people to do it for you."

Hayes opened his briefcase and took out a single piece of paper. He held it up for Knox to see. It was the order signed by Hayes cutting off further discussion of John Carr receiving the Medal of Honor.

"When you called and told me that the 'country' folks around this filthy hole in the ground might rally around the *persecuted* Vietnam vet, I wondered what you might have meant by that. *And* how you found out about it. I went to the military archives. They were very helpful in showing me what you'd looked at. Unfortunately, the boxes weren't inventoried, but this page had left a bit of the print on the inside of the box wall. It was enough to have my people search your house. And they found this. I thought it had been destroyed a long time ago. Just goes to show that no one is truly omniscient."

He glanced over at Stone. "And I'm sure John here has told you all about our little disagreement in the jungle."

"I've told him nothing. He was working for you. You think I'd trust his ass?" Stone snapped.

Hayes sat back and rested his hands on his lap. "John, you're a much better killer than you are a liar. Prevarication is my bailiwick. And I could always sense it in others."

"You could never let it go, could you?"

"Why should I? You hurt me a long time ago. Where's the justice in that?"

"Justice?" bellowed Knox. "You kept him from getting the Medal of Honor!"

"And he kept me from the promotion that was rightfully mine."

"You're comparing what this guy did on the battlefield to making you wait a couple extra months to get your crappy pair of oak clusters?"

"He was a grunt. We had millions of them. But there weren't that many officers of my caliber. I'm certain he hurt the war effort by doing it."

"You really think we would've won the Vietnam War if you'd been made lieutenant colonel sooner?" Knox said in disbelief.

"I admit I have an ego."

"That's not an ego. That's freaking psychotic."

Hayes pulled out a lighter, clicked it against an edge of the old paper and in a few seconds it crumpled to ash.

"Now let me get this right." He pointed at Knox. "You're an armed robber and murderer. Nasty business. If I'd only known." He turned to Stone. "And you're Anthony

Butcher. At least that idiot warden has a sense of humor if not style. Triple murderer. How perfect, though that tally hardly does you justice."

He rose and clicked his briefcase shut. "I believe that's all. I'll leave you two to serve out your debt to society. I've told the warden to be especially attentive to you both. I'm sure you appreciate the significance of that."

"Hayes!" Knox screamed as he strained against the shackles. "There is no way in hell you can pull this off. Not even you."

Hayes stopped at the door. "Well, the fact is, I just did. Oh, and one more detail. The guard who contacted Marsh on your behalf? I wouldn't wait around for his help again. You see, we traced the call to his home phone. I've shared that information with the good warden. I'm certain he'll follow up in an appropriate manner."

He closed the door softly behind him.

CHAPTER

75

"THE HUMAN RIGHTS WATCH people and Amnesty International, among others, have been trying to get into Blue Spruce for years," Caleb said after he'd informed them of many particulars of how the prison was run. They were all back at Tyree's house, which they were now using as a base.

"The list of alleged human rights violations there is very lengthy," Caleb continued. "But the prison has refused all requests for visits by Amnesty and other organizations. God, even Russia has allowed those folks to visit its prisons. And when several inmates had stun guns used on them at Blue Spruce, lapsed into comas and died, additional requests were made to enter the prison, but they were denied."

Alex looked at Tyree. "I know he's your brother, but

all that going on right next door and you never did anything about it?"

"That's another reason Howard and me aren't close. Who do you think turned Amnesty International on to the place?"

"You?" said Caleb.

"I went up there once on a prisoner transport. Poked around a bit when nobody was watching me. I guess my big brother thought I could be trusted. Stuff I saw, heard. Yeah, I called it in. Howard found out later. That was the official end of our brotherly love and I haven't been invited back to Blue Spruce since."

"Let's just call the place by its *real* name, okay?" said Annabelle sternly. "Dead Rock!"

"With all that stuff how come the Justice Department or the Civil Rights Division hasn't opened an investigation then?" said Harry Finn. "Or at least the Virginia Department of Corrections?"

Caleb looked at his notes. "Apparently, the current state and federal administrations don't have the rights of prisoners as a priority. There was talk of a state inquiry but it went nowhere, and the Justice Department has nothing pending. And for the last two years the prison has been more or less shut down to all visitors."

"So Howard Tyree has his own personal little fiefdom and can do what he wants. Including selling drugs," growled Reuben. "And holding innocent men."

"Looks that way," said Caleb.

"What about the mineshaft?" asked Annabelle.

"I did find some info on that," Caleb answered as he pulled out some pages he'd printed off at the library. "It was cut on a parallel course to the shaft the miners were trapped in. I read a couple newspaper articles about it and then compared it to records I was able to access about the prison construction. I can't be certain, mind you, because it's not like they publish the blueprints for supermax prisons online. But it seemed to me that that rescue shaft ran all the way up that ridge because that's where the miners were trapped. When the explosion happened it collapsed the tunnel the trapped miners were in, but the rescue tunnel survived. I know that because the other miners were able to get out okay. It says that the mine was sealed up at the entrance, but it doesn't say anything about the rescue shaft entrance."

Reuben said, "But if you build a supermax on top of a mine and you know there's a shaft running underneath, you sure as hell are going to plug it up."

"Plug it up, sure, but maybe in a way that allows you to unplug it," replied Annabelle as she paced the room in front of them.

"Howard was involved in the construction planning, that I know," said Tyree. "It would be just like him to allow himself some flexibility."

"But why would anybody do that?" asked Alex. "Prisoners could escape that way."

Annabelle turned around to face him. "From what Caleb has been telling us about Blue Spruce, there's no way that escape is that serious of an issue. Every prisoner is kept segregated, and then shackled and searched when they need to take a leak. There are almost as many guards as cons, and they only get one hour out of their cells a day. The setup is perfect for a drug-dealing operation that requires some of his men to routinely leave the prison in the middle of the night to take care of business."

"But if some of the guards are involved why wouldn't they just leave from their houses?" asked Caleb.

"Howard Tyree sounds like a real control freak to me. He'd want every man right under his thumb."

"You're right about that," agreed Tyree.

"If these shipments come in routinely to the courthouse with some of the boxes diverted, where do you think those boxes are going?" asked Alex.

"To the prison," answered Tyree simply. "It's easy enough. Prisons get deliveries every day of food, supplies."

Alex added, "And the courthouse records filings are a great way to ship the drugs. DEA or ICE agents would just let it right on by."

"So they make the switch somewhere en route," reasoned Annabelle, "and the diverted boxes go to the prison until they're ready to be shipped out using addicted miners as couriers. Which brings me back to my point. You're not going to have a bunch of guards walk out the front door every night with boxes of illegal pills. And you can't fly the chopper out every night, because people will start wondering."

Harry said, "So you go out the back door."

"You go out the back door," echoed Annabelle. "Which I believe is that mineshaft."

Alex looked at her incredulously. "So we're going to find this mineshaft entrance, get in somehow, even though it's been sealed, and then somehow make it through there alive? And then break into a supermax prison where there are guards armed to the teeth and who also happen to be drug dealers?"

"Sounds like a plan," said Reuben eagerly.

"It sounds like suicide," shot back Alex.

"Actually," said Annabelle, "you're both wrong."

CHAPTER

76

"I SWEAR IF IT'S the last thing I ever do, I'm going to kill Macklin Hayes," Knox muttered to Stone. The two men were back in their cell and many hours had passed since Hayes had come to put the proverbial nail in their coffins.

"But that would be against the law. And people will come and hunt you down and put you away," said Stone, as he peered out the slit the prison called a window. It overlooked the front parking lot but it was very difficult to see through because of the opaqueness of the window covering attached to the bars.

"Yeah, I realize the irony, trust me, but I'm still going to do it."

"*If* we get out of here."

"Yeah, I also realize the impossibility of that at the moment."

"I think you might be wrong about that."

Knox sat up. "Really?"

"Don't get your hopes up. It's for a bad reason, not a good one."

"What are you saying?"

"Have you noticed that ever since Hayes left they haven't bothered to feed us or let us out of the cell?"

"Yeah, my stomach is reminding me of that pretty much every second. So?"

"So that tells me that our stay here is coming to an end."

"Don't waste food on corpses? How unlike our esteemed warden."

"There's no reason to keep us here any longer. There's always a chance that someone might show up and search the place. Why risk it?"

"Where do you think they'll take us?"

"I know from firsthand experience that there are abandoned mines around here. A drop down an old shaft, seal it back up. Apparently people up here are used to dead men being inside these mountains. That's how this place got its name, in fact."

Stone pressed his face against the wall, trying to wedge it between the edges of the slit so he could see out better. He squinted and could see the outline of the mountains in the distance. They might as well have been on Mars. Three feet of concrete, a hundred yards of open space, killer wire and a battalion of snipers with aggressive trigger fingers was all that stood between them and freedom.

No way out.

Knox said, "You get into this business you know any

day your number could come up. And you deal with that. But you keep going because it's your job, a job you swore to do to the best of your ability. Serve your country to the end."

"Or until your country screws you," amended Stone.

"When I was assigned to come after you, I really didn't know what to expect. I knew you were a dangerous guy but figured you'd just gone bad like some do. But the more I found out . . . Well, if anyone ever deserved an apology from his country, you sure as hell do."

"Funny, I was thinking the same thing about you, Knox."

"My friends call me *Joe*, Oliver."

Stone turned back to look at him. Knox was standing and holding out his hand.

Stone took it and the two condemned men shared a brief but heartfelt handshake.

"When do you think they'll come for us?"

"Tonight." Stone looked out the slit again. "And best as I can tell that's about six hours away—" He stopped talking and then desperately tried to squeeze his head into the slit. He was barely making out a group of people climbing out of a car and heading to the prison entrance. Yet one tall, bushy-haired gent stood out from the others.

It has to be.

"What is it?" Knox said, "what do you see?"

Stone turned to look at him, a smile spreading across his face. "I see hope, Joe. Damn if I don't see hope."

CHAPTER

77

"Mr. Tyree, I think you better come down here, sir," the guard said into the phone.

"What is it?" barked Tyree as he sat behind his large desk with a bird's-eye view of his little kingdom. "I'm busy."

The guard turned to the group facing him.

"He said he's busy."

Alex Ford yanked the phone out of the man's hand.

"This is Alex Ford, United States Secret Service. I'm here with a joint federal agency task force and we have some questions for you, Warden. And if you don't get your butt down here, the next person you'll be talking to is a U.S. attorney as he reads the charges against your ass."

In his office Tyree nearly dropped the phone. "I have no idea—"

"Get down here, now!"

Sixty seconds passed and then Tyree walked stiffly into the front entrance area.

Alex flashed his creds before motioning to the others. Reuben, Caleb and Harry Finn wore blue FBI windbreakers. Annabelle had on a DEA jacket. "Agents Hunter, Kelso, Wright and Tasker."

"What the hell is this about?" said Tyree angrily.

Alex looked askance at him. "You really want to do this out in the open? Wouldn't you prefer some privacy, or is every son of a bitch here in on it?"

"In on what?" Tyree said indignantly.

"Tyree, you can't be that stupid. In fact, I've got a file on you an inch thick that says you're a pretty smart boy."

Tyree glanced at the nervous-looking guards and hurriedly motioned Alex and the others into a small room off the main entrance.

Alex shut the door behind them. "Okay, your little drug ring is falling apart."

"What drug ring?"

Alex looked at Annabelle. "Agent Hunter?"

Annabelle walked up to the diminutive Tyree, towering over him. "I thought you'd be a bigger guy. I rarely see shrimp like you in charge of an op this large."

"I am the warden of this prison. You will address me—"

"Screw you! You're lucky I'm not cuffing your scrawny ass right now. We have the shipments coming up from down south. Either the real oxy or manufactured pills. They're addressed to the courthouse, which gives them cover. That's where the old judge came in. That's where the old judge on the run. When we find his ass he'll turn government witness faster than I can say lethal injection. And you can kiss your butt so long, unless you killed him too. Like you did Shirley and Bob and Willie Coombs. And let's not forget Debby Randolph and your bean counter in crime Rory Peterson. How much did he skim off the top before you stopped him?"

"You're a lunatic!"

"I'm just getting warmed up. Then you'll see how crazy I can really be when I have your ass with a grand jury indictment painted all over it. So where was I? Oh, then part of the shipment is peeled off en route and comes here. Maybe in the chopper rides where you *transport* prisoners. Then the stuff gets moved out to the back edge of the Riker farm. And the miner train comes by and picks it up in the dark of night, and slings it on up the pipeline under the guise of the poor addicts going to get their methadone. And the money comes pouring in." She glanced at Caleb. "Agent Kelso?"

Caleb stepped forward. "And then the town *investment* fund is used to launder the drug proceeds. That's where Rory Peterson came in. He kept the cooked books and parceled out checks to the good folks of Divine, with you and your partners keeping the lion's share of the profits. What the citizens of Divine thought were payoffs from brilliant bets in the stock market were really drug monies. I believe that an investigation will show that you all have an ownership interest in all those businesses. Then you dump the laundered funds into offshore accounts. Peterson was killed because he was skimming. Josh Coombs was killed because he got wind of what was going on up here. You killed Shirley because after you killed her son you figured she might just turn on you."

"Why the hell would I kill her son?"

Annabelle looked confident, because Tyree had told them what Stone had figured out. "Because he was close to Debby. She saw whoever killed Peterson because she was working at the bakery across the street from his office. Your goons killed Peterson and Debby and made her death look like a suicide. But Willie never believed she killed herself. He was making a lot of noise. You were probably afraid Debby might have called him back and told him something about what she saw before she was killed. You tried once to get him and failed. The second time it worked."

Tyree slumped down in a chair.

She counted off on her fingers. "So let's see, that's at least half a dozen murders in addition to the federal drug charges. And on top of that we have reason to believe that you're holding two federal agents here against their will."

"What?" Tyree snapped.

"Right, I forgot to tell you that part. Where are they? One answers to the name Joe Knox, the other John Carr."

Annabelle studied him closely. The man was a good poker player, but she saw the truth simply in how his blinking kicked up a notch and his fingers quivered just a hair.

"These accusations are ridiculous. And where's your proof?"

"Our proof will be when we search this place and find our two agents. And the rest of the puzzle is coming together quite nicely. And when we nab the judge we'll have our key witness against you."

"You can't search this place without a warrant."

"Oh, we'll have a warrant. By the crack of dawn to-morrow morning. And just in case you get a hankering to travel anywhere, we have a roadblock set up. So don't even think of trying to slip them out that way. And leave the chopper grounded. Because we've got two of our own waiting to lift off the moment yours does."

Annabelle leaned down close into the man's sweating face. "By the way, we're well aware of your rep as being an asshole to every con that's ever walked through these doors. You like dishing out the pain, *little* man? Well, after your conviction, our strong recommendation to the correctional folks will be that wherever you go you're to be placed in the general prison population. Might save the Commonwealth the cost of an execution. Get my drift?"

"How dare you!" Tyree suddenly moved to strike An-nabelle, but a massive hand was placed on his arm by Reuben.

"I would not advise that," the big man said. "Because then they'll have to shoot you."

Tyree looked around to see Harry and Alex pointing pistols at his head.

Annabelle said, "We'll see you bright and early tomor-row morning, Howie. Oh, and if I were you, I'd definitely get my affairs in order."

CHAPTER

78

"THEY'RE COMING," Stone said.

He and Knox stood and backed against the wall as the pounding of the approaching boots echoed down the hall.

"I hope you're right about what you saw," Knox said nervously.

"Cuff slot!" a voice barked.

Stone started forward but Knox stopped him.

"This one's mine. They tend to kick the crap out of the first guy. Guess they run out of energy."

"Joe, you don't have to do that."

"Why should *you* have all the fun?"

Knox backed to the door and put his hands through the slot. Someone grabbed them and pulled hard, causing Knox's head to slam back against the door.

As he shook the pain away, he said, "You'll have to do a lot better than that, jerk-offs."

That got him another slam, but he'd braced himself against the door so the damage was negligible. Knox smiled at this small victory even as his headache grew worse.

The two guards didn't bother to search them this time, and they weren't shackled. And it was George, the crotch-grabber. Manson was apparently still in the infirmary.

Or with any luck, dead, thought Stone.

"Where are your uniforms?" Stone asked George.

"Changing occupations?" Knox added. "I'm not sure that's the drug dealer look you want."

"Shut up!" roared the man.

They were hustled downstairs and through more corridors and then down a sloping, winding passageway until Stone could smell the pungent odor of wet dirt and slimy rock.

Up ahead they saw a light. When they approached the man came into view. Howard Tyree was dressed all in black and didn't look nearly so smug as usual.

Stone looked down at him. "I see the visit today triggered some things."

"How did you——" Tyree began, but Knox cut him off.

"Macklin Hayes has been under internal investigation for a year for basically being a deranged asshole. They were following him. He led them right to us. *And* you. You moron."

"Shit!" blurted out Tyree.

Stone said, "So you might just want to surrender, Warden. It's over."

Tyree smiled, a dangerous look on his face. "They

might be the feds but they're not from around here. Don't know our ways or our land." He gave Stone a hard shove in the back. "Now move!"

They walked, the ground sloping down more with each step. Mold clung to the walls, and the heavy smell of damp gripped just as fiercely to their lungs. They finally came to a heavy steel door. George unlocked it. They all stepped through, navigated another short passage and came to yet another massive door. This was unlocked and they stepped into what had to be a mineshaft. Stone and Knox were told to wait as the other man headed off down a side corridor.

Stone looked around at the long tunnel and brace posts in the dirt floor and beams and thick wire across the ceiling holding back the rock. It reminded him of the place with the snakes. And there were rattlers with him tonight too, just of the human variety. Low ceiling, dirt and rock, massive beams holding back the mountain along with the tonnage of the prison. It was claustrophobic, all of it. Stone didn't know which was worse, the cell or the mine.

Maybe, in a way, they are the same.

His philosophizing stopped when he saw the guard coming back and leading another person with him.

"Abby!" As she grew closer, Stone's rage swelled. In the beams of the flashlights carried by Tyree and her guard Abby's face clearly showed the beating she'd endured.

Stone lunged at Tyree, but with his hands behind his back, he was easily subdued.

"I will kill you," he said quietly to Tyree.

"I see it the other way around," the warden replied calmly.

They walked on, Abby next to him while Knox shot curious glances at them.

"Abby, what happened?" Stone whispered to her.

"They came to the house and got me. Maybe killed the man Tyree had guarding me, I don't know for sure."

"Why would they want you?"

"Something to do with Danny."

"So he *is* mixed up in this?"

A sob slipped from Abby's mouth. She just nodded mutely.

Stone was going to say something else, but a billy club hit him in the back.

"No more talking," the warden snapped.

Stone lost track of time. Minutes or hours, he couldn't tell down here in the black of a mountain's bowels. He couldn't imagine spending his life down here on his hands and knees digging out rock. Digging his own grave.

Knox, Stone and Abby were suddenly grabbed and told to stay still. The two guards ran ahead and Stone could hear scraping sounds, large things being moved and the grunts and curses of the men doing that heavy moving.

Up ahead the darkness suddenly turned a bit lighter.

Tyree pushed them forward. Stone and Knox exchanged a glance. Neither knew exactly what was going to happen in the next few seconds. Stone kept as close to Abby as he could. If need be he would shield her with his body. He strained against the cuffs, trying to free himself. They probably only had a few seconds left.

They ducked down and came out into a moonlit night. Freedom at last from Dead Rock. Except for the cuffs and the men with guns surrounding them. And except for the fact that their lives were about to end. Stone could hardly believe that what many men with special skills had tried to do and failed, a pudgy warden from a backwater hole-in-the-wall was going to succeed in doing. Kill him. And yet as he glanced over at Abby, he felt far worse for her. The truth was he should have been dead long ago. He had done things that he deserved to die for. But not Abby. It shouldn't end this way for her. And he told himself he would do everything in his power to prevent the woman's life from ending violently here on this high rock.

Stone glanced around. They appeared to be in the middle of mountainous forest, but as his eyesight adjusted he was able to make out a wide path that had been cut through the heavy brush.

Tyree took ahold of Stone's arm and propelled him forward. He tripped over a rock and fell awkwardly to the ground. He rose to his knees and looked at the warden.

"They have this place completely locked down."

"There are ways out of here that I know that nobody else does. You don't think I didn't plan for something like this?"

Knox looked at the guards. "Must've been more guys than this involved. You just going to leave the others for the feds?"

"What do you care? You'll be dead," Tyree sneered.

"Would it sound really stupid if I said you'll never get away with it?" said Stone.

"Yeah, it would."

"How about if I said it?"

Tyree and the others whirled around to see Alex Ford step from the shadows of the trees, his gun aimed at the warden's head. When the guards pulled their weapons, a bullet sailed over their heads and the men froze.

A wisp of smoke floating from his gun's muzzle, Harry Finn moved forward while Reuben leveled a shotgun at the men. Annabelle and Caleb stepped out of the woods and stood next to Reuben.

Tyree suddenly pulled Abby toward him and leveled his pistol at her head. He said, "You folks better back the hell off or this lady is dead."

"Put the gun down, Howard."

Tyree jerked at the sound of the voice and then looked for its source. His gaze stopped and held as Lincoln Tyree stepped from the tree line. "Put it down, Howard."

A smile eased across the warden's plump face. "You know you were never any good at telling your big brother what to do. Now why don't you stop playing detective and just go on back down to your little town and pretend you know what you're doing."

"I know what I'm doing, *big brother.* I'm arresting you for enough stuff that you're the one's who's gonna end up at Dead Rock."

Tyree jammed his pistol against Abby's neck, causing her to cry out in pain. "Maybe you didn't understand what I said. If you don't back off, this lady is going to die."

"Put the gun down," the sheriff said again. "Killing her gets you nothing. It's over."

"Gets me nothing? Nothing? I tell you what it gets me. Satisfaction."

Alex said, "Last chance. To all three of you. Weapons down, now!"

"Go to hell," screamed Tyree.

He started to pull the trigger. But his gun never fired because Stone slammed into him, knocking the pudgy man off his feet, his pistol flying away.

"Run, Abby," screamed Stone, as he struggled to get up.

Tyree stopped rolling and sat up. Unfortunately, he'd stopped right next to his gun. He snatched it up and aimed for Stone's head.

The shot rang out and the round caught Tyree in the forehead. For a second or two the warden didn't seem to realize that he'd been killed. Then he fell on his back, his eyes staring up to the sky, the guard towers of Dead Rock visible in the distance, though he couldn't see them anymore.

Alex shouted, "Where did that shot come from?"

No one had time to answer that question because another man emerged from the tunnel and opened fire. And the weapon he carried was an MP-5 submachine gun that laid down a solid wall of fire all across the tree line. Stone had been in position to see this before anyone else. An instant before he fired he had gotten to his feet, lunged and tackled Abby as she was trying to run for cover.

Alex, Reuben and the others fell to the dirt as rounds zipped past overhead, shredding tree bark and anything else in their path. Ripped leaves rained down on them like snowflakes.

Sheriff Tyree yelled out as a round caught him in the leg. He fell heavily to the earth, grabbing at his thigh.

Stone glanced at the mineshaft opening. It was one-eyed Manson wearing a neck brace now along with the eye patch trying to kill them all.

God, I should have finished the son of a bitch when I had the chance.

Knox had thrown himself behind a large boulder, while George and his buddy had run off toward the woods. His buddy didn't make it very far because one of Manson's errant rounds caught him square in the back and he fell facedown in a wash of blood.

Stone got up and ran with every ounce of speed he had. He made a flying tackle on George and both men went down hard. Stone was still handcuffed so he couldn't hit him with his fists. He did the next best thing. He head-butted George flush in the face and the guard fell limp under him. Stone flipped over and, using his cuffed hands, tore at the leather pouch on George's belt. His fingers closed around the key. He felt for the opening and un-locked the restraints. He grabbed George's gun but looked down in dismay. The pistol had landed on a rock and the trigger had snapped off.

A moment later Stone ducked down as MP-5 rounds roared overhead and Abby screamed.

"Abby!" Stone slid like a snake through the dirt and rock, his clothes ripping and his skin tearing as he made his way frantically back to her. He'd done this exact same maneuver a thousand times through the jungles of South-east Asia, yet never for a reason more important than now.

On his belly too, Knox had dragged himself over to the dead Tyree. He wrenched the gun from the dead man's hand and slid back toward where Stone was heading.

Manson was barely ten feet from Abby. He stopped again to slam in another clip. Alex, Harry and Reuben opened fire, but Manson had wisely taken up cover behind a large rock outcrop. When he came back out with fresh ammo his firepower would overwhelm them at the short-ened distance. But clearly Abby would be the first to die.

"Oliver!"

Stone looked up at Knox's shout.

Still cuffed, Knox held up the gun between his feet and Stone nodded. Using his feet like a catapult Knox tossed and Stone caught. He had bare seconds.

"Stay down, Abby," he warned.

She frantically dug into the earth with bleeding fingers, trying to get as low as possible.

A second later Manson stepped out, the muzzle of the MP-5 searching for and finding her lying feet from him. Alex and the others had no line of fire because of the chunk of mountain lying between Manson and them.

Stone had no direct line of fire from where he was either. The first rule of the sniper was that any unintended movement of gun and shooter would spoil the shot. Steady hand, breath exhaled, heartbeat in the sixties and weapon locked in position against a stable surface—that's how one killed successfully. And Stone had mostly followed those rules in his career as the best assassin the U.S. ever had.

Mostly, but not always. Because sometimes what looked good in planning went to shit in the field. When that happened the merely good and competent failed nine times out of ten.

The best cut those odds down to fifty-fifty.

The very best improvised and upped the percentage of success by twenty points.

And then there was John Carr.

John Carr, who had come back from the dead at least one more time, to save a good woman who did not deserve to die at the hands of a maniac wielding a weapon of mass destruction.

Stone leapt, his pistol arrayed out at the sharpest angle

he could hold it and still get a shot off. Manson's finger closed on the trigger.

Stone fired. Joe Knox would later claim that he had seen the damn bullet actually bend around the chunk of rock. No one argued with him.

Manson pulled the trigger and the MP-5 roared. But all the rounds went straight up into the air because there was a massive hole in the side of Manson's neck. The shredded arteries released their rich blood supply high into the air and for several horrifying moments a red rain poured down on the dying Manson. Then he hit the dirt, his one eye open but now as unseeing as the other.

CHAPTER

79

STONE RACED TO ABBY and helped her up. She was scared, but okay.

Alex and Harry Finn were putting a tourniquet on Tyree's leg using a stick and a piece of Finn's jacket. The tall sheriff was sitting up now, grimacing with pain.

Stone and Abby came over to him and she knelt down next to him, took his hand.

"Tyree, are you okay?"

He tried hard not to show the pain. "Hell, take more than this to get me all worked up."

The shout made them all turn toward the woods.

Caleb was running back to them. "Hurry. Hurry."

They raced after him, Stone and Reuben in the lead. They plowed through the brush and vines.

When Stone saw what Caleb was pointing to, he felt like he had just died. He rushed to the fallen man's side.

"Danny? Danny?"

Danny Riker was lying on his back, a scoped deer rifle in the brush next to him. Stone wasn't focusing on the weapon, but rather on the large splotch of red on Danny's chest.

Danny's eyes focused on him. He managed a smile. "Don't think I ducked in time," he said weakly.

Stone looked back over his shoulder toward where Manson lay. That first blast from the MP-5 had hit right here. He turned back and counted no less than three bullet holes in Danny's shirt. And they were placed at locations that Stone knew did not allow for survival, even if they could get him to a hospital in the next few minutes, which they couldn't. He had brought Willie Coombs back from the dead using the juice from a spark plug wire. There would be no such miracle for Danny Riker.

Reuben squatted next to his friend and picked up the rifle. "He was the one who took out the warden."

"Damn right," Danny said, his voice growing stronger for an instant. "He killed Willie. Told the little son of a bitch what I'd do if he did that." His hardened features softened. "Get my ma, willya, Ben?"

Stone felt rather than heard the presence behind him. He rose and stared at Abby, whose gaze was only on her son.

"I'm sorry, Abby," Stone said. "I'm sorry."

Blood was spilling out of Danny's mouth. "Ma?"

She dropped to her knees next to him, taking his hand in hers. The sob burst from her with such force that all the others, who'd clustered somberly around mother and son, felt tears rise to their own eyes. Her features looked like those of a child fleeing a monster in a nightmare. Yet then Abby almost instantly calmed, perhaps sensing that her son needed her to be strong; that her boy's last moments on earth would not be taken up with the sight of a hysterical mother.

"I'm sorry, Ma. For all the stuff."

Stone knelt and held the young man's other hand. He felt it growing cold.

She said, "I love you, Danny. I've always loved you more than I loved anything."

"Shouldn't got mixed up in all this drug stuff. But didn't want to work the mines. And didn't want to take the death money either. You know?"

"I know. I know, baby." Tears were spilling from them both.

"Didn't have nothing to do with any killing. 'Cept the bastard warden." Danny's pupils were losing their focus, receding into the white pools of the eyes, as Stone had seen on many a dying man.

"I love you, Danny."

He looked over at Stone. When he spoke his voice was so weak Stone had to bend close to hear. "Me and Willie. State champs . . . Boy caught everything I threw at him. Shoulda played at Tech together. You know?"

"You two were the best, Danny," Stone said, gripping the cold hand. "The best."

"California dreaming, man."

He turned back to his mother. "California dreaming . . ."

Danny's eyes grew hard and flat, and the fingers that had gripped his mother's now fell away. Abby bent down and kissed her son and then wrapped her arms around him. And just held him.

Just held him.

CHAPTER

80

THE CAMEL CLUB sat at Rita's Restaurant. The place was not open for business today, but Abby had insisted that they use it and her home for as long as necessary. Sheriff Tyree was expected to make a full recovery. He had summoned the Virginia State Police, who were currently sorting out the mess in Divine. Since transport of drugs across interstate lines had occurred, the feds had also been called in. Knox and Alex had run interference with their government colleagues and Stone, Annabelle, Caleb, Reuben and Harry were not part of that questioning. Prison guards had been rounded up, bodies collected and other evidence secured. Judge Mosley had been stopped at a small airport in West Virginia trying to board a regional jet for Dulles International Airport with a travel itinerary that included several countries that had no extradition agreement with the United States.

Stone and the others watched the street through the front windows of Rita's. Along with the cop cars and black sedans swooping up and down the road, they observed several citizens of Divine walking around as though in shock, some holding dividend checks that they now knew were nothing more than drug money.

Danny's body had been taken to the morgue in Roanoke along with Howard Tyree's. Only when the police had zipped him up in a black body bag did Abby relinquish her grip on her son's hand. And even then she walked down the road after the slowly departing medical examiner's wagon.

When everyone had had some food and coffee, Stone stood in the middle of the small circle of the best and perhaps only friends he had in the world.

"I would like to thank you for what you did," he began, looking at each of them in turn.

Reuben immediately piped in, "Oliver, don't go sappy on us. You would have done the same for any one of us."

"You *have* done the same for every one of us," said Annabelle.

Stone shook his head. "I know how much you risked. I know what you sacrificed to come here and do what you did." His gaze settled on Alex Ford. "I especially know what you did, Alex. Even though it went against all your instincts as a Secret Service agent. And I appreciate it more than I can ever express."

Alex could only meet Stone's heartfelt gaze for a few moments before he looked down at his shoes.

When the door opened, they all turned to see who it was.

Abby had changed her clothes and washed her face,

though the imprint of the tears she had bled ~~with Danny's~~ death seemed to linger. Apparently, no soap could reach that. When Stone rose and went to her, the others silently made their way out of the restaurant and out onto the street.

Abby and Stone sat at a back table. When Stone handed her some napkins she shook her head. "I've got no more left. No more tears."

"Just in case then," he said. "What will you do now?"

"You mean after I bury my son? Haven't thought that far ahead."

"He saved us, Abby. But for what he did, you and I would be dead. He was a brave man who tried to do the right thing. That's how you have to remember him."

"I told you I lost my husband. Danny was all I had left. Now he's gone too."

"I know it's hard, Abby. It's harder than anything else you'll ever have to do."

"You lost your wife, but you still have your daughter."

"What?" Stone said, startled.

"That woman out there said she was your daughter."

"Oh." Stone looked embarrassed. "That was a cover story, I'm afraid. My daughter." He stumbled over what he was about to say. "My daughter died, like I said."

"How?"

"Abby, you don't—"

"Please tell me. I want to know."

Stone slowly looked up to see her gazing at him pleadingly. "She was shot right in front of me when she was an adult. And the thing was she didn't even know I was her dad. The last time I'd seen her she was only two years old.

I found her again after all those years and then I lost her. Forever."

Abby reached out and took his hand. "I'm sorry . . . Oliver."

"But you do survive it, Abby. You never get over it, but you can keep on living. Because you really don't have a choice."

"I'm scared. I'm alone and I'm scared."

"You're not alone."

She laughed halfheartedly. "What? Tyree? The wonderful town of Divine?"

"Me."

She sat back and looked at him. "You? How?"

"I'm here. Now."

"But for how long?"

Stone hesitated. He could not lie to the woman. "I have to go away."

"Sure, of course you do. I understand," she said offhandedly.

"I have some things that I have to take care of. Some wrongs finally need to be righted."

"Okay, whatever you have to do."

"Abby, I mean it. I will be there for you. Even if I'm not physically here."

He caught her gaze and held it with a pleading one of his own.

"I want to believe that."

"You can believe it."

"When do you have to go?"

"Soon. Sooner than later."

"Are you sure things will work out for you?"

"I won't lie to you, there are no guarantees."

"The trouble you might be in?"

"Yes."

"Will they put you in prison?"

"It's certainly possible," Stone admitted.

A quiet sob escaped her lips and she rested her face on the back of his hand.

"Will you promise me one thing?"

"I'll try my best."

"If you can't come back here, will you never forget me?"

"Abby—"

She sat up and put a hand against his lips. "Will you never forget me?"

"I will never forget you," he said truthfully.

She leaned across the table and kissed him on the cheek. "Because I'll never forget you."

A few minutes later Joe Knox came in. Stone looked over at him.

"You ready?" he asked Stone. "We need to get this done."

Stone gave Abby's hand one final squeeze and rose.

"I'm ready."

CHAPTER

81

THE FRONT DOOR to Macklin Hayes' stately brownstone in Georgetown was thrown open so hard it smacked the wall hard enough to make a dent in the plaster.

"What the hell?" began the man as he half rose from his chair, the book he'd been holding falling to the floor. When he saw who it was he sat back down, stunned.

"Hey, *sir*, how goes it?" Knox said as he strode in.

"Knox?" Hayes began nervously. "How did you get past the guards outside?"

"Oh, that. One of them is a buddy. I said I'd only be a few minutes. So they went down the street for a cup of coffee."

A panicked look came to the general's face. "Knox, let me explain—"

When Hayes saw Stone walk into the room, he could only gape in astonishment. When he observed that Stone's hands were manacled together, he started to breathe again.

"Mack," Stone said. "Nice place you have here. A lot nicer than the one Joe and I were in. But then you know that, don't you?"

Hayes finally wrenched his gaze from Stone.

"Knox, this will earn you that retirement you've been after, plus anything else in my power. Anything! I swear it."

"Thank you, sir."

Obviously encouraged by this, Hayes rose and put a bony arm around Knox's burly shoulders, drawing him aside.

"You really shouldn't have brought him here, though. Particularly since you sent my guards off. He is a dangerous man, handcuffed or not."

"There was really no other place to take him. And after you left my ass in that hellhole, well, there weren't a whole lot of options once we broke out."

"So you . . . broke out? The police are looking for you?" he said nervously.

"I would think they are. I mean, we killed five or six guards along the way." He turned to Stone. "Was it six?"

Stone said with an impassive expression, "Eight. I got two more while you were strangling the warden."

Knox turned back to a stunned Hayes. "Okay, so it was eight. I gotta tell you, we weren't in there all that long, but that place just drives you insane. Frigging out of your mind. I would've killed my own mother."

Hayes took his arm away, his hands visibly shaking. When he spoke, his voice shook as much as his hands. "Listen, Knox, I know what happened was unfortunate. But it was necessary until I could get a handle on what to do with Carr. As you can imagine, it was a highly delicate situation. In fact, I was about to send my men up there to do an extraction. Rest assured, I was not going to let one of my best men rot in that place one second longer than necessary. I swear to God."

Knox shook his head sadly. "I appreciate that, sir. I really do. But it would have helped to know that *before* I killed all those people to get out of the place."

Hayes' face was paper white now. "I'll talk to someone for you. We'll figure something out. This is a national security issue."

"I doubt that's possible now. In fact, that's why I brought Carr along with me."

Hayes glanced sharply over at Stone. "I don't quite understand."

"Well, *I* might forgive you. But he sure as hell isn't about to. So since we're both wanted for murder, I mean . . ."

"What the hell are you saying, Knox?"

Stone answered. "What he's saying is we've already done eight. Who the hell cares about one more, especially if it's you?"

Hayes staggered back against the wall, his hand to his chest. "Knox, you can't allow this. I am your superior."

"You *were* my superior. At least in rank. In reality, I've always considered you quite inferior."

"How dare you—"

Knox uncuffed Stone and then slipped a knife from his pocket and handed it to him. Stone automatically gripped it in his favored killing position.

"Knox!" Hayes screamed.

Stone advanced. "Do you know how many times I've done this on behalf of the United States government?"

"Knox, for godsakes."

"You should have given the man his medal," Knox said.

Hayes screamed, "I'll give you your damn medal, Carr. It's yours."

Knox sat in a chair and said, "You were a piece of crap for pulling the plug on it just because he wouldn't follow your order to slaughter an innocent village in Nam."

"I know that now. I'm sorry. I should never have given that order."

Stone stopped next to the quaking Hayes and looked him up and down, apparently deciding on the best place to deliver the lethal blow.

Knox added, "And you shouldn't have come up to that prison and made a deal with that warden to keep me there because I'd found out the truth."

Stone was now holding the knife against Hayes' throat.

"I've dreamed about this for nearly forty years, Mack," said Stone.

"Knox," wailed Hayes. "I'm begging you. I'm sorry for what I did at the prison. I never should have left you there. I'm sorry. For God's sake make him stop."

"Okay," Knox said. "Oliver, go ahead and stop."

Stone stepped back and flipped the knife to Knox, who pulled out a walkie-talkie and said into it, "Okay, come on in."

Five men came rushing through the door seconds later and strode up to the still cowering but confused-looking Hayes.

One of the men said, "Macklin Hayes, you're under arrest for obstruction of justice, false imprisonment, war crimes, covering up a drug ring, conspiracy to commit same and for using government property to blow up a civilian car in a public place resulting in reckless endangerment." The man then gave him his Miranda warning.

Knox pulled out a DVD from his pocket and tossed it to Hayes. "You can share that with your lawyers."

Hayes looked down at it. "What the hell is it?"

"The place where you met with us at the prison and told us everything because you figured we'd never get out? It was an *interrogation* room, you dumbshit. Warden up there was real keen on surveillance. There was a hidden camera and it recorded every syllable you said." He looked at the men. "Take his ass away. I'm sick of looking at him."

As they pulled Hayes from the room in cuffs, he screamed, "That man is John Carr. He killed Carter Gray and Roger Simpson. Arrest him, arrest him right now."

One of the men said, "Shut up!" and then pushed Hayes out the door.

After they were gone, Knox and Stone left the house and walked down the dark, quiet, lamplit streets of Georgetown as a chill wind blew in off the nearby Potomac.

"You know," Knox said, "Hayes was the only one who was after you. I reported only to him. He was doing this on his own authority, it wasn't an Agency thing."

"He's a man who holds his grudges," agreed Stone.

"My point is, as far as you're concerned, it's over." He put out his hand and Stone shook it. Knox continued,

"Now, I'm going to walk that way." He pointed to his right. "And I suggest you go the other way."

"I can't do that, Joe."

"Oliver, get out of this place and go start over somewhere. I'll even get you some money and a new ID. But you have to go. Now."

Stone sat down on a weathered stone step and gazed up at the man.

"I've been *going* for thirty years and I'm just tired."

"But the FBI is still investigating the murders. And with Hayes out of the way any impediment to them turning in your direction is gone. Sooner or later, they're going to knock on your door. Particularly with Hayes screaming his head off about you."

"I know that."

"And, what, you're going to just wait until they come get you?"

Stone stood. "No. I'm not going to wait. I'm going right to the top on this. But first I need to go get something."

"Get something? Where?"

"At a graveyard."

CHAPTER

82

THE SECRET SERVICE examined the contents of the box that Stone had brought with him. It was the same one he'd hidden at Milton's burial plot before leaving Washington. Knox had driven him over to the graveyard where he'd gotten the box, called Alex Ford and made the arrangements to be where the three men were now.

The White House looked particularly impressive in the crisp morning sunlight. Alex knew the agents on duty today at the northeast gate entrance and he talked to them as Knox and Stone went through the metal detector and security process.

After that Alex led them up the driveway and into the White House. They passed the guards stationed at that entrance. As they walked toward the West Lobby, the security badges issued to the three men bounced against their chests. They arrived at the small West Lobby and were cleared. Stone and Alex sat while Knox nervously paced.

In a calming voice Alex said, "Down that hall is the Roosevelt Room. It's got a painting of FDR over the fireplace mantel and one of Teddy Roosevelt on the south wall. Straight ahead of that is the reception room, and to the immediate right of that is the Oval Office. The president doesn't actually work there. He's got another office nearby where he can get some real work done."

"Interesting," said Knox as he continued to pace the room, shooting glances here and there. All three men were dressed in suits. Alex and Knox had chipped in to buy Stone some appropriate clothes and he looked distinguished, if uncomfortable in his jacket and tie.

"You sure he's going to see us?" Knox asked Alex.

"We're on the schedule. So unless war is declared or a hurricane hits somewhere, we're going to see the man."

Knox let out a deep breath and slumped in a chair. "Jesus, Joseph, Mary."

As soon as he said the last name, a woman appeared and said, "The president will see you now, gentlemen."

In the Oval Office, President Brennan rose from behind the Resolute Desk and shook hands with all three, lingering over Alex, who'd taken a bullet while trying to prevent the president from being kidnapped in Brennan's hometown.

"Great to see you, Alex. You all recovered, I trust?"

"Yes, sir, thank you, sir."

"I can never express how grateful I am for what you did for me back then."

"Well, Mr. President, that's partly why we're here."

Brennan looked confused. "The schedule said you

wanted me to meet some friends of yours?" He looked at Knox and Stone. "These gentlemen, I'm assuming?"

"It's a bit more complicated than that, sir, if you could spare us a few minutes."

The president motioned them to sit down in chairs set in front of the fireplace.

Alex started speaking and didn't stop for over twenty minutes. Nor did Brennan, known for being an inveterate questioner, ever interrupt him. He just sat in his chair absorbing what Alex was telling him about the events in Pennsylvania and up to what had happened at Murder Mountain and then on to the confrontation at the Visitor Center underneath the U.S. Capitol where Milton Farb had been killed and Harry Finn's son rescued. Knox took up the tale from there, and though clearly nervous in the presence of the commander in chief, his voice was strong and his details meticulous as he took Brennan through his part of the story, including Stone being denied the Medal of Honor, their time in prison and ending with Macklin Hayes' arrest.

Brennan sat back. "My God, this is incredible. Truly incredible. I can't believe this about Carter Gray. He was one of my most trusted advisors." He glanced over at Stone. "And you are John Carr?"

Stone nodded. "I am."

"With this entity called the Triple Six?"

"Yes, sir."

"It's amazing to me that we engaged in that sort of thing."

"It wasn't amazing to me. I was just following orders. It was only later that my conscience got the better of me."

"But to kill your family. To come after you like that.

I'm sorry, Alex, it just doesn't sound like the people I knew."

Stone held up the box. "Do you mind, Mr. President? I have something here that might convince you."

Brennan hesitated but then nodded.

Stone opened the box and took out the small recorder. He hit the play button and a voice came on loud and clear. It was Carter Gray. At Murder Mountain.

"I thought you had to give that recording back to Gray," said Alex as he hit the stop button. "And Finn said they had a device there that could tell if it had been duplicated, and it hadn't."

"Before I gave the phone with the recording on it to Gray I just held this recorder up to it and copied it. Sometimes people forget all about the low-tech ways."

He hit the play button and as they listened they came to the part that Stone had particularly wanted the president to hear. When it was over, Brennan stared at them, his face flushed.

"He was going to kill me. Carter Gray was going to kill me so he could start an all-out war with the Muslims!"

"Yes, sir," said Stone. "He was."

"And you were the one who saved me," he said to Stone. "That was your voice on there convincing him not to do it. After the woman was killed. Who was she?"

"She was my daughter, Beth."

Alex quickly explained to the president how Roger Simpson and his wife had come to adopt Stone's daughter.

Brennan sat back in his chair, his mind obviously whirling. "They killed your wife and took your daughter.

The man who had your wife murdered and tried to have you killed took your daughter and raised her as his own? And Gray, what he did to you. What he almost did to me. It's . . . it's beyond horrible, John. I'm rarely at a loss for words but I don't know what to say."

"There's something else I need to tell you, sir."

Knox and Alex both took deep breaths and then held them, their bodies tense as boards.

"What's that?"

"Carter Gray and Roger Simpson were both murdered, Mr. President."

"Yes, I know that—" He broke off and locked gazes with Stone.

"I see," he said. "I see." He sat back and looked over at the fireplace.

Nearly a minute went by and no one broke the silence.

Finally, Stone said, "Thank you for your time, sir. I plan to turn myself in to the authorities. But I wanted you to hear the story from me first. After thirty years of lies I thought it was finally time for the truth."

As Stone and the other two rose to leave, Brennan looked up at him.

"Listen to me, Carr. You've put me in a difficult position. Probably the most agonizingly difficult spot I've ever been in, and that's saying something for a two-term president. And yet with all that, I don't think it approaches the pain that you've suffered at the hands of a country that should have known better." He paused and stood. "I tell you what I'm going to do, since I wouldn't even be alive now and this country would be in the middle of a disastrous war but for your efforts, I'm going to take this under advisement. I don't want you mentioning this to anyone, much less turning yourself in. Do you understand me?"

Stone looked at Alex and then Knox and then back at the president. "Are you sure, sir?"

"No, I'm not sure," he snapped. "But that's the way it's going to be. I don't condone vigilantism. Never have and never will. But I also have a heart and a soul, and a sense of honor and decency despite what some of my political opponents claim. So until you hear from me you are to do *nothing* except carry on with your life. Understood? I know you're no longer technically in the military, but I am still the leader of this country. And you will obey that order."

"Yes, sir," said an obviously surprised Stone.

As they turned to leave Brennan added, "Oh, and it'll be a long term of taking it under advisement. So long in fact and with all the other issues I'm confronted with as president, it is highly likely that I may completely forget all about it. Good-bye, Carr. And good luck."

As they closed the door behind them, both Knox and Alex exhaled in relief.

"Holy shit, do I need a drink," said Knox. "Come on, I'm buying."

CHAPTER

83

OLIVER STONE OPENED the gates to Mt. Zion Cemetery and walked up to his cottage. The front door was unlocked, and when he went in he saw that the changes Annabelle had made were no longer there. Everything was just as he had left it.

He sat down behind his desk and ran his hand over the old wood, squeaked back in the chair and gazed over at his wall of beloved books. He made a cup of coffee and carried a mug with him as he explored the grounds of the cemetery, noting where work needed to be done that he would get to the next day. He was once more the official caretaker of hallowed ground. It was where he belonged.

That evening, the others came by to see him. He hugged Reuben, Caleb and Annabelle, thanking each in turn again for what they had done for him. Reuben brought a few six-packs while Caleb had a nice bottle of red wine. Later, Alex, Finn and Knox joined them.

As Knox and Stone sat in front of the fireplace, Alex and Annabelle were engaged in animated conversation in one corner of the room. She held a glass of wine and he had a beer.

"Why did you really come to help us?" she said suddenly.

"Friends don't let friends die by stupidity."

"Gee, thanks."

He drew closer to her. "Well, actually, I did it because it occurred to me that we had left things on the wrong foot. And I wanted to tell you that despite all the mean, nasty things you said about me, I'd still like to hang out with you on occasion."

"Oh, is that right?"

"That's pretty right, yeah."

"Is that the best 'please come back to me' line Secret Service agents are taught?"

"We're more the strong and silent types."

Annabelle hooked her arm through his. "What you did was pretty wonderful," she said into his ear. "And I am sorry for the things I said." She glanced over at Reuben. "He really set me right on things."

"Let's just start over and see where it goes."

Reuben, who was watching all this from the other side of the room along with Caleb, said, "Oh, man, I'm going to puke."

Caleb replied, "Don't be jealous, Reuben. He's younger and much better-looking than you are. And besides, I don't have anyone either. I'm as big a loser in the female department as you are. I hope that makes you feel better."

Reuben drank down his entire beer and stalked off muttering.

Everyone looked over when Alex's cell phone began to ring. He answered it.

"Hello? What?" He suddenly snapped to attention and almost dropped his beer. "Yes, sir. Absolutely, sir. I'll make sure he's there. You can count on it, sir."

He clicked off and looked at the others in complete astonishment.

Knox said, "Who was that? Not the president?"

Alex slowly shook his head and walked over to Stone and put a hand on his shoulder. "That was the chairman of the Joint Chiefs of Staff."

"What?" Reuben exclaimed, his features growing pale. "What the hell did he want? You know, technically, I'm not AWOL. It was a misunderstanding."

"He called about you, Oliver," said Alex.

Stone looked up at him. "What *about* me?"

"We're taking another trip to the White House. Tomorrow."

"What? Why?"

Alex smiled. "Something about a medal, my friend. A long-overdue one. The top brass reviewed your war record, made the recommendation and the president immediately accepted it."

Reuben roared, "That's fantastic." He slapped Stone on the back as the others crowded around him, offering their congratulations.

When things quieted Stone said, "Alex, will you

please call them back and tell them I appreciate the gesture but I can't accept it."

"What!" exclaimed a stricken Reuben.

Alex added, "Oliver, no one turns down the Medal of Honor. No one. Hell, a lot of soldiers who get it are dead."

"I'm not turning it down. That would be a dishonor to everyone who earned it. But I just want them to withdraw the offer. They made a mistake."

"Mistake, hell. You earned it," Finn said. "I read your record, Oliver."

"Maybe I did deserve it. Back then. And back then I would have accepted it. But I don't deserve it now. And for me to take it would dishonor the memory of every soldier who was awarded it."

Annabelle said, "Oliver, please, don't do this. Think about it. You'll be a part of American history. How many people get a shot at that?"

"I already *am* a part of American history, Annabelle. I know what I did on that battlefield. And I did it because I couldn't let my men die. But I also know very clearly what I did *after* I left the army. Very clearly. And that's the difference."

"But you were just following orders," said Alex.

"Sheep follow blindly. We're not supposed to be sheep."

Caleb went over to Stone and put a hand on his shoulder. "I never served in the military, so I can't really speak to any of that. But I do want to say one thing. I was very proud of you when they offered you the medal. But I think I'm even prouder of you for not accepting it."

After they all left, saying they would be back soon, Stone took the box out that he had kept the recording in. It also contained two other items.

He looked first at the photo of his baby daughter, Beth, who had grown up and then died never knowing that he was her father. Then he turned to the other faded picture.

In this image his wife Claire was suspended forever as a young wife and mother. In his mind every day it was Claire Carr who kept him going. In that prison while Tyree and his men were brutalizing him it had been her memory to which he'd clung.

He could never part with that image because in a visceral way it was the only shred of identity he had left. It was the one memory that kept alive the spirit of a young soldier, husband and father named John Carr. Not the assassin, not the killer. Just him, or who he used to be.

With his fingers he touched her hair, her face, skated along the line of her mouth. She and his daughter had been the only good things in a life that otherwise had been filled with scars and hurt and violence.

And yet memories of them were enough to take away all of it. Gone, like the cleansing force of the purest water.

He sat in the chair holding his wife and daughter.

And at least for a few moments everything again was all right.

After he put the box away he pulled out the new cell phone Annabelle had given him and punched in the number from memory. With each smack of his finger against the pad, Stone was growing more and more confident of what he was about to do.

After all, how much time could a man like him really expect to have left? He told himself he could not afford to waste another minute of it.

When the voice answered, he said quietly, "Abby, it's me."

Acknowledgments

To MICHELLE, the ride continues. And your incredible enthusiasm always keeps me going.

To Mitch Hoffman, for another superb editing job. Your thoughtful comments guided me to where I needed to go.

To David Young, Jamie Raab, Emi Battaglia, Jennifer Romanello, Martha Otis and all the rest at Grand Central Publishing who take such good care of me.

To Aaron and Arleen Priest, Lucy Childs, Lisa Erbach Vance and Nicole Kenealy for good counsel and warm friendship.

To Tom and Patti Maciag and their wonderful children, Stephen, Colleen and Emily. The Tall Family truly rocks.

To Maria Rejt and Katie James at Pan Macmillan for always being there.

To Grace McQuade and Lynn Goldberg for letting the world know.

To Dr. Catherine Broome, Sohan Makker, Dr. Alli Guleria, Mark Poplawski and Harvey Watkins for technical support and making a cool scene even cooler.

To Bob Schule, for his boundless knowledge of all things political and his incredible generosity in sharing it.

To Tom DePont, for being a great friend, wonderful advisor and the guru of NASCAR for yours truly.

To Lynette, Deborah and Natasha for always steering the good ship Columbus Rose straight and true.